Walking Into Her Heart

by

Susan JP Owens

A First Realm Novel

Walking Into Her Heart

Cover Art by *Diana Carlile*

The Wild Rose Press, Inc.
PO Box 708
Adams Basin, NY 14410-0708
Visit us at www.thewildrosepress.com

Publishing History
First Faery Rose Edition, 2013
Print ISBN 978-1-62830-068-0
Digital ISBN 978-1-62830-069-7

A First Realm Novel
Published in the United States of America

Kyle's stomach clenched as remorse flooded his gut. "When you touched my arm, I responded. I didn't mean to scare you."

Shelby hugged him and gazed into his eyes. The connection of her trust, coupled with his conviction to protect her, created an inconceivable force within him, producing a stimulus for something deeper, an impetus toward a commitment. He sucked in a breath and admitted there was more.

A visceral reaction drew him to her—where no woman had taken him in a long time. He visualized his hands in her thick brown hair spread on his pillows, tangled in sheets after a night in bed…with him. Sweet Jesus, it'd been ages since he'd had this type of response.

Her hazel eyes danced. Shelby tilted her head, and her silky hair cascaded down her back. The creamy skin of her neck invited him and his body answered in a primal way.

Her lips turned into a smile and her natural beauty smacked him on target. He shifted minimally to relieve the pressure in his jeans but not to dislodge her from his thigh. Hot streaks of desire shot through his veins, while tiny sparks set his skin on fire. He shivered, recognizing the irony. Reining in his thoughts, drawing back his fervor, he blinked long, inhaled fully, and released the air.

With Shelby's arms wrapped around his waist, their gazes still locked, her eyes were a window to her soul. He wanted to mind walk with Shelby. No. He intended to keep his vow. Damn, what was he thinking? What had this woman done to him?

Praise for *WALKING INTO HER HEART*

"From the first paragraph, I was hooked. The story has extraordinary turns and kept me reading far into the night. The scenes are beautifully orchestrated and stunning. The author doesn't hold back and each emotional turn left me hoping that she has more books waiting for me."

~J. Juergens, author

Dedication

To my fellow author,
Nese Lane,
who "walked" every footfall with me.
~
And to my husband and "Soul Mate,"
Jimmy,
for his love and unwavering support.

Acknowledgments

This particular novel took a tribe that I'd like to acknowledge for their technical help, valuable resources and information: Captain H.D. "Dusty" Spain; John St. Germain, Operations Manager, Jackson Hole Aviation; LtCol. Wren Meyers, USMCR (Ret); Sergeant Kim Wolff, TPD; Megan Gersbach, PA; Nancy Livingston; Judy Juergens; Margaret Wilson; Pat Holloway; Keith Moninger; Martha Tutor; Gina Veillon; Jodi Fields; Margaret Bryant; Cindy Schleede; Jake D., and the members of the Heart of Texas, RWA chapter. A special thank you and kudos to my editor, Ally, and cover artist, Diana.

Chapter One

Columbia, South America—Ten Years Earlier

Kyle Pressley scrubbed a hand over his face as he led his team through the thick jungle north of the Ecuadorian border. His beard and mustache itched. Sweat trickled down his back, the salt stinging the mosquito and God only knew what other bites. He gulped the sultry air. Damn, the humidity made it difficult to breathe and clung to everything including his weapon. He swiped his palm down one thigh then the other. The acrid smell of the lab one klick south hovered with no breeze to carry away the fucking obnoxious odor.

The two-by-ten-foot boards settled in the mud marked the path to one of the biggest known cocaine work-camps. Once the team found the site's position, they were to reconnoiter, then provide GPS coordinates, but not engage. His superiors wanted any shipments tracked to the drug cartel's new mode of transportation, a submarine. Their intel had been based on a paid informant, and he hoped like hell this wasn't some wild goose chase.

He set a parallel course to the planks, hacking his way through the dense undergrowth. His instincts howled. Adrenaline shot through his system. The hair on his neck rose. His gut wrenched. He stilled. Catching movement to his left, he clenched his fist and held his arm up to call a halt to his team, then melded by a tree.

The Assistant Secretary had asked his SEAL team to try out the new video gear, including a screen detailing each member's position and point of view in real time. The usual load-outs used for this type of assignment went back to basics, a machete and a mere compass because of the rain forest's impenetrable canopy.

His team had practiced for several months before testing the advanced equipment in a live situation. The special rig was integrated into their helmets and pierced the jungle's substantial covering. All he had to do was think which team member's POV he wanted, and the images would appear on one of the screens. Processing what he was seeing on both displays and multi-tasking his thoughts, the high stimulus caused his brain to seize, which changed the screen to snow. The innovators had called it a white-out. His team called it something else. "Did you see it?"

"Affirmative," Dan's voice whispered through his ear piece. "I have a bad feeling."

He did too.

Kyle had joined the Navy and risen through the ranks at breakneck speed. Dan, nearly a decade his senior, had become his mentor. Together, their team was a force to be reckoned with. He'd declined a vote of his constituents to join SEAL Team VI. Those men were the elite, intelligent, had guts, courage, and were bound together by one hell of a brotherhood. He'd been honored, but he didn't see himself doing this for another ten years, and he sure as hell wanted to see his thirtieth birthday.

Bark chipped off the tree above his head. Kyle counted until he heard the gunfire report. The guerrillas had exposed their position. He dropped to the ground, using the thick trunk as protection. Bullets sprayed where his chest and face had been seconds before.

Out of the corner of his eye, he caught an asshole trying to hide. He double tapped. His target crumbled.

The barrage of lethal ammo flew by his head while shredding nearby foliage.

"Jesus Christ, engage the fucking bastards," he yelled while he squeezed the trigger, inundating the area with lead. The hail of gunfire rose close to Dan's position.

"Two?"

"A little bit busy right now. Ahh!"

"Fuck this shit." Kyle snatched a grenade, pulled the pin, and threw. "Fire in the hole!"

The eerily quiet minutes that followed slithered into what seemed an eternity. Kyle spoke into his mic. "Red One here."

"Red Three."

"Red Four."

"Red Five."

He waited. "Two?" Kyle eyed Dan's video feed. All he saw was snow-fucking-white.

"Red Three to One. I'm looking at Two, and he's down."

Kyle's right lens picked up Two's position and Three's image. "I see him. On my way. Secure the perimeter."

He backtracked and spotted Dan's body, lying at an odd angle. He knelt beside Dan. His severed femoral artery spurted blood with each heartbeat. "Stay with me. We'll get you out of here." He swallowed the lump in his throat and applied a tourniquet then compressed the wound.

Kyle keyed his mic. "One to Three, request medevac." His neutral voice belied the urgency screaming through his gut.

Dan's eyes opened. "I'm done...go."

"Don't be a dickhead, Forbes. Remember when you were stabbed last year? The knife had pierced your lung and you pulled through." Kyle tore the corner of a packet and sprinkled the blood clotting agent. Every man on his team had medical training. Their lives depended on it.

"Leave, prick. Fuck me, that shit burns." Dan winced.

"Stop being a pussy and grow some balls. You've survived worse." His injury was life threatening. Dan might have a chance based on a few things going his way, like an extraction—stat—a little help from lady luck, and a damn strong conviction to live. But Dan acted like he didn't care if he lived or died.

Dan groaned. "I don't want to."

"What? Why?" Fuck, he never expected Dan to give up, not this fast. This wasn't the man he knew and admired. No matter what team a man was on, they were bad asses to the end, especially when the damage had been caused by the cock sucking enemy. A SEAL lived just to piss them off. And each man faced death, head-on.

"None of your business."

"Pull your head out of your ass." Kyle swallowed hard, fearing the worst. He wouldn't let Dan concede, not on his watch. He had to figure out what was going on.

Kyle closed his eyes to journey into Dan's mind. He concentrated on his spiritual self, some call it the third eye, but he preferred to think of it as a portal. While clearing negative energy, Kyle released his physical form and embraced his spirit. He had been given the gift and the name Mind-Walker, which was one of the reasons he had excelled working with the new military equipment and had been chosen as the team leader.

Traveling to other realms was different than journeying into people's minds. In most instances, he had to cloak his presence, but not this time. He wanted Dan to know he was there and pushed his positive consciousness within Dan's. Dan's physical pain struck Kyle like a freight train. Kyle's leg throbbed. He blocked the excruciating agony and opened to his best friend's thoughts. Dan's memories flashed before him. Both of Dan's children, Aaron and Katherine jumping into their father's arms, happy their dad came home. Kyle was Aaron and Katherine's godfather, and he loved these kids as if they were his own. Another recollection unfolded before Kyle, Dan's wife smiled, then betrayal and heartbreak.

"You bastard, you're mind walking. You told me this was a bunch of bullshit."

"Would you have believed me?" This was the first time he had walked in Dan's mind and he opted not to veil his presence. Not too many people understood his ability and the ones that had… No. He didn't want to go there…Ever again.

Dan chuckled then grimaced. *"No. What happens if you're still here when I die?"*

Kyle discerned his best friend's life slipping away, the lack of oxygenated blood damaging Dan's heart as his will to survive diminished. *"When did Becca ask for a divorce?"*

Mail call...two days ago. I can't live without her, man."

"You should've told me...Don't give up...For your kids."

"She wants custody...Taking them on her symphony tours...Hiring a tutor."

Kyle willed his strength to Dan. *"Stay with me...We'll fight this together...I'll help you...I've means."*

"I know who you are, prick."

"Then you know I can hire the best damn attorneys money can buy and we'll win."

"Will you look after them?"

Dan's energy and light faded with each breath. Frustration seared every neurological wave. Why couldn't he change Dan's outlook, make a difference? *"I'll make sure the twins will want for nothing, but you can give them more than I can, by staying alive, being their dad, watching them grow up, graduate, get married and have your grandchildren."*

"Tired...Cold."

The love Dan had for his wife and children rendered Kyle silent. His heart ached for his buddy. He pleaded, not only for Dan's family, but for him too. *"Don't do this."*

Dan heaved a sigh. *"Tell Aaron, Kat, and Becca, I love them."*

"I will." Kyle drew on his own energy, expounding further to his surroundings. *"Hang on."*

Still not enough, he expanded to cull the positive forces in the sky, space, then the universe. *"Stay with me."* Kyle called on his spirit guides and the angels for their help.

Dan gurgled, *"Please go."*

"No, I need you to live." Kyle gathered all the lifesaving influences and launched the potent power into Dan. *"Come on."* Kyle filled his lungs and released the life giving oxygen to Dan by telepathy. *"Fuck, fight damn it."*

"No more, let me go."

Kyle stilled then honored Dan's last request and walked out.

"So damn cold."

He gathered Dan in his arms keeping him warm in the hundred-plus temperature. "I love you, man."

Dan nodded. "Me too." Then he was gone.

Tears blurred Kyle's vision. "Fuckin' A." If he'd known about Becca's letter, he would've kept Dan from this mission. He would take the responsibility to tell the twins their father had died, on his watch.

For the first time and when it counted most, he'd been unable to make a difference mind walking. If he was incapable of accomplishing such a simple task as to help Dan live for his children, then what good was his gift from the First Realm? He managed to have the right stuff for covert operations, slip in the enemy's head and step out without them knowing he'd been there. Hell, he could plant ideas into the fucker's subconscious, and they'd believed it was theirs. He'd had saved numerous agents from certain death and gave up the positions of the rogues who'd put them there. How had he failed to keep Dan alive?

A hand on his shoulder jostled him. "We found the camp several meters west, and everyone scattered. I've sent the coordinates. They're on their way...Pressley, give Forbes to me. We need to get the hell out of here."

"Fuck off." He hoisted Dan over his shoulder and carried him to the helo rendezvous.

With each step, his desolation grew. His heart ripped in two, then fragmented into tiny pieces. He cursed. The loss of Dan was like a death of a brother.

His brother.

They were trained in stealth, movement, and extraction. This mission was supposed to be a cakewalk, new equipment tests, keeping undercover, not engaging. The worst part, this job was their last. Kyle had planned a vacation with Dan and his twins. He should've keyed in when Becca wasn't able to join them.

He sighed. Dan was going home all right, in a damn body bag. He had screwed up as the team leader, and the hardest fact he had to accept, he failed Aaron and Katherine. Not only them, but also, his spirit guides, the First Realm, and his ability to help his world when needed.

The rotor wash whipped from the black hawk, lowering to the ground. He climbed in. When the medic stretched to take Dan's lifeless form, Kyle growled. Dan's blood covered him, some of it still tacky, some of it dried. The coppery smell filtered to his nostrils. Life had always been uncertain in their line of work. He sure as hell expected more from himself.

He had a duty to Dan. Aaron and Katherine would have everything...except a dad. All the hurt and anguish boiled inside his gut and the repulsive mixture spilled to every part of him including his soul. He had pledged to use his ability for good without undermining destiny. Did he really think he could change Dan's outlook, snatch his best friend from death's clutches, and alter fate? The simple answer was yes. He held himself accountable and vowed never to use his gift again.

Chapter Two

The First Realm
Present Day

"You have done well, but you need help," One-Who-Soars-With-Eagles communicated telepathically to Tim.

The aura surrounding the medicine man's spirit demanded his attention. "I don't want Shelby to die like I did."

The bell tinkled as his wife left the book store. From above and within the First Realm, Tim watched with the shaman. The sun bathed Shelby's skin and the golden highlights of her brown hair shimmered. He longed to touch the silken shafts, her soft skin, to walk hand-in-hand. He'd give anything to make love to her one more time.

One-Who-Soars-With-Eagles' methodical cadence dissolved his thoughts. "Observing her struggle is difficult."

Shelby's tireless effort to find his murderer put her in danger. Why hadn't he told her? Taken the time to share with her about the fetish, the exposure, and risks involved with the Kachina doll? Now in this so-called afterlife, he was forced to accept the medicine man's plan. Even if it meant an eternal damnation from the First Realm, he wanted Shelby safe, happy on earth,

10

and a kinder death than his.

"However, she is the key," One-Who-Soars-With-Eagles continued. "We can guide her much like we directed you."

Tim's guttural laugh stung with distaste. "You helped me? Based on where I'm standing, she doesn't have a chance." Having to follow the shaman's divine guidance disgusted him. He preferred intervention, but had no choice.

"There's more at stake than your woman's life. Potent powers are within Ten-Blue-Sun. Little-Dove-Feathers must have possession of the doll, for she will know how to harness the energy to win the upcoming battles and heal the scars. Shelby is an important step. Dangerous entities will be countering our efforts not only on Earth but here too. When the baby is born, we will have a chance to right all the wrongs."

"Shelby's going to have a...babe?" Mixed emotions inundated him, the light of Tim's spirit dimmed. He understood One-Who-Soars-With-Eagles. This wasn't an immaculate conception. Shelby would have a lover, a partner...or a husband.

"Her life's path is crucial."

"Let me get this straight. You used me and now you want to take advantage of Shelby too, all for a damn doll and a baby who's not born yet?"

"You'll learn many things in our spirit world, but first, your wife must release you."

Tim peered down on Mother Earth while Shelby window shopped. He would bet she wasn't ready to let him go. For that matter, he wasn't either. Now, when they were together, she'd talk to him for hours and he'd answer the only way he knew how. He had discovered how to bundle his energy to communicate through physical means, to grasp, to blow wisps of air, and he reveled in Shelby's presence.

To acquire the skill of manifestation was a long process. But he had wanted, no, needed to seek out his soul mate. He was pleased Shelby never feared his spiritual existence.

The first several times were tough. She'd cried at the injustice. But her perseverance and resolve prevailed. She had made several promises to him, to find out who murdered him and never marry again. Pledges he wasn't sure she should keep. He'd have a hell of a time getting her to break those oaths. Between the medicine man and him, they could influence Shelby to find his killer and whatever else, the shaman had up his proverbial sleeve, but until the baby was born, their powers were limited, only to navigate, not intervene.

Maybe she would find someone, a friend, one who wouldn't be threatened by her strengths and her strong sense of commitment. He vowed if the right man entered her life, he'd give Shelby his blessing. For now, he'd have to take the only course available to him, to follow the shaman.

One-Who-Soars-With-Eagles' whispered, "Good, I'm glad you have come to this conclusion. When Shelby releases you, you'll be able to go on to your next step and receive more power for our war. Shelby's spirit guide will take over and assist."

The medicine man's next words brooked no argument. "Come. We have many things to do, many levels to complete."

Chapter Three

4th of July - Jackson, WY

When Shelby Littleton caught a glimpse of the ice cream parlor, her mouth watered. The icy treat promised a reprieve. She'd take a short cut through the town square where the tall trees and evergreens would provide shade.

A humming sound buzzed around her. The cool clasp of her husband's hand on her elbow reassured her. "Tim, I have a feeling our Kachina doll has more history than my research has unfolded, but I intend to learn everything I can. My gut feeling tells me you were murdered for her. Babe, you've never left my side and I'll always be grateful." Air brushed over her ear giving his approval.

Even though she'd much rather have her husband's physical presence, she would take any form of him. At first, she thought she was losing her mind, but now, she'd accepted his corporeal death, her earthly life without him, and his spirit. Her first call of business was to find her husband's murderer.

A sudden noise came from her right. She stilled, tilting her head away from the buzz of the cars and people. There it was again, a whine. Cautiously, she pursued the sound. A poor dog ensnared in twine, cowered on his belly. She crept forward and dropped to her knees. The canine shied from her. Shelby's eyes connected with its dark brown ones quieting his cries.

"You're scared. Why don't you have a collar?" She stretched to stroke him, her efforts rewarded when he offered his floppy ears. "Let's try to find an end. How did the rope get so tangled, huh?" He nosed her and allowed her help.

"Give me a little more time, I can't find the beginning. "Roll over on your side. Good baby. What do you know, you're a girl."

The high pitched frequency associated with her husband's spirit screeched. "Tim, what are you trying to tell me?"

"Pardon me?"

In her peripheral vision, she glimpsed a pair of tanned cowboy boots stopping alongside her.

"Looks like you could use an extra hand."

His baritone voice ignited tingles down her arms and resonated to her fingertips. Shelby's gaze hooked onto his mahogany eyes. Her mouth opened to answer but nothing came. Sable brown hair brushed the starched collar and his square jaw sported a five o'clock shadow even though it was just past noon. The corner of his lips inched higher transforming into a smile sending warm sensations to her belly then lowered to her feminine folds.

"Here, let me." He retrieved a penknife out of his pocket and knelt beside her. "Hold tight. I don't want the dog to move and get cut with my blade."

She nodded, forming the words to thank him, but her jaw quivered. She clamped her lips together. Goosebumps rose over her skin. She stared at his deft fingers, full of strength as they gently finessed the rope

14

loose. Now free, the canine jumped onto Shelby's lap taking every inch.

The handsome man sat on his haunches, leveled his luscious gaze with hers and chuckled. "I think you found a friend."

Her id swung into action along with her body. The ripples of pleasure aroused her in places where only her husband had given her full satisfaction. Shocked by her response, she processed her reaction. Since Tim's death, her desire for physical release or emotional attachment had been nonexistent. Who was this guy?

He shucked off his hat, gliding his hand through the thick locks of hair. "Can I help you with her?"

His eyes shined with life. She couldn't break their contact, didn't want to, but in the end, she shook off the moment, ending the connection.

This time her voice didn't falter. "I guess I should find a shelter and see if anyone claims her."

The cowboy settled the Stetson on his head. "I happen to know of one down the street. It's within walking distance. I'll show you. Can you coax her off your lap?"

Shelby relaxed her grip guiding the dog up on all fours. "Thanks."

The gentleman helped her to stand. "My name is Kyle. What's yours?"

As she stood, she wobbled. "Shelby. Nice to meet you."

He steadied her. "Same here." His words were sincere, then his gaze turned introspective.

"Is something wrong? Kyle?"

"No, ma'am…this way." He gestured with his arm.

She quickened her stride to walk beside him. The

cool shadows gave way to sunlight while she coaxed the dog to follow.

They approached a cross walk where a group of older women waited for the signal light to change.

A single voice rose above the din. "My dear, how are you today?"

Kyle panned to the right, searching, and then smiled. "Well, Mrs. Dent, I'm doing just fine. How are you?" He waited for Mrs. Dent as she shuffled through the ladies.

Her sun bonnet bounced with each word she spoke, "I'm doing well. We've missed you at our bridge tournaments, but most of all, I miss my partner. We always won and I don't take too kindly to losing."

Kyle nodded. "I've been out of town on business."

Mrs. Dent's alert eyes landed on her and the dog. "Looks like you're busy. Spreading yourself too thin isn't good for you."

"Yes, ma'am, you're right. This is Shelby. Shelby, Mira Dent." The signal changed and Kyle extended his arm. "May I help you, Mira?"

"I'd like that. Shelby, nice to meet you." Mira grasped Kyle's elbow.

"Nice to meet you, also." Shelby lagged a few paces behind, instantly liking the spritely woman.

Mira shuffled with a slow gait and resumed her conversation with Kyle. "Please come and see me sometime. I miss your mom and dad. Tell your brother he's invited too. We can reminisce about old times." Mrs. Dent grasped Kyle's forearm for his support and stepped up onto the sidewalk, then released him. "Thank you. Kyle, you don't have to be a stranger. I know we miss our loved ones, but we shouldn't be remiss and forget them."

He kissed her cheek. "My pleasure…You've always been thoughtful of my family. I'll take you up on your offer and bring something for that sweet tooth of yours."

Her smile brightened. "I'll have the tea ready."

Kyle straightened and winked. "I'll look forward to it. You take care now."

Mira's head bobbed. "You know I always do."

Kyle had extended kindness to his lovely friend. Surprisingly, his strong body adapted to guide Mira with gentleness.

"She seems like a very sweet woman."

His focus hinted he was a thousand miles away, then his awareness returned. "She is."

****

Shelby grinned at how the young and vivacious veterinarian's assistant greeted them with a pleasant smile. "Mr. Pressley, what can I do for you today?"

He held the door open while Shelby entered coaxing her four-legged friend inside.

Kyle wiped his boots on the entry rug. "Hi Liz, I see you have volunteered for holiday pay."

Liz's expressive face amplified her jovial attitude. "Oh yeah, several of us did."

Kyle removed his hat. "I appreciate everyone's dedication. The reason we're here, has anyone been looking for a lost dog? We found this one downtown."

Liz peered at a list hanging on the wall. "Give me a moment to check."

When Shelby sat in the closest vinyl covered chair, the canine scampered over and nuzzled her thigh. She stroked the red coat. The dog's brown eyes fasten with hers as though she was trying to tell her something. Although, Shelby didn't understand her, she did discern one thing. She had a connection with the brown-eyed renegade.

Liz poked her head over the counter. "Nope."

Kyle's hand whisked through his hair. "Is there a vacant kennel available?"

Shelby vaulted from her seat. "No. I mean, until someone comes forward, I'll keep her."

Liz's calm voice echoed in the room, "This facility is a no-kill-animal shelter, compliments of Mr. Pressley here, if that helps."

"How nice." That sounded tongue-in-cheek, she rephrased. "Truly, that's terrific. Do you think you'd have time to bathe and groom her for me? Also, I'll give you my cell number, in case someone comes for her."

"Of course, I can have Delores start on her right now. Would you like to wait or come back?"

"I'll stay, thank you."

Kyle stepped beside her. "How about a cup of coffee? I'm buying."

Liz rounded into the reception area with a leash in her hands. "I just made a fresh pot. Let me have your new friend. I'll feed and water her for you too."

Kyle led the way into the cozy lunchroom. He directed her to sit while he poured the java and set the mug in front of her.

She raised her arm in a cheers salute. "Thanks. I needed this."

He joined her across the table. "Where are you from?"

She sipped the hot steaming liquid and set the drink

on a coaster. "Texas." Her to-do list seemed never ending, but the first item was to find her husband's killer. Would she be able to recognize the right clues, understand them, and devise a plan to catch the bad guys? Sure, no problem, she could become Sherlock Holmes or Hercule Poirot...fictional characters. Her stomach curdled.

Shelby remembered the next decision she had to make. Should she change Alessa's position to president? Her youngest sister ran the business with efficiency and her new marketing ideas had outstanding results. The old adage timing is everything still held true. She shook her head. Her mind drifted a lot lately. There were times when life and stress were overwhelming.

She sighed. "You?"

"Wyoming. Are you on vacation...maybe with your husband?"

He noticed my wedding band. "No, I'm widowed." Shelby glanced away. When would the pain stop and her heart feel whole again?

Kyle murmured, "I'm sorry."

She raised her eyes to meet his. No other man compared to her soul mate and his presence never wavered. She stilled. Except today when she met Kyle, Tim's spirit had been AWOL ever since. Her gaze pierced Kyle's, taking his measure. He didn't back down or blink. She gave in first and focused on his strong fingers wrapped around his cup. "Thank you. It's hard."

Kyle's whispered. "I'm sure it is." He cleared his throat. "Where in Texas do you live? It's a big state."

Shelby grinned. "Everything is bigger in Texas or

so the saying goes. The heart of Texas. How about you?"

"Near here…Are you enjoying your stay?"

"I am."

Kyle eased back in his chair. "So tell me, what have you seen?"

"Not a lot, been doing some research."

His eyebrows rose. "For what?"

"A book." She was here for research, just not her current work in progress—truth by omission. She didn't see a need to discuss her real task.

He angled forward. "What kind?"

"It's fiction." She hoped. The Kachina doll, known as Ten-Blue-Sun, had many powers for good, but her husband's death pointed to murder. She didn't have any evidence to take to the police. If she voiced her opinion, one of two things would happen. Either, she'd be branded a lunatic or her husband was a thief. As far as she was concerned, the latter didn't have merit. Tim had an exceptional moral standard.

Hell, when he drove, she'd cut her eyes to the speedometer, begging him to set the cruise control one mile per hour over the limit. He'd say, "Laws must be obeyed even if we don't agree with them." Nope, not him, no way would he have stolen anything.

"Is it about this area? I could help since I know most of the places around here."

"Thanks, but I shouldn't."

Kyle's head cocked. "Why not?"

"For many reasons. I don't know you for one." And second, for the first time since his death, Tim's presence left her. Third, she had to figure out the significance of the doll, and fourth, would she be killed next?

A chuckle rumbled deep from within his broad chest. "If you let me help, we can get to know one another."

Her insides melted at the sound of his mirth. "Point taken. But what I need the most is a shower." She stood and washed her cup. "Do you want any more coffee?" She turned and met his gaze.

"I've had enough. Will you let me walk you to your hotel room?"

"No, you don't have to." She wiped the counter with the paper towel.

He rose from his chair. Reaching for the grounds to dump in the garbage, their hands met. "But I want to. I can help baby sit." Kyle nodded at the dog Delores had brought in a few minutes ago, now curled on the floor asleep. "Then, we could take in the fireworks, all three of us."

Her lower lip quivered from the jarring reaction of his touch. She gauged his character. His eyes shined with sincerity, his posture and manner open. She'd enjoy company who would actually talk back to her, unlike her conversations with Tim. As a local, he could possibly give her insight into the history of the Indian tribes.

The Kachina doll came from the Hopi people, but Tim wrote several unexplained entries in his journal pointing to the Shoshone and the Comanche. Through research she'd learned, the Shoshone language was a mixture of all three. She understood the connection with the Shoshone and the Comanche, but had questions concerning the Hopi lineage. She'd have to dig further.

Since she had met Kyle, Tim's spirit vanished. She didn't want to think about her husband leaving for good simply because she had male company. Her life hadn't been threatened since her arrival in Jackson, but her home had been burglarized several times. She weighed all the factors. "I'd like that."

Kyle winked. "We'll have a good time. Have you ever been to the Fourth celebration?"

"No, this will be my first time."

"You'll like it. I'll be waiting for you outside. I need to make a few phone calls."

After paying the bill and leaving her cell number with Liz, Shelby led them to her hotel. Out of the corner of her eye, she checked out Kyle. His stride gave him a self-confident air of command; she didn't think anyone would try to test him. For the first time since her husband died, she felt safe.

At the hotel door, she withdrew the keycard from her purse.

"I should check your room before you go in."

She added distance between them. "What? Why?"

If it were possible, he stood straighter, his chest heaved. The way he stated the words, "Anyone can get in your room" had more meaning than she could ascertain.

He strode inside and checked the premises. "All clear. I'll wait for you out on the porch."

****

As she closed the door, Kyle exhaled. Memories bombarded him. His dad sat him down with his brother, never shedding the tears that gathered in his eyes. 'I have bad news...Your mom didn't make it.' She'd been oblivious to her surroundings and men had kidnapped

22

her. They abducted her from her hotel, ending her life. He shook his head to end the foul flashback.

Kyle settled on the top of the wooden steps leading to her small veranda. The dog plopped down beside him. He wouldn't frighten Shelby with the dangers of keeping his company. Obligated for her protection, he made the appropriate phone calls to his security detail. Knowing he wouldn't see her again after the holiday, he opted not to tell her. Why invite questions?

If he were honest, there was something special about this gal. When he met her trying to free the dog, his gut rolled. Her bright eyes welcomed him. At that moment, he'd wanted to walk through her mind.

His gift had many benefits. The ability to journey into the recesses of someone's subconscious, to understand the person's intentions, gave him insights into their character and world. The pure of heart blessed him immeasurably. It always sounded corny even to him when he explained his experiences to his older brother, Jude. His sibling never believed in spirits or any other world except the one he was in.

At first, the lack of control bothered him. He'd project when he hadn't meant to do it. Through discipline and direction, astral projecting became manageable. By the time he'd mastered the power within, he'd kept the occurrences to himself. For the most part, people were good and decent. The evil ones…

Not many people could withstand the horror. His gut clenched, then churned with revulsion. He had first-hand knowledge of the heinous people walking this earth, corrupt perceptions of life left little doubt about their sanity.

During his military service, beyond enemy lines, he'd traveled into many adversarial minds. Appalled by the interrogation techniques inflicted upon prisoners of war, he'd sworn to help his fellow soldiers. Which he did with success, but his superiors used him unmercifully for other things. He'd saved lives, but many people benefited by prostituting his gift. After Dan died, he had kept his vow.

Kyle's insides roiled because he wanted to mind walk with Shelby. A woman he didn't know, a lady in all practicality he wouldn't see again, however, a soul he wished to visit.

He wanted her company. The challenge to get her to agree to watch the fireworks with him became paramount. In the break room when their hands met, the unexpected jolt traveled from his fingers through his body and landed on his third leg. He was an instant believer in the saying stiff as a fencepost. His groin tightened, again. As the evening progressed with Shelby, he'd know whether he was acting like an addled teenager or if his instinct was correct. He voted for the last.

Shelby stepped out of her room. He rose, and made modest adjustments. "Shall we go?" He gently tugged the leash. The sleeping dog yawned, then ambled to all fours and shook. "Little lady, you need to come with us."

"How do you think she'll react to the fireworks?" Shelby pursed her lips.

"We're about to find out. But I think she'll do fine."

At the town square, he led Shelby through a curved structure made of elk antlers held together by wire.

Once past the noted arch entrance, he guided her by the small of her back to a great view of the night sky.

****

The man glared into the lady's eyes, hoping to intimidate her. "How much are ya' talkin' about?" He didn't trust this one.

"Enough so you can have a fresh start…somewhere else."

He peered over the spectators to see Kyle and Shelby. "What about her?"

"If she gets in the way, deal with her."

He squinted, giving his evil look he practiced. "It'll cost ya' more."

"Just do the job correctly and you won't have any problems. But I understand what you want and agree to double the amount."

"You can count on it bein' done right." He laughed inwardly. His luck was changin'. He fixed his gaze on his paying customer ploddin' through the crowd. His tongue swiped across his lips. When he'd hesitated to take on Ms. Littleton, the ante upped immediately. He learnt that from his cousin playin' poker and it worked. Sweet vengeance, he'd be paid twice for the same job.

As for the wench on Kyle's arm, he'd already accepted that assignment. She'd be an easy target, unless she continued to hang with the asshole from the multi-millionaire's club. When the time was right, he'd play his hand.

Pressley had bodyguards. Ha! People thought he was stupid. He'd show them. Soon, the high and mighty Pressleys would be mournin'. He rubbed his hands together. Yep, an eye for an eye, that's what the good book says. A plum fact, hell is where he was headed, but he'd have plenty of money and fun getting there.

****

The hairs on the back of Kyle's neck rose. He shifted. Kyle widened his stance, balancing on the balls of his feet and searched the crowd noting first Shelby's position, then each group and person. No one stood out. His Navy SEAL training took over. Senses on high alert, he zeroed in on anything suspicious. His gut instinct kicked into gear, adrenaline coursed through his veins, his hands curled into fists at his side. His taut muscles readied for action.

He'd asked his two bodyguards to keep their distance so Shelby wouldn't question the need. *Shit*, if anything happened, he'd have to wing it until they could get across the square.

Hands grabbed his arm. Startled, he whirled to face his adversary, shoved his attacker back with one hand and cocked his arm to throw a haymaker. When he focused, Shelby stood in his grasp, her eyes rounded in horror. Anger gave way to relief. He captured her shoulder, tucked her to his side as he scanned the multitude of people. Not giving her a choice but to move with him, her arms wrapped around his waist while he circled, covering all three hundred and sixty degrees.

Her voice wavered, "My God, what's wrong?"

How would he explain the ominous instinct? He couldn't, but he understood something wasn't right. One of the many lessons he learned in the military, you act because by the time you react, it was too late. Another factor that was innate as breathing, assess the situation, then decide a course of action.

He glimpsed at the two men striding for him,

taking note everything was in order, he gave the sign and his bodyguards backed off.

As the youngest son of the Pressley empire, there were ups and downs living a privileged life. Money didn't make him any better than anyone else. The majority of occasions he felt luckier and other times, it was downright harder.

This was one of those instances. He didn't go around telling people he was worth a fortune, and as a newfound friend, he hadn't told Shelby. He expelled his breath and calmed.

"Nothing, we're good."

She hugged him and gazed into his eyes. The connection of her trust, coupled with his conviction to protect her, created an inconceivable force within him, producing a stimulus for something deeper, an impetus toward a commitment. He sucked in a breath and admitted there was more.

A visceral reaction drew him to her—where no woman had taken him in a long time. He visualized his hands in her thick brown hair spread on his pillows, tangled in sheets after a night in bed…with him. Sweet Jesus, it'd been ages since he'd had this type of response.

Her hazel eyes danced. Shelby tilted her head, and her silky hair cascaded down her back. The creamy skin of her neck invited him and his body answered in a primal way. His cock rose to the lure of her feminine appeal.

Her lips transformed into a beautiful smile and her natural beauty smacked him on target, and blood rushed to his dick. He shifted minimally to relieve the pressure in his jeans but not to dislodge her from his thigh. Hot streaks of desire shot through his veins, while tiny sparks set his skin on fire. He shivered, recognizing the irony. Reining in his thoughts, drawing back his fervor, he blinked long, inhaled fully and released the air. "When you touched my arm, I responded. I didn't mean to scare you." And he hadn't.

With Shelby's arms wrapped around his waist, their gazes still locked, her eyes were a window to her soul. He wanted to mind walk with Shelby. No. He intended to keep his vow. Damn, what was he thinking? What had this woman done to him? Or had he found a trustworthy lady? Everything was out of sync.

He had learned to listen to his premonitions. His gut told him something big was going down, but he couldn't tell if they were included. Shit, he had the ability to search, seek, and find what he needed to know, but with his oath, he closed the one path he could use to find answers to his questions.

At this juncture, he'd placed the shift, if that's what he could call it, in the back of his mind and chose to enjoy the rest of the evening.

****

Shelby unfolded her arms from Kyle. "You didn't, but I think I frightened you." Very strange…The familiar hum of Tim's presence echoed. The comforting sound changed into a horrible staccato rhythm she had never experienced. Her heart paced with the beat. Just as quick, the discordant pitch stopped. Then his spirit left again. Tim's warning and Kyle's response occurred at the same time, were they related? She didn't know and retreated one step.

When she touched Kyle, an unmistakable surreal contact melded their forces together, very close to a spiritual connection. The attraction between them could be attributed to yin and yang, male-female. Shadows don't exist without light, but there was more relevance. She couldn't attach a description to their bond...yet.

"Did you lose your balance or want to tell me something?" His fingers lightly held on to her arm, then slid down to the inside of her wrist, gliding further, tickling her palm.

Her heart rate accelerated, she opened her mouth and gasped. "I've...I named Annie."

"The dog? How did—?"

"Orphaned...Red coat."

He let go and smiled. "Annie, I like it."

She enjoyed his company and his handsome features attracted her too. The tailored western shirt outlined his broad shoulders and molded to each ripple of his sinewy chest. Her gaze marched on to his slim waist and glanced lower. He emitted sex appeal. She reacted like any other woman. Every time he chuckled, her insides twirled, sending erotic flames, building a wild fire she didn't want to put out.

The hissing rockets streamed into the ink black sky, detonated and twinkled down to the earth with phosphorescent colors and a montage of patterns. Shelby joined the cacophony of oohs and ahhs.

Shelby angled toward Kyle. "This is great." She pointed at the ball of red fur. "I can't believe she's sleeping through this."

Kyle closed the space between them and lightly touched her with his arm and shoulder. "Annie has a full belly and she knows we'll keep her safe."

Shelby turned. Their gazes met. Her heart hammered inside her chest. There were two sets of fireworks, one in the sky and one between them.

Boom. The pyrotechnic exploded and the profound sound waves broke the spell. To ease the mind numbing, searing impact of his touch, she mentally scanned over her to-do list. *Damn.* She struggled to collect her thoughts. First, she'd try to figure out who killed Tim and why his spirit disappeared. The doll had to be the connection to his death.

Kyle grinned and amplified his voice over the continual barrage of noise. "This is my favorite part."

Shelby kept her vigil, watching the display, the night sky bright with painted colors. "On the account of it being so beautiful or because it's the climax?" She glanced at Kyle and winced when he smiled at her double entendre.

"They never seem to have enough to satisfy me." She rolled her eyes, clamped her lips together, maybe that would keep her mouth shut.

Kyle chuckled, drifted close, placing his mouth near her ear. "I would have to lie down. My neck would get a crick in it if I had to watch the fireworks like this for very long."

His moist, heated breath danced across her skin sending waves of delight to every nerve ending. She swore they were all connected to her clit. Her eyes closed. Did the fairies spread pixie dust over her? When she opened them and pivoted to face Kyle, his gaze met hers.

He winked, his regard eased into a gentle caress. His intent shifted. Entranced, she sank into the liquid brown depths of his eyes fully aware she'd give herself willingly to him, right now.

Awareness detonated, discharging an electrical

storm within her. Bolts of lightning shattered the involuntary response to breathe. Finally, her lungs expanded and her vertigo disappeared. This nexus between them was mind bending and soul altering.

As though in another world, she sensed rather than saw people shuffling around her. Someone bumped into Kyle and all the fireworks ended.

Protectively, he drew her to his side and led her through the crowd. Kyle guided her to an empty bench. After they sat, Annie maneuvered between their feet and curled underneath them.

Her nerves settled and she listened to the music drifting from across the street. She grinned as the patrons' voices buzzed with the night celebrations high up on a balcony. "This reminds me of Bourbon Street, on a smaller scale of course. People are having fun and enjoying the evening."

Kyle arched his eyebrows. "You've been to Mardi Gras?"

"No, especially not during the celebration. I visited under more sedate times. Mardi Gras is a little wild for me. You?"

Kyle smiled. "Ah, the Big Easy. On several occasions."

For the first time, she noticed his dimples. He had two on each side. Kyle's focus drew her in and held her captive. His gaze radiated an emotion she couldn't quite place. She cleared her throat. "So tell me, what other fun things do you do for entertainment? I know you've been to Mardi Gras and the Fourth of July celebration here in Jackson."

A huge smile lit his face and he laughed out loud. "I've been to a few places over the years. But my favorite place is right here." His baritone carried a warm sound.

"Really, I would never have taken you for a man who lets dust gather on his boots."

"If the dust gets a chance to settle, I'd prefer to be at home. What about you?" He draped his arm along the back of the bench resting his hand near Shelby's shoulder but not touching her.

"I like to get away." Vacations were always fun, but this trip was purely for answers. "Do you do a lot of traveling?"

He crossed his legs. "Yeah, guess I do. That's why I like being at home."

"Me too." Shelby's voice trailed off thinking of her ranch and family. She stopped her woolgathering and rose. "I should call it a night. Thank you for your help with Annie. I enjoyed your company and the lovely evening." Not waiting for an answer, she called, "Annie, time to go."

****

Kyle stood and hoped. "Wait, I'll walk you back to your room."

She bent down and picked up the leash. "You don't have to, thanks." When Shelby straightened, her eyes journeyed from his face down to his chest and then traveled lower to his midsection.

He didn't want her to leave. Her bright smile put sunshine in his drab life. With his extensive travel schedule, he met professional women all the time. Hard and fast rule number one, he never dated them. When he did meet ladies, they usually knew his background and their intentions were clear, they wanted his money, not him.

But Shelby was different. The few hours of making her acquaintance, he had learned she was educated, writing a book, gained strength to continue after losing her husband, and a genuinely gracious woman.

He didn't refute the sexual attraction and wanted her in every way a red-blooded man desired a woman. But there was a difference. He wanted to caress every inch of her with his hands, tongue, and body. From their reactions when they brushed against one another, he discerned their releases would be erotic and on a different level than any he'd ever experienced.

When he saw where Shelby's gaze landed, his heart raced and his ego soared to new heights. Her cheeks blushed to crimson. Blood rushed to his groin. His hustler reacted and he adjusted his jeans. He wouldn't let her wiggle out of the few minutes they had left to share. Plus, he couldn't shake the dark foreboding he had earlier.

Her safety was his responsibility. The guard he had placed at Shelby's room kept him updated via texts. He could delegate the task, but he didn't want to. He wanted to escort her.

She lifted her long, fixed stare to connect with his. He wanted a few more minutes with her. "Dance with me?"

"On the sidewalk?" She rolled her shoulders. "I'd like that." Her lips drifted up at each corner.

He noted her "tells" as a signal for a positive outcome. She wouldn't be good in a poker game. He had to remember, if she ever partnered up with him, make sure she wore sunglasses and loose clothing. Nope, the lift of her mouth would be a dead giveaway.

Patsy Cline's song "Crazy" drifted from the bar. In

several paces, he stood in front of her. He gathered her right hand in his left and the other rested on Shelby's hip, letting her chose the distance between them. As he shifted his weight, she closed the space and laid her cheek against his shoulder. When the music ended, his palm slid to her lower back, holding her responsive body, willing her to continue dancing.

Vince Gill's "Go Rest High on That Mountain" played and she hadn't stepped away. With each sway, she leaned against him in full contact. Pleasure scuttled down from his head to his balls because her position showed trust. Yes, there was a connection. The summer night's breeze wasn't enough to cool the heat of their movement. Shelby's face burrowed into the crook of his neck and her breath skimmed across his skin. The heat glazed his flesh. His heart pounded, raising his temperature. Beads of sweat trickled down his back and he grasped her tighter.

Drops of moisture rolled down his chest. Shelby sniffed, her gaze found his. Tears dripped off her chin and he froze. "Shelby?"

"Sorry...I should go."

He nodded and draped his arm over her shoulder. The sidewalk narrowed, people milled about and he didn't get a chance to talk.

At the hotel, she used her keycard, opened the door and crossed the threshold.

"Let me check your room."

She turned to him. "No, I'm fine. Nice meeting you and thanks again for everything."

"It was my pleasure. You take care, Shelby...what's your last name?"

"Littleton. And yours is Pressley? Did I remember

correctly?"

"Yes, ma'am."

"You too, Kyle Pressley."

"Can I help you with Annie? I could take her home with me tonight and bring her back in the morning?"

"No, she'll be fine. I'll tell the front desk about her tomorrow."

"Then have a good night, Shelby Littleton."

"You too."

He spun and headed toward his bodyguard. "Hey, Sam, thanks for watching."

Sam nodded. "Never seen you like this before."

Kyle kept walking past the man who waited for his response. "What are you talking about?"

Sam caught up to him and smirked. "Son, I've known you since you were a teenager and you're taken with the lady. Don't try and deny it."

Kyle released all the air out of his lungs then filled them again. "I'm interested in getting to know her, that's all."

He wanted to know Shelby Littleton's favorite color, flower, and music. Something about the last song made her cry and he questioned if he'd ever get the chance to ask. Hell, he could come up with a reason…morning coffee and donuts…who could turn down pastries and a caffeine jolt?

Sam waved. "Goodnight, I'm meeting Linda for a late dinner."

"'Night and tell your lovely wife I said hello."

****

Shelby closed the door and sighed. How could a simple phrase, *have a good night Shelby Littleton*, convey so much tenderness? Her stomach fluttered.

When they had touched, explosions the size of Texas blasted through her body and blazed a fiery trail over her skin.

God, she would miss getting to know Kyle better. What was she thinking? She should have reminded him about his offer to be her guide. Instead, she let a perfect opportunity slip out of her grasp. She leaned against the doorjamb. It was probably for the best. Her home was with her family and work, twenty-four hours south of here.

Shelby stroked her arms warding off the chill, her tired muscles begged to be stretched. Wyoming nights were cold and a hot shower would warm her. She focused on the welcoming bed with Annie comfortable on top of the bedspread. "Humpf." She straightened her shoulders and squared them. Tomorrow was a new day and she'd get back to researching her husband's journal entries.

A hum whispered near Shelby. She smiled. Tim would join her in a few seconds. His presence drifted around her. "Hey, sweetheart, why did you leave, do you have a to-do list in your world? No, don't tell me. I won't get the humor, I promise. Listen, we have a lot to talk about, but I'm going to get my shower first."

At last in her nightgown, Tim's company soothed her. Shelby breathed, "I love you and miss you so." She stretched her hands to touch him. The ambient temperature dropped, his spirit skimmed over her fingers, traveled up her arms then enveloped her body. She shivered from the cool air and quivered with anticipation. Her ears popped. "What are you trying to tell me?" She followed the air differential to where he hovered above her backpack. She understood.

On the bed, she carefully unwrapped and held the doll. A vibration coursed through her and an odd aura emanated from Ten-Blue-Sun. "Tim, what's happening?" A pure light encased her while a loving and healing sensation stroked her soul. She relaxed and her heart opened to a world she never knew existed.

Chapter Four

Shelby floated through the air, weightless, traveling further from her physical body. Surrounded by beautiful prismatic lights, time or the lack thereof had no meaning. There wasn't a background, any buildings, no biomes of earth, just an ethereal beauty. The brilliant refracted spectrums didn't hurt her eyes and lent to a more spiritual, unworldly sphere. She peered down at what should've been her human form. A translucent field took the space, but within the boundaries, pinpoints of white light sparkled like stars in the night sky.

The intensity of another presence drew her attention. She recognized Tim and extended her essence to touch him. When their life forces comingled, peace and tranquility surrounded them. He drew her close. The thrust of his energy encapsulated hers and propelled her to a pinnacle, an edge. Multi-colored points of light emerged and exploded, enlarging the field of their joined powers. Tim withdrew and stayed at her side, his love evident.

"Tim, where am I and who are these people?"

"You're in the First Realm."

A being approached them.

"This is She-Who-Smiles. You'll get to know her."

Shelby didn't understand the camaraderie she shared with the woman. "She-Who-Smiles is lovely and her spirit really does seem to smile."

"I want you to meet one more, he's a medicine man."

Finally, she was getting answers and the one disclosure she wanted to know. "Wait, Tim, were you murdered?"

"Yes."

"Enough." One-Who-Soars-With-Eagles dictated.

This wasn't a request. She beheld the dominant one and his strong presence overwhelmed her. Dark colors inundated her vision. Scenes of slaughter, death, and destruction appeared. She felt rather than heard the screams. Intolerable pain and absolute horror flooded her consciousness. Frightened, she searched for Tim and he wasn't there. She turned for She-Who-Smiles and she too had disappeared.

Shelby tumbled down, whirling, everything blurred before her. Her stomach flipped, then flopped, gravity overtaking her entity. She plunged into her earthly form. Gasping for breath, her chest heaved. Her eyes opened and released the doll. Tears rolled down her cheeks and heart-wrenching despair possessed her. Her body temperature climbed until perspiration trickled down her face.

"What just happened?" She glanced at Annie still sleeping. "Tim, what's going on?"

His presence cooled her down. Remembering the love and commitment they shared in the First Realm. "I do believe and trust you." She cautiously placed the sacred doll back where she belonged…for now.

****

Shelby woke to the ringing of the telephone. Instinctively she grabbed her cell on the night stand.

Nope, not the mobile. The intermittent jingle continued. She picked up the hotel phone and in the seconds it took to get the handset to her ear, she cringed thinking something must be wrong at home. "Hello."

"Good morning sleepy head." The masculine baritone articulated in her ear.

"Kyle?"

"How many guys do you have calling you?"

She skipped his question. "I thought I recognized your voice. Hey, thanks for walking Annie and me back last night."

"Get up and open the door. I have coffee that's burning my hands. I'm juggling a cell, and pastries from the bakery. In a few more seconds, everything will be on the ground."

Shelby threw the phone in the cradle, put on her robe, ran to the door, and squinted through the peep hole. *Yep, his hands were full.* She yanked the door open holding her skimpy robe closed and helped him get everything to the small table.

He looked magnificent. *God, my hair isn't combed, my teeth, yuck. Ah hell.* "Give me a few minutes, I'll be back to take you up on all the goodies you brought."

"Great, then I'll give you my tour."

She nodded. "I'd like that."

****

Kyle smiled. Shelby couldn't help being sultry and beautiful in the morning. With her hair messed and her sleepy look, he was aroused just seeing her. A wicked idea crossed his mind. *Did the goodies include him? Maybe, just maybe.* He yelled to the closed bathroom door. "I'm taking Annie for a quick walk."

Waiting for Annie to finish her business, he

contemplated the odds on meeting a lady like Shelby, who fit into his world. He'd had his share of relationships over the years and across the globe, but none could come close to the desire she inspired in him. Except one.

The memories of Christine had been buried successfully. Why were they popping into his mind now? He reflected back in time. He loved Mira Dent and having her as a grandmother would have been heaven on earth. Bile rose and scalded his throat at the recollection of his ex-fiancée. He shoved the offensive reminder away.

In the past, most women were too fixated on his money and family, but Shelby knew nothing about him. But she liked him for who he was and he damn sure wanted to get to this woman better. Much better. His heart skipped a beat. He involuntarily ruffled at the idea she would have other men calling her this morning. Wow, where did that reaction come from? He mentally tucked those thoughts away to examine later.

Annie's morning rituals completed, he knocked on Shelby's door. When she opened, Kyle stepped across the threshold. "Ready to get started? We're burning daylight."

"I'm ready. Annie, time to go."

"I'll get her for you. I want to stop by the grocery store and buy something for us to eat."

"A picnic sounds wonderful."

Kyle ruffled the red-coated renegade's ears. "I'll drive my old truck, I call her Jalopy. It'll give Annie more room and she can't do any harm."

Shelby froze in place. "I don't know, maybe I should take my car."

"Whatever makes you feel more comfortable."

She adjusted her shoulders, her body relaxed. "Your truck sounds fine. You're right, Annie will have more room and if she gets muddy, we can put her in the back."

Her body language gave away the exact moment she'd come to her decision. What were her actions when her answer was no?

He attempted to remember all the situations. Damn, it'd be nice to have Jude's ability. His brother had a photographic memory. Jude hated his gift and didn't perceive it as such. On numerous occasions, Kyle would've rejoiced at having the power of recollection and retention.

Kyle followed Shelby and smiled. He enjoyed getting to know her "tell" signs.

Shelby opened his truck door and Annie jumped up to the floor, then settled on the middle of the seat. In one easy motion, Shelby climbed inside and shut the door.

Kyle leaped out of the way, shook his head and muttered, "Independent woman...and I get to sit beside the dog."

****

Inside the grocery store, Kyle pushed the cart as she walked beside him. "How about cold cuts?"

He shrugged.

She questioned him again. "Do you like sandwiches?"

"I like healthy food, if that helps."

"Good, so do I." She picked up a small loaf of organic multi-grain bread from the bakery department. "Do you exercise too?"

"Every day. You said 'too', what's your regimen?"

He admired her physique as Shelby jammed her hands in the pockets of her light jacket. "Aerobics, lift a little weights, walk and jog. What about you?"

"I have a gym at home and run. Maybe we can work out together?"

Shelby grimaced.

He laughed enjoying her reactions. "What was that expression about?"

She headed for the ten-items-or-less register. "I don't exercise in front of anyone."

At the check-out, he quit unloading the basket. "How old are you?"

Shelby emptied the remaining items. "That, dear sir, is none of your business."

He liked the way she bristled under his scrutiny. "Well, I think you look terrific."

****

Kyle led Shelby down a Grand Teton National Park trail into a lush meadow. Annie's nose lowered scouting the distinctive scents. Green sage and spring flowers wafted in the air. Giant waterfalls flowed down from the melting snow caps giving the valley much needed moisture for the summer months. The nearby rippling stream had a calming effect. The rocky spires projected toward the open sky, the highest pinnacle possessed a power beyond him and beyond man.

Shelby stilled beside him and sighed. "This is beautiful."

He shifted his stance and stood in front of her. "This is one of my favorite places. I'd thought you'd enjoy it."

Surprise and something else crossed her face. "And

43

you're sharing it with me? Thank you."

He lifted her chin with his index finger to connect her gaze with his. "You're welcome."

"This means more to me than you could know." She glanced away. Her focus appeared to land on the distant mountain range. "I didn't mean to say that out loud."

Her cheeks changed to a reddish tint. He grinned delighted in recognizing her little nuances. The vermillion hue of embarrassment changed to a full blown glow. He angled toward Shelby. "Today, with you, this means more to me too." His nostrils flared, drawing in her scent, wanting to haul her into his arms, but waiting for her to calm down.

"Are you hungry?" Her throat pulsed then she swallowed hard, her voice low and sultry.

"Sure." He doubted they had the same things in mind but he'd settle for a turkey sandwich.

After eating, Shelby lay beside him on his western quilt with Annie at their feet. He lifted the arm covering his eyes, leaned forward and relaxed on an elbow. He gazed down at Shelby. She was bewitching him. The notion she could have this much power over him needled his conscience.

The fragrance of her silky hair seduced him, along with the spring breeze carrying the familiar aroma of new growth and life. Her reactions increased his enthusiasm to pursue a relationship, well, at least to get to know her better. And he sure in the hell didn't want to stop the sexual connection.

Her sensual lips beckoned him to kiss her and he craved her lithe body. He hungered to taste the thin, sensitive skin behind her ears, neck, and wrists.

Fascinated by her pale skin, he wanted to compare his tanned hands against the gentle curve of her hip and the slope of her thigh.

Yet her physical appearance wasn't the only thing that enticed him. She shared some of his passions. Exercising and eating healthy were important to him. He envisioned perspiration sliding down her temples. Tempted to lick the salty dew, his tongue swept over his lips. Decadent thoughts immerged, drifting to more seductive advances, his mouth lingering at the pulse in her throat, coasting down to play with her nipples, his cock lengthened with his erotic musings. This woman stirred a need in him to take her to his bed.

He wished to let passion set the course, to allow their minds and soul connect. Yes, he wanted to walk in her mind. For the first time in years, he considered using his gift, but he'd given his oath. He wouldn't employ his ability for his own benefit. In fact, he would never apply his talent again. He cleared his throat. "I like being with you."

****

Shelby inhaled deep, the weight of Kyle's eyes constricted her chest. "I'm enjoying this too..."

She sat up, braced her hands behind her to bear her weight. She peered over her shoulder at Kyle still resting on his arm. "The picnic was a good idea."

The outdoors and peaceful setting had dissipated most of what happened to her last night. She wanted to think everything that happened in the First Realm was real. Tim was murdered. And she couldn't shake the horrible scenes One-Who-Soars-With-Eagles had shared with her. All the pieces of the puzzle didn't fit together. She didn't have a clue how this involved her and Tim. For today, she wanted good, positive thoughts, not murder, death, and destruction. The lack of Tim's presence still nagged the back of her mind. In fact every time Kyle was around, Tim left.

Kyle rose to a sitting position and held one knee with his elbow while the other leg stretched out. "I want to show you so many places."

Her gaze wandered. Kyle's T-shirt encased his broad shoulders. The cotton fabric tight against his chest tapered down to a trim waist. Her eyes journeyed lower to his muscular thighs where his snug jeans wrapped around them. The bulge hidden in his denims—
"I'm sorry what did you say?"

She glanced and his double dimples deepened. His full smile revealed his perfect teeth against his bronzed skin. He had caught her ogling. "Crap." She sprung to her feet and strode away.

Kyle's footsteps pursued hers, getting closer. He grasped her hand and swung her to face him. "Shelby, stop."

As she turned, embarrassment threaded its tendrils from the top of her head down to her feet. Kyle lifted her chin with his thumb forcing her to look at him. Heat from her cheeks added to the humiliation.

He whispered, "No harm done."

Kyle cupped each side of her jawline and feathered kisses across her lips. He slowly added pressure and caressed her mouth. Her knees wobbled, his arms encircled giving her support. He stroked her back with one hand and when she buried her face to his chest, he massaged her neck and shoulders. "That's wonderful."

His breath tickled her ears when he whispered, "Your muscles were hard as a rock."

"And now?"

His head lowered to take another taste. "Much better."

Annie barked and her front paws landed on their hips. Her bright eyes greeted them.

Kyle pushed her down. "Great timing, Annie."

She moaned and slid her arms around his waist.

He returned her embrace. "I want you, but you're not ready."

Shelby nestled deeper into his warm body and didn't reply. Her mind reeled with all the reasons she shouldn't go to bed with him so soon, but her eager body wanted him in every physical way imaginable.

He rested his chin on top of her head. "Let's take Annie for a walk, okay? There's a stream down there."

Shelby gazed into his understanding eyes that still held molten desire. "I'd like that."

Annie ran ahead and plunged into the water. She laughed when Kyle picked up a few stones and she excitedly counted the skips out loud. This was perfect and serene.

Add nature's pristine beauty to the mix and her soul calmed. The slight breeze caressed her skin. She closed her eyes. For the first time since her husband's death, she let herself enjoy life.

Did she have a right when his murderer ran free? She had vowed to find the perpetrator. Saddened again, her spirit tumbled.

She stood beside her husband's closed casket. Memories flooded her mind, the reflections as clear as a pool of mountain water. Gut-wrenching sorrow tore her apart, piece by piece, knowing she would never see him again, to touch, to laugh and cry. Life would've been easier had she been killed too, a bullet to end the mind-numbing emptiness. Without her family, she'd have been lost.

She was grateful her sisters never left her side. Alessa clasped her elbow. "Shelby, are you all right?"

She stared at the coffin. "No, Al. God, no."

Kyle's distant voice rifled through her conscious. "Shelby, are you all right?"

When she opened her eyes, she met his worried gaze. "I'm sorry, what did you say?"

Kyle grasped her shoulders. "Are you okay?"

Shelby nodded.

She swayed and his grip tightened to steady her. "Are you sure? You don't look good."

"I'm fine." Her arms slipped around his neck and she gave him a hug. She drew strength from this man she hardly knew. The bond surpassed their physical attraction. Could there be a connection to the doll? She had to figure out the answers and soon or she'd end up in a psych ward.

When she drifted away, Kyle's head tilted. "Who's Al?"

"I said that out loud?" *Damn.* "My youngest sister." She was losing her mind. And what if she really hadn't astral projected to the First Realm? Did her imagination transport her to fantasyland? Maybe this whole doll thing was her soul searching for answers that simply weren't there. Then she'd have to admit she fabricated Tim's manifestations. She would be forced to side with the authorities that Tim committed suicide.

The premise of those thoughts meant the trip to Jackson was worthless but also meeting Kyle held no special meaning. Everything that had happened so far, she'd blown completely out of proportion. The physical attraction between them was human pheromones at work. *No.*

She wouldn't allow confusion to rule. This man in front of her was real. And Tim wouldn't have killed himself. Those statements were true, absolute, genuine, and irrefutable.

"Ah, what were you thinking about or am I prying?"

"Nothing." Like she'd share where her mind wandered. "Nothing at all."

Kyle guided her to sit and lowered himself beside her. "Your husband?"

"I don't know what I would've done without my family's support and my work to keep me busy."

His hand rubbed her back. "Family is important, especially when you lose a loved one." The comforting strokes eased her chaotic thoughts and his words of encouragement alleviated the turmoil.

Annie barked, pranced over and sat on both of their laps.

The cold water seeped into her clothes and she frowned. "We need to teach you some manners."

"Since we're wet, let's head back." He scooted Annie off, and he helped her to stand.

****

At the hotel, Shelby slid from the bench seat landing steady on both feet while Annie bounded from the back of Kyle's truck trailing behind her.

Kyle rounded the front of Jalopy. "I would have helped you."

"Oh, that's okay." She walked to her door then fished for her keycard in her purse, while Kyle waited beside her.

Shelby stilled and glanced at him. Her eyebrows rose in question.

"I want to make sure you get in safely."

Shelby inserted her card in the slot. "Thanks."

Kyle crossed the threshold first and Shelby followed. His hand stopped her at the doorway.

"Why are you so...You have a penchant for safety?"

He ignored her question. "Let me check things out."

Annie bolted past and hopped on the bed.

"No, get down, you're wet." Kyle snapped his finger and thumb, then pointed.

Annie hopped off, circled several times before she plopped on the floor with a huff.

"Good girl." Kyle's voice softened.

He entered the bathroom. The click of the shower door unfastened then closed. He made his way back to her. "Everything is fine."

"No robbers or ghosts?" She doubted he'd take her seriously.

"Ghosts?" Kyle chuckled and stopped in front of her standing toe to toe.

Hearing his mirth, she locked her knees. His strong but gentle hand cradled her cheek. She tilted her head and pressed against his palm soaking in his strength and tenderness.

Kyle's body tightened under her touch. He hovered over her ear, his breath danced through her hair. Desire laced with warm moisture cascaded down her neck to land at her feminine juncture. "I'd like to kiss you again."

An intense heat generated low in her belly creating a need, a craving. "I'd like that."

"Hmm," Kyle murmured, closing the distance. He cupped each side of her jawline with both hands, whispering his lips across hers then maneuvered to add several inches between them. His hooded eyes spoke volumes, he wanted more and so did she.

She feathered a kiss on his palm. As she inclined away from him, she relished the hunger and yearned to satisfy him. Kyle gathered her in his arms, parted her mouth and she opened. As new lovers on an exploration, she stroked and he caressed in return.

A low moan reverberated in his throat as she pulled on his shoulders to get closer. Her mind reeled with the consequences of what she wanted. His erotic touch woke her body from hibernation, hot passion streamed through her veins. She had refused all relationships since her husband's death. Now, she wanted this man. Her hands slid to his back drawing his chest to rub her achy breasts.

The pressure from his muscular abs against her firm nipples added to the fire that burned deep in her belly. Erupting low, the heated cauldron churned, simmering down to her feminine nub. She hefted her left leg around his hip massaging her apex. Her strict moral codes and standards had vanished. In all honesty, her promise to Tim was still secure in her mind.

She undulated at Kyle's side, aching to have him. All at once, the spewing steam bubbled in all directions. The potent force detonated sending a storm of passion she'd gladly dance in.

Chapter Five

He angled to her throat and Shelby eased her head back, her climax just out of reach. His sweet kisses journeyed to her jaw. His tongue trailed moisture to the thin skin behind her ear.

He whispered, "You taste like honey on a spring day."

Shelby opened to refute his comment, but gasped as his mouth wandered to her earlobe. He nipped the soft skin with his teeth then soothed it with his lips before he released her and traveled to her neck.

She guided his palm to her breast; the lacy bra abraded her nipples adding to his erotic caress. She arched. Her hands roamed down his sinewy chest to his flat abdomen. His muscles tensed under her fingertips. But she didn't stop, slowly, drifting down to his midsection. The outline of his shaft sent shivers of anticipation to her nipples.

Kyle moaned. "You're not ready and I can wait."

"Mmm?"

He gently steered her backward. "Look at me."

Her eyes adjusted, latching onto his.

"I literally ache to have you and believe me I can tell you want me. But earlier today, you were still thinking of your husband…I don't want to be his stand-in. When we join, I'd prefer it'd be my name on your lips."

She blinked long. The heat of humiliation flooded her cheeks. She cleared her throat. "I understand." Trying for lucidity, she straightened her top and attempted to disentangle her thoughts.

This was the first time she'd have let a man take her to bed since her soul mate. She'd rejected plenty, but it had been at the beginning, not after heavy petting, primed and ready for sex. Rejection was a bitch.

Although she couldn't explain the attraction she had for Kyle, ultimately, he was right. She had no business making love to a man she hardly knew. "Thank you for a wonderful day." She twisted the handle, opened the door and gave him room to leave.

He cocked his head to the side. "Shelby?"

Unable to face his censure, she took a giant step backward and focused on his boots. "No, Kyle, you're absolutely right."

Kyle answered her retreat by advancing, leaving an arm's length between them. "I'd like to see you tomorrow."

She shouldn't. When they kissed, sparks ignited an explosion. The chemistry between them would blow up a lab and burn the building down. After the fire, all that would remain would be the charred pyre of her remains. "I'm sorry, but I…"

He shifted his weight to his left foot. "Can I see you again?"

She inhaled and pegged him with a stern gaze. "Please go. It's for the best."

His lips thinned into a straight line, then he spun and left. Her focus tracked each strike of his boot heels, replaying Kyle's conversation.

No way had she used him as a stand in for her

husband. What had prompted all the memories of the funeral earlier?

Maybe the trigger had been while Kyle skipped the stones across the water and Annie frolicked beside him, she had laughed, enjoying the moment. Something she hadn't experienced in a while. It was then she'd flipped back in time. This wasn't about Tim. This was about letting herself be happy and live.

Although Kyle had been the first man since her husband who brought her libido back to life, she'd never once believed Kyle to be Tim. With the heat in her belly still percolating, there was no disguising her desire for the Wyoming cowboy. Given another minute, she would've climaxed right there against him.

She closed the door. Kyle had pushed her away. The reason he gave was understandable, but the crux of the matter, he'd refused her intimate invitation. When she had brought his palm to her breast and she touched the outline of his erection, he had stopped cold. Embarrassed again, her stomach lurched. "Dear God, what am I doing?"

Tears ran unchecked down her cheeks. She sniffled. A moan escaped, rendering a horrible sound, even to her ears. She knew one man, okay, spirit, who wanted her around.

She strode to her backpack, retrieved the doll, and relaxed on top of the bed. Leaning against the headboard, her hands shook anticipating the familiar hum, the vibration to escape this world.

Neither appeared. "I need you. Why aren't you letting me in?"

After several hours, nothing happened. Frustration stormed through her veins. "Damn you and damn your

First Realm."

Annie nudged her hand with her nose. "Hey, pretty girl. I'm all right, just discouraged. You and I are alike, waiting for answers. Maybe if no one claims you, we'll have each other." She laid the doll on the nightstand and curled on her side waiting for sleep.

The next morning, Shelby tried once more to astral project without success. Disappointed again, she attempted to summon Tim's presence and failed. What was happening? Confused and disillusioned, she packed her bags. Maybe she'd have better luck in Texas, because she wasn't giving up. Or was it possible none of this really happened?

Had she journeyed to another plane? Was the passage to the First Realm and talking to her husband's spirit a product of her vivid imagination? Strife settled into the pit of her stomach, and her muscles involuntarily tightened. She plopped one of her suitcases on the floor to keep the hotel door open and returned to the bed to close the other.

****

Annie wagged her tail at the threshold while Kyle scratched her ears. His gaze fixed on the bag holding the door ajar. Kyle kicked himself mentally. Damn he'd screwed up, but he had to stop last night. It took everything he had not to take what Shelby offered, and what he craved. He'd wanted more than a roll between the sheets, demanded more of himself, especially for this beautiful woman and their budding relationship.

She was stubborn to a fault. He admired her tenaciousness and questioned if that same trait would keep her away? The knight in shining armor defending her virtue blew up in his face, but he liked challenges and she was worth fighting for…He paused. She was different than the women who sparked his interest.

Usually he preferred petite women. When he held her close, her tall, lithe frame conformed to every nook and cranny of his six-four body. In the back of his passion-hazed mind, he considered having her as a significant part of his life. Fire burned through his veins and his blood pumped, tightening his groin. Her scent drove him wild. Every place she touched him, galvanized his skin with a scorching desire for more…Oh yeah, she was definitely worth the fight.

He'd determined she had some skeletons in her closet and for that matter, so did he. His life had a few bumps and bruises along the way. Didn't everyone? But there had to be more than what she was telling him.

A bad feeling roiled in his gut. He gave Annie one last pat and knocked. "Shelby?"

"Come in."

He stepped into her room and a noise caught his attention. A doll vibrated on the table. "What are you doing with Ten-Blue-Sun?"

Shelby stared like a deer caught in head lights at the wooden figurine. "What am I doing? What the hell is she doing and how do you know about her?"

"Answer my question."

Shelby gaped at the fetish as Ten-Blue-Sun shimmied across the surface on its own accord. "When you answer mine."

The yellow eyes of the figurine glowed and her long black bangs waved in the air as though a brisk wind whipped through the room.

She pointed. "She's made out of wood. How can this be happening?"

"Semme' Mugua." The doll stilled. "Wahatehwe Tsoap." Her bangs leveled. "Bahaitee Dabai." The glowing stopped. "For the last time, how are you in possession of Ten-Blue-Sun?"

Why and how did Shelby have this particular Kachina doll? The reappearance had enormous consequences for his step-mom and blood-brother's tribe. He never imagined it would be in his lifetime. Who in the hell was this woman?

Shelby had more skeletons in her closet than she'd let on, and this by no means was a small one. She had in her possession the very key to winning a war that had been talked about for generations. Whose side was she on?

He refused to believe a lady from Texas, taking a holiday in Jackson Hole would be the catalyst against his people. She was here for research...Jesus...had he been blind to her true nature, and missed her motives?

Shelby hadn't moved. She stood shell-shocked, still staring at the damn doll, no one can act that well, can they? He'd hear her out, then make his decisions based on her replies.

She spun to face him. "What did you say?"

In two steps, Kyle towered over Shelby using his bulk as intimidation. "Who are you and how did you get her?"

****

Speechless and confused, Shelby deciphered which parts to tell Kyle. His anger surprised her and the doll had come to life when he stepped through the doorway. Explanation for the vibrations would have been easy...well maybe, but not the saffron glow or the movement of her bangs. Whatever chant he used, he'd halted her. "You think I've given you a false name?"

"She's not a fake." He slipped his hand on her shoulder and guided her to the bed. "Sit for a minute." He leaned against the table and folded his arms across his chest. "Where did you get her?"

Funny how circumstances dictated false truths, but what part to leave out? Their meeting may not have been by chance, but she couldn't believe Kyle would harm her. His penchant for safety conveyed otherwise or had he afforded her protection for another reason?

Automatically converting to her business voice and demeanor, she distanced her emotions. Truth. "My husband." Distortion. "You already know I'm a writer and I'm researching Kachina doll customs for my book."

"How did your husband get her?"

He expected her to answer all of his questions, but he wasn't reciprocating. "I don't understand your interest."

He sighed. "Let's just say, I'm familiar with her attributes."

No crap. The doll must have recognized him. Had he astral projected to the First Realm? Was that part of Ten-Blue-Sun's power? "Will you share with me what you know?"

He unfolded his arms and his hands curled around the edge of the table. "Why don't we grab something to eat and we can talk there."

Eat? Was he crazy? "No, thank you, I'm not hungry."

"Okay, how about coffee?"

Shelby stood. "I was about to leave."

Kyle straightened. "I thought you wanted me to tell

you what I know."

Oh, he was slick all right, but she could handle this. He wanted to reposition for an offensive and she'd be stupid to go on the defensive. She wanted every tidbit of data she could get her hands on, but how to parry? Humor. "If you show me yours, I'll show you mine."

He grinned. "Perhaps I've been too harsh. Ten-Blue-Sun is rife with symbolism. She's a tenacious warrior and a powerful medicine woman. Her bangs represent the life bringer's souls she guides, she directs paths, helps conquer evil on Mother Earth, a great healer, and follows the spirit guides in the First Realm and beyond."

Shelby gasped. "You know about the other world?"

He raised his hand to stop her. "Ah, now your turn."

"You didn't tell me anything new." But he knew of the First Realm. What other information did he have? "Tell me something I don't know."

His chest swelled with air, and he rose to his full height. "This fetish has powers. Exactly how did your husband find Ten-Blue-Sun and what are you doing with her?"

Rational thoughts clamored around in her brain, bouncing inside her head, coherent signals never making it to her mouth. Damn. "Me...doing? You're the one—"

"Shelby, I'm surmising you're in possession of stolen property, and I could have you arrested with one phone call."

Reasoning broke through. "You think I'm a thief? Please do call the authorities because I'd rather deal with them."

"I've given you every opportunity to tell me." He slid his cell from his jean jacket pocket. "You've given me no other alternative."

She had a hunch he would be able to help her and knew more than he let on. This wooden figure represented something beyond what she understood. Kyle seemed to be in the know. She needed answers. Right now, she figured the truth would be the best approach. "My husband was the director of the archaeological department for the university. His responsibilities included but certainly weren't limited to the inventory of their digs. I discovered a key belonging to his safety deposit box and found her there."

Kyle let a long whoosh of air escape. "Do you think he stole it?"

Her hands whipped to her hips standing against the accusation. "No, absolutely not. I believe someone murdered him for this doll."

Kyle's eyebrows rose. "Why?"

Oh, because Tim told me in The First Realm and by the way, I met She-Who-Smiles and One-Who-Soars-With-Eagles too. It would be easier for Kyle to believe she was a thief rather than to give credence to a far-fetched place and a story even she had questioned ten minutes ago, claiming she lost her mind.

Her best bet was to keep with the facts. "According to Tim's journals, he found the doll without documentation. Tim figured Ten-Blue-Sun had been stolen and he hid her until he could ascertain the rightful owner. That's all I know."

Kyle headed for the door. "I need to make a phone call."

She picked up her purse. "Don't bother. I'll drive

to the police station myself."

Kyle faltered in mid-stride. "You're not leaving. I believe you're in danger."

Oh crap, just what she needed another person to affirm what her intuition had been shouting. "Okay."

He slid her bag inside the room with his booted foot. "I'll be back around six and take you to dinner."

Her shoulders automatically drew upward. "Is that a good idea?"

His eyes connected with hers and he cocked his head to one side. "Yeah, it is." He stepped outside and closed the door.

She opened her mouth to tell him forget it, but then she would've been talking to Annie and promptly clamped her lips together.

Grabbing her cell, she tapped the number to her office, and asked for Alessa. "Hey Al, how are things going?"

"Great and up there?"

A reflection against the wall drew her attention. She twirled to see the doll's eyes glowed again. "Fine…Just touching base." *What the hell? Al? So Kyle and Alessa are the connections to the doll?* Great, she had a long-ass road to haul to figure this shit out.

Chapter Six

Shelby's sister cleared her throat. "Whenever you're ready to talk, I'm here."

Alessa had an uncanny sense, an ability to know what people were thinking, one of the many reasons she excelled in business. "Thanks. How's everything there?"

"Good."

If she could project one more time, Tim should have the answer. "Listen, I need to go. I'll be in touch and thank you for being there for me."

"Anytime, that's what family is for…Hey, be careful, I love you."

"Love you too. Bye." When the call ended so did the glowing.

Scooping the doll up with her hand, she scooted across the bed, her back against the headboard. She checked the time, nine in the morning. Her eyelids closed, taking slow breaths, in…out. Brilliant lights danced around her mind's eye, then showered down. The journey began, releasing her from the boundaries of her earthly body; the pinpoints of white stars and a steadfast peace settled in her being.

She-Who-Smiles greeted her. "I see you've learned how to relax and be open."

Mesmerized by her energy, Shelby admitted she liked She-Who-Smiles. "Your spirit is so beautiful."

"Come, I want to share some things with you."

"Wait, I'd like to see Tim."

Her spirit guide nudged her. "He'll join us later."

"I'm new at this, how do I follow?" Shelby peered down.

"I'll lead you."

Instantly, they were outside, hovering over a valley floor. She-Who-Smiles had transported her life force. "Where are we?"

"In Texas, what use to be known as Comancheria. The significance of this location will become known with each person's sojourn."

A bare-chested man climbed up a rocky canyon, his muscular legs flexing. The leather leggings billowed in the wind as it whipped through the crevices of the gorge. With each step, he tested the rugged earth, his moccasins protecting his footfalls. The morning sun erased dawn's pink and purple hues. The eastern horizon gave way to a brilliant sunrise. The rays of light glistened at the top and slowly illuminated the arroyo's gulf. Midway up, he slipped inside what appeared to be a cave.

She-Who-Smiles guided her inside the grotto. He had removed his outer covering to reveal a beautiful breechcloth decorated with colorful beads. He painted his face, arms, and legs with berries and ash. The satchels he carried appeared bulky, filled with what, she didn't know. He chanted, withdrawing the contents.

Her spirit guide narrated the components of the ritual. "For protection, tobacco from the east; cedar of the south holds blessings and purification of air; to cleanse the mind and body sage from the west; and sweetgrass from the north guards against bad influences." All were placed into an exquisite tooled hide.

Thank the heavens she didn't have to remember them, the relevance would be imparted in due time, according to She-Who-Smiles. *Whatever the hell that means.*

Carved obsidian in shapes of a crescent moon, a star, a raindrop, and the sun dangled from the fringe of the medicine bag. There were many other configurations symbolic of life everlasting, but the ten dove feathers caught Shelby's eye.

The shaman continued to add an arrowhead for food and protection, an adolescent eagle feather for keen eyesight, a wolf's incisor tooth for cunning and intelligence, a claw from a bear to bring bravery in the face of danger, and a bone teething ring. He closed the flap and burned outlines in the shape of a buffalo symbolizing all the basic needs, food, clothing and milk. He added a depiction of a horse, which meant good hunting and wealth. The last was an engraved dog, a faithful, loyal companion, a protector during good and bad, giving unconditional love to his master.

He withdrew a doll from one of his sacks. Six midnight-blue translucent stones were embedded in a vertical line down the front. Unsheathing a knife from his belt, he pried open the piece of wood and placed the medicine bag inside the hollowed figurine. His song grew louder. The cave walls echoed his wails. All six of the gems illuminated emitting an azure luminescence.

The intensity of the light drew her in, compassion welled deep in her heart, a love she couldn't explain. Not understanding why, she wanted to know more about the medicine man.

One-Who-Soars-With-Eagles' sad eyes connected to hers. He nodded and tears slid down his angular cheek. He grasped the fetish in his right hand, which meant an offering to the living or immortal spirits. Pointing the statue to Shelby, he then guided it back to his heart. As he closed the doll, the crystals slowly dimmed to their original state.

"I don't understand. He's a living human being, what year is this?"

"Mother Earth's nineteenth century. He's my father's brother. My Hopi grandfather whittled the Kachina doll and told my uncle he'd know what to do. One-Who-Soars-With-Eagles readied the wooden figurine, also known as the 'life bringer.'

"This powerful warrior woman will be used in a naming ceremony for Ten-Butterflies' baby. But this will never happen. A journey of death he knows that must come and a rebirth of a child destined to be a leader."

"I—I met your uncle earlier—He showed me images of a tribe being slaughtered, but I couldn't tell who was killing them. Is that the same Ten-Blue-Sun I have?"

Shelby sensed a shift within She-Who-Smiles. "Yes. You must complete a quest, but don't worry, you will know what to do."

"Quest? This is crazy." She's insane…Jeez, I'm the one losing my mind… "You can hear me…Can't you?"

She-Who-Smiles giggled. "Yes."

"No wonder everything is beautiful here, no lying, cheating, or stealing. Hell, no pun intended, my husband died because of that damn doll. I'm not qualified and I'm certainly not the best candidate for your crusade. Please, I need to see Tim."

"You must release him. Lean on Kyle. He and I will help guide you through your walk."

"No. I want my husband, now. And I don't want another sad journey. I've had my quota, thank you very much. And...And...I don't need you adding to my to-do list..." Panic and confusion slammed into her. The pinpoints of her light dissipated.

"I cannot hold you in this realm when you have negative thoughts."

The mass of energy plummeted into her body. This time she gasped for air, fear wrestled in her soul, apprehension of facing life without Tim and that her spirit would turn dark with sorrow. She groaned. The crushing sensation felt like an elephant sat on her chest. Slowly, she relaxed, regaining her breath, and the pressure receded. Shelby focused and Annie whimpered, nudging her hand. Leaving the doll on the bed, she crawled out, slid into her flip-flops to take Annie for a walk.

Outside, the sun hung in the western sky. Her wrist flipped to see the time...six. "*Mon Dieu*, I'm so sorry Annie." Time didn't have relevance in the First Realm, past, present and future were the same. If she had to guess how long she'd been gone, she figured sixty minutes, not nine hours.

Dread inundated her very being when she realized she'd have to give up Tim, while tingles of anticipation skittered across her skin thinking of his journey. "Oh, Annie, I'm frightened. I have to release Tim so he can continue his course...I didn't mean to hold him back." Goosebumps rose over her flesh and she shivered from trepidation when she remembered the first item on her to-do list.

Shelby exhaled an audible sigh. "I've been given a mission of sorts. I'm to pass Ten-Blue-Sun to the rightful owner and I'll know when the time comes." Annie grunted then something caught her attention under a hedge. "Yeah, right, that's what I thought too. I'm thinking Kyle and Alessa should decide who retains guardianship. They're the ones who make her light up and defy all laws of physics, damn redundant but metaphysics too."

Annie sniffed her way around a pine tree straining the six foot leash. "Hell and that's not all, for no extra charge, I'll be guided by She-Who-Smiles, but wait for an added bonus, I can lean on Kyle."

"Lean on me for what?"

She jumped. "You scared...I was talking to Annie."

His baritone timbre softened. "Why do you need to rely on me?"

Honestly, she tried never to lie, but she had to draw a line when it came to revealing her whereabouts today and no way would she admit it. "I said I was keen on style...Hanson's...Her new line is all the rage."

****

When he left her this morning, Kyle had run through what he remembered about Ten-Blue-Sun. The fetish had great powers over the forces of good and evil. According to legend passed down orally by songs and dance, she'd defend her people and the legitimate owner. In the wrong hands, nothing but death would follow. Shelby claimed her husband was murdered for the warrior woman. Would he end up calling the police and have her arrested? Or were Shelby and Tim victims?

He hoped for the latter because the proper possession of the medicine woman would bring removal of curses, healing, and rebirth of a powerful human shaman. Now that fit Shelby more than a thief, but where did she belong in all of this?

For some reason, he truly believed she had found the figurine secured in her husband's safety deposit box. A chill slithered down his spine like a snake at the idea of mercenaries carrying out orders to do whatever was necessary to apprehend the powerful life bringer. She didn't have a clue of what she was up against.

Shelby paraded around a tourist town probably buying souvenirs. She had rescued Annie in the town square, went on picnics with him, and the fireworks with who knows how many people around. There were plenty of riffraff out there who'd die for a cause. Worse yet, would think nothing about taking a life and according to Shelby, they've already killed for the doll. Ah hell, the Fourth…just like that night, the hairs on the back of his neck rose.

He had to think…what was supposed to happen next? Ultimately, battles would be fought in the First Realm, as well as on Mother Earth, and lives lost. Damn, he never thought this would happen in his lifetime.

There would have to be a sequential ownership of the statue, stages of tenure, she would be a dominant figure in every holding. First, he would have to find out who Ten-Blue-Sun belonged to and let the why present itself.

Kyle shoved his hand through his hair. "Ready to grab a bite to eat?"

"After Annie does her job, then I'll need a few minutes."

He withdrew the happy-eyed canine's leash from Shelby. "Go on. I'll watch her."

"Thanks, I won't be long."

Kyle followed Annie's exploration to an evergreen bush.

Earlier, he had called Rain, his second mom, and then speed dialed his brothers Jude and Garrett, leaving a succinct message for all three, "Call me." He had tapped the next number, knowing there wasn't a choice.

He had relayed the information to his private investigators, including the make and license plate of Shelby's car. After giving his instructions to the team leader, he drove out of the parking lot and headed home. He needed his computer to look up a few things.

Within two hours, his PC beeped. He had opened his email, read the attachment "Shelby Littleton," and wanted to dance the proverbial jig. No one had that clean a record, but she did. She lived on a ranch in Texas and owned a successful business. In Shelby's absence, her youngest sister ran the concern.

Another sibling, Joni, a couple of years older than Alessa, lived on the west coast. Joni's colleagues acknowledged her having foresight, a special gift of design, and her clients were multi-millionaires.

Shelby wasn't wealthy, but very comfortable, which meant she wouldn't try to sell the medicine woman. Her husband's report would take a little more digging. After releasing his bodyguards to spend some time with their families, he looked forward to being a regular guy on a date. He had hesitated, but in the end made the decision to watch over her without their help.

Her apprehension accepting his invitation for supper was evident, but never reached her eyes. They held something else. When Shelby's gaze connected with his, the enticement to bond and the lure to unite arose. Yesterday when he'd stopped their petting, she immediately erected a wall to keep him out. But her regard said more.

Anytime he was near Shelby, there was a strong magnetism drawing him to her and the air charged, perfect for an erotic seduction. He'd try to take things slow and easy, easier said than done. He wanted a way to keep her here, wanted her luscious body in his bed, but most of all, he wanted Shelby to make love to him, not her husband...him.

****

The owner of the café had set up a private table outside in a secluded corner. Kyle thanked the proprietor while singing a hallelujah chorus for giving Sam and his entourage time off. He looked forward to having an intimate dinner with Shelby.

Kyle peered over the rim of his wine glass as Shelby sipped on a pinot noir. Her hair glistened from the setting sun and her skin glowed. He ached to taste her beautiful body and weave his fingers through her silky locks.

"Kyle Pressley, as I live and breathe."

He cringed from the familiar southern drawl. How in the hell did Bobbie Jo find him? If she could discover their whereabouts, then who else would be able to locate them?

Kyle shifted and stood. "Bobbie Jo."

She had a perfect coiffed hair and extended her hand. "How have you been, darling?"

Kyle lightly grasped her hand and turned it for a handshake rather than the kiss she expected. "Fine, you?"

Clad in a business suit and stiletto heels, she let her arm drop to her side. "Oh honey, you know I can't believe I'm seeing you here," she purred like a cat.

Since he couldn't think of one nice thing to say to her, he resolved to end this as soon as possible. His gut contracted when he figured this supposed surprise meeting was clandestine.

Her eyes darted to Shelby. "What do we have here, a friend of yours?"

He traced her gaze. "Shelby, this is Bobbie Jo Brown. Bobbie Jo, I'd like you to meet Shelby." Kyle refused to give her Shelby's last name.

Shelby nodded and a burly man sidled next to Bobbie Jo.

Bobbie Jo twirled her dangling earring causing the already stretched lobe to twist and right itself. His stomach soured. "I'd like you to meet a friend of mine, David Lamb."

She pointed her pinky finger. "He's in construction and I told him you might have work for him."

Kyle measured David. He had on a muscle T-shirt that didn't cover his pot belly. His dirty blue jeans fell below his hips and appeared like they'd slide down any second. Not that he meant to judge a book by its cover, but taking care of oneself implied a shit-load in any profession. "No, ma'am. I don't."

Bobbie Jo winced. "Oh, well…" She slid one of the chairs out from the round wrought-iron table and sat. "I need your help."

Kyle settled in his seat. "What do you need?"

Bobbie Jo spun to face him then inclined toward him. "A loan."

He angled away putting more distance between them. "You should be talking to your financial advisor, not me."

Bobbie Jo glanced at David, then back at him. "I fired her."

Of all the foolish things Bobbie Jo could have done, dismissing her consultant was downright stupid. "Why?"

She bowed her head, covered her face with her hands and he could barely hear the garbled words. "She's horrible, Kyle. How could you have hooked me up with her?" She withdrew from her palms and her chin quivered.

"What—"

"The nasty woman wouldn't let me have any of my own money. She gave me a pittance for an allowance. My God, I couldn't buy any clothes or go out. I felt like a teenager asking my foster parents for cash."

He wanted to tell her she was acting like one but thought better of it. "I helped you once and gave you the means to overcome your dilemma."

She twisted her earring again taking the long skin with it. Damn, he wanted to tell her to stop it.

He had known Bobbie Jo for a while. The president of a corporation requested his presence and he'd flown in for the meeting. The office building lost the air conditioning. Enduring the heat to finish what was on the agenda, everyone shucked ties, suit coats, rolled up the shirt sleeves, except for one person.

By the end of the conference, perspiration dripped down her face. He waited until everyone had left and asked if she wanted to talk. When she finally relinquished her jacket, untied the frothy scarf around her neckline, her neck and arms were covered with hard-core bruises from her husband.

She'd explained the bastard kept full control of her paycheck, finances, home, and her body. Furious that any man would strike a woman, he had checked her story out and everything was true.

He struck a deal with Bobbie Jo. Provided that she'd use a financial advisor, he'd assist. He contacted Sharon Brenner, wired money and let her work her magic. Within a year under Sharon's wing, Bobbie Jo sported designer clothes, shoes, the works.

During the first couple of years, he'd made several calls to Sharon following up on Bobbie Jo's progress and happened to know she had divorced her spouse, made a boat load of money, but she must have made some foolish choices since then.

Recently, Bobbie Jo's advisor had e-mailed him. According to Sharon, Bobbie Jo had become a spendthrift, unwilling to make the necessary changes in her life to get back on track and to anticipate Bobbie Jo to get in touch with him to bail her out again. He expected a telephone call from her not a personal visit.

Sacrifices were a part of life no one liked. He'd had his share, no, not with money. With a much more personal gift, he had given a part of himself for this beautiful country. Mind-walking helped find his fellow soldiers from missions that had gone from bad to worse. The numerous POWs saved provided a balm to his soul.

Of course, the military loaned him out to other agencies. One in particular used him to find agents who should have reported in to their superiors. He attributed the experience to keep freedom of choice, speech, and the right to choose how to live your life. His code of honor demanded no less.

At one point, assistance became exploitation. But it wasn't until his last mission that he closed the door and refused to use his ability under any circumstances. He often questioned why his gift hadn't manifested itself to help his mom. His stomach knotted into a tight ball, he missed his mom and dad.

He glanced at Bobbie Jo fiddling with her diamond ring. She grew up in the foster care system. Maybe under the best of circumstances, her parents would have taught her about money.

As wealthy as his mother and father were, they kept him grounded. Raising two boys who were hell-on-wheels challenged them. They had replaced his bicycle twice. His mom sat his carcass down and shook her index finger at him. "This is the last time, buddy. The next one will be out of your own pocket." After buying the motor and accessories two times, he had a grand total of thirty-seven cents to his name. Well, that cured him of trying to convert a bike into a hog.

True, that had been a boy's lesson, but he still carried the experience to this day. He inspected the woman in front of him acting like a young girl in junior high. If she was unwilling to change her lifestyle and he helped her now, then he'd only be enabling her careless imprudence.

"I suggest you call Ms. Brenner and ask what can be done. I sent extra to start a savings account for you. You should have plenty of funds."

Bobbie Jo's manicured fingernails played with the edge of the table. "It's all gone."

Kyle whistled.

Indignation surged in her voice. "Well?"

He unfolded from his chair and waited for Bobbie Jo to stand.

The server ambled to their table and placed the plates in front of Shelby then him.

David grasped Bobbie Jo's arm. "He ain't gonna help us."

She thwarted David's hold and stood. "You're being so mean to me. How do you live with yourself?"

As David dragged Bobbie Jo away, Kyle caught the plural "us" and grimaced.

He sat and mumbled to Shelby, "Sorry about that."

Her lips tightened then relaxed. "No problem, how do you know her?"

"She's an employee with one of our largest distributers in Georgia."

Shelby's mouth curled into a cute smile. "Sounds like you helped her when she needed you. I'm impressed." Then she picked up her fork. "Dig in before the food gets cold."

Instead of a utensil, he grabbed his glass, swigged long, taking every bit of liquid and then set it back on the table. "Bobbie Jo had a hard life. I'm guessing with David at her side, she hasn't improved her situation." He hadn't meant to verbalize his thoughts and Shelby never commented. It was probably best the subject remain closed.

After a quiet dinner, she rubbed her hands up and down her arms. "Do you mind if we call it an evening?"

"Sure. Let me get the check."

****

When Kyle parked at the hotel, Shelby clutched the

door handle. "I'd like to see you tomorrow. Can you wait and leave later?" He had been silent through the meal and introspective so his rich baritone words surprised her.

Shelby nodded. "I need to talk to you about Ten-Blue-Sun, but I'm really tired. So yes, I'll stay until we find a solution. Thank you for dinner. Good night." She slid out of the truck and closed the door. When she glanced through the window, their eyes locked. Sad, the sole purpose of meeting Kyle was the custody rights of a doll made over a century ago. Tears welled, and she blinked them back.

A sense of dread enveloped her again. The thought of losing Tim twice, once through physical death then releasing him to continue his spiritual journey was too excruciating for her to think about. What about this beautiful gentleman? In all probability, she'd lose him too. Kyle had somehow given her strength.

Shelby wanted to connect with Kyle. The desire wasn't for sex alone. She wished for a close relationship with him. As long as Kyle assumed he was a stand-in for her husband, nothing would come of it and she would miss his companionship.

Hell bells, she waved goodbye. She needed to get a grip.

****

Early morning's dawn light sliced through the curtain opening. Shelby blanched and scrunched her tired eyes shut. She peeked through her lashes, letting her pupils become accustomed to the sun.

Without luck, she had attempted astral projection yesterday evening. Tim didn't come to see her. Had he continued on without saying goodbye? Did She-Who-

Smiles abandon her too? She tossed and turned all night, until she made a decision. She would ask Kyle to contact Alessa and together, they would decide what to do with the doll.

Disappointed she'd lost contact with Tim before finding his murderer; she threw the covers off and strode to the bathroom, hoping the shower would cleanse away her failure. Maniacal laughter escaped. A mental breakdown would not be in her best interest, God, just deal.

When a knock reverberated inside the room, she tossed the last of her cosmetics into her bag.

She double checked who was on the other side, opened the door and invited Kyle inside. With a wave of her hand, she asked him to sit. The coffee he placed on the table smelled wonderful and would be a welcome caffeine boost. "Thank you for the java and treats."

"Are you okay? What's going on?"

Chapter Seven

Shelby cleared her throat. "I don't know where to begin. But I'm about to tell you some things you can believe or not. At this point, I really don't care." She sipped the hot liquid, gathering strength to start at the beginning.

Kyle never interrupted and listened to the crazy story.

"That's it." She waited for his response.

"I've spoken with Garrett's mom, Rain. She's a shaman. Ten-Blue-Sun is in the right hands...yours."

"I'm not being disrespectful, but she's wrong...terribly so." Earlier, she'd bought a small treasure chest, some pretty material, wrapped the precious cargo and placed the doll inside. She retrieved the special box from the floor and set it in front of Kyle. "I'm giving her to you."

"No, Shelby."

She raised her palm to stop him then withdrew the piece of paper. "You can reach Alessa at this number."

When he didn't take it, her breath shortened, heat rose to her face as exasperation crept in. Why wouldn't he listen to her? She'd had enough of these insane events and laid the information on top of the chest. "Do whatever you want. I'm through. I've done my job." One of them at least. She could only guess she had released Tim since he hadn't been around.

She erected her tired body from the chair, the boost from her drink diminished. "If you'll excuse me and my manners, let yourself out. I need to get ready to go."

Kyle grasped her arm. "Wait, we could try to astral project together?"

"No, I'm finished with the quest. I do have one question, what did you say to calm Ten-Blue-Sun?"

He released her. "One—the Great Spirit, two—the Ghost, three—the Sun."

She nodded.

"Shelby, I think it's worth a try to project and yes, the doll's eyes glowed for Alessa, but your spirit guide shared the ritual only with you. That is significant. I shouldn't take her when I've been told you are the rightful owner…at this time."

She scooted the case away from him. "Fine, I'll give the damn thing to Alessa." A whoosh of air escaped. "Sorry, I didn't mean to take my frustration, my resentment out on you. I guess I've had enough of this situation, I'm irritable from lack of sleep, furious that I accepted such a cockamamie…I'm exasperated that's all."

****

Kyle winced. Shelby had reached her limit, she was exhausted and disappointed. The special light in her eyes had vanished, her shoulders slumped, polar opposite of who she was a few days ago. When she recounted her experiences, the monotone words revealed her state of mind. His first instinct was to embrace and comfort her, but that wasn't what she needed.

She had narrated her encounters, fear laced every word. By the end, Shelby perceived she had failed and anger radiated from her normally happy features. Rain warned him dangerous entities would try to attack her to retrieve the doll for the use of the powers held within. Her advice, help her, and then she'd laughed and added Ten-Blue-Sun works magic for the people closest to her.

Maybe, Shelby would be relieved if he kept the life bringer for now. Her mental state would settle and he'd bet she'd look at the situation differently. He didn't want to leave her disjointed with his world, with the First Realm, and the new life she had yet to accept. He'd offer her a reprieve.

"For now, I'll take the box with us for safe keeping. How about we go to Pogonip, my brother's ranch? We can enjoy the outdoors and relax."

By her tells, he knew the minute she acquiesced. Her whole demeanor shifted, her back straightened, and a slight smile curved at the corners of her mouth.

"Fresh air…sounds great…I bet it would be wonderful stress reliever."

****

Kyle cracked his window. The wind whistled inside the cab of the Jalopy.

"Tell me about your family?" Shelby palmed her thigh.

He smiled. "I have an older brother, Jude. My mom and dad have passed, so Rain is like a second mother. Garrett, her son, is my blood brother. That's where we're headed now, to his ranch."

She angled her hips and propped the side of her knee on the seat. "Rain's the Shaman. Wow, that's how you knew so much about Ten-Blue-Sun…Where does Jude live?"

"Across the border, in Idaho."

"Do you get to see him much? Are you close?"

He glimpsed at Shelby with his peripheral vision. Her open body language revealed she was honestly interested in what he had to say. How could he be pleased from simple questions? "We work together…we're tight."

Her thumb pushed the corner of her sunglasses, edging them up her pert nose. "What is your line of work? I know you travel frequently and you have regional distributors."

"It's a family business, like yours."

A puzzled look crossed her face.

****

Kyle parked the truck near the horse trailers on the gravel lot and Shelby jumped out first, then Annie. "Take your time. You don't have to open my door."

He rounded the corner of Jalopy, grasped the handle, and closed it. "That's not the point. I want to be there for you, if you'll let me."

Her chin descended about an inch and her cheeks changed to a pretty pink. "Maybe I've been on my own too long. Tim always opened and shut…Never mind."

He maneuvered in front of her. "How long has it been?"

"Eighteen months."

He raised his right hand, allowing his fingers to trace her jawline. His heart rate increased from the simple touch. He used the pad of his thumb to caress her lips hoping his blood pressure would drop a little. "It's okay to talk about him. Tim was a part of your life, a part of you, so yeah; I'm interested in what you have to say. I want you to know, you can tell me anything and I'll keep it in confidence."

He released her before another part of his anatomy hustled to attention and he whistled. "Come, Annie."

By the small of her back, he led Shelby toward the stables while Annie darted to and fro, her nose sniffing the ground, taking in the new scents.

He spotted Grey Wolfe, coming out of the round pen. "Uncle Grey, it's been awhile."

The old man ambled his way to them. "To say the least, how are you doing? You just missed Garrett, if you can believe this, he ventured into town."

Kyle shook the age-wrinkled hands of the head foreman. Evidence of the many hours in the sun, Grey's crow's feet inched higher with his pleasant smile. "Really must have been something special for him to be traipsing through the city. I'm doing well...you?"

Uncle Grey nodded. "I'm fine. Come to ride?"

"Yes sir."

"What?" Shelby gasped.

Kyle wheeled a ninety degree to check on her. "What's wrong?"

Her face answered his question. "We don't have to—"

"I'll try but I'm a beginner." She grimaced.

His mind raced through the detective's report. She owned a ranch...it must have been her husband's business. "Shelby, I'd like you to meet Grey Wolfe, Rain's brother. Grey, Shelby Littleton."

They both nodded, reciprocating each other's greeting.

Kyle headed toward the barn. "I'm going to take Mosey for Shelby with a lead halter. But first, she'll sit with me."

"I'll get her." Uncle Grey volunteered. "And I'll get Bridger ready too."

Grey led a sorrel gelding and a dun mare over to where they stood. Kyle grasped Shelby by the hand and lifted her up on the sorrel. He sensed Shelby's apprehension. "Don't worry we're going together for a little bit. Then I'll see if you can handle Mosey." He took the stirrup from her foot, and in one fluid motion settled behind her.

Kyle wrapped his arms around her and held the reins in his right hand. He appreciated Grey's help by putting a halter under Mosey's bridle, then attaching a lead rope so the mare could follow behind. Even Annie running to and fro hadn't scared Mosey.

He squeezed his knees against the horse's sides. "Let's go nice and easy, Bridger."

Shelby relaxed and nestled against his chest. "This is strange, I'm so comfortable and I feel safe when I'm with you."

Kyle hugged her waist with his left arm. "I'm glad. You've been through enough to frighten any woman. I'll make sure no harm comes to you."

"Don't make promises you can't keep, Pressley."

Irritation gave way to fury. He didn't like what Shelby had implied. Was she used to people not keeping their word? Shelby would find he kept his, at any cost. He'd forego a retort and let the creak of the leather saddle and Bridger and Mosey's hooves striking the ground fill the air.

He wanted to know more about Shelby and there was still a question she had refused to answer earlier. "When's your birthday?"

"It's… Smooth, very smooth. How old are you?"

"Thirty-five. Well?" He loosened the reins so Bridger could have his head.

She blew air out of her lungs and sighed. "Where are we going?"

Kyle rested his hand on her hip. "I don't think age is the issue. I think it's about fear and trust."

Her body stiffened and when she didn't reply, he didn't press her further. "Let's give Bridger and Mosey a rest by that copse of trees. There's a stream nearby too."

After Kyle dismounted, he helped Shelby down.

"This is great...feels warmer today." Her voice quivered.

Kyle ground tethered the horses and strode to her. "Are you discussing the weather?"

She exhaled, her gaze darted in every direction. "Yes, I am."

Kyle shook his head and grasped her shoulders. Her eyes finally locked onto his. "You've been through some traumatic experiences and I'm here to help. You're beautiful and have a good spirit. As for us, we're attracted to each other. I want you and you want me. We'll know when the time is right and I have a feeling we'll both be surprised when we join. Until then, are you hungry or thirsty? Would you like a sandwich?"

"Absolutely." Her muscles relaxed under his hands and she smiled.

He released Shelby and untied the bindings holding the heavy saddlebags filled with the food, drinks, and the blankets. He slid them from the saddle.

Shelby's nervous energy had the picnic spread before him and jammed a sandwich in his hand. He took a bite watching her fiddle with the bread rather than eating it. Her life had changed and she was handling the transition as well as could be expected. He wanted to help, but she had chosen not to be a part of his world. Her path would be filled with good things, and Rain had assured him, evil as well. Even though that scared the hell out of him, there had to be a way to alleviate Shelby's fear of the unknown and encourage her to take the journey with him.

He placed the leftovers to the side. "Come here, I want to hold you."

She scooted next to him and he gently laid her in front of him. He extended his arm to cradle her head and rolled a blanket for his. She clasped his hand that draped over her waist, relaxed and content that he spooned her. Annie dozed at their feet.

The clop of a trotting horse drew closer. He peeked over Shelby. "Rider…going by or…stopping it is. Let me up so I can find out what they want."

****

Shelby shifted to release his arm. When he rose, she snuggled to rest a few more minutes. From under her eyelashes, she peered at Kyle waiting for the equestrian to approach. His long legs held his beautiful frame erect. For the first time, she noticed the multi-faceted lights surrounding Kyle. She crunched her eyes together and opened them. The same refracted rays from the First Realm glowed around his body. She blinked again.

A soft feminine voice filtered through the air. "Grey told me you were out here. I decided to try and find you."

Kyle's head tilted. "Lisa?"

Shelby strained to see through his emanation. Kyle smiled his full luscious lip smile. A muscle spasm ripped through her chest. Her lungs froze. *Breathe, Littleton.* How could the sight of one man stop an involuntary response?

"Grey didn't tell me you were riding with someone. Am I intruding?"

"No not at all, please join us." Kyle helped her down. They kissed one another politely on each cheek with a quick embrace. Lisa ground tethered her horse then stepped forward in rhythm with Kyle.

"Lisa, this is Shelby Littleton. Shelby, Lisa Clarke."

Shelby rose to her feet. "Nice to meet you."

"Same here."

Kyle gestured, pointing at the blanket. "Shelby. Lisa."

Shelby thumbed over her shoulder. "I'm going to check out the stream that nearly lulled me to sleep so you two can visit."

"Please be careful." He followed Lisa and settled on the quilt.

The wide creek revealed deep green foliage. She found a flat, smooth boulder, climbed up and pulled her knees under her chin. She listened to the babbling water, stared at the clear liquid reflecting the sun's rays and the sparkles dancing across the ripples. An audible sigh of contentment escaped.

Her thoughts drifted to Kyle, a kind and gentle soul. She enjoyed learning about his family and business… Come to think of it, how did he know she ran a "family business"? She'd ask him later.

The flip side of Kyle intrigued her. He stood strong

when pushed into a corner. Bobbie Jo pressed him hard for money and Kyle had handled the situation well.

On the Fourth, she still wasn't sure what happened when he acted like a soldier, ready to fight and protect. *Note to self, don't get on his bad side.*

Even when he met Myra, his strong hands and body adapted, gingerly helping the lovely woman. Hell, he accepted her and the crazy experiences without ridicule, kept the treasure chest and Alessa's number. Maybe, she could depend on him.

She speculated how long Kyle had known Lisa. According to their greeting, she surmised a long time. Lisa was petite, waist-length black hair with sky blue eyes, a beautiful woman. Oh my God, she didn't have an aura, no lights, nothing. What did all this mean and when in the hell did she start seeing auras? She gasped. Kyle was the first one. Was this an omen for her and Kyle? It's not like there was a neon sign or a waving banner with directions for her to follow.

She lay back and closed her eyes. The warmth of the rock seeped through her clothes. All she needed was a couple of minutes.

The brilliant lights showered down, she emerged from her body, weightless, the agile transition to the First Realm happened fast unlike the previous times. "Tim, I thought I'd never see you again."

He opened his energy, but this time he held back the passion they experienced earlier. Instead, he enveloped her with a soothing embrace.

Intuition fluttered through her when other souls arrived. "What gives?"

"They're spirit guides. This is Bear-Claws, Shadow-of-Elk, and Long-Feather."

"I asked them to watch over you with She-Who-Smiles."

"Why? I've done everything I said I would. Ten-Blue-Sun is in the right hands."

"Sweetheart, you're partially right, but the quest isn't finished. Because of your bravery, I can move on and learn more. I'm so proud of you, darling, thank you for your strength and your never ending love. Bear-Claws is Kyle's spirit guide. He's in agreement, Kyle is a good man and you can rely on him. I'll never forget you, good-bye, my love."

Tim vanished. Sadness gripped her and then anger. Gradually, her pinpoint of lights faded and slowly dissipated.

She-Who-Smiles appeared. "You'll learn to overcome your negativity…soon."

Shelby sighed. She had returned to her earthly form without the physical problems she had before. She scooted off the boulder to tell Kyle the bad news, Tim was gone and the good news, she met his spirit guide. Just as she crested the stream's bank, she caught Kyle and Lisa arm and lip-locked. That was a lover's embrace. Tears burned the back of her eyes and she commanded her muscles to respond, but they didn't budge. Finally, the paralysis ended. She backed down the embankment seeking a place of refuge, to her boulder and ended at the stream.

She tried to swallow and couldn't. Her mouth parched, she cupped some water in her hand and grimaced as an emotional upheaval erupted. Her gaze fixed on the surface of the stream. The reflection reminded her of She-Who-Smiles advice. *Yeah right, lean on Kyle, depend on him.*

Since when did she count on anyone other than her husband? Never. Even then, Tim had to win her over. He gained her trust with patience, gained her admiration with his unwavering respect, and won her adoration with his unyielding love. She inhaled. Instead of drinking, she splashed the cool liquid over her face. Now, she didn't have Tim anymore or Kyle for that matter. Shivers of trepidation traveled down her spine.

Everything between her and Kyle had been a farce. Kyle's kindness didn't usurp the harsh anger swirling deep within. She thought their relationship was different, special beyond the powers of earth, involving the forces of the Kachina doll and the First Realm. Did he have that effect on all women? Hell, he'd been the one to stop her advances and at this point, she had to agree he'd done the right thing. Not too many times could she be taken for a fool, but admittedly, she was the sap this go-around. Again, a timely intervention she'd heed.

Get up, get back to work and live the life you made for yourself. Kyle had kept the doll so be happy he accepted and stay with the status quo. She squared her shoulders, thrust her chin in the air and returned to find Kyle cleaning up.

"There you are. I wondered where you were." Kyle carefully placed the picnic paraphernalia back in a saddlebag.

"Where's Lisa?" She grabbed the blanket and folded it.

"She wanted to ride some more and didn't want to infringe on our privacy."

"I don't want any special considerations and solitude is the last thing we need." Shelby knelt and rammed the remaining items in the other leather pouch.

"Are you okay?"

She straightened. "I'm fine. I'm ready to ride back on Mosey."

His one eyebrow cocked. "You sure?"

"Oh, I'm not sure of anything anymore. But that's what I'm going to do." She marched over to Mosey, stroked her neck a few times while Kyle readied the horse. She placed her foot in the stirrup and hefted her leg over the saddle. Kyle balanced her with his hand on her thigh and bottom. She swatted them aside, denying his help, perhaps psychologically pushing him away. At this point, she refused to analyze her actions. Her thoughts were a tangled mess, her emotions lost in a labyrinth, her body and spirit seemed disconnected. Determined to ride by herself, she squeezed her knees and held on tight.

****

Kyle left Shelby alone in her thoughts. The trip was long and silent. When they arrived at the stables, Grey took their horses.

"I'll cool them down for you."

Kyle gratefully accepted. "Thanks, Uncle Grey. I'll owe you one. Is Garrett back?"

"No, not yet."

"Thanks again." Kyle grabbed the saddlebags and followed Shelby.

Her rigid back and stiff gait shouted her ire. Shelby settled inside the truck with Annie perched in the middle and stared straight ahead.

He hopped in, headed Jalopy toward Jackson. He concluded Lisa was the root of her fury. Lisa had the rapid ability to irritate a human soul. His mind wandered back to the memories of his long-time, family friend and his ex-fiancée, Christine. The three of them had an extensive and entangled history.

Catching Christine in his bed with…he shook his head to dislodge the scene. Fast forwarding to Lisa's condo, Christine invited…no, she coaxed him to come and talk to her. He flew to New York City and made his way to the posh Manhattan apartment. The images played out before him.

Christine prodded Lisa and him to sit on the couch while she diligently played the hostess. "Let me get the ice tea." When she returned to the living room—he stopped the horrific flashback from unfolding.

In no time at all, he was at Shelby's hotel and turned into the parking lot.

She slid out of the truck. "Annie, come. No need to get out, I'm calling it an early night. I'm bushed."

"Okay, see you in the morning. But I should check your room." He peered out the passenger side.

She scrunched her face. "That's not necessary. I want to spend tomorrow going over my notes. I'm sure you need time to do…whatever it is you do. I had an enlightening day, thanks." Not waiting for his response, she slammed the door closed and strode away.

Kyle exhaled. "My pleasure." He waited until she entered her room then backed out and waved at Sam.

****

Kyle slid onto the stool at his favorite pub. "Hey, Jude, I'm glad you called."

His brother nodded once. "What's going on buddy?"

"I took a gal to Garrett's ranch today."

Jude grunted.

He wanted to tell Jude about Shelby, confess for the first time in years, he wanted to use his gift, but he held back. Jude didn't believe he had the ability to mind walk, let alone a spirit guide that talked to him.

Instead, he changed the subject. "Never guess who I ran into."

"I'm not going to guess." Jude pulled a long draught of beer from the bottle.

Kyle shook his head. He loved his brother, but Jude took life too seriously. "Lisa. Lisa Clarke."

"Well, I'll be damned. How is she doing?" Jude smiled which meant only one corner of his mouth tipped a fraction. There were two places that Jude showed his emotions, in the set of his jaw and the eyes.

"She's doing great."

The bartender eased in front of him and extended his hand. "Kyle, haven't seen you in a long time. How've you been?"

Kyle stood and accepted his gesture. "I've been good, Chester, you?"

"Business is better, so I'm happy." Chester dropped the handshake. "What can I get ya'?"

"Draft. Thanks, my good man."

"Coming up and don't leave without telling me what you've been up to. It's my job to know what's going on around here."

"You got it."

Kyle eased onto the chair and braced his arms on the bar.

"So, how are Hank and Sarah?" Jude scratched the edge of the label on the bottle.

"Lisa said they are doing great, but have slowed down on the theme parties until Hank recuperates from his triple bypass. Funny thing."

Jude raised his chin for him to continue.

"We talked for a while. It was like old times. It brought back a lot of good..."

"Good what?" Jude swiveled to face him.

"Memories. A lot of good memories…"

"You two thinking of getting back together?"

"No, No. But she did give me a big goodbye hug and kiss."

"Are you sure? Sounds like you want to drink from the well again."

"No. I had to push her away because I'm not interested in Lisa that way… I couldn't help but think of all the good times Garrett, Lisa, you, and I had together. Remember, she coined the phrase fearsome-foursome."

"Yeah, we had a blast. Hell, Hank and Sarah made sure to include us after Mom and Dad passed. I remember Mom always calling them events, clam bakes, yacht races, and beach parties…those were fun times."

Kyle waggled his eyebrows at his brother. "My favorite, the Monte Carlo theme, gambling, eager women, and I won money that weekend."

"Don't let her go." Bear-Claws' voice reverberated interrupting his next thought, Kyle released an audible sigh. Of course, he'd watch over Shelby. Though, at times, she sure made it difficult.

Kyle listened to Jude walk down memory lane; soon, Chester joined the conversation and they reminisced until closing time.

****

The rain continued for the next three days. Kyle

called Shelby every morning to offer his assistance which she had politely declined. He wasn't sure if he was following through with Bear-Claws' instructions or his own wishes.

"Grrr." Kyle's frustration mounted with each sunrise. Shelby was pulling away from him, he didn't want to lose her, the magic they shared, but the expression "it takes two," hit the mark. Opening the door of the refrigerator, he scanned the contents. Not seeing anything appealing, he closed it.

Hilda, his housekeeper, had taken a day off to help a friend. He'd told her not to worry about preparing any meals for him, he was a twenty-first century kind of guy and he could fend for himself. However this morning, he didn't feel like it and wanted to grab something downtown.

He chose a favorite of his, the Bun's Café & Bakery. After parking, he strode to the column of people and waited to be seated. As the line shortened, he could see the patrons inside. His heart skipped a beat when he noticed Shelby sitting alone. *No, I won't bother her. She doesn't want to see me.*

Shelby grinned and his gut knotted. He had to talk to her first. If she didn't want him, he'd let her go, because the most important thing was for Shelby to be happy. With a purpose that meant everything to him, he headed toward her table and dug deeper for the tenacity it'd take to cross the bridge of doubt she harbored.

Shelby's skepticism of the First Realm and the acceptance of her gifts were like a churning river during a flash flood, full of debris. To navigate her lack of faith, he'd have to calm the waters and drain the negativity.

Then, he could approach the subject of their relationship. Yes, he wanted to get to know her. He knew basic things, but wanted more. What was her favorite flower, color, author…Did she prefer flip-flops or tennis shoes…A backrub or an overall massage…Making love, did she like the top or the bottom, would he ever find out?

He ambled near her chair and cleared his throat.

Chapter Eight

As Shelby perused the menu, a crack of lightning pierced the air, then the thunder rolled. This morning, she'd thrust aside the curtains to watch the turbulent clouds release a torrential downpour. Then the deluge changed to a steady rain. The monochrome shades of gray had matched her mood. Maybe, she should've trusted her instincts and left, but she'd stayed. Tired of psychoanalyzing her actions, thoughts and emotions, she delayed her departure to face her demons.

Over the past seventy-two hours, she'd come to terms with Tim's departure. She'd lost the ability to astral project to the First Realm since her trip to Pogonip. After three agonizing days, she'd edged toward giving up on finding Tim's murderer. Suicide still listed as his official cause of death grated against her nerves, but her research had come to a standstill. Tim had moved on, maybe she should too.

When she'd stretched across her bed, a flute played several soft, lyrical notes. She-Who-Smiles' voice resonated and centered in her heart. "Brave-One, don't give up."

Alarmed that she had been transported to the First Realm without her consent, she jumped off the mattress, inspected her body, patting her arms and legs. She panned a one-eighty, taking in Annie, the table and all the fixtures. "Yep, all's well here on earth." A delirious laugh spewed from her lips. After several minutes, she calmed, threw her hands in the air declaring she had lost her mind.

She shook her head. Surely, she must have dreamed those words and the beautiful music. "Bah, humbug. Annie, you ready for your grooming appointment? It's time for me to get the hell out of this room."

She'd left the happy canine at the shelter. Liz had badgered her to let Annie stay all day. How could she say no? Preferring not to be alone, she chose from the many restaurants in town. Determined to test her mettle, Shelby chose the café where Kyle bought their coffee and pastries. She had grabbed her umbrella, laptop along with her research material and ran. She spied an empty table in the back with plenty of space to spread out and had asked the seating hostess for that particular one. She had made the right decision.

Her gaze drifted to the customers. Each person's emanation was different, in color and abundance. Some were closed-in, tiny, others were large enough she walked around them. What haunted her the most? The people who had none, void of anything, nothing—her spirit guide informed her they weren't part of the First Realm or part of the upcoming battle. A dusting of folks sitting around had auras. However, the largest percentage lacked the radiations.

She had to admit Kyle had helped her accept the other world. God, she missed Kyle. No matter how hard she attempted to distance herself from him, a word or phrase would remind her of what he had said or done. She had to admit, they did have something magical, that transcended words...the writer in her smiled at the anomaly.

Drawn to a masculine sound, she focused to pinpoint the familiar pitch and her gaze found the source. Kyle's baritone voice sent shivers of want and, yes, need to be in his presence. "Want to join me?"

Kyle closed the distance, bent down, and kissed her cheek. "Thank you."

He slid the chair out and sat. Kyle gathered her hands inside his. "I've missed you."

"Same here." Tingles of excitement danced across her skin. Her tummy quivered and her pulse increased. Blood rushed through her veins carrying what must have been a copious amount of oxygen. She blinked to rid the dizziness. A euphoria of happiness blitzed to every nerve ending. Bless him, she felt alive. This man had brought her out of the pits of hell and self-pity to highest mountain top in heaven in less than fifteen seconds.

Without a doubt, not only had she invited him to her table, but she'd welcomed him back in her life. Her world shifted again.

The busy waitress stopped at their table. "What can I get for you?"

Shelby clicked off her order. "I'd like the vegetarian omelet and orange juice, please."

Kyle offered both Shelby's and his menu. "I'll have the special with coffee."

The woman nodded. "Be right back."

Kyle's angelic smile hinted at a touch of devilry. "Would rather have something else, but this will do for now."

Afraid he'd reject her again, she refused to acknowledge his comment, but she could only hope.

"What have you been up to these past couple of days?"

"Not much with the weather. I visited with Jude and read. Nothing was in the fridge that I wanted, so here I am. What about you? Did you get some work done?"

"Yes, I did." She hesitated for a couple of seconds then decided to take the plunge, the hell with her insecurities. "I want to say something, and I hope you'll understand what I'm trying to tell you."

"Sure, what's on your mind?"

"Remember when I walked to the stream at Pogonip?"

He nodded.

"Do you know you have a prismatic aura? It's the same refractive light in the First Realm and I have a hunch—this is going to sound insane." She paused, sipped her coffee and wouldn't tell him what She-Who-Smiles talked about. Not that she was keeping a secret, but she still had to think through the implications of her gifts. The fact she saw Kyle's aura and intuited his soul was good and trustworthy…maybe, she had let her imagination roam wild again. She'd skip that part. "I astral projected without Ten-Blue-Sun. I thought I had to have the doll. I met your spirit guide."

"Why would that sound crazy? But, you were going to say something else, then you changed your mind. When you're ready to tell me, I'll listen."

She squeezed his hand. Kyle understood she still grappled with these new and startling revelations. "I encountered several guides…and I wanted to tell you about it. Have you met your spirit adviser?"

His head tilted to the side and his brow furrowed. "Yes."

"Good, then this will make sense to you. I've released my husband and he's continuing his journey. Bear-Claws said I was to rely on you, that you were a good man. Of course, he confirmed what I already knew in my heart."

His lips formed his next word, but she held up her hand to stop him.

"Wait, I'm not finished. On my way back from the creek at Pogonip, you were kissing Lisa—"

"Shelby—"

"When I saw you together, something happened to me that I didn't want to put a microscope to and analyze. That's why I've been avoiding you."

"Shel, I'm sorry. I didn't mean to hurt you. Lisa gave me a goodbye kiss, that's all. In fact, she was happy that I had met you and hoped we would have dinner with her sometime."

Hearing Kyle use the endearment of her name, an emotional attachment lodged in several feminine places at the same time, the folds between her thighs, her heart, and deep within her soul. "I'm the one who should apologize. I'll be gone in a few days and doubt you'll ever see me again. This is your life and I don't have a right to—"

"I want you in my life and for more than the next few days."

Her tummy fluttered as if hundreds of birds took flight. She smiled. "I'm glad you decided to eat here this morning."

He returned the grin. "Me too."

The waitress balanced the huge tray on their table. The myriad of plates and glasses were shuffled around them.

After the serving attendant left, Kyle hovered over her ear. "What's your favorite dessert?"

She tilted a few inches away and glanced at him. "Dessert?"

****

Shelby maneuvered her car beside Kyle's truck in the parking lot of her hotel. She jumped out, closing the door.

Kyle had wanted Annie with them. They had picked her up and he put her in the back. Standing on all fours with her chin on edge of the bed, Annie waited. Shelby scratched the top of her head. The little tuft of hair between her ears stood straight in the air like a cowlick. She added definition with her fingers. If it had been larger, she would've put a small bow there.

Kyle rolled down the passenger window. "Please join me."

He scooted over as she climbed in and settled next to him. "What's wrong?"

Although he had said he wanted to spend more time with her, was Kyle placating her in a public place? Now, was he going to tell her how he really felt? She couldn't handle another rejection from him. Not wanting to hear the answer, she grabbed the door handle.

"Wait, Shel." He grasped her elbow. "We have something special, you know that, don't you?" He wrapped his arms around her shoulders.

She nodded, pleased he wasn't pushing her away. Air rushed out of her lungs succumbing to the immeasurable relief.

Lifting her, he shifted and set her on his lap. She nestled her head into the crook of his neck. The cologne and his masculine scent drifted to her nostrils. His smell was unique in every way. She indulged again, taking in his distinct aroma.

His fingertips kneaded the muscles of her back, soothing her jittery nerves. He kissed the hair at her temple, then angled to her throat. She gasped as goosebumps rose over her flesh. Her hand found the nape of his neck and she tugged him closer. When his mouth grazed back to hers, she opened for him, lost in the sensations she had missed for so long, spellbound by his touch, she absorbed his affection.

A minty taste blazed across her taste buds. His lips were a set in contradictions, soft, asking, summoning her to respond. At the same time, they were firm, issuing a directive, follow me. And she planned on it, because this wasn't the action of a man who wanted to disappear.

His kisses morphed into a possessive pleasure. She relished his attention and matched the pace. Mimicking the intimacy of a lover's dance, their tongues advanced and retreated.

He encircled her in his arms. A sense of security cloaked her and she angled against his hard chest. With his mouth, he wove tenderness yet his desire was domineering, creating a need within.

She groaned swirling into a maelstrom of his ardor and passion. She gathered his hand to cup her breast. Kyle paused. His gaze connected to hers then his lips followed her guidance. He suckled. The heat and moisture infused her shirt percolating to her skin. Shards of erotic tingles pulsed from her nipple to her clit.

She wanted to take everything he gave, give him

the same in return, eclipsing any doubt he may still harbor about her not being ready. "I want to make love to you, right now."

He released her and leveled his gaze. "Baby, are you sure?" Kyle's smooth baritone voice offered her another chance to stop, to end the passion without retribution.

"I am."

He whispered kisses over her cheek. "Whose face and body will you see when I take you?"

"A man who for some reason hasn't given up on me, a gentleman who shares acuity of mind and spirit, an ethereal bond that I'm not sure I understand yet."

A moan rumbled from his chest. He opened the truck door, balanced her while she gently slid out and guided her to the room.

She shivered, anticipation raced through her blood. "Where's the key?"

She withdrew the card from her purse. "Here."

Kyle held the door for her as she crossed the threshold, he whistled for Annie, who bounced through the doorway. He slid the Do-Not-Disturb sign into the slot then with his boot heel, he closed out the world.

Shelby turned to face Kyle. "I want you to hold me like you'll never let me go. I know you will, just don't let it be right now, today."

Kyle stepped closer and hugged her. "Baby, I don't know what the future holds, but are you ready to make our memories?"

"Ours?"

He murmured, "Shh, let's hold on to now."

His kisses streamed from her ear to her cheek then flowed to her mouth. Nipping her bottom lip, he laved to sooth the pleasant pain. When she parted, he delved in and once again, spearmint exploded on her tongue.

Her palms stroked down his spine. At the base of his back, she kneaded his muscles. They tightened under her fingertips. As his shoulders curled, she arched her back creating erotic pressure against her breasts. Desire erupted deep in her belly then lowered to her clit. He drew her to his chest. Her nipples ached from his heat and friction and she wanted more.

Her hands slid to his bottom, she shifted undulating against his erection. As she oscillated, and caressed his shaft, the intensity escalated. Her juices flowed from her feminine folds. She was wet and ready.

"What name will be on your lips when you climax?" Words from a distant voice tumbled through her mind. Kyle? Had he asked a question?

She struggled to make sense of the surrounding presence. Finally, she surrendered.

A fog drifted around her. "Mind-Walker." The haze of damp air and moisture filled her nostrils. She allowed the strange sensations to swallow her subconscious.

"What?" He withdrew a few inches and searched her gaze.

She blinked several times and adjusted her focus. "Did you say something?"

He rested his forehead on hers. "What's my name?"

"Sweet Jesus, Pressley."

He flicked open the top snap of her jeans, gathered her long-sleeve henley shirt above her breasts. As he unhooked her lace bra and lifted them, the abrasion accelerated her hunger to join with Kyle. Yes, she wanted sex, but there was something more she strove for, something beyond two physical bodies uniting.

When he released her clothes, the material drifted to the floor. His hands coasted to her bottom warming her skin. He edged her close again, nestled and cradled against his pelvis.

In his firm hold, she shook from the passion surging through her blood, wanting him to take her, to fill her.

A deep rumble resonated in his chest as though he was fighting for control. He inhaled and calmed. Kyle lightly traced his palms from her ass, up each side of her ribs until he found her breasts. He held the weight gazing in reverence.

His hands shaped and squeezed while his long fingers kneaded. A quiver sluiced over her flesh from his potent offering. With his thumb and forefinger, he twisted her nipple. Pure bliss raced to every nerve ending.

She craved to touch his skin, her palms and fingers explored, but his denim jacket and T-shirt were in the way. Her fingertips slid up to his shoulders, then down his arms, relieving him of the outer obstacle.

Kyle gathered the ends of his jersey, removed the shirt over his head and let it coast down one arm falling on top of her clothes.

She closed the distance to rub her breast against the dark-curly hair on his broad chest. "I want you."

Shelby unzipped her pants, shimmying to let them pool around her feet. Her toes worked the back of her tennis shoes and with one foot whisked the pile to the side. Taking both index fingers to each side of her hips, she scooted her panties down, stepping out of them then waited for Kyle to do the same. His seductive gaze touched her heart.

Bereft of his clothes, he stood before her. Comfortable in his skin, desire in his gaze, with him fully erect, Kyle's physique was like a god. She wobbled, as though her bones were melting.

He gathered her in his arms, and eased onto the bed until her backside met the mattress. "Birth control?"

"Taken care of."

Lowering on top of her, he rested his forearms on each side of Shelby's shoulders, his hands cupped her cheeks, and his thumbs followed the lines of her lips. "I'm clean. No condom. I want to feel your wet warmth surround me."

"Then make love to me." Her mouth engaged his.

His hands explored while each moist kiss aroused her, giving her pleasure. The tantalized trail of his pursuit from her ear lobe to her breasts, provoked, teased, and enticed her. The white outline of her tan lines contrasted against his dark hair, he hovered above her nipple, not touching, just looking...driving her insane. She wiggled with impatience. He licked a swath across her areola, then shifted several inches away to watch the bud tighten.

Kyle murmured, "Oh, sweetheart, what you do to me."

Shelby whimpered. "Inside me now."

He rolled over and helped steady her as she straddled him. She guided him in and he delved to the depths of her core. She clenched her inner muscles. His moans matched hers. The ecstasy of his hard-as-steel cock filling her to the brim transported her closer to the edge. With each plunge, his groin tapped her clit. She widened her legs to meet his advance needing more, wanting the slap of pleasure. With every thrust, her muscles drew tight holding his velvet-hardened shaft, reveling in the ancient dance of lovers.

She increased the tempo, enjoying the unequivocal power and control of being on top. Deliberately withdrawing to the tip, she stopped and smiled. In slow motion, she eased down taking an inch at a time and halted.

As she rocked forward teasing his length, Kyle growled and grabbed her hips, dragging her wet sheath down his shaft. Fully seated and in one fluid move, he spun until she was on her back. Still joined, he mumbled, "Baby, it's my turn to be in control."

He angled her hips for deeper penetration and each stroke found her G-spot. His raw act of possession catapulted her to the bliss of euphoria. "Kyle." She shuddered. Lights danced in her mind's eye.

She sailed to another plane while Kyle embraced her. "Hold on, there's nothing to fear."

When she opened her eyes, she was back in bed. With the last of her spasms ending, her muscles relaxed.

Kyle's eyes twinkled. "You're beautiful. Next time, we go together." His lips met hers giving her a thorough kiss, he advanced and withdrew, metering a steady rhythm.

She milked him, wondering if she'd travel with him during his release. Her fingers found his balls and teased. Not wanting to wait any longer, she gripped his shaft with her inner muscles as hard as she could.

He eased away from her swollen lips, his eyes darkened. "Come with me." His thumb rubbed her clitoris. With each plunge, he accelerated, rapid and electric.

The play on his words didn't escape her, and she'd surrender for either one or both.

"Stay with me." Kyle flexed his hips.

His muscles stiffened under her hands and a guttural growl thundered from his corded neck. The pressure exerted on her clit, and the force of his thrust launched her again.

As though traveling through a black hole, lights flickered as her weightless body passed by them, alone.

"Open your eyes, you're not alone."

When she did, excitement coursed through her energy. A Utopia, perfection, a place she wanted to stay, but only with her cowboy.

"Time to go." He held onto her, returning to their hotel and safely back into their bodies.

He lowered himself onto her, the sheen of sweat cooled by his quick gasps rushing over her skin. Kyle rolled to his side and gathered her into his embrace. No words were necessary. Contented, sated, she reveled in the mind-blowing experience unique to the ties she and Kyle held to the First Realm. Or was it? The latter thought pulled her out of her reverie.

He kissed her forehead. "Shower?"

He didn't seem taken aback by what had happened. Did this occur all the time? Was this normal for him and other women? "I don't know if I can walk."

Kyle chuckled. "I'll help."

He rose, put one arm around her back, the other under her knees and whisked her into the bathroom. He lowered her to the counter. "Give me a minute."

He turned on the water and adjusted the

temperature. Kyle tucked her against his chest carrying her inside the glass enclosure.

His beautiful mouth kissed, laved, and loved every inch of her and she reciprocated. He fondled, licked, and grazed. The desire for another release broiled deep in her belly. She wanted to go to the highest peak, the pinnacle of another world. This wasn't just sex, well maybe it was, but she didn't care as long as he didn't stop, and as long as they both came together. And they did.

Kyle twisted the handle, cutting off the water, grabbed a towel and dried her. After he finished dusting the moisture from his skin, his whiskey irises changed to molten-lava chocolate. He stalked her steps out of the bathroom until the back of her knees hit the bedside. "Want to go again?"

She nodded.

He gently lowered her and helped her shimmy across the sheets then he closed the distance lying beside her. His legs entangled hers, as he nuzzled her neck. The swath of moisture from his mouth laid a trail beginning at her collar bone to the underside of her breast. She grasped his head. His wet hair cooled her palms as she guided him to her nipple.

A chuckle resonated. "Patience, baby."

He blazed a path down to her belly then further to the one place she wanted him. His knees hit the floor and he grasped her calves pulling her to the edge of the bed. With his shoulders, he widened her thighs and streamed kisses marking the distance on the inside of her legs to her juncture. When he opened her folds with his fingers, his tongue lapped from the bottom to the top, stopping at her clit, he suckled. She wanted more pressure. He released the tiny bud, and his tongue journeyed to her opening, probing, piercing, fucking her while his thumb added the force she had desired. The ecstasy of his intimate love shoved her closer to the apex, but she wanted him to travel with her.

"Stop." Her hands still on his head, she tilted him away as she sat up.

He rose. Her palms trailed down his side until they found his balls and her mouth welcomed him. She stroked the underside. His fingers weaved through her hair guiding her to take him fully. His erection rasped against her tongue and she swallowed.

He groaned and withdrew. His forearms tucked under her arms, he hurled her across the bed once again. In the time it would take her to say "fuck me," he had her legs spread and was buried inside her.

Kyle grunted while their skin slapped and his balls smacked her ass. She liked the animalistic side of him. Yes, gentle, attentive, and loving had its place, but rough, hard, and feral gave a pleasurable dimension of wild lovemaking she wanted to explore with him. This wasn't darkness; it was creating an unyielding appetite for one dominating the other by a master controlling the release of pleasure.

Kyle led then she'd eclipse him into the exotic territory of the untamed. When they climaxed, they met once again in the other plane. How, she didn't know. Why, she couldn't care less as long as they were together.

With only short rests between their lovemaking, her sore muscles stretched to accommodate his amorous affections. She wasn't used to this much sex. As if he understood, he held her under the sheet and used his body as a tranquil blanket of repose.

He enveloped her in his arms, kissed the top of her head, speaking through her hair. "I noticed...your two children are Tim's?"

She nodded. "I'm learning, if you're lucky enough, love transcends all boundaries."

He gently squeezed her. "Do you want children?"

"Seriously? Wasn't this just sex? Yes, we have something special, but we're not there yet. To answer your question, I'm not in a position for that to be an issue. You?"

"Just sex. I'm going to let you in on a little secret, it wasn't for me, but we'll come back to that. And yes, I'd like to have some. Right now, I'm ready to refuel my body. How about you?"

"I'm famished. Let's order in."

"You know, we need to talk...about us."

She buried her face into his neck. "What about?"

"We have something extraordinary and I want to explore the possibilities."

Her gaze connected with his, a devilish smile spread across his face. She giggled and laid her head on his chest. "I feel it too, but I'm not sure if there's anything to discuss." Obviously, they shared an emotional experience together and making love to him had advanced to another level, beyond sex, physical attraction, and an ordinary release. But her roots were in Texas, his Wyoming.

Their worlds collided because of a doll. What remained were spiritual ties and those could be severed as well. The bonds with Tim had been broken, twice. Could she handle another loss? She had enough gut-wrenching despair to last a lifetime. Would she be able to endure her heart ripped to shreds again? She didn't think so.

"How about I order some Chinese food?"

She clung to the subject change. "Kung Pao chicken, if they have it."

He unlocked his arms and legs and climbed out of the bed. "One spicy poultry dish coming up."

He crossed the room and she admired the flex of muscle in his tight butt. She shivered in anticipation of having his ass under her hands.

With the pangs of hunger gone and Annie taken care of too, Shelby relished the down time cradled in Kyle's arm. The sheet drawn to cover her breasts while his beautiful body partially lay on top, she draped a leg over his. The crisp hair tickled her sensitized skin.

"I wish you would've let me take you and Annie to my house. I don't understand your reluctance." Kyle bounced her against the mattress.

How could she explain to him that by accepting his invitation she would've been making a commitment? She ignored his statement and his search for an answer. With the inside of her hand, she stroked his cheek. "I'm glad you keep your shaving kit and extra clothes in your truck."

"I always have to be ready to travel." He gently cradled her hand in his and kissed her palm. "When do you have to leave?"

"Tomorrow."

His lips found hers and before he closed his eyes, desire radiated from his gaze along with something else. She refused to think about leaving him and departing this part of his world. He took his time making sweet love to her. With Kyle by her side, she'd make the night. Facing tomorrow would be no small task, but for now, she'd relish every minute and memorize every inch of his body.

****

The next morning, Shelby handed Kyle her bags. He loaded them into her SUV, put Annie in the back seat and buckled her in with the doggie seatbelt while she scooted behind the wheel.

He ambled to her door and placed his hands against the open window frame. "I want to see you again, Shel. We haven't discussed how we can be together. I need to go back to work, but I want us to make plans to see each other." He winked. "Remember I get visitation rights with Annie."

His comment erased her sad disposition. Would he really visit her and the canine she loved? "You can see Annie any time you want."

"What about us?" His palms grasped the door, and he waited for her answer.

She sighed. "Kyle, what we had was wonderful, but this—" Shelby waved back and forth from her to Kyle. "Can't work out, I just don't see how."

"Let me worry about this." Mocking her movements, his lips curled into a big smile, deepening his dimples, and he winked again. "I'll call you. Be careful, I'll be in touch. You're special to me, Shelby Littleton, don't you forget that."

Kyle kissed her one last time, a kiss she hoped would last her a lifetime.

Not out of Jackson yet, her cell phone rang. The caller ID illuminated KP. "Hi."

"Baby, I miss you already. What we have is great and we're going to make more memories together.

Gotta' run. Bye."

"Bye, Kyle." Tears clouded her eyes. *Damn.* His goodbye shouldn't hurt this bad. How did he think a long-distance relationship could work out? Someone always had to give up something, the hurt comes, then frustration, and finally anger.

Ten-Blue-Sun was still in Kyle's possession. Along with his spirit guide, they'd finish the quest. After all, the doll came from Rain and Garrett's tribe. She wasn't needed anymore and she had figured out, she and Tim had been used to get the doll to Wyoming.

Kyle had his life in this beautiful state and she had hers in Texas. She'd made love to her cowboy and just like Tim, she had to let him go, lessons well learned from She-Who-Smiles but hard as hell to accept.

Chapter Nine

Kyle gazed out his kitchen window. The August breeze blew through the screens, cooling his skin. The weeks had passed at an agonizing slow pace and frustration had changed his normal easy going self into a near maniac. Jude threatened he had better get his head out of his ass before he personally made him a proctologist appointment. He admitted, at least in part, he had a rough time keeping his mind on work. As for the doctor, he reminded Jude, bad karma was a bitch.

Finally after the last of his many requests, Shelby had said yes. He'd bet she'd enjoy a break from the relentless Texas heat. By the end of the week, she'd be here, and he wanted to have a plan. This is what he did for a living, find a win-win situation for all parties concerned. All he had to do was come up with…something.

Just in case his strategy worked, he had contacted the attorney for a prenuptial agreement. He wanted to be upfront with Shel, put all the cards on the table. The time had come for him to tell her who he was, the intricacies of the trusts, including the one he'd set up for his future children. He scoffed. His estate alone would last for the next ten generations.

Would she hightail it and run? Shelby's independence would be a hurdle he'd have to overcome and that's why he wanted to wait until she was here, to see her reactions. The next step would be a doozy; she'd have to take off her wedding band to accept his engagement ring.

His fingers curled into his palms. What if she said no… He let out a ragged breath. She responded to slow and easy. He'd have her here for seven days and he'd make every moment count. In his bed, he'd take her unhurried, manifest a loving tribute even she couldn't refute.

When his fantasies considered the various places he would make love to her, inside and outside his home, his cock hardened. He moaned. *Remember slow and easy.*

Even though they had a multitude of things in common, they still hadn't shared all of them. She refused to exercise with him. Of course, he considered making love an excellent way to increase their heart rate and burn calories.

He had kept in touch with Shelby, calling her twice a day, once in the morning to wake her and at night to wish her sweet dreams. At first, her voice held reluctance, but eventually, she'd dropped the fortified bulwark and warmed up to him. He had known the minute her wall tumbled down. After he had hung up that day, he was as high as a kite and shouted, "He makes the shot, cleared the rim, three points."

He slid his cell from his back pocket and tapped Garrett's number. "Are you free to fly to Texas, then deadhead back here this Saturday?"

"Sure, where and who?"

"Waco. Shelby Littleton."

"Is that the same gal you brought to my ranch?"

He paced around the island and eyed the orchid

arrangement Hilda had placed on top of the granite counter. Damn, Shelby would look beautiful with those scattered throughout her hair. "I'm assuming Uncle Grey told you."

"He said she was a pretty filly."

Kyle stopped. "Yeah." His stomach tightened, jealousy speared into his gut. This was a foreign reaction to him. He had never met a woman he thought of his own, not that he considered Shelby a possession. He wanted her with every fiber of his being, that's why he'd called his attorney. The barbaric feeling had hit him hard. He needed to get a grip. This was family, and his elder.

Garrett chuckled. "Earth to Pressley?"

"I'm here."

"It's normal for men to appreciate the female form."

Kyle harrumphed. "Let's get back to my question."

Garrett whistled. "You got it bad. I already said I was free."

He ignored his brother's jibe. "I'll need to handle a few last minute things at work so I won't be going with you, but I'll meet you at the airport."

This time Garrett laughed out loud. "See you then."

Kyle cleared his throat. "Wait. This deal with the doll, you know we're going to have hell in the next few years." Only silence greeted his statement. "Garrett?"

"Even though you refuse to use your gift, you're still Mind-Walker."

Kyle didn't want to go there. "Gotta' run, call me if something comes up."

"Sure."

Kyle pocketed his phone. Garrett's words rang

true. He'd always have his ability. Inherent with any oath, obstacles arise to question the validity of the promise. Case in point, during the Fourth of July celebration, he knew something wasn't right. He could have searched for the problem and handled it.

The more he thought about it, he could count off several other times. When Shelby called him Mind-Walker, he wanted to jump in to see how she knew. She had been in a trance, not cognizant of what she had said and he could've been in and out in a matter of seconds with the answer.

Hell yeah, he wanted to walk in her mind. When the intense desire rose, it scared the shit out of him. No situation or person prior to Shelby had tempted him to the extent she had. He could've had said, this time would be okay because and click off the numerous reasons, justifying his actions. His word meant everything to him so there would be no excuses, none. He would not succumb and break his vow.

He sighed. Garrett was a good man and Kyle trusted him with his life. His blood brother's gift of visions helped many of their people. Kyle thought highly of him, proud as hell to call him family.

In their previous life, they were cousins, had the same Hopi grandfather. He remembered the day he had accepted the concept of reincarnation, but prior to that, he'd thought he was losing his mind.

At the age of nine, his ability had scared the bejesus out of him. Jude, who was eleven and even then, only believed in what could be scientifically proven, had made fun of him. The many months after the collision of beliefs between them, he slipped in and out of people's minds. Terrified of what was happening to him, he developed introverted tendencies. As time passed, he'd gained finesse with his ability and transformed into a secure young man.

Two years later, the fearsome foursome, Jude, Lisa, and Garrett had played kick the can and he was it. He had found the first two. However, Garrett had been a tough nut to crack. He knelt and concentrated, he'd find him.

Garrett grasped him by the shoulder. "Get out, now."

Kyle smirked. All he could think about was that he had won and laughed. Garrett didn't get the humor.

Garrett grabbed the front of his shirt and lifted him to meet his face. "We need to talk."

Uncle Grey and Rain had helped him with his gift, taught him the ways of their people, his people. He overcame his fear, learned customs, language, created intrinsic bonds and acknowledged he was a part of a larger history.

This was his life and he wanted to share it with the one woman who understood.

****

Shelby placed the phone in the cradle, conjuring a picture of the company airplane picking her up and couldn't. *God*, she missed Kyle. Could they make a go at a relationship or was it doomed from the beginning? Her stomach churned. She preferred to think of the former, but if the latter proved correct, she'd leave, take her heart, and store the broken pieces to mend later.

Much later.

She speed dialed her sister. "Alessa."

"Yes, ma'am."

"Can you watch Annie for a week and handle my

things at the office."

"Sure, what's up?"

Her youngest sister had a boundless source of energy. "I'm going to Jackson for a week."

"No problem. Wyoming? Sounds a bit more serious than you led me to believe."

Shelby balked. They're scouting the possibilities, not acting on them...Right? "To be honest, I don't know. I'm not sure..."

"Go and have a good time. Besides, he sounds like fun and his voice is erotic." Alessa giggled.

"When did you hear—?"

"At work, you answer your extension with the speaker phone." Alessa clicked her tongue.

"Oh." Shelby made a mental note to stop using the hands free option.

"Give the guy a chance....allow yourself the opportunity to have a good time."

Shelby softened her big sister tone she had a tendency to use with Alessa. "He calls me every morning and then the evening...to say goodnight. Oh hell, this has disaster written all over it."

"You still look for the negative in everything."

"That's been my job, Alessa. All because of...Never mind, will you take care of Annie and the business?"

"Of course." The catch in Alessa's expression caught her attention.

"I'm sorry. I shouldn't have gone there. It's been ingrained since...Al, we've talked about this, they're my problems, not yours."

"When do you want me to come by?" Alessa's usual vigor changed to resignation.

"I'll drop her off at your house on the way to the airport tomorrow morning. Alessa, thanks."

"Anytime."

She'd give her little sister an extra big hug in the morning. Shelby would remind Al that she had chosen to put both of her sisters first many years ago.

****

Garrett had met her at the designated place. Along with the escort of the Fixed Base Operator, he led her to the plane and boarded. Cleared for take-off, the jet didn't take long to reach altitude.

Garrett angled over the harness like seatbelt, peering out of the cockpit. "Would you like to join me?"

Shelby jumped at the chance. "Love to, feels strange to be the only one in the cabin."

Once settled in the right seat, she kept her hands folded in her lap for fear she'd bump the wrong knob.

When Garrett introduced himself, she immediately noticed his aura shined like Kyle's, his Indian ancestry apparent with his onyx eyes and coal-black hair. The immediate camaraderie created an irreversible bond. At the same time, her nerves jangled because they all shared the knowledge of the First Realm and what was to come.

She didn't have to wonder if he knew about Ten-Blue-Sun, the blessings that were forthcoming and the eventual battles. A strange phenomenon, the unsaid acquaintance of truth forged a strong link between them.

However, the puppet syndrome kept popping in her mind. Had she been used to transport the life-bringer to their people? Either way, being exploited rubbed her the wrong way.

Garrett had given her a headset. "You're Kyle's blood brother, who owns the ranch called Pogonip?"

"Yep, heard you were there." He nodded.

"Does Pogonip mean anything and how did you come up with the name?"

"My mother is Shoshone and depending on which words you use, the meaning can be thunder fog, ice fog, or valley fog. The literal translation is the fog that settles in the mountains and valleys."

"Shoshone must be a beautiful language to know." Shelby fiddled with the dangling wire from the headset.

"Excuse me a minute, I need to speak to D/FW. I'm switching you off." Garrett flipped a toggle then adjusted his headset.

She waited for him to finish. Garrett's voice resonated through her receiver, but not the other person. Pilot talk was another language all its own.

"I'm back."

"How did you two meet?" Her curiosity peaked, wanting to get to know more about Kyle.

"We grew up together and now his family's company, Pressley International, is a customer of mine. But this particular aircraft is Kyle's."

Shelby angled in her seat to see if he was joking. His raven eyes focused and settled on hers. "Kyle belongs to 'the' Pressley empire?"

Her tummy jerked into a tight knot. The name Pressley ran synonymously with Rockefeller and the Hunts. How she could have missed the signs? She had assumed this ride was a company perk, not his private jet.

Small business my ass, she moaned under her

breath. "I think I need to go back."

"Sure, help yourself to anything in the galley, and I'll let you know when we are about to land."

"No...I mean...I need you to turn around and take me to Texas."

"Can't do that, I'm paid to get you to Wyoming. You didn't know who Kyle was?"

"I thought I knew." She disconnected from his potent stare and looked out the side window. "No, I guess not."

"He's a good man."

"I've never doubted that."

"Even when he lost his mom, he didn't harden his soul. Any man who preserves my mom's upbringing holds a high account with me. You were supposed to laugh."

Recollections unfolded before her. On the day of their picnic, Kyle had shared his favorite places with her and Annie. He had sweetly kissed her. When she had the terrible flashback, he held her in his arms giving her comfort. She would hold those fond memories close to her heart.

During their drive to the national park, Kyle had said he worked with a family business just like hers. She'd meant to ask him how he had known. She hadn't shared that tidbit of information. In the overall scope of things, did it matter? The answer resounded loud and clear. Yes, it did.

"Shelby?"

She twisted to face him. "Sorry, I was woolgathering."

"After Kyle received his sheepskin, then his masters, he served our country. When he returned, he went right to work beside his brother and opened the no-kill animal shelter in memory of his mom."

"That explains a lot...I know he's an honorable man."

Garrett cleared his throat. "We all agreed."

"On what?"

"You should take back Ten-Blue-Sun on this trip. Bear Claws directed Kyle to watch over you and he's accepted the responsibility. No matter what you may face, Kyle will be there...he'll take care of you."

Kyle once made the statement Garrett barely talked to anyone except his equestrian friends. She'd beg to differ. What she needed right now was time to think.

"I'm going to get some water, want any?" Shelby removed the headset and carefully, rose.

"No, thanks. Maybe, I shouldn't have said anything, but I wanted you to know, we've all come to the same conclusion. For right now, you're the chosen one." Garrett grasped her elbow and steadied her until she cleared the seat.

"When you land can you point this plane toward Texas?"

"Sorry, I'm heading to New York. I can be back in a few days to take you home."

Shelby patted his shoulder. "That won't be necessary. Thanks for your offer."

When she slid into the plush cabin seat, the tan leather creaked. Shelby drank the bottled water and reflected. She-Who-Smiles had beckoned her a week ago. Astral projecting, her spirit guide introduced her to Many-Horses, her uncle's Hopi grandfather, who'd whittled Ten-Blue-Sun. Then, Many-Horses asked his powerful son, One-Who-Soars-With-Eagles for help.

Shelby met Many-Horses and his second wife, Sunlight, a Comanche.

She-Who-Smiles asserted, "Listen with steadfast diligence. Enraged that his daughter fell in love with Many-Horses, the Comanche father cast a curse on Sunlight's man and their entire lineage. Sunlight had given birth to Ten-Butterflies."

Then she imparted. "Hear carefully, Brave-One. Ten-Butterflies' baby was to be 'the' next shaman, but the naming ceremony never happened, for they were slaughtered."

Garrett's voice echoed through the cabin. "We're descending to land, buckle up."

The scenes of death and destruction deluged her memory again, the same dreadful acts One-Who-Soars-With-Eagles had shared. Without a doubt, Shelby knew the possession of Ten-Blue-Sun lay solely with Kyle and his family. Although she couldn't explain Alessa's involvement, that was for the rest of them to figure out. She and Tim had merely been pawns in a treacherous game initiated by an irate father.

She'd taken this journey to explore a relationship with Kyle. Kyle's integrity would bind him to Bear-Claws' request. How could she tell the difference between Kyle's love given from his heart or a love dispensed through honor-bound vows, traditions, family, and commitments?

She couldn't, and there was no way in hell she'd allow Kyle to stay in an obligated relationship. Yes, she cared for Kyle deeply and what she had to do would hurt like hell. Her path was set now that she had knowledge of Bear-Claws' petition. It was up to her to sever Kyle's duty.

Funny the men she had chosen in her life, she had to say goodbye and walk away, twice. Anger coursed through her veins. She-Who-Smiles lessons were getting on her nerves.

When they landed, she gazed out the window. The FBO, Jackson Hole Aviation, directed the plane to a stop, the sun shined and Kyle leaned against Jalopy.

She gasped and her tummy somersaulted. Kyle's wide grin spread across his handsome face. God, from the bottom of her heart, she desired this man. She wanted to caress the outline of his jaw and give him an everlasting kiss. She more than cared, that's why she was here to explore what their future might hold. Well initially.

Although, why didn't he tell her who he was? What was this trip about? Perhaps, Kyle's agenda was different from hers or maybe not. Damn, should she throw caution to the wind, to cast the sails and see where the next port-of-call for their mighty ship would anchor?

No, the First Realm had dictated her course, again. She'd cut the ties that bound Kyle.

Garrett opened the door and the stairs unfolded before her. "JHA will help with your luggage. Good luck, Shelby."

"Thanks, Garrett, you take care."

She greeted Kyle, giving her cheek instead of her lips that he aimed for, and his smile disappeared. "I need to return to Texas, something came up that I don't want Alessa handling alone. If you could take me to the rental car place here, I'd appreciate it. Plus, I need a few moments to talk to you."

When Kyle didn't acknowledge her, she hurried.

"Never mind, I'll ask the FBO to take me."

"What's going on?" Kyle extended his hand to cup her cheek.

Shelby took two steps backward knowing if he touched her, she'd lose her resolve. She wanted to leave without a long dissertation dissecting and psychoanalyzing her thoughts and discussing lessons from the First Realm.

"Alessa called and I have to get back. If I leave now, I can be there late tomorrow evening for the Monday morning meeting." She quickly lowered her gaze because she never lied well. There had to be a continuous scroll across her forehead, "Liar, Liar, Liar. Kyle would see the bright banner and right through her fib. But she was doing this for a good reason, wasn't she? No, two wrongs never made a right.

Out of the corner of her eye, Shelby spotted Garrett descending the steps. He shook his head and mouthed silently, "Sorry."

Kyle's brows drew together, and he focused over her shoulder, and then panned back in her direction. "Give me a minute."

He strode toward Garrett and talked to his best friend, but she couldn't hear what they were saying. After Kyle shook Garrett's hand, he paced back to her.

His chest heaved then he released a breath into an audible sigh. "There's a car rental at the main terminal, I'll take you."

Shelby spat. "Thanks, Mr. Pressley International, a family business just like mine, right." Her words were sharp and laced with hostility. What was wrong with her? She hadn't meant to speak so harshly, just state the logical reasons with diplomacy, and leave.

Kyle visibly stiffened. He opened her door, and she slid in the passenger seat and waited for the slam. It never came.

A gentleman even in anger, Kyle placed her bag in the back and slipped inside the cab. He grasped the steering wheel, his knuckles whitened. Kyle never bothered to look at her. "Why?"

All her thoughts were jumbled, her mouth was dry from her erratic breathing, and she couldn't form a word let alone a sentence to save her life. Resigned her feelings had the best of her and definitely tongue-tied, she set her vision straight ahead and didn't answer.

Kyle drove around the circle and stopped curbside. "We need to talk before you leave. Will you follow me home?"

He'd earned her respect, deserved an answer and she had to correct the lies she had told Kyle earlier. He had to know the real reasons that she needed to leave. She rescued her drowning thoughts and revived her voice. "Yes, I'll meet you at the exit."

The gamut of emotions ran rampant while she tagged behind Kyle's truck. Her heart rate increased and perspiration beaded on her lip. The First Realm held Kyle hostage and she was a marionette. Embarrassment crept in and her cheeks burned with heat. She wouldn't be a pawn to the whims of the First Realm. Soon, she cooled under the resignation that most things were out of her hands.

Except one, she had the ability to release Kyle from Bear-Claws' demand. Kyle shouldn't be burdened with a Texas thread in his Wyoming tapestry. She calmed and accepted the fate. She'd finish the job she set out to do, break off their relationship, and head back to her ranch.

She parked beside him and clamored out of the car. Kyle placed his hand on the small of her back guiding her to the house.

A wrap-around porch encircled the massive log cabin with five stone chimneys. The porch had several grouped seating arrangements which suggested familial places to gather, along with rockers and the bench swing tempted her to test the soothing lull of motion.

Inside, the foyer welcomed her with a staircase of ornate balustrades and the massive newel in shape of a horse's head. The mane of the stallion flowed as if he galloped on the open plain.

Shelby spoke softly and was surprised there wasn't an echo. "You have a very nice home. It's beautiful and comfortable. It's you."

"Thanks, did the plans myself. Care for a drink?"

"White wine, if you have it."

"Follow me to the kitchen." Kyle strode ahead of her.

Houses of this ilk usually had formal foyers, but warm wood gleamed from the sun shining through the large floor-to-ceiling windows inviting her to enter.

To the left, the library ensconced an impressive stone fireplace. Thick beams stretched along the ceiling and books lined the entire height and length of the walls. *Ahh, surely a room from heaven.*

Following Kyle down the hall, he stepped across the curved threshold into the gourmet kitchen and motioned for Shelby to sit at the bar. He poured her a glass of pinot gris, a scotch neat for himself, then slid onto the barstool beside her.

Kyle sipped his drink then set it on counter. "Are

you ready to talk?"

"Sure, but you go first."

"Do you have any questions?"

"About a zillion."

His boot heels hooked on the bottom rung of the stool, forearms braced against the granite counter and his hands relaxed around the monogrammed glass. He blinked long, then his gaze eluded hers to focus through the window, on something outside. "I think it's safe to say, you don't really want this relationship. If you're calling it quits, then I am too. I can't force or fix what you don't want. Do you agree?"

"Yes, but first, I should apologize for being rude. Second, Garrett told me about you accepting your spirit guide's directive—" She inhaled fully, then expelled the words in rapid fire. "Kyle, I'm not going let you—"

"That's not your decision to make."

She had to reaffirm her stand. "I'm not taking Ten-Blue-Sun and I don't want you to yield to Bear Claws' request."

When he had looked at her, his eyes were an open wound. He grimaced, then adjusted his attention outside again. "Yes. You. Are."

She waited for Kyle to insist she take the doll. His physical presence sat on the stool, but mentally, he was somewhere else. "Kyle, what's going on? What are you seeing? Where are you?"

After several minutes of silence, she bowed her head. "I understand." Moving behind him, she raised her hand and lightly touched his shoulder. When he didn't respond, she let her arm drop to her side. *He's letting you go, take the offering as a gift.* She made her way through the foyer, opened the heavy front door and in a sotto voce sent a prayer. "Good luck and I wish you well."

When her car eased to the control panel, she waited for the gate to open. Instead, Kyle's voice echoed over the intercom. "Shelby, come back. I'm ready to talk."

Would returning change the outcome? At this point, she had her doubts, but she turned around and headed to the house. Something terrible must have happened to Kyle. What problems had he gone through to affect him with deep emotional wounds? As she drove, she replayed the hurt in his eyes, the rejection, then the inability to acknowledge her.

Kyle stood on the edge of the driveway. She parked, took a deep breath and climbed out of the rental. The need to comfort him overwhelmed her. She stretched her arms toward Kyle to embrace him. Her hands circled around his neck and she drew him close and hugged Kyle as though this would be the last time she'd ever get to touch him. She choked back a sob. Their relationship had to end. She was only being fair to Kyle, right? He didn't respond right away, but soon, his palms found her waist, finally they encircled her.

He swayed a few inches back, his eyes glassy. "Shelby, come with me."

He threaded his hand with hers leading her around the house. The back had a fire pit with several cushioned lawn chairs with throw pillows on them. The pool and Jacuzzi were beyond the patio and beside those, water cascaded down a stone fountain into a self-contained pond. The sound would've been calming, tranquil, but at this moment, the setting was incongruous with the turmoil between them and the acid churning inside her tummy.

The silence continued and her tension increased. Her nerves knotted. A burning sensation crept up her chest taking residence at the back of her throat.

He lit the gas pit, slid onto the chair beside her then whispered. "I guess I should explain."

Shelby waited for him to talk. His contorted face revealed his thoughts, and he was reliving memories in high def. Several minutes elapsed before Kyle's low haunting voice revealed his hurt and her heart fluttered hearing his pain.

"Earlier, you said 'Pressley International' like it was a disease. When we were in the kitchen, I recalled how my fiancée always threw that in my face as though my family including myself, were heathens of our democratic society. I'm not comparing you to her, but the similarities are there, enough I can't refute it."

She had done exactly what he said, although for different reasons. They'd been on the way to Pogonip when he told her he worked for the family business. That's what pissed her off, not that he was worth more than she'd see in her lifetime. Some people had more money, some had less, and she couldn't give a crap where someone put the measuring stick for worth. The lines of wealth wavered from year to year, gains or losses in the stock market, all of which can be here today and gone tomorrow. One thing she knew for sure, his fortune would be here for a long time.

She'd listen and the way things were going, her intuition told her the outcome wasn't going to be good. This wasn't exactly how she imagined her day. She hoped for an amicable split, but she'd take the lumps due and keep on going. "How?"

Chapter Ten

"I'll start by stating, I found my fiancée in my bed with a college buddy of mine and...another gal."

Kyle didn't trust her? That sliced her soul in two. "I'm sorry you experienced something so heart wrenching."

He grunted. "Back then, I worked full time, took a full course load finishing my masters and started a home for her...for us. My parents had set up a trust fund. Rain encouraged me to take the dividends and Jude suggested I work part-time, but I turned them down. I wanted the satisfaction of attaining my goals, fast and my way. Between work, classes, and course studies, I was exhausted. When I did find some free time, I shared it with Christine...problem was I usually fell asleep. She didn't care for the decisions I made, nor understood why I had refused the money. Christine resented the Pressley fortune, but at the same time, never hesitated to tell me I was foolish for not using the wherewithal I had at my disposal."

Call it intuition, but he had something else on his mind. Eventually, he'd drive his quarry and hit the target. She had the distinct impression, she was the wild game and his bulls-eye was going to be her soul. "What did your fiancée do for a living? Didn't she help?"

"She started her own business as an interior designer."

"Starting a new venture is hard. That still doesn't explain...did you live together?"

"No. She lived with her grandmother and I lived in our...the house."

Shelby gently prodded. "And?"

"Christine wanted to decorate. We had remodeled several rooms into offices with a separate entrance. She could give her clients a tour of the downstairs to show off her talents and the upstairs would have been our private quarters."

"Not a bad idea. But, something happened."

"I had rearranged my schedule, took several days off. To surprise her, I made myself available to help with some of the designing decisions. Maybe, I was hoping to rekindle the romance that had dwindled from...When I returned to the house, I had caught her unaware all right...found her with two people...in my bed."

"I've never had that happen to me, but I can empathize."

He snorted. "You know what? Yeah, it hurt, but I bounded back pretty fast from that diabolical situation. I knew she wanted a third, wanted me to be the Dom. My tastes didn't follow hers. I won't judge her or the others for the lifestyle they choose."

****

Kyle shifted in his chair and met Shelby's hazel eyes. "The outcome was as synonymous as the catastrophic failure of the Hindenburg landing in New Jersey, just as volatile and just as unstoppable. Several months later, she killed herself in front of...I didn't have time to act. I couldn't stop her. I never knew she was in that bad a shape."

He swiped his right hand down his thigh. "Ah, the million dollar question, did she give up because of me...was I the catalyst for choosing death over life...probably both...Not too long after, the bottle became my best friend as I tried in vain to recollect any sign or indication she had gone over the edge. I finally realized there were no answers."

Kyle connected with Shelby's gaze. He slipped in. The beautiful colors heightened his senses. Now in her mind, he discerned how torn she was with him. His stomach jolted. She was hurt and confused by—

He jerked out. She acted like she didn't know he was there. He closed his eyes. He had lost control and broken a promise. Damn it. As much as he wanted Shelby, the temptation was too much.

He had wanted Shelby in his life and wished to marry her. She had wiggled her way into his heart and infiltrated every thought. When she stood beside him, he ached to have her in his arms, to hold and comfort her. In his embrace, he could stroke her with tender affection. Sleeping together, he filled her with love. Sheathed in her warmth, she gave him back his heart. Shelby had passion for life. He honestly believed the years ahead could've brought joy and happiness. He'd had confidence in their union.

But he was wrong. He had too many demons and Shelby didn't deserve to be shackled to him. The skeletons in his closet overwhelmed him sometimes. Issues ranged far and wide. His mom's murder meant tightened security. The SEAL missions plagued his nights with nightmares of innocent women and children slaughtered. With Christine, trust had been the first significant factor.

Another reason their relationship wouldn't work out, Shelby had given up on the quest and abandoned the First Realm. The very things he desired to share with her.

He opened his eyes in time to see Shelby stretching her hand to touch his, immediately, he withdrew. "I don't want your pity."

He met her surprised gaze. "In more ways than one, you're not any different from Christine...Maybe even worse...You've surrendered Ten-Blue-Sun and your spirit guide. Hell would freeze over before I'd ignore the First Realm's mission. I'll keep the doll and hope for the Great Spirit's help to complete the quest."

Plus, he had mind walked with Shelby and he refused to have temptation anywhere near him. He may still be Mind-Walker, but he'd committed a horrific blunder. He could control what happened in the future and the time was now.

"For your information, I knew you were angry when you found out that I am part of the Pressley fortune, but we still consider Pressley International a family business. Since you wanted to end our relationship, consider your goal accomplished. I'll buy a plane ticket for you." He grabbed his cell to call his personal assistant.

Shelby's voice seemed as though she was a million miles away and her focus off in the distance. "No, don't bother. I can take care of myself. I don't want or need your money. To be honest, I can't say I wouldn't have been daunted by your fortune, but one thing I do know, I'm not intimidated by you. I can find my way out and home. I don't require your guidance...I'll always think fondly of you...We both have dragons that need to be slain…with any luck, that too shall come to pass."

Kyle drew deep, pulling strength from every fiber, he had to do this. "You can go now."

"I do wish you well." She left and never glanced back.

His gut heaved. This is why he never had relationships, just mutual flings. In point of fact, he hadn't been with a lady in over two years. Back then, they were just faces and hadn't meant anything to him. He actually wanted more with Shelby. She had been the first woman he'd desired since Christine. He had fallen hard and fast for her. Ending their relationship hurt. He exhaled to gain better control.

"Anyone home? Kyle?"

Kyle rolled his eyes. He didn't need this. "Back here."

Jude sauntered to the patio. "Who's the girl? Same one Garrett flew in today? You look like shit."

"Don't concern yourself, yes, and thanks."

Jude cocked his head to the side. "Want to talk about it?"

"Damn sure don't."

His big brother talked over his shoulder as he made his way to the back kitchen door. "Looks like you could use a drink and so could I."

In a few seconds, Jude strode back to him. His throat and face red. "What in the hell is going on? A full glass of wine and a half empty scotch are on the bar and I'm betting yours isn't the fluted goblet."

Kyle thrummed his fingertips on the arm of his chair, holding his temper. "Then you would have won."

"Don't go there, Kyle. It isn't worth it."

He grasped each side of his seat, ready to bend the

ornate metal. "You're right."

"I meant the liquor. Don't start on the scotch again."

"You're too late because right now, I don't give a damn."

"Who is she? You never told me about her."

He released his grip and massaged each side of his temple. Would his questions ever stop? "Her name is Shelby Littleton, end of story."

"I don't think you were counting on this as the finale. This should've been the beginning."

"You'd be—"

"Anyone who goes to the company attorney requesting a prenup and flies her in, I would put my money on the latter. Of course, she was supposed to say yes. I'm throwing the dice here. But I'm damn sure she didn't."

"Jude, just…go away. If you are going to be a pain in the ass, you can make yourself useful and get me a drink. Scotch."

"Buddy, she had wedding ring on her finger."

"It's not mine."

"What the hell? You could have any woman you want."

After a long moment, Kyle gathered his breath. "She's a widow. I'd like my scotch if you're going to stick around and play twenty questions."

"Sure. I see you need some beer and some company."

"If you bring me a beer, you can go out the way you damn well came in," he yelled as Jude entered the house.

Jude returned, restocked the fridge under the

outside bar, kept two bottles, popped the caps and gave him one.

He chuckled when the stubborn bastard sat his ass in the chair next to him and gulped a mouthful of ale. They were tight and he would love his brother forever.

Chapter Eleven

Kyle relaxed on a stool cradling his glass. He glanced at the mirror behind the bar, the reflection of everyone keeping to themselves, swigging their drinks and playing pool. The dive had caught his eye, a shit-hole by most standards, but that's what he wanted, no one to recognize him, nobody to bother him.

He'd told his security to fuck off and leave him alone. Probably not the nicest way to get rid of Sam and his crew, but he didn't give a rat's ass. His boots rested on the bent rail of his chair and he listened to a country western song about lovin' and leavin'.

He had taken a sabbatical from work against his brother's wishes. To keep his mind off of Shelby, Jude tried to talk him into traveling to Korea with him. After his brother had lost his wife and unborn child in a car accident, his motto had been, go to work. Then there isn't any time to ponder the reason for existence.

Nothing would remove Shelby from his mind, his job certainly hadn't and the scotch made him numb half the time. The other half, his past demons pressed around him making sleep impossible.

Three weeks ago, he'd shared beer and his plans with Jude. When he flew Shelby in, he had a week to convince her everything would work out. He would've been happy watching the sunrise or set with Shelby. She more than pleased him in bed, hell that particular area was exceptional, but most of all, he didn't have to be doing anything with her. Just holding her would've been enough. Somehow he'd let Shelby get beyond his walls and deep into his heart.

She deserved better than an issue-weary man. Telling her to leave had been hard and in the end, Shelby paid the price. Her tormented eyes haunted him. He wasn't proud of what he'd done, deplorable wouldn't begin to describe his actions. His heart ached remembering another broken vow, he promised to keep her safe. Was this him protecting her?

His mind preyed upon his memories. The passion and the reckless abandoned moments they'd shared. Her giggles bursting into graceful laughter echoed around him. Shelby's touch sent his nerves screaming for more, her sweet kisses, delectable, and the simple act of her gentle caress gave him immeasurable joy.

Shelby had strength and fortitude. When he'd told her to leave, she struggled for composure, a second later squaring her shoulders, she wished his sorry-ass well. *God, he hurt without her*. Damn, there wasn't anything he wanted more right now than Shelby. He loved her and for the first time, acknowledged this feeling touched the very depths of his soul.

Would she be willing to try again? Maybe, together they could battle the monsters they both harbored, find peace, build a life and seek the answers for Ten-Blue-Sun.

His gut roiled. Did he have enough strength and control to stay out of Shelby's mind? Even though Jude didn't believe in the gifts from the First Realm, his big brother had come up with all sorts of excuses to ease his guilt. Justification was like licking lime and salt before and after the shot of tequila. It only made the burning liquid palatable. He'd have to exercise restraint and resist temptation by discipline.

His resolve gave him stamina to initiate the first step. He slid the glass away. The scotch had to go.

Since he hadn't been sleeping well, he needed to rest. Then, he'd call Shelby and ask to see her. If he had to, he'd beg. Maybe, he'd insist on visiting Annie. She had a soft spot when it came to the red-coated creature and if he had to, he would use that tenderness. Energized for the first time in weeks, the cloudy haze of liquor shifted, empowered again, he'd call her in the morning.

As he stood to leave, someone knocked him down and fell on top of him. "What the hell?" He shoved the guy. "Get off of me."

Both on their asses, Kyle mirrored the sneer of the other man, ready to fight.

Kyle took the guy's measure, his elongated face with a long skinny nose appeared like a swordfish. He remembered him…from somewhere.

The man's fist barreled toward him. His head flung back when Swordfish's knuckles connected to his cheek below his left eye. *Fuck that hurt.*

His rage channeled to his hand, he clenched his fingers and threw a haymaker hitting Swordfish's nose.

Dazed, his adversary shook his head, blood spurted, flying in all directions.

Kyle threw another punch to his attacker's stomach.

Swordfish doubled over and moaned.

Three men approached. A tall, big boned guy picked him up and held his arms behind his back while the other two took their turn punching his face, stomach and ribs.

Because of the liquor, he couldn't hold his muscles taut. The blows kept coming. He fought to keep away from the blackening hole of unconsciousness. His legs crumbled underneath him, but they held him up by his elbows. *Fuck, that hurt too.* He battled not to pass out.

One of the men helped Swordfish up.

The other two dragged him outside.

Swordfish seethed. "I wanted ta' take care of this sum-a-bitch. Why did ya' push me on him?"

The tall one retorted. "'Cause you weren't gonna' get around ta' it. I just harried things up a bit." He laughed sarcastically.

If it wasn't for the two men holding him by his armpits, he would've buckled to the ground. He doubted he would forget the missing two front teeth of the big man.

"Well, I wanna' teach him a lesson he ain't never gonna' forget." Swordfish threw his fist into his stomach.

He doubled over. *Air, just a breath.* The intense pain seized his lungs. They burned. Finally, he gasped inhaling oxygen, then groaned.

"He ain't gonna' forget ya' fer awhile."

Swordfish ground out. "No, I don't want him breathin' my gawd damn air. He's gonna' die."

"Throws him in the truck and I couldn't give a shit whatcha' do with him or his pickup."

Rough hands threw him in Jalopy. He bounced against the seat and crumbled. Darkness snaked all around him and the bar's neon light faded.

Daylight seeped into his consciousness, and he

gingerly touched the crusted blood on his lips. He slipped a hand to his ribs and rubbed. *Damn*, he hurt. He rose, then moaned, his injuries screaming with each movement. "Fuck."

Kyle peered into the rearview mirror. Swollen to a small slit, his blackened left eye contrasted to the purple hue of his cheek. The right didn't look much better, but he could see out of it. "The proverbial Mack truck."

The next task proved to be harder. To retrieve his keys, he wiggled his fingertips and grasped them from his pants pocket. He jammed the piece of metal into the ignition, and paused to rest his head on the steering wheel.

He wouldn't call Shelby this morning, maybe after he healed and felt a little better. Where did those guys come from and why did they beat the shit out of him? He hadn't recognized anyone except Swordfish, but where had he seen him before?

Hell, he clamped his molars together to withstand the intolerable pain shooting from his head down his spine then exploding in his chest. In between the unbearable throbs, he started Jalopy. To drive he had to move, he gritted his teeth together, backed out of the parking lot and headed home.

Several miles down the highway, the truck careened to the right, off the highway, down an embankment, hitting a tree at the bottom. Even though the last thump against the evergreen happened in a matter of seconds, he had an eternity to think. Damn, he never had the chance to tell Shelby he loved her. Was this the end? Regrets, he had plenty of them.

Chapter Twelve

While Shelby's left hand rubbed the back of her neck, she rolled her head in a circle to ease the tense muscles. She stared out her office window catching a glimpse of a chipmunk gathering food.

She-Who-Smiles called her Brave-One. She scoffed, yeah right. If she had an ounce of game in her, she'd would've kept Ten-Blue-Sun and found Tim's murderer. She wasn't as courageous as Kyle. He'd had the fortitude to break up, keep the doll, and continue his life without her.

She couldn't imagine the betrayal he must have felt when he had found Christine in his bed with two other people. Funny, he said his college buddy, then gulped down the third person's name. Not that she'd know who the hell his friends were back then.

The thread that had unraveled him was Christine's suicide especially since she chose to end her life in front of him. The burdens he carried were laden with onerous duties and stormy emotions. She didn't pity him, but from the depths of her soul, she ached to comfort him. No one should have to live through that.

A paralyzing dread rippled down her spine. A frightening tingle danced in her chest and around her heart. She realized she missed him. The last bitter memory of him casting his poisonous venom haunted her. Yet, she still yearned for his presence, touch, and most of all, his heart.

She muttered her mantra, "Family, work...Family, work."

She shook her head and plopped in her office chair.

Tears stung the back of her eyelids. Giving in wasn't an option. If Shelby did, she wouldn't be able to stop.

Her thumb found the wedding band and she twirled it on her finger. "Tim, I hope your journey is going well. Mine? I've landed in the silage pile and the shit stinks. I guess She-Who-Smiles and Bear-Claws are disappointed in me too...Jeez, this melancholy mood has to cease now. I can't stand myself anymore."

When she returned from her trip, she had shared with Alessa what had happened. For the most part, Alessa supported her, but her little sister relegated herself to be her conscience. While sitting outside at a coffee shop, she remembered how Alessa's voice thrummed her take...

Alessa huffed. "No, that's your answer to every problem you face. You bury yourself in work at the office, the ranch, family, and if there is any time left over you give it to yourself."

"Give me a break."

"I may be the baby of the family, but what I see is a woman who is hurt and didn't fight for what she may have wanted. But you'll never know now."

"Thanks. I didn't need an evaluation of my actions."

"Shelby, I love you. Don't do this to yourself. Meanwhile, keep your head up. It sounds like he got scared. He'll be back. If he does call you, what are you going to do?"

"You're not listening to me, that scenario will never happen. The only plan of action is filling my days with work and family."

Alessa smirked.

"Al, please...don't say I told you so. This is how I keep myself sane."

"I know, sis...I'll be here for you."

Shelby extended her arm across the table. The flashback of her hand stretching to meet Kyle's fleeted before her eyes. She hesitated, Alessa never moved, she grasped and squeezed. "Al, you've always been there for me."

Alessa had rescued her in more ways than one. Shelby heaved a long sigh and stared at the calendar on her computer. Al had purposely scheduled physical activity every day from cleaning the offices to painting them. Shelby owned the building so maintenance didn't bother her. She laughed. She had plenty of exercise completing all the ranch chores, but what bothered her the most was lying in bed each evening. All the "what if" scenarios rifled through her mind until exhaustion reigned and she fell asleep.

Alessa peeked around the door of her office. "That was healthy. The cilia in your lungs are doing double time."

Shelby grinned. "Speak of the devil."

"Huh?" Her gaze panned the office. She shrugged her shoulders. "End of a marvelous Thursday. What are you doing this weekend for Labor Day? Got any plans? Shelby? Did you hear me?"

"Yes. I'm waiting for you to take a breath. You don't give anyone time to answer your questions."

"I do give people time, nobody speaks fast

enough."

"I know you have a lot of energy, but slow down."

Alessa's mouth and face exaggerated each syllable and pronunciation. "Okay, what are you doing for the holiday?"

"Nothing, smart ass." Shelby dropped to her knees, crawled underneath the desk to pick up the shoes she had kicked off earlier. The company telephone rang. "Hannah has left for the day, please get the phone for me."

"This is Alessa, how can I help you?" After a few silent seconds, Al responded to the caller. "Yes, you have the right Shelby Littleton. Hold on. Shelby, you need to take this. I'll be in my office if you need me."

"It's past five, I thought you were leaving."

"I'll wait."

Shelby rose from the floor. "Okay." Then, she grabbed the receiver. "This is Shelby, how can I help you?"

"This is Jude Pressley, Kyle's brother."

She lowered to the edge of the leather chair. "Yes?"

"Kyle's been in an accident."

Shelby's sharp intake filled her lungs and her nerves jangled. "What happened? How is he?"

"The authorities think he fell asleep at the wheel. His truck plunged down an embankment and he fractured his ankle and a few ribs. He's still unconscious and—"

"Oh my God, is there anything I can do?"

Jude cleared his throat. "Could you come up here…to the hospital?"

Shelby let out a whoosh of air. "I don't think that's

a good idea. You may not know this…Kyle asked me to leave. No, that's not true, he demanded. I'm the last person you would want around him, unless you're looking for an adverse reaction like anger to pull him out."

One memory continued to haunt her, Kyle retracting his hand and his eyes…"He loathes me. Truly, I want to help, but I don't think I'm the best choice. I'm sure Garrett or Uncle Grey would be more advantageous and probably safer, then there's Lisa too."

"Kyle told me what happened. I'm making a bold statement, but I don't think he wants to come to without you and the doctors are concerned that he has stopped fighting. For the few seconds he's conscious, he calls your name. When he realizes you're not there, he falls back into a comatose state…You may be our answer."

Shelby hesitated. "Are you sure?" Was it possible Kyle still liked her?

"Yes, I am."

Kyle had called out her name? "Okay, if you think I can make a difference."

"Thanks. I'll have a company jet pick you up in Waco. Do you remember Garrett?"

Of course she did. Garrett was taller than Kyle and his shoulders were wider. According to Kyle, Garrett was an accomplished rancher, an astute pilot, and an exceptional horseman. Her hands shook because the last trip hadn't turned out well. "Yes, I do."

"He'll get you here and I'll set up a rental car for you at the airport."

Animosity barreled through her veins. "That's not necessary. I can get my own ticket and transportation.

All, I need is the name and address of the hospital."

Jude never answered.

"I'm sorry. I didn't mean to sound…spiteful."

"Accepted, here's the information."

****

Shelby tensed as the automatic doors opened into the hospital. *What if he doesn't make it through this?* She stopped in her tracks and her whole body trembled. Nervous, she spotted the restroom, ran through the door and splashed water on her face. *God, what if Jude is wrong? What if her presence makes his condition worse?* If he fell further away from life because of her, she wouldn't be able to handle it.

She cupped her hands under the spigot then drenched her face allowing the moisture to cool her forehead and temples. *Composure, Littleton.* She dabbed the cold droplets with the paper towel. Her eyes weighed the reflection in the mirror and she drew in a deep breath for strength, then exhaled for courage. *Just do what you have to do, one step at a time.*

On the way to the ICU wing, a chapel caught her attention and she entered the octagon-shaped room. A sleeved quote from Emily Dickinson gifted those who took the time to read it. "Sometimes when I consider the tremendous consequences from little things…a chance word…a tap on the shoulder…or a wink of an eye, I am tempted to think there are no little things."

She panned the room taking in the altar which had a kneeling bench, a cross, the Star of David, and two flat glass dishes containing smoothed pebbles and stones. A small bookshelf perched on top of the piano held a cross section of inspirational books encompassing nearly every religion.

Shelby settled into one of the chairs against the wall and peered at a stained glass window. Hummingbirds drew nectar from the flowers, a depiction of being fed…She bowed her head and prayed.

Shelby shoved the ICU room door open, then let the hydraulics close it quietly. She tiptoed to Kyle's bedside. She bit her lower lip to keep from gasping out loud as she studied his ragged body. Cuts and contusions marred his face, arms, and what she could see of his chest. Butterfly stitches arced across his shoulder. His right foot and lower leg was encased with a boot similar to a cast.

Her gaze followed the intravenous lines taped on his left arm to the hanging plastic bags filled with fluids.

She cradled his chafed and bruised right hand in hers. Tears welled and blinking to rid the moisture, she spoke in hushed tones, "Kyle. I know you can hear me. Can you wake up…for me?"

Her stomach twisted. Struggling for composure, her ragged breaths burned her lungs. She couldn't hold back and lost the battle. Tears flowed down her cheek, she cried for what could've happened to Kyle, mourned for what might have been between them and maybe, she sobbed for herself.

A flute played the familiar soft whispery notes then She-Who-Smiles' words centered. "Brave-One, all is not what it appears."

She'd beg to differ.

After a few minutes and back under control, Shelby whispered. "Come back to us. You need to for Jude, Garrett, Uncle Grey, and Lisa. Don't forget about

Bridger, Mosey, and Annie, they'll be waiting for you too."

Her temples pounded with every heartbeat. She lowered the bed rail, scooted a chair close to his bedside and sat. Her hand lightly clasped his, refusing to let go, she braced her forearms against the mattress and waited.

Her head drifted down and nestled in the crook of her arm. From this position, she could still see Kyle's face. She fought to keep awake.

When Shelby woke, she straightened in the seat and blinked the haze from her eyes. Her gaze found a handsome man sitting across the room watching her. Still groggy, she licked her lips. "I'm sorry. I didn't hear you come in. I can leave."

The legs scraped against the floor when she rose.

"You don't have to leave." The man trailed her lead, unfolding his tall frame and stood. "You needed some rest and I didn't want to disturb you. I'm Jude."

Jude and Kyle could have been identical twins except he had cobalt-blue eyes and hair the color of espresso. The aura that surrounded him was exactly the same as his brother's.

"I'm Shelby. Nice to meet you."

"The pleasure's mine." Jude nodded once.

"What have the doctors said?"

His thumbs rested in his jean pockets. "Nothing's changed."

Shelby's gaze traveled to Kyle, then back to Jude. "He's groaned a couple of times as though he was hurting. Are they giving him anything for pain?"

"They have him on medication that doesn't interfere with coming around." Jude shuffled his feet. "I want to thank you for getting here so fast. I believe you'll make a difference."

"I hope you're right. If Kyle gets worse or anything happens to him because I'm here…I don't know if I could cope with that." She had handled Kyle's withdrawal from her life, but losing him in death would be a road too soon traveled.

"My hunch is you'll be the one to pull him through."

"You keep saying that." She shook her head. "You weren't there. Truly, I don't think I'm the wisest choice. Surely, Garrett would have more of a positive impact or Uncle Grey."

Jude reflected for a moment. "We talked the day you left." He cleared his throat. "Kyle may not admit it, but he's fallen in love with you and those same feelings scare him. Like everyone, he has a lot of history. Are you willing to work through it with him?" His right hand rose as if to stop her. "I'm not the one who deserves your answer."

Jude paused. His gaze took in Kyle's listless form then met hers. "I received the news about the accident from our personal physician, Andrew Humphreys. I canceled my business meetings and Garrett flew me back from Korea."

His hand glided through his short hair. "When I arrived, Andy explained his injuries will heal, none of them are bad, but he's choosing not to come to. It's possible he won't respond to your presence, but I'm betting on the scenario he will. You'll be the wake-up meds…so to speak."

"I'll do whatever I can to help. I need to find the ladies' room, excuse me." She grabbed her purse and left.

Once inside, Shelby rested against the closed door. Jude thought she could make a difference with his brother's prognosis. She knew better. The last memories of Kyle replayed again. She winced. *Wow, no pressure from the Pressley men.*

She plodded to the basin and swiped her fingers across the infrared motion detector. She cupped her hands under the flow and splashed her face. The refreshing water strengthened her resolve to continue her doomed mission. Each stroke of the wet paper towel across her skin helped bring positive thoughts and a renewed determination to support Kyle and his brother in every way possible.

Shelby returned to Kyle's side. Jude told her Kyle had become aware again but slipped back. He slid the chair closer to the bed for her to sit and Jude returned to the recliner in the corner.

"Shel?" Kyle fingertips curled as though looking for her hand.

She threaded her fingers with his. "Yes, it's me."

Kyle relaxed. A slight smile crossed his face, and he mouthed, "Baby."

Shelby peered over to Jude and grinned, then Kyle's hand went limp.

He hadn't moved for several hours. When Kyle awakened and said her name, she assumed his status had changed. But now, she wasn't sure.

The door clicked softly when Jude left to make a few phone calls.

"Kyle?" She whispered, "Please fight this. I need to talk to you...We need to have a heart-to-heart conversation. I've been thinking...You don't have to carry your burdens by yourself. If we communicate to each other, share our thoughts and concerns, then maybe we can mend or even fix them."

She-Who-Smiles' words entered the forefront of her mind. "Maybe you need to learn to lean on me."

She feather kissed Kyle's palm. Talking might make a connection and help rouse him. "What would you like to do when you get out of the hospital? You said you had a gym and you ran. You may have to wait for a while and let your body heal. What else do you do? You must read a heck of a lot. Your library was jammed packed with books. What's your favorite kind? Fiction? Non-fiction? Do you have a garden? I don't remember seeing one. Do you mow your lawn? No, I bet you don't. I'm pretty sure you'd have it hired out."

Shelby waited a few seconds, still no movement. "I mow mine and the weed whacker is the worst part of the whole chore. I enjoy working in my flower garden, that is, if I haven't killed them by over fertilizing, watering too much or sometimes the lack of. Overall, my thumbs are a light green."

A grin crossed Kyle's face. The corner of his mouth split open, then he moaned.

"Let me help you." She retrieved lip emollient from her purse and gingerly applied the wax.

"Water."

Not seeing any, Shelby hustled toward the door. "I'll be right back."

When she returned to his room, his eyes were closed, had he drifted back? "Kyle, you ready?"

"Yeah," he rasped.

"I'm going to move you up a little." She mashed the directional button, the motor hummed lifting the head of the bed. She supported his shoulders, held the insulated container directing the straw. He drew several small sips. When he had his fill, she braced her feet and gently lowered him. He relaxed on the pillow with a sigh. He found and slid his hand in hers. "Shel. I'm glad you're here."

"Really?"

"Uh-huh, yeah." His voice was hoarse and his thumb rubbed a circle in her palm. He licked his lips. "Is this St. John's? What day's this? How long have I been here?"

"Yes, you're in St. John's. Jude said you wrecked Jalopy last Sunday. Today's Friday."

"How did you know I was here?"

"Your brother called me yesterday."

Kyle smiled. "He got you up here faster than I could. Did you fly in? How's Garrett?"

Shelby answered part of the question and changed the subject. "Yes, I flew here. How are you feeling? Are you in any pain? Do I need to get a nurse or doctor? Can I do anything for you?"

He smiled again. "Some more water." She held the container steady. He drank more this time.

The nurse barged in with bright smiles, congratulated Kyle for joining them today and shooed Shelby out of the room. The RN spoke over her shoulder. "It's going to take a few minutes if you want to grab something to eat."

Pausing at the doorway, Shelby glanced at Kyle, his gaze had pursued her steps. She answered his question. "I'll be back."

Chapter Thirteen

Shelby breathed a sigh of relief. The doctor released Kyle the following Monday. Jude briskly took over the orderly's job and wheeled his little brother out of the hospital.

Jude latched the brakes on the wheelchair. "Shelby, mind watching him while I get his new truck...the one he never drove."

He winked at Kyle. "And no wheelies or races with the other patients."

"The Pressley boys...didn't think the attending would release Kyle this fast."

The older man pumped Jude's hand then Kyle's. "You look a dang sight better than a week ago."

"Doc, good to see you today, this is Shelby Littleton. Shelby, I'd like you to meet Dr. Andrew Humphreys, our family physician." Kyle nodded in her direction.

Dr. Humphreys extended his hand. "Good morning, nice to make your acquaintance."

Shelby reciprocated. "Same here, Dr. Humphreys." His aura shined sweetly.

"I'll have none of that, call me Andy."

Kyle repositioned the leg with the boot. "How's the family?"

"My wife is as ornery as ever and that honey-do list just keeps on getting longer." Andy barreled out a contagious laughter. "My boy decided to go in partnership with me so when I retire, he'll be taking over my general practice. Funny thing, his specialty is sports medicine." Again, he chortled. "Imagine my surprise and delight."

Kyle grinned. "Now you can take your beautiful wife on that elusive vacation."

Andy reflected for a moment. "That would be nice indeed. Well, I better skedaddle. Shelby, nice meeting you. Kyle, you have any problems call me and stay away from fights. You're not as young as you use to be. Jude enjoyed our visit a couple of days ago. I'll be seeing you."

Jude spun toward the parking lot. "I'll be right back."

Kyle's eyes squinted. "Where's your car?"

"At your place. I didn't think you'd like climbing in and out."

"Your Porsche is a nice ride, but I'm glad you thought better of it. I'm going to miss ol' Jalopy."

Jude coasted to a stop curbside. He helped Kyle settle into the passenger seat and closed the door.

Kyle rolled the window down. "Shel, are you getting in?"

Shelby stepped closer. "I should head back to Texas. You're doing great and I'm proud of you."

"Is that what you want to do?"

Shelby hesitated. "I've finished helping—"

"Is that what I am to you... a job?"

"Jude called me to..." She lowered her voice. "No."

"I assumed you'd hang around and I shouldn't have. Will you stay with me? In my home?"

When she didn't answer right away, he lifted her chin with his finger and caressed her lower lip with his thumb. "Baby?"

For the second time, she gave in to his gentle touch and his endearment. "Okay. I have to check out of my hotel."

Kyle's fingertips glossed over her cheek. "You remember how to get to my place?"

"Yes, I'll see you there."

"Come here."

She angled toward him.

"Closer." He guided her to him.

His hand cradled her face and his lips brushed over hers. "Thank you." His mouth opened and bathed her in his moisture.

Jude cleared his throat. "We're blocking the flow of traffic, we should head out."

****

Shelby rang the doorbell.

Jude's muffled voice echoed from inside. "The door's open, come in."

She entered Kyle's house, set her suitcase on the floor and tracked the masculine conversation into the kitchen.

Kyle raised his sandwich in the air. "Want some lunch? Jude will make it for you."

"I'll have some ice tea. Tell me where the glasses are and I can get it."

Jude volunteered. "Top cabinet, to the right of the double sink. Are you going stay with Kyle?"

Kyle swallowed his food. "Yes. She is. What do you need?"

"Not a thing." He turned his attention to Shelby. "If

you need help, let me know."

Shelby savored the refreshing drink and set the glass on the counter. "Don't worry, I can handle him. But if he gets unruly, I promise, you'll be the first one I call."

Kyle straightened in the seat. "Me? Not a chance. I'm a good patient."

Jude ignored Kyle and swiveled back to her. "Thanks. I appreciate your time and effort."

Getting up from the stool, Jude stuffed the last bite into his mouth, finished the remnants of his tea and stowed the dishes in the washer. "I need to get back to work." He slapped Kyle's back. "Glad you're better. Need anything, call me."

After Kyle finished his turkey club, Shelby coaxed him. "You should put your leg up and relax. I'll clean up here."

"Leave it for Hilda."

"Hilda?"

"My housekeeper. She's not here today but—"

"I can handle a plate, two glasses and a knife. Do you need help?"

He slid off the barstool and balanced on his crutches. "No. I'll be in the library."

Shelby smiled. "Give me a few, then I'll join you."

In a matter of minutes, she had the kitchen in order and anticipated perusing Kyle's books.

Shelby had filled her afternoon reading while Kyle labored at his desk completing the backlog of work.

After a light supper of soup and salad, he appeared wiped out.

"Time to get some rest, what do you say? Where are you going to sleep? Here on the couch or in your room. I can help you up the steps."

He stretched. "Definitely in my own bed."

Following him up the staircase, she braced her arms in the ready position in case he lost his balance. At the top, she whistled. "Wha-hoo! You go!"

He shook his head and his lopsided grin appeared. By the time he crossed the threshold of his bedroom, his features changed, first serious then focused. "Will you join me?"

"No. You need your rest."

"You can choose from any of the guest bedrooms, make yourself at home." He limped entering his room and closed the door.

Shelby exhaled a long sigh and she whispered, "Good night."

"Night."

She jumped when he answered.

****

Shelby's hair fluttered from the crisp September breeze blowing through the library's open windows. She chose another book from the plethora of novels. For a week now, she had avoided intimate conversations with Kyle and she thanked her lucky stars he never pushed her.

She bit her bottom lip, closed her eyes, inhaling a long breath through her nose and held the captive air in her lungs. Acknowledging, and to her surprise without remorse, she loved Kyle, but remembered he'd compared her to Christine. She exhaled. Her gaze found the man she had fallen for. He nodded at her perusal and returned to his work.

"Kyle?"

"Hmm?"

She closed her book and stood. "I'm going for a walk."

His pen stilled then he set it down. "What's bothering you?"

"Nothing. I just need some fresh air." The breeze flowing through the room reminded her to pick another excuse. "I mean exercise."

"Maybe when you get back, we can play cards and talk, if you're ready."

"Yeah, maybe." She shifted to leave and the sound of a lawn mower blared inside and fresh cut grass wafted in the room. "You have a gardener?"

"Michael. Don't be surprised or afraid if he introduces himself to you."

"Why would I be frightened?"

"Sometimes he gets a little overzealous trying to help."

"I don't understand."

"He has a heart of gold and one hell of a green thumb. I have a friend of a friend, you know how that goes, who told me his parents had divorced and then his mom passed away. He needed a place to stay and a job."

"He stays here?"

"I bought and renovated a building downtown. Michael lives on the second floor, pays his own rent and collects from the others then gives it to me. I opened a retirement account for him and match the funds. It sounds like I'm tooting my own horn, but I'm not. He works for every cent he earns. When he learned how to count, you should've seen his face. I've never seen a man so proud."

She remembered asking him while he was in the

hospital about mowing his own lawn. Now, she had her answer and then some. "Pressley, I'm proud of what you did for him."

"Michael does more for me than the other way around. Wait until you taste some of the fresh veggies from the garden out back."

Shelby nodded. "Hmm, can't wait. I'll be sure to say hi to him. Be back shortly."

As she closed the front door, the hum of the blades and engine were off to the side of the house. When she returned, she'd be sure and talk to Michael.

Kyle's alpha-man exterior belied the tender spot he had inside. Shelby grasped the fact that if anyone crossed family or friends, he'd deal with them in one swift action. When it came to control, Kyle had exceptional discipline. Even with her, he'd exhibited patience and managed to restrain his inner tormoil.

That evening, Hilda peered into the library as Kyle shuffled the cards. "Is there anything else I should do before I head home?"

Kyle dealt from the pile. "No, thanks. See you tomorrow."

Shelby pounded the table with her hand. "Hilda, you can tell Kyle to stop dealing from the bottom of the deck."

"You kids keep me out of your disagreements and Kyle play fair." Hilda winked at her. "Have a good evening."

"Thanks, Hilda, you too."

When Kyle slammed the deck on the eight-player-table top, she leapt several inches off her chair. "For Pete's sake, what's wrong?"

He pointed his finger. "You've got Hilda in your

pocket."

"No, she knows you better than you give her credit for."

Kyle gathered the cards. "Yep, I'm sure she does. How did you know?"

Shelby stood in indignation. "Ah-ha, you admit it."

He squared the deck, set them off to the side. "I'm ready for a break, how about you?"

She placed her hand on her cocked hip and offered a saucy smile. "Oh yeah, sure, now that you're caught."

Kyle snagged her wrist and pulled her to his lap. His hand smoothed her hair. His long fingers rested lightly at the base of her throat, and he gently applied pressure with his palm in the V of her blouse. He nestled his forehead against her temple. "What do you want from me?" She withdrew several inches, his face scrunched in question and yet…was there a measure of uncertainty?

Kyle's words had haunted Shelby since August, when he likened her to Christine. "I don't want anything. I'm only here to help you." How could he doubt her again?

She tried to stand, but he held her to him. Her erratic breaths accelerated. She stumbled over her thoughts and blurted, "I guess…I didn't make myself clear the last time." Moisture welled, blurring her vision. "Oh my God, you're still accusing me of wanting your money, and not handling Ten-Blue-Sun correctly." He still mistrusted her. Pain splintered her heart. This time she successfully stood erect. "What do I want from you?" The back of her hand swiped the traitorous tear that escaped. "I didn't realize I still threatened you." She hurried through the open door.

"I'll call Jude and let him know I'll be leaving in the morning." She didn't realize her soul could shatter, but it had.

"Wait. You took my question out of context." Kyle stood.

Shelby paused at the bottom the stairs. "I don't think so."

She turned and scrambled up the steps. Numb from Kyle's consternation, Shelby wondered why she had opened herself to another failure to add to the growing list. There were times she wished life were kinder and gentler, but in the end, she had no control over other people and their thoughts. How could she have been so naïve?

****

Kyle knocked and waited for Shelby to answer. When he peeked in the bedroom, he cleared his throat. "May I come in?"

Packing her suitcase, she acknowledged him over her shoulder. "This is your house."

Quiet minutes followed and she must have misunderstood his silence.

"I can leave now. It won't take me long. I'll just be a few more minutes. I didn't realize how uncomfortable you were with me." She shook her head. "I should've known. Oh the hell with it, I'll buy more damn clothes." She zipped the luggage closed, headed for the door keeping her back to him.

His temper rose, the heat flushed his face, he curled his fingers into his palms. He'd waited a week for her to come to him, on her own accord, but this new revelation just flat out pissed him off. "Shelby. Stop right now."

She halted.

"I've never seen a more stubborn, mule-headed filly in all my born days. Do you really think I don't want you around? Why would I have asked you to stay with me? Why would I ask you to join me in my bedroom? I...Grrr." He inhaled a full breath for control then released it. "Shelby Littleton, there are times when you exasperate me and all I want to do is shake some sense into you."

He inhaled fully again, then let the air flow between his teeth. "Then...I'd make sweet love to you."

Shelby pivoted to face him. "You...would?"

He nodded. "How about you?"

"Yes...a thousand times over and I'd start again."

Hot damn. He cupped his hand to his ear. "I'm sorry, I didn't hear you?"

"I love you."

Yee-haw. "Good because...I've waited a long time to tell you. I love you too." He stretched his arms toward her and waited for Shelby's response.

She released the handle of her bag. In two steps with tears streaming down her cheeks, she joined him. Shelby buried her uncontrolled sobs against his chest.

He stroked her back. "Honey, shh...sweetheart... everything will be okay, you'll see." Shelby calmed. Her tense muscles relaxed under his ministrations. He drew the small circles on her back crooning soft assurances. When she quieted, he lowered his lips to her ear. "Follow me."

He led her to his bedroom, sat her down on the bed, pulled off her shoes and guided her to lie down. He discarded his tear soaked shirt, removed the boot-cast, leaving his jeans on, he eased down beside her. Taking the quilt from the bottom foot rail, he pulled the hand-made blanket over her. His arms embraced her, holding and comforting Shelby until they both fell asleep.

The next morning after breakfast, keeping warm by the crackling fire, Kyle lowered his book and waited for Shelby to acknowledge him.

From the other side of the leather sofa, her feet under her, Shelby must have sensed his heavy gaze.

She closed the paperback and locked her eyes onto his. "Do you need something?"

Kyle cringed. He had to tell her about issuing an investigation. Would Shelby understand why, would she respect his motivations, tolerating what he'd done? The ultimate question, would she capitulate to Pressley security protocols? "Have you projected anymore?"

"Not lately."

He catalogued her comment to review later. "Do you still believe your husband was murdered?"

"Yes. Why?"

He cleared his throat. "You had several home break-ins. Did the perpetrators steal anything?"

"Not that I could tell…I'm not stupid, Pressley, where are you leading me?"

He let out a sigh and plunged into the topic he'd been putting off. "My reports indicate a possible connection although the PIs haven't found any tangible proof."

"Reports? PIs? Who initiated them?"

"Me."

She scooted to the edge of the sofa, her back ramrod straight. "When and why?"

"When we first met…security. I received yours in a matter of hours, clean and your husband's too. I asked for more research concerning his death and the doll. They're still digging, but the preliminaries agree with the authorities."

When Kyle stood and approached her, she sprung from the couch and paced to the floor-to-ceiling window, away from his grasp, away from him.

"Hear me out."

Her gaze lingered on something outside, she crossed her arms. "Go ahead."

Definitely not a good indicator. "I wanted you to know what I'd done, wanted to be truthful with you. And I want you to understand, I believe that you believe all of the conspiracy theories exist."

"Thanks." She faced him. "You should get some rest."

He limped across the room and took her hand in his. "You're right, I could use some."

"I'm going to go to the public library."

He questioned if he'd hurt her feelings. For a fractured second, she appeared put out then she drew her eyebrows together, squared her shoulders and a mask covered any indications of her thoughts. "Walk with me to my room."

When he crossed the threshold of his bedroom, Shelby released his hand. "Penny for your thoughts."

"I'm exhausted."

She nodded. "You've been working close to fourteen-hour days since you've been out of the hospital. I'll see you in a few hours."

"Okay, till then." He crawled on top of the bed and stretched out. God, he hoped she understood.

That evening, hypnotized by the fire-pit, Shelby kept an arm's length away from him.

Kyle broke the silence. "How do you do it?"

"Do what?" Long lines furrowed across her forehead.

"You've been attentive and taking care of me while successfully pushing me away. I get it, Shelby, you're unhappy. But I won't apologize for hiring the PIs."

"I didn't ask you to...I understand. We live in a crazy world that dictates certain actions from you. Actually, I'm honored you were interested enough to check on me and ecstatic I've held up to your scruples."

"Then why are you angry?"

"I'm not. I'm fine." Shelby pursed her lips.

"Anytime I hear a woman say I'm fine, it means the exact opposite. Damn, baby, I'm not good at this. Something's bothering you and I want to know so I can help."

"I'm disappointed that's all. No biggie. You can't mend or fix me, okay? I need to be alone. I'll be in my bedroom, if you need me."

"Tell me why you're unhappy?"

She worried her lower lip, her gaze shot to his. "The police report and your investigators concluded my husband committed suicide, never mind that I found a damn doll and his journals pointing toward something else entirely."

Shelby rubbed her temples with her fingertips. "What bothers me most is I find this whole situation ironic. You believed me about the First Realm and spirit guides then hesitate to accept my hypothesis about his death. Maybe I am just a crazy lady from Texas who thinks her husband's murder is related to Ten-Blue-Sun."

She held her palm out to halt the discussion. "I

need to be alone."

"Don't walk away. Listen, all the evidence points toward a man taking his own life." He hesitated. Shelby needed him to trust and accept her word. "All right, I'll redirect my investigators from your perspective."

"I don't know whether to thank you or tell you to stop for fear I'm a stark raving maniac."

"Come here, Shel." When she edged closer, he weaved his fingers in hers, maneuvering her to sit on his lap. His arms enveloped her, her face tucked in the lee of his neck while his hands soothed her tense muscles. "I want to hold you for a bit." There were a multitude of other subjects that needed to be discussed between them, but he'd save them for later.

****

By the end of the second week, his endurance lasted longer. The bruises had faded into burnished yellows and the red angry cuts were reduced to a healthy pink.

To finish a perfect Indian summer day, he had grilled fresh vegetables and salmon for supper, then they relaxed in the Jacuzzi. The fire-pit shed an appreciable amount of warmth to stave off the chilly evening air. Wrapped in robes, he held her in the glider for two.

The sun had long since set when she shuddered and goosebumps rose. He helped her rise. They changed, and he led her to her favorite book-lined room.

Once the fireplace was lit, Shelby joined him on the couch, lying beside him. Her head nestled in the crook of his hip, her arm draped over his thigh while she cradled the paperback in her palm. His book about global economics balanced on his chest.

Shelby's moist breath permeated through his jeans, sending chills across his skin. The last thing on his mind was how his business decisions affected worldwide commerce.

He caressed her shoulder. The pads of his fingers slid to her neck, massaging the sensitive area behind her ears. One of the many places he had wanted to sample when he first met her and he wasn't disappointed. She tasted like honey, responded to him when his tongue grazed her curves. He fondled her ear, the soft swirls guiding his fingertips to trace the outline. His palm shifted to her jawline, his thumb brushed over her full lips. Lips he wanted wrapped around his cock.

Shelby was beautiful, attentive, and a caretaker. Since he'd been back from the hospital, tonight was the first meal he'd cooked for them. Hilda had offered, but Shelby told her to go home, be with her family, and get some rest. Hilda had let Shelby coddle her too.

He thanked the powers that be she'd come back into his life. These weren't the circumstances he envisioned, but he wouldn't look a gift horse in the mouth. Right now, all he wanted was to make love to her. He bowed his hips.

She changed her position and her gaze met his. "Am I hurting you?"

"Yes, but not in the way you're thinking." He rose again.

Her hand coasted up his inner thigh. She palmed the outline of his throbbing hard-on.

His hand covered hers, adding pressure. Her book hit the floor and his followed.

She finagled off the sofa, knelt beside him and flicked the top button then unzipped his jeans, inching his pants and briefs down. Her fingertips retraced their path. Shelby's fingers and palm found his cock and she stroked him while her tongue slid over his crown. The velvet heat of her mouth closed around him sending shivers to his toes.

Nothing seemed more important, not even his business or the outside world, only the sensation of her mouth making its way down then back up his entire length. Not even the reminders of unanswered questions concerning the doll or the temptation to mind walk, only the gratifying diligence she gave to his cock. He wallowed in the pleasures of her concentration.

Kyle groaned as she took all of him. He swept a stray lock of her hair from her face to watch while he weaved the length through his fingers. With every plunge, he twirled the highlighted fall colors of her mane. Not only did her soft tresses sensitize his flesh, but her wet, satin skin of her mouth harboring his cock carried him closer to the edge as she loved every stretched inch. He was in heaven. When her hand grasped his balls, erotic flames roiled inside him and the bliss of his release was imminent.

He closed his eyes to draw control, nearing the edge, he stopped her. "I've got a better idea."

When he stood, he shucked his remaining clothes and draped a blanket on the floor. He removed Shelby's, settled her on her back and nestled beside her. At the base of Shelby's throat, he nuzzled planting wet kisses then ventured down the valley. Stopping to nibble and relish her taste, he nipped and smoothed her taut nipple. Crossing to her other breast, he suckled, eliciting goosebumps and shivers from her.

Shelby arched her back. He loved her responses

and continued his trail to her navel leaving a swath of moistened skin. Her moans begged him to coast down and sample her honeyed nectar. He greeted her with light touches of his lips and blew puffs of air across her sweet swollen nub. She bucked asking for his full attention and he gave his undivided concentration, savoring every delicious lap. It was like an ice cream cone melting under his tongue.

"Kyle."

"Let go, baby." He sucked the sensitive flesh and spasms shook her body. He closed his eyes and traveled with her. She had a healthy, positive energy, one that flowed into his.

The first time they journeyed together, she was scared of being alone. When he told her to open her eyes, and her spirit connected with his, Shel was his woman. They were meant to be together. He'd been told of such things from the elders, but never had any personal experiences.

What he did know, his little filly was still skittish from when he'd acted like an asshole. He had a long ways to go to earn her unwavering trust, to build a strong foundation for a future and commitment for a lifetime relationship. He didn't care how long it took, just that he would.

Gradually, he embraced her spirit and drifted back into their bodies.

"I love watching you climax and our sojourns together."

Shelby smiled. "Your turn, cowboy."

"Hell, yeah!" His balls burned for release.

He rose from between her legs and assisted her to sit. "You'll have to be on top. Cowgirl up."

Chapter Fourteen

Kyle helped Shelby straddle his hips and she guided him in. When he filled her, her intimate muscles gripped his cock. This was his promised land.

He lifted the weight of her breasts, tugged and squeezed. With each stroke, he was in Eden, his Utopia. If he had his druthers, he'd stay in her forever. Seated deep on each immersion, he found her G-Spot and let her choose the tempo.

She increased the rhythm. Under the report of another orgasm, her body quaked, uttering his name again.

Her prolonged contractions energized his thrusts. His heart pounded, blood coursed through his veins, and his balls tightened, then erupted.

He grabbed hold of her spirit and soared to a place he now called Cameahwait. Named after the Western Shoshone Chief, One-Who-Never-Walks, it seemed appropriate. As the tremors diminished from their climax, he led her back.

She collapsed on top of his chest and laid her head on his shoulder.

Her gasps rushed around his neck. Hell, yeah, this lady was his woman. His arms circled her heated body and with his fingertips, he kneaded her back, following the linear length of her spine.

Slowly, her panting breaths receded to a normal

pace, then she sighed.

He murmured, "I didn't think making love to you could get any better."

She moaned.

"That an affirmation?"

Shelby nodded.

Satiated, dressed, and mesmerized by the silhouettes dancing across the book shelves from the fire's flames, Kyle's gaze caught hers. He wanted their relationship on the next level. The only way to obtain that step would be for her to reside in Wyoming. All he had to do was ask her. She should be ready, all the signs pointed in that direction.

Her face illuminated by the orange glow was a study in contentment...complete satisfaction which gave him the courage to venture into the unknown. "I want you to live with me."

Damn, he meant to lead in with a hell-of-a-lot better line. "I called Garrett and inquired about his schedule to fly us to Texas, in case you needed to run home for clothes, handle anything and get Annie. He said he would be available in a few days. He questioned me as to why you didn't fly on home with your ticket then he could pick you up on his way back. But he'd do whatever I needed."

Shelby cleared her throat. "So what's on your mind?"

Did she hear his question or did she choose to ignore it? First things first, he guessed. "I didn't know you flew up on your own. I understand why you didn't want to return your rental. I should be paying for the car. That's my responsibility."

"Responsibility? Don't worry about it."

"How about my treat?"

When she didn't illicit a response, he groaned under his breath. "We can work out a time frame." *Still no answer.* "Stay…All I'm asking for is a while."

Her brow creased. "You want me to stay with you…for a while?" She emphasized the last three words.

He answered quietly, "Yes, I think we're ready."

"I see."

This was easier than he thought. "You do?"

"No and yes, I understand you want to test the waters, but you're asking me to give up my life in Texas for the sample run…and I can't."

He'd have to reason with her and hope she'd follow his lead. "You're loyal to the ones you love. Do you love me?"

"Yes."

"Enough to concur we should devote time to each other?"

"Yes." Shelby's hazel eyes transformed from a droopy trance to desire.

"Good. We've reached a milestone." He gave her the lopsided grin that she succumbed to. And she did.

He threaded his fingers between hers and guided her upstairs.

In the shower under the multi-directional jets, he caressed her, hoping to wash away any doubts she harbored. He added the overhead rain spigot and drank the water running down her body and she responded in kind. With each swath of his tongue, his hands pressed firmly to establish she could trust him. He turned her around, placed her back against his chest to assert a united front, then embraced her demonstrating she'd be safe, and held her arms within his own showing he'd carry her burdens. When she sighed in relief and leaned on him, she'd unknowingly signaled he'd won her over. Maybe soon, she'd even tell him her birthday.

She exposed her neck for him to nibble, but he wouldn't stop there. Gathering the weight of her breasts, he massaged and pinched her nipples. Shelby mewled.

Damn, he installed a bench in the guest shower and now wished he'd done the same in his. "We'll have to use the bed." Shelby shut off the water and he dried her with his towel then wrapped her in it. He led her into the bedroom.

In his bed, he supped again. Making love with her did get better each time.

Exhausted, he cradled her beneath the covers until sleep overtook her, then him.

The next morning, his cell rang. Letting go of Shelby nestled in his arms, he grabbed the mobile from the night stand. "Kyle."

He let out an exasperated sigh. "What's wrong, Jude?"

Kyle planted both feet on the floor. He glided his hand through his hair and rested his elbows on each knee. "You can get someone else to handle the problem. What about Jefferies? Abbott? Dugan? Hell. Don't 'buddy' me....All right, I'll be ready. See you there."

He bowed his head and tapped the phone against his temple.

Out of the corner of his eye, Shelby stretched and slid her chin onto her palm. "Anything wrong? Can I help?"

Kyle stood. "Yes and no...I've got to attend an emergency meeting." You can stay if you want. I'll be back...I don't know when. One of our distributors has their tail feathers in a spin. Jude and I will smooth them down so they can fly again...preferably with us. Garrett's dead heading here to pick us up."

She crawled out of the bed and donned her bathrobe. "I should be going too."

He had to ask even if it meant disappointment. "Baby, are you coming back?"

"Go take care of business, then we'll discuss everything after."

"Sure...later." Kyle headed toward the bathroom for his morning ritual.

He splashed water across his face shedding the last bits of shaving cream and wanted Shelby one last time before she left.

The shower from the guest bath echoed into his room. He strode toward the sound and found her.

He stood before her and loosened his wrap, letting the towel fall from his waist.

In one movement, she shrugged and the garment coasted down her arms to meet his on the floor.

Once in the shower, he directed all of the spray heads to the seat. On the bench, with streams of water jetting from every direction, he made love to her then held her long afterward.

Her legs straddled him and her head rested on his shoulder, his arms embraced her while the steam rose around them. He wouldn't push her to make a decision. The quiet repose spoke volumes for neither knew when would be the next time they'd see each other.

****

Shelby peered out her office window reflecting on the three weeks that had passed by at a snail's pace. After several days home, her cat forgave her for the extended absence and Annie loved Aunt Alessa so no scars there. For her, the groove of normalcy would never arrive.

"Kyle flying in?"

She whirled to find Alessa standing at the threshold. "No, he sounded exhausted. I told him to go home and get some rest. Then, we could schedule some time together."

"Then let's go to Austin's Central Farmers Market tomorrow. I know Saturday is crowded, but we'll have a blast together. Besides, I haven't had any big sister time in ages."

"That sounds like fun. What time?"

"Let's start out in the morning and spend all day there. I'll pick you up say…around nine?"

"I'll ride with you if you promise to keep your speed down."

Alessa laughed and yelled over her shoulder as she left. "Nag, nag, nag."

"My nerves will be shot by the time we get there."

"Bye." The thump of the outside door reverberated through the office.

"How does she always get the last word in?"

The next morning, Alessa talked ninety miles an hour, drove the same speed, and described how she found her now ex-boyfriend in bed with another girl.

Shelby laughed at Al's description of them getting caught. "You amaze me, sis, how you can bounce back so easily from disappointment."

"My doctrine, be happy instead of sad. In fact, I

choose to not be around people who are constantly depressed. Take you for instance—"

"You're not going to go there. I forbid it." She pointed at Alessa.

"You are miserable, admit it. Since you've been back from Kyle's, your dog ears are sweeping the floor." Al waggled her finger back at her.

"Yeah, I know."

"Ah, but that's why we are on our way to Austin. Sixth Street here we come."

"I thought we were going to the market." Since Alessa insisted on visiting Austin's Sixth Street for music, food and fun, she had a long day ahead of her.

"We are, but we'll have to eat."

After a long afternoon being on her feet, Shelby wanted to relax, have a libation, and eat a scrumptious meal. The thirty minute wait enticed them to sit at the bar.

The bartender set a chardonnay before Shelby and a vodka martini for Alessa. Within minutes, he placed another napkin followed by a glass of wine.

Shelby pushed the bottom of the goblet which slid easily across the polished surface. "I didn't order—"

"This is compliments of that gentleman over there."

Not following the direction of his nod, she pleaded, "Please tell him thank you but—"

"You tell him, he's on his way over."

"Damn."

Alessa whispered, "Be nice. He's a hunk."

Shelby gave Al her best go-to-hell look.

"Hi, my name's Ben." He bellied up to the counter next to her.

"Ben, I'm Shelby and this is Alessa." She extended her left hand to shake his while her wedding band glistened from the directional lighting.

"Nice to meet you both." His grin faded when his gaze caught her ring. "I…didn't see you were married, forgive my intrusion."

"Quite all right. May I buy you a drink so we can call it even?"

He chuckled. "No. Buying your wine was my pleasure. Have a great evening."

"You too and thank you." His soft laugh hadn't affected her, her insides never twirled. Kyle had all of her.

It was time she told Al about the First Realm, astral projecting, and the distinct possibility of families being reincarnated.

There were so many people void of auras. Alessa had one, but she'd have to call the emanation a small one. She concluded that there were different levels, a graduation of sorts going from tiny to large luminous ones.

Al had summed up her repertoire, giving her the third degree, something about living a life not shadowing. She had heard it all before.

Hedging on her deliberations, she peered over her sister's shoulder and a man at the end of the bar glared at her.

His aura was huge, ugly, and black with blood-red rays flicking like flames around him taking up a vast amount of space which meant he was stronger. Hairs rose on her neck, she glanced at Al then back at the sinister flares implying a God awful evil. *Holy shit, was he Lucifer?*

The repulsive appearance emanating from him was an exercise in equations. Should she run like a scared ninny even though he'd catch up with her within seconds of trying to escape or should she stand her ground and be slaughtered?

The only thing she could think about was the likeness to the nefarious scenes One-Who-Soars-With-Eagles shared with her. Damn, had he been reincarnated, but for what reason? Of all the people on this planet, why would the man across the room be chosen? Maybe he was a helper or a soldier. Right now, it didn't matter what he was, she wasn't going to stick around and find out.

She angled closer to Al and whispered, "We need to leave."

Her sister's face scrunched. "Why?"

She grabbed Al's arm and yanked her off the stool. "Now."

Back home, drained from the all-day excursion, she relaxed on her bed. She sifted through her thoughts about the devil reincarnate and Alessa not accepting her limp explanation. Maybe after a good night's rest, her mind wouldn't be so jumbled.

The next morning, the telephone rang. Groggy, she squinted and found the clock, six thirty. She grabbed her cell. "Hello."

"Shelby?" The bass voice was loud and clear.

"Yes." A strange foreboding shimmied down her spine and landed in her tummy while the acid churned.

"This is Jude."

She sprung to a sitting position, finger combing her hair out of her eyes, dreading the next few words. "What's wrong? Something happened to Kyle?"

"No, he's fine."

A smidgeon of ease crept through, but her hands trembled. "Thank God." Obviously something was amiss and trepidation niggled at the edge of her mind, and she had to know. "What's up?"

"I'm sending Garrett down to pick you up."

"Why?" Every nano-second ticked into infinity.

"You have an interview with the sheriff's office this afternoon in Jackson."

"For what?" Her stomach clenched.

"I don't want to discuss this with you over the mobile. Kyle retained an attorney for you. Your first appointment will be with our lawyer, then he'll be there during your interview."

This wasn't even close to what her imagination had conjured a few seconds ago. "What's going on?"

"I'll fly down with Garrett and tell you then. See you about noon in Waco."

"Where's Kyle? Will he be there?"

"He's with the detectives right now. You'll probably see him later on tonight."

"You're not certain?"

"I can't say for sure. Twelve sharp."

"Jude, I need to see Kyle and make sure he's all right. I'll see you then."

Shelby disconnected the call. Why hadn't Kyle called? She phoned Alessa.

"I don't know why Kyle didn't contact me or why I volunteered to go."

"Sis, you love Kyle so you're going to help him anyway you can. As for Jude giving you a ring, my first thought is he felt comfortable enough to pick up the telephone and ask for your help. I'd say they both think highly of you."

"I'm sure you're right. As soon as I shower and pack, I'll drop Annie off."

****

On the plane, Jude motioned with his hand for Shelby to pick a seat. Shelby recognized the arrangement. The leather couch nestled on the starboard side and the grouping of individual seats was port. She chose one and Jude comfortably folded his tall frame opposite of her.

Succinct in every word and phrase, listening to his base voice, Jude's cadence stated only the facts. She shivered not from being cold, but from terror gripping its grimy tendrils around her.

"What we do know. One, Kyle didn't fall asleep at the wheel, someone tampered with the steering linkage. Two, his house was trashed and there were messages."

"My God was anyone hurt, Kyle, Hilda? Oh God, Michael?" She shuddered. Hilda was a sweet woman and Michael didn't have a mean bone in his body. She refused to think about something horrific happening to them.

Jude scowled. "No."

"Do the authorities think Kyle is in danger?"

"Yes."

Was this Jude's usual laconic self or did he not like talking to her? It didn't matter, she needed answers. "You said he's with the sheriff. After he leaves, what happens? Kyle will need some sort of protection. Are bodyguards a feasible solution?"

"Yes."

"I do have one more question."

He acknowledged her with a nod to proceed.

"I'm willing to help anyway I can, but why do they want to interview me?"

His gaze met hers. "You had access to Kyle's truck, his house and were estranged on occasion."

"They suspect I sabotaged Jalopy and broke into his home?" She resented her vocal cords relaying the tension barreling through her nerves.

"They must eliminate you."

Her hands trembled and she clasped them together placing them on her lap. "I'm curious as to what Kyle thinks…and you?"

"I can't answer for Kyle and it doesn't matter what my opinion is."

His words slammed against her heart, alarm bells rang, issuing red flag warnings. Fear snaked through her. No, she wasn't a brave one at all. "What were the messages?"

He cleared his throat. "I can't tell you."

"Hmm…Kyle's attorney will be representing me?"

"Pressley International's. His name is Lindbergh, Ed Lindbergh," he hissed as though she squandered valuable company time and resources.

Well, she didn't have to wonder anymore. Kyle's brother could give a flip whether she caught her next breath. Shelby unlatched her seatbelt. "I need some water. Would you like anything?"

Jude vaulted from his seat. "I'll get it."

His reaction wasn't a gentleman volunteering. He wanted her to stay exactly where she was. "Do you want to check my backpack? My purse is right here, if you need to inspect it."

"I had my security team inspect your bag and you walked through another check point. I'm satisfied." His tall and broad frame filled the aisle and within several strides arrived at the galley.

When Jude returned, he held the bottle for her to take, but for the life of her, she couldn't move and stared at the clear contents.

He put the drink in the well, settled into the leather seat, and closed his eyes.

Shelby gazed out the window mentally recapping what had happened so far. Since, the authorities viewed her as a person of interest, Kyle sent the jet, hired a lawyer and his brothers escorted her…why? So she would be rested and not fatigued from the long drive for her interview? Perhaps, so she wouldn't feel alone and frightened.

But Jude's words and actions suggested another reason. There was a distinct possibility Kyle had doubts about her. Maybe, his investigators found something and Kyle didn't like what he read in the reports? That idea was ludicrous. What would they have uncovered? That she was right all along about Tim's death?

A horrible premonition anchored. Her tummy lurched. Suspicion slithered over her flesh. Her intuition rang loud and clear, she was in the fight for her life. If it wasn't so serious, she'd laugh.

How was this going to happen? She'd walk into the police headquarters and proclaim her innocence? They'd all laugh at her and throw her ass in jail. Shelby grudgingly accepted she needed Pressley's corporate attorney.

Damn, this was one hell of a predicament. She repeated to gather her strength, "Put away your heart and put up a shield of protection. Cautiously, take each step forward." *Shit*. She wasn't ready for this.

The plane landed and the FBO directed Garrett. Within a minute, the jet stopped and the drone of the engines halted.

Jude opened the door and the steps descended. Her gaze drifted to her ride, a sheriff's car parked on the tarmac.

She carried her overnight pack and purse with her. When her foot hit the pavement, the deputy snatched the bag, opened the back door of his cruiser, and motioned for her to get in, like a damn criminal.

She thought back to her first visit at the airport. Kyle had leaned against Jalopy with his sensuous smile. She cringed. That didn't turn out well and from the rigid set of the policeman's face, this wasn't looking good either.

A uniformed officer led her into an interview room and placed her backpack in the corner. "Sit down. The detectives will be with you shortly." He prompted and headed out.

Shelby panned the room, the proverbial reflective glass, a table, three chairs, and a camera mounted high in the corner. She marched to the mirror, pointed her finger and checked for a gap. It was a two way. The old saying 'no space leave the place' tolled a warning, however she didn't have that option. The dull gray cement blocks should've calmed her, but had the opposite effect. Instead her anxious energy accelerated, ripping through her nerves at warp speed. Her hands shook. She jammed them in her jean pockets then settled in the seat the man indicated before he left.

She'd been fingerprinted, photographed and swabbed for DNA. The deputy didn't take her purse or suitcase, which should be a good sign, she guessed, okay, fervently hoped.

The combination of the stark surroundings and being watched spurred her to seek solace. Wanting reassurance, she folded her arms across her chest, but it wasn't enough. She wanted, no needed Kyle by her side for his encouragement that everything would be fine. If he had given her the slightest affirmation of trust, she would have been comforted. And wouldn't it have been delightful if he'd hugged her and said they would get through this together.

The door opened, a gentleman entered and introduced himself as Mr. Lindbergh. He placed his brief case on top of the table, grabbed the back of the chair and hauled it into position. The metal feet screeched against the floor and he plopped down. His thumbs dragged the two buttons to each side and the echo of the metal clasps releasing bounced around the room. He withdrew a legal-size tablet, grabbed a pen from his shirt pocket and wrote, without saying a word.

She seized the opportunity to take his measure, a portly, older man. Maybe age was good, he should have plenty of experience. But what was his specialty? Did he practice criminal law? Had he ever handled a defendant's case? How many did he win? Most important, could she trust him?

She scrunched her eyelids shut hoping this was all a bad dream and she'd wake up in her bed with Annie nudging her with a wet muzzle to take her outside.

Mr. Lindbergh cleared his throat. She opened her eyes and gazed at true reality. *I'm really here and the very person she trusted didn't have faith in her.* Her stomach heaved violently. She clenched her jaw and her hand covered her mouth afraid she was going to hurl.

"I'm Ed Lindbergh." He didn't look at her. "State your full name."

The unemotional voice slapped her face and the stark realization of her situation struck her again. *Damn.* She dug deep for courage. Her tummy ceased the contractions and she lowered her arms then clenched her fingers together on her lap. "Excuse me, Mr. Lindbergh, you're representing me?"

"Yes, I've been hired as your legal counsel." For the first time, he met her gaze over his glasses perched low on his bulbous nose.

She ignored his first question. "What are your fees?"

"Pressley International will be paying all costs."

She propped her elbows on the table. "I'm sorry, but I'm concerned. Isn't this a conflict of interest for you?"

He scooted his glasses up a half inch. "No, ma'am. You're my client."

The door opened again. Shelby breathed deep and exhaled, she was on the carpet.

With the interview complete, hell, she hoped the inquisition was over, she was alone and sighed with relief. Mr. Lindbergh left directly after the two men who'd grilled her.

The detectives had asked the same questions several times in varying ways and not in sequential order. Some of them were personal, the heat of embarrassment climbed from her neck to her cheeks just thinking about it. Alessa would be interviewed to collaborate times and dates. The scariest part of this convoluted mess, the person or persons responsible were still out there.

One of the detectives who had interrogated her returned. "You are free to go, Ms Littleton."

"I'd like to see Kyle now."

"He's left."

Her breath hitched. "That's Mrs. Littleton."

"Someone will be here shortly to escort you out."

She gathered enough air to acknowledge him. "I'll be waiting."

He excused himself and retreated from the room.

She closed her eyes. Kyle didn't want to see her.

Her body ached as though someone had kicked the crap out of her for the past several hours. Out of the growing list of emotions swirling inside her, she never thought she'd be adding abandonment. What else would go wrong? What else could possibly happen? Frantic to knock on wood, she glanced around and there wasn't any.

Another gentleman entered, she rose from the chair, both legs swayed beneath her. She grasped the table until her feet stabilized under her weight. "May I go now?"

"Yes, ma'am. I'll take you to the front door."

Shelby slung the straps of her bag and purse over a shoulder, trailing him. When she stepped outside, the bitter-cold October air assailed her lungs giving her a jolt of strength and fortitude to find a place to stay. She lowered her backpack to the concrete, extended the handle letting the wheels take its own burden.

Up ahead against the night sky, a neon sign flashed vacancy and for the first time today, relief swept over her.

By the time she checked in, set up a courtesy car for seven in the morning to take her to Zip Away Car rental and had let the balm of a hot shower fortify her frayed psyche, it was too late to eat or call Alessa. She collapsed on the bed.

Her cell rang, the caller ID read KP. She switched her phone off. Her stomach heaved again and she curled into a fetal position. Unchecked tears slid across her cheek. She'd been right all along. Kyle had taken her under his wing only because of Bear-Claws' request. Without a doubt, he'd loved her. He was a man of his word. Kyle didn't know it yet, but she had released him.

She groaned. Kyle thought she was capable of murder? Well, that sure would put a damper on his emotions. Obviously, he gave her enough credit to sabotage his truck...A mechanic? She had to read the manual just to change the damn clock twice a year.

Shelby flipped a pillow over her head to drown out her thoughts. This horrendous day ranked in the top three worst she'd lived through. She honestly couldn't define the moment when everything in her life had turned upside down.

She-Who-Smiles was right, all is not what it appears.

Nothing helped to silence her ramblings, sleep never came. At five-thirty, she gave up and called Al. The detective had interviewed her over the phone late last night. She heaved a sigh of relief that Alessa didn't have to come here.

After her shower, she headed to the buffet, breakfast bar and devoured eggs, bacon, and toast. She chased her food with cold milk and a hot cup of coffee then hurried to meet the van.

Dropped off at the airport, she strode for the

automatic doors. The cold air felt good last night, but this morning, she shook from head to toe and her teeth chattered.

Once inside, the warm blast of heat helped. Before she made it to the car rental counter, two men resembling professional wrestlers asked her name.

"Shelby Littleton. Why?" She stated it without thinking.

Both men grabbed her and barreled outside. One on each side of her, the muscle-bound guys escorted her toward a long, black suburban, the windows too dark to see in.

Shelby shrieked, fearing the worst. Her lungs constricted. Oxygen, she needed air. Her heart rate increased and her temples pounded. The adrenaline rush kicked in. "What the hell? Where are you taking me?"

Neither of the men spoke, but their fingers squeezed tighter.

Her mind recounted the entire dos and don'ts of kidnapping. Don't go to the second location and bring as much attention to the situation as possible, fight, because your life depends on it.

She inhaled and shrieked a blood-curdling scream. Their grip lessened. She kicked and thrashed.

They jerked her to cease, but she refused to give up. The next jolt from her abductors nearly pulled her arms out of the sockets.

Her muscles burned from the abuse, but she wouldn't be defeated. Shelby lashed out with the words she had been taught. "Fire." She flailed her arms and swung her legs, anything to get away.

Chapter Fifteen

"What the fuck?" Kyle flung the door open of the armored car. He launched toward Shelby. "Cease and desist. Unhand her."

Kyle clenched his fist. He cocked his arm to give momentum to a haymaker. A powerful gridlock stopped his throw. His punch halted.

The forearm belonged to a man. He forced Kyle into a stronghold and yanked his back against a broad chest. Survival training kicked in gear. He refused to surrender. Kyle's left hand followed his assailant's shoulder finding the subclavian nerve while his right thumb found the attacker's throat. He simultaneously applied pressure. Kyle balanced. The aggressor's kneecap would discover a boot heel next.

Words rasped from the intruder, as Kyle crushed his windpipe. "Buddy, it's me."

Kyle's head whipped around to see Jude's face turning red, his older brother's grip yielding under the intense compression he administered. Kyle released Jude and cursed.

Jude massaged his throat. "Get in the car." Although a bit rough, his voice echoed control.

Kyle denied Jude's request and didn't move. He eyed the two men. "Let her go, before I kick the shit out of both of you. Now." They immediately freed Shelby and he nodded once.

In two strides, Kyle paused by the limo door. His hand fanned an imaginary line across his waist gesturing for Shelby to get in while the two guards slinked into the front.

Shelby stepped inside and slid into the seat facing backward.

Kyle settled beside her. "Did they hurt you? Let me see." He checked her shoulders, arms and hands. "Damn, you're bruised already. I'll call Andy."

"I'm fine."

"Bodyguards are hired to protect, not hurt their clients. Where are my people, Sam and his team? I trust them, not these yahoos."

When Jude didn't respond, Kyle scrutinized Shelby's black-and-blue marks again. "Are you sure you're okay, baby?"

"I said. I'm fine."

Obviously, Shelby was pissed and he wouldn't contradict her when she repeated, I'm fine, or for that matter, any woman. "Why haven't you answered your cell?"

Shelby squinted. Her eyes dripped with disdain, panning from him to Jude then out the window.

"We were concerned whether you were kidnapped or something worse happened to you."

She continued her vigil through the bullet-proof glass. "I heard you."

"Will you look at me?"

Shelby twisted to face him, her fierce gaze pierced his. He finally had her attention even though it wasn't in a good way. "We are going to a penthouse where we'll have guards that won't kill us."

"I can't afford a penthouse."

At least she was talking to him. "I'm paying for it. The elevators have a special key and we'll have men posted throughout the resort and with us."

"I'll be safe at home, in Texas. Take me back to the airport."

"You don't have a choice," Kyle said quietly.

"I need to call Alessa so she won't worry."

He fingered a stray lock of hair that fell across her cheek and placed the strands behind her ear. "I've already talked to Al, that's how I knew where to find you."

She withdrew from his touch. "Am I allowed to make any phone calls?"

"You shouldn't."

"Are telling me...I would be endangering my loved ones if I talked to them?"

He nodded not wanting to sound too drastic. "Only until we figure out what is going on."

"How dare you take away my family, work, and free will." Shelby scooted low in the seat, crossed her arms below her breasts and resumed her vigilant attention out the window.

He guessed he had that coming. Most people didn't understand the ramifications of fortunes. Everyone assumed having money meant a life of leisure and fulfilling your every whim. Security protocols were a bitch to live by, but a necessary evil.

He still faced solving the conundrum of a bungled burglary for Ten-Blue-Sun, someone wanting revenge and why.

"How many people knew you had the Kachina doll?" Jude's question pierced the silence.

"Rain, Garrett, Shelby and myself."

She stiffened beside him.

"I'm wondering what the black market would give for it. For someone to commit a crime for the damn thing, the logical explanation would be a monetary gain." His older brother postulated.

Shelby turned toward Jude. Her mouth opened then promptly closed.

Kyle clasped his fingers together and placed them on his lap. "You don't really accept that theory, do you?"

Jude's brows drew together. "Why wouldn't I?"

"Dude, we know what the appearance of Ten-Blue-Sun means."

Jude scowled. He scrunched his eyelids until they were small slits. "You know I don't believe in that garbage. Kachina doll, First Realm, reincarnation were created by people who were bored to death. I can see it now. Everyone sitting around a campfire, telling ghost stories for entertainment and somewhere along the line, someone took it seriously."

Kyle shook his head. "You amaze me. Rain, Garrett, and Uncle Grey are family. We were raised with the handed down traditions, seen miracles beyond what science can explain, and yet, you continue to deny a supernatural existence."

Jude swiped a hand through his short hair. "We have real problems and concerns that demand our attention. Have you been able to remember the people involved in the bar fight?"

"You're a stubborn fool and you've left yourself wide open to be proven wrong." Kyle grinned. "I can't wait for the day when you realize you've been wrong all these years and I get to see the what-the-fuck expression on your face. You're going to flip the fuck out and when you do, I'm going to be there for you because I love ya', man."

Jude scrubbed a hand down his face trailing the middle finger down his nose. "Watch your language around a lady, you moron."

Kyle laughed. "Shelby's already pissed at me." He placed his hand on her thigh. "Besides, she usually looks past my flaws just like I do yours."

Jude smirked. "Just answer my question."

Shelby's palm covered his and squeezed. He shuddered under the warm sensation racing from his hand to his dick. He adjusted his position to relieve the pressure. Absence did make his cock grow fonder.

"I don't know their names. I remember thinking I had seen one of them before, but I can't place Swordfish."

"Swordfish?" Jude's eyebrows quirked.

"Yeah, that's what he resembled."

"You told them about Bobbie Jo and her friend?"

"No, I decided to keep that tidbit to myself." Jude usually didn't miss a beat. "There are times you really aggravate the shit out of me, of course, I did."

"You better start thinking about all the people you met personally and I hate to say this, as a possibility, with Pressley International. Have you had any falling out with some of the crew at work? What about your gas and cattle leases? Would your neighbor be a consideration?"

"I had to ask for a guy's resignation about six months ago. His name was Haines. He wasn't happy about it, but I don't think he'd kill me over it. Besides, Haines would be too far back in time to know about

Shelby.

"The renewal on the cattle contract has been the same for the past ten years so that wouldn't be a problem.

"And I terminated the agreement with Pressley International's energy division, several years ago." Kyle shook his head. "Like I said, none of this makes sense."

"The latter two don't seem like there should be a problem, but firing a guy could be one. Just because you didn't know Shelby back then, we can't assume or follow he wouldn't know her now and somehow found out about the Kachina doll."

Jude had an innate fault that drove him nuts. His brother mulled over a problem until he solved it.

Usually, that would be a strong point, but damn, he'd rather be burned at the stake than rehash the same subject that put Shelby and him at odds. He needed a break. Therein lay the catch, how could he distract him?

With every heartbeat, Kyle's ankle throbbed. *Screw it.* "Calm down, Jude, I'll let the authorities know if I think of anyone else who might be of consequence—We're here."

Kyle rolled down the privacy glass.

The sunshades on the team captain belied where his gaze landed. "They want to do another sweep before you go in."

Kyle nodded.

When cleared, numerous guards encircled the three of them.

Kyle kept Shelby in front of him shielding her from behind. Once inside the penthouse suite, suitcases were lined neatly in the entry and the smell of sausage, bacon, and fresh bread wafted through the air. "Hmm, breakfast."

"What bedroom is mine?" Shelby asked.

"I'll show you." Kyle carried her backpack, guided her upstairs and opened the door to her room. He placed her bag on the floor waiting for her to enter. When she didn't, he retreated beside her, lifted his hand, and cupped her cheek.

Shelby leaned into his caress, then took a sudden step back, crossed over the threshold, and quietly closed the door.

Even though she drifted into his palm for just a few seconds, then jerked away, he'd take any amount of time and affection she was willing to give to him. He raised his voice a smidgen. "I'll wait for you so we can eat together."

"I'm not hungry. I'm going to lie down for a while."

Kyle strolled down the steps and helped himself to the breakfast buffet. "Jude, she's really upset. I've never seen her like this and I'm worried. I want to talk to her before I call Andy. Or maybe, I need to leave her alone so she can rest."

"The two guards were a little rough and scared her. I'm with you, let her process all that's happened and give her some time. I think having the doctor look her over is a good idea too. He can talk to her and evaluate whatever her needs are. And right now, I'd say we're not on her best-friends list."

"You do have a way of stating the obvious." Kyle picked a chair at the dining table and sat. "This whole situation is a bunch of bullshit."

"Yeah. I'm going to stay a few days, then I'm

heading out."

"Where? Besides, the detectives wanted you corralled too."

"I've hired a couple more bodyguards, but they won't be available for another couple of days. By then, we should know more. I'm sure we'll need a break from each other. You and Shelby on the other hand, should use this time to talk things out, mend, and heal. I don't want to be here when you're mending and healing."

Off the top of his head, he could think of a several ways to say he was sorry to Shelby. And all of those ideas would start in the bedroom. "I particularly don't want you around either, but you shouldn't leave and become a target."

Jude waved his hand. "I'll be fine."

Kyle wiped his fingertips on the cloth napkin. "Let's get a game plan for the next couple of days. We should talk to management and see if they'd close the workout room, swimming pool and such to the guests during the early morning hours. We could use some of the amenities the resort has to offer and shouldn't get too bored. They should be able to handle the closings during the slow times since this isn't the peak season yet.

"Also, we could buy a couple of laptops and use the company's secure server, since ours are being checked out. Surely, the authorities will know whether it's someone avenging me or directed at Pressley International in a few days."

"I'll talk to the manager and you can call for the computers." Jude snatched a link sausage with his fingers, then popped the whole thing in his mouth.

Kyle grabbed his plate and silverware and headed for the kitchen. "Consider it done."

Shelby hadn't come down for lunch and Kyle bounded to the second floor and knocked. "Baby, you okay?"

"Yes, I'm fine."

She was still at the "fine" stage. He softened his tone. "Would you please let me in?"

The knob rotated and the door opened. He entered. She crossed the room and sat on the edge of the chair, her spine straight.

Kyle trailed her steps and knelt beside her. "Are you all right?"

Shelby nodded…stopped…then slowly shook her head. "How could you believe that I'd want to kill you?"

"Shel, I never did." Kyle cradled her hands in his, turned them over and kissed her palm, first one then the other.

Shelby withdrew from his hold and stood then strode to the glass doors overlooking the ski runs. "I'm not certain I believe you."

Kyle rose, and followed. He wrapped his arms around her waist, nestling her back against his chest. His mouth lowered to her neck moving her hair with his chin.

He hovered over her ear. "I'm sorry the detectives had to interview you by yourself. Hiring Lindbergh was the only way I could have someone in your corner. Afterward, they were instructed to bring you to me. I waited for you in another room. When Lindbergh sought me out and I realized you weren't with him, I inquired and found out you had already left. I tried to call you."

She rested her head on his shoulder. "I know."

He ran his cheek down her jawline. "When I couldn't reach you, I started putting a few things together and figured you would be at the airport. I confirmed my suspicions with Alessa this morning." Kyle chuckled. "You sure are giving a lot of business to Zip Away car rental."

She pivoted to face him. "They demanded to know everything about us. I answered as truthfully as I could."

"Truth goes a long way." Obviously, Shelby needed to talk to him about what had happened. Maybe he should listen while she vented her frustrations.

"You don't understand. They interrogated me. What was our relationship, when it began, when it stopped, how close we were to each other, were we intimate and for how long. Did we have any disagreements, fights, and when did we make up. How I could afford the plane tickets, rental cars and absence from work weeks at a time. Did I use Pressley International's perks, did you give me money, and was I expecting more. Some were like the wife beating questions any answer produced a negative connotation."

"I didn't think it would be a walk in the park."

Shelby released his arms from her waist, pacing across the bedroom, her voice rose with each step. "Walk in the park. I don't think you have fully grasped my position. In fact, I'm sure of it."

He bristled at her accusations. "I did understand your circumstances and took the correct actions necessary for your well-being."

"I was implicated for tampering with personal property and attempted murder, accused of using you for money and power. Do you know what the next lines of questions were?"

She didn't give him a chance to respond and he wanted to.

"They may open Tim's case with me as the suspect because the detectives knew you were investigating us. Jesus Kyle, this is blowing my mind. I didn't realize how far people go to protect you. And why in the hell am I a damn suspect?"

A few seconds slipped by and her eyes locked onto his. "Unless, you're the one calling the shots...You are... aren't you?"

He steeled against her condemnation and tempered his anger and words. "No, if I had any control over this situation and you wanted to go home, you'd be in Texas with my damn army to protect you.

Her eyes widen and her mouth drew into an O.

"However, I do admit to handling your travel arrangements and legal counsel." Any man worth his salt would have done the same thing.

"Everyone thinks I'm guilty." Her head dipped a few inches.

"And I know you're not." Damn, he loved this woman.

"Thank you, I really needed to hear you say that."

He held out his arms. Thank God, she launched across the space and embraced him willingly. "I missed you." He kissed the top of her head. "I'd like for you to see Andy."

She angled several inches away from him. "Why?"

He placed his forehead against hers. "Because I

want to make sure those yahoos didn't do any damage beyond what I see."

"You're being ridiculous, but if it would make you feel better...I will."

"That's my girl." He removed the wisps of her hair that had caught on his whiskered jaw, making a mental note to shave again.

He speed dialed his personal assistant to contact Dr. Humphreys.

"Done...now where were we?" Kyle slid the phone into his back pocket.

He ached to kiss her. His gaze found her lips and she swiped her tongue across them. The plump and moistened skin called for his attention. His mouth lowered and danced lightly over hers, then she opened. He tasted, loved, and paid homage.

His cell rang. He released Shelby and a curse flew from his mouth. "Sorry, give me a second." He yanked the mobile from his blue jeans. "Kyle."

Jude explained the circumstances to him and told him to call the flip. "Heads...Damn, call and tell them I'm on my way."

He glanced over his shoulder to find Shelby watching him. Her eyes questioned, and her lips quivered as if she wanted to ask, but wouldn't. "I need to go down to the police station...I'll be back in a few hours."

Her chin notched a few inches in the air. "Did something new happen?"

For some reason he couldn't put his finger on, she was still scared. "No. It has to do with Pressley International and I lost the coin toss with Jude...Shelby, I'll protect you with every available resource I have at my disposal—"

"I don't do well with fifty-fifty chances either." She pivoted from him changing the subject.

He sidled next to her. "You believe me right? If you let me, I'll take care of you."

She shrugged.

Kyle locked his arms around Shelby. "You can count on me, baby."

Her squeeze answered him.

"You should grab a bite of lunch. I'll be back for dinner and we'll eat together."

Shelby nodded and angled into the haven he kept just for her. Kyle swore he'd keep her safe.

After Shelby promised him to eat, he closed the door then strolled downstairs. Sam leaned against the threshold waiting for him while his team was outside.

Kyle stuck out his hand. "Good to see you. Ready to head out?"

"You know I'm going to stick to you like a duck on a June bug, no matter how many times you tell me to go be somewhere or how ornery you get. I'm not having you get beat up again especially on my watch."

He slapped Sam on the back. "Remember, I'm the one who told you to—go be somewhere as you put it. Quit lambasting yourself over something you had no control over. Now, let's get going, we're burning daylight."

****

Shelby opened the glass door and stepped onto the balcony into the rays of the October sun. The frigid blast of air scurried around her, but the warm stream of heat saturated her skin, trickling into her bones. It felt wonderful.

She drew in a deep breath. Kyle had believed she was innocent. His opinion allayed her trepidation and he had bequeathed an intangible inner peace. She trusted him to protect her.

Twenty-four hours ago, this horrible journey began everything beyond their control. She had to admit she'd given up on him and thought the worst when all she needed to do was to talk to him. Communication, a simple act, sometimes it didn't even require words, a true art form in itself. In her instance, she should've accepted his phone call last night, demanding an explanation. Hindsight was always twenty-twenty.

As for Bear-Claws' request, Kyle had a mind of his own and he damn sure walked to the beat of his own drum. For the first time since her husband's death, her perception changed, purging all the frightening what-if scenarios, fear no longer dwelled in the far recesses of her subconscious, and she entrusted Kyle with her life.

She felt free, as though she had sprouted wings and soared through the sky. If worries were clouds, there wasn't any as far as she could see. Her endorphins kicked into high gear, giving her a euphoric high and making her giddy. She giggled and she spun lifting her hands as high as they could go then she broke into laughter.

A man's voice called out, "Hey!"

She squealed, then lowered her palms to her side and panned to pinpoint the origin.

Her gaze met a gray-haired gentleman dressed in black from his turtleneck to his sports jacket and trousers.

His aviator sunglasses reflected the light and he adjusted his timbre to a more paternal tone. "It's safer if you stay inside."

She nodded. "Sorry." Then she chuckled again. She wouldn't allow anything to bring her down.

Just as she stepped inside, a knock echoed inside the room. "Come in."

Jude crossed the threshold along with another gentleman. "Shelby, this is Andy's son, Dr. Chris Humphreys. Chris, I'd like you to meet Shelby."

Dr. Humphreys ambled over and shook her hand. "I finally get to put a face to your name. My dad spoke highly of you."

Several inches taller, he was certainly handsome in every detail. He could've been a model for a romance book cover or a designer cologne ad. He probably had every nurse in the county or for that matter, the surrounding states flirting with him. She figured a few of them propositioned their bodies as a sacrificial offering too.

His shirt defined every muscle. His thick chest, well-honed arms and thighs had a balance that came by many hours of hard exercise and a propensity for proportion.

"Thank you and I think your father is an exceptional man. He bragged on you and seemed very happy when you chose to join his practice. I'm glad to meet you also. I expected him, is he all right?"

"I told him to go home and spend some time with Ma." He set his case on the floor beside the coffee table, motioned for Shelby to sit on the couch and followed suit. "I heard the bodyguards decided you were their morning workout session?"

His gray eyes twinkled at his own joke and she couldn't resist the banter. "I felt like I was Olive Oyl caught between Popeye and Brutus."

"Let me see what they did to you."

She rolled up her sleeves. "It's nothing really."

"Let me be the judge of that."

Marcus, the head of security, popped his head in the room. "Jude, can I see you for a moment."

"Sure, I need to step out for a few minutes." Jude said in more of a statement than a question.

Chris gently took her arm in his hands. "Leave the door open, this won't take long. Her bruises look superficial, but I want to make sure."

"Will do." Jude disappeared with Marcus.

"Shelby, Shelby, Shelby." Chris' fingertips curled into her flesh.

Chapter Sixteen

"Doctor, you're hurting me." Shelby attempted to extricate out of his grasp.

He jerked her toward him. "Don't scream or move…You're going to listen and obey me."

His hypnotic gaze had a profound effect and his words commanded her attention. She couldn't break the connection.

Chris released her, rose and tapped the door closed with his foot then turned. He smirked. With a flick of his wrist, a black aura oozed from his frame. The emanation engulfed her, suffocating any thoughts of running. "Don't look surprised, my sweeting, I know about your gift."

She recoiled, drawing her legs up until her knees settled below her chin then she wrapped her arms around them. "What do you want from me?" If the man in Austin was a warrior, Chris was a five-star general.

Snakes of fire whipped, cracking in front of her face like a bullwhip. "You, my dear, will give me Ten-Blue-Sun when I tell you to do so."

"The Kachina doll?"

"Come now, you seemed surprised."

"I can barely breathe from your stench, do you mind?" She blanched when he released his evil, guttural laugh.

He retreated giving her a foot of space. She sucked

in a clean breath of air and sighed with relief.

"When Ten-Blue-Sun's stones light indicating all the stages have been completed, you will bring her to me."

Confused, she stared waiting for him to clarify what he meant.

"Hell, you're about as clueless as your husband."

"What about Tim?" she asked scared witless he had everything to do with his murder.

"My pet—"

"I'm not your—"

"Silence." Blood-red slime slammed against her.

He lowered his voice. "At each level of completion, the warrior woman will gain significant strength to pass on to those who have possession. After all the phases have been obtained, you must freely give her to me."

She brushed her hair behind her ear. "And what makes you think I'd do that?"

"Ah, my Comanche princess, you will or I'll have your family members killed one by one. May I remind you, I didn't hesitate to have your husband dispatched."

Her head pounded. She couldn't tell whether it was from his foul miasma creeping up her nostrils or knowing Chris' hands had Tim's blood on them, probably both. A thick knot in her throat swelled, she swallowed hard. "Why?"

Chris sneered. "He told me Ten-Blue-Sun wasn't his to give away—"

"You were there? You killed him?" Acid churned in her belly, rising until the bitter taste of dread, disgust, and death mixed with her saliva.

"I don't do the dirty work, my dear. Maybe you'd

like to know his last words? Eh?"

Her hand closed over her mouth, she was going to hurl.

"Tim asked me not to hurt you because you didn't know anything about the doll and to tell you he loved you. What an obnoxious emotion." Chris goaded.

She jumped from the couch, her fingers curled into fists. "You bastard. You won't get away with this."

His irises swirled. A narcotic suggestion emerged for her not to move, threatening talons surfaced from the ominous cloud surrounding him. They hovered above her shoulders then dug in, her flesh burned as the claws hooked, each nail piercing her skin. All at once, they shoved her and retracted. She fell onto the sofa.

"You will make sure that I do." He taunted.

Chris wrestled his backpack open, withdrew a syringe and a rubber tourniquet. Within seconds, he had the elastic around her arm and uncapped the needle. Liquid spurted then he inserted the metal tip and dispensed the contents. "You have about sixty seconds to make it to the bed. Go."

She rose and wobbled. Her eyes blurred and she couldn't talk. She summoned the strength to make two more steps. Chris had the quilt and sheet drawn and she crumbled onto the mattress.

He covered her. "Remember, the lives of your family rests in your hands. If you tell anyone, I'll know and your loved ones will pay the price. And the cost will be death. Sweet dreams, Brave-One." Chris smirked again.

Shelby awoke. The dark room matched its silence which conflicted with the battle of emotions roiling inside her heart and mind. Anger and fear battled for first place. Her life had changed from the second Chris made himself known.

She would be signing her family's death warrants if she revealed the part he played in Tim's murder, asked for help, or didn't freely relinquish Ten-Blue-Sun to him when asked. His threats were real and she'd heed them.

Everything fell into place. Kyle had told her of the stages of tenure and how powerful the doll would become with each one. How rightful possession was the key and in the wrong hands, warrior woman would be a curse. That's why she had to voluntarily give Chris the life bringer.

The memory of One-Who-Soars-With-Eagles' placing the medicine bag inside the doll and all the stones illuminating barreled to the forefront of her mind. Especially, how he had lifted the wooden figurine to her with tears running down his cheeks. Oh God, the battle had begun the moment her husband had found the doll.

Groggy and in a haze, she cast the covers off and headed for the bathroom, clinging to the walls for support. She flipped a switch and groaned until her eyes adjusted to the light. Carefully, she made her way to the sink and peered into the mirror. Her eyelids were puffy and red. She recalled her skin burning, her flesh giving away to each claw and slung the material off her shoulder. Nothing. She shook her head in disbelief.

After completing her morning ritual and in her crumpled clothes from yesterday, she slipped downstairs to make some coffee then after, she'd get a shower.

In the kitchen, fresh brewed espresso filled the air.

She glanced through the dining room, a man stood guard watching her. He acknowledged her with a dip of his chin, she reciprocated then she scampered back to her room.

After finishing her much needed caffeine kick, she freshened up and rested for a moment on the couch to gather her thoughts. She perched her feet on the table in front of her and crossed her arms over her tummy to relax and think.

She leaned her head back and remembered when she had first met Kyle at the town square. He'd made sure she was safe then, even went so far as to check her hotel room. She grinned. Her mind fast forwarded to the last days at his house. The fond recollections warmed her. When he made love to her, he covered every inch of her body with affection. She wasn't sure of the reason, but he'd always fanned her hair out whether she lay on the pillow, mattress, or floor.

Kyle expressed his passion with his sweet kisses. His caress soothed the jolts of despair in her life. He had massaged her with his strength to endure and his breaths extolled his love, wrapping her in a cocoon of happiness.

She savored the memories of his love making. Kyle had stroked her arms and shoulders with care and devotion. The pads of his fingers drew circles at the small of her back which tempered her anxiety. His moist mouth meandered from her neck to behind her ears. She loved Kyle's touch. He had finesse to apply the right amount of pressure at every one of her erogenous zones. Drifting to the crevice of her shoulder, his moisture lingered on her skin and her favorite part, with every breath he heated her damp flesh.

His soft lips journeyed to her breast. Laving with his tongue, he'd nipped and smoothed her hardened nipple. The erotic tingles zinged to her clit. He'd traveled to her other breast bathing her with sweet affection. His mouth widened to suckle. She arched her back to give him more, to get more and wallow in the sensual sensations racing to her clitoris. Her body greedily accepted his long fingers kneading her ribs and hips. His kisses trailed his palm to the inside of her thigh, behind her knee, then on to her ankle. Strong hands massaged her foot and instep. His ministrations sojourned up to her yearning slick folds. He cupped his hand applying the right amount of force to bring her near the edge. With ecstasy close, she welcomed him. These were the memories she would hold close and keep for a lifetime.

Succumbed to lethargy, she made her way to her bed. Lying across the quilt she gazed through the glass of the french doors to find dawn breaking as the beauty of nature came to life. The leaves swayed in autumn's allure of colors from copper to gold, carmine, and sienna, the awesome change of seasons stirred a memory that always moved her. In the words of John Muir, "When we try to pick out anything by itself, we find that it is bound fast by a thousand invisible cords that cannot be broken to everything in the universe." How appropriate and yet for survival, she needed to cut a few of those strings.

Instead of lying here, feeling sorry for herself, she ought to be clearing the drug-induced cobwebs from her mind and come up with a plan. At least one of her missions had been accomplished, she knew who had killed Tim and yet couldn't do a damn thing about it. She sighed, don't ponder life's complexities, Tim's moved on, get with the program and figure something out.

To counter the blackmail strategies, she would have to put numerous miles between her and Kyle. Obviously, his and Jude's life were in danger because she'd brought Ten-Blue-Sun into their lives. Someone had attempted to kill Kyle already. The Pressleys had plenty of help with the army of men, but Chris finagled his way through the obstacles and found her.

This situation didn't make sense. She never made the doll light or move, only Kyle and Alessa had. One thing she did know, Chris couldn't give a shit whether she had any abilities or not, but he mentioned he knew about her gift of seeing auras. When he had called her my pet and my dear, she'd gagged. Chris was repulsive in every way. Then he had said my Comanche princess. She scowled. What the hell was up with that?

Shelby remembered his last words to her as she had fallen into oblivion. She froze…Brave-One. Damn, this was too much. She had to get the hell out of here before anything happened to her family and before Chris had a second chance to kill her with the crap he'd injected into her system. And with distance, keep Kyle and Jude alive.

She stood. The room swirled. Willing her equilibrium to return, she inhaled hoping more oxygen would clear the cloudy effects of the drug. A few minutes later with her balance restored, she packed her things.

With the two straps of her backpack secured on each shoulder, she snuck out of her room. The sound of

Kyle's shower filtered through the hall so his uncanny radar couldn't zero in on her. As she crept down the steps, she listened for voices and heard several in the kitchen. The old bodyguard in black must be on break or a shift change. He would recognize her, but if she could slip by him, she had a much better chance.

She tiptoed to the door, quietly twisted the knob, and slipped through. Gently, she released the handle until it clicked. Looking down the hallway, she spied the fire-escape stairwell. She breathed deep and exhaled slowly bringing her jittery nerves under control, clearing the hazy fog hovering in her head.

This evening, she would figure out what flight to take, staying away from the car rental since Kyle tended to think she used them all the time. Disgusted, she breathed heavy. She wasn't any good at this subterfuge shit.

To her surprise, the staircase led to an outside exit and she was relieved when no alarms sounded. The frigid air hit her. She had stowed her jacket in her overnight bag so she'd wait until she left the premises to don it. Although this whole impromptu scheme to leave wasn't the best idea she had, the slap of the October wind and temperature cleared her mind.

Not wanting to bring attention to herself, she fast-walked with her face down. She inhaled the sweet vanilla aroma of the ponderosa pines lining the driveway to the main road and stayed within the shadows of the long boughs. Her feet hit the hard pavement. She'd have to hitchhike to make it back down the mountain by sunset. Swallowing past the lump of fear, she hastened her stride.

The sound of a truck engine approached and she

prayed no one would recognize her. She pivoted to face the vehicle putting her thumb out at the same time. The young man smiled as he slowed bringing his pickup to a stop.

She ran up to the window. "Where you headed?"

"Jackson," His teen voice echoed through the cab.

Shelby nodded, opened the door, hopped several times and jumped in, clearing the four-foot height to the seat. Pleasant conversation made the time go quickly. The cowboy competed in high school rodeos. He team roped, road bare-back broncs and bulls. With the money he won, he saved for college and hoped for a scholarship or a sponsor from Rodeo-Round-Up for Education, set-up and headed by Jude Pressley. He praised Dr. Chris Humphreys who volunteered for any doctoring a guy might need.

She choked. "Excuse me a minute…I swallowed my gum." She wasn't chewing anything, but it was the only excuse she could come up with.

The sports doctor was slick. Even if she had turned him in, the authorities would have laughed at her. He was a pillar of the community. The five-star general was smooth, proficient, and had easily mastered his strategy. He'd carried out an effective course of action to his benefit. For the second time, she was reminded she was just a pawn.

The young man stopped under the portico of the hotel and left his engine idle.

Shelby opened her purse, grabbed some money for the cowboy, and offered the folded bills to him. "I wish you all the luck."

"No, ma'am. I can't accept that."

"Put the token amount in your college fund." She

left the money in the drink well, slid out and landed on her feet.

His eyes gleamed. "Thank you, ma'am."

She smiled and closed the door.

The cold air whipped around the building, the wind blasted across her face and her stomach growled. She'd call Alessa after she checked in and grabbed a bite to eat. By tonight, she should have a seat on the next flight out. If not, a rental car or bus would have to do, as long as the ride ended in Texas to check on her family.

At the restaurant, the soup and sandwich combo looked yummy. The steam rose from the bowl and the turkey club smelled terrific. While she ate, her cell rang. She refused to look at the caller ID, let alone answer the calls, and slid the toggle to mute.

After eating, she flipped the mobile over and noted the number of missed calls and voice mail messages. Again, she declined to tap those menus opting to speed dial her sister. Just as her finger touched the screen, she connected with an incoming call.

KP appeared at the top. She slipped the phone to her ear without saying a word.

"Did you leave on your own?" The angst in his voice tugged at her heart.

"Yes."

"Are you alone?" Kyle's distress was evident by the anxiety in his tone.

"I am."

A rush of air came across her cell with a whispered, "Thank God."

An understanding smacked her in the face, he thought she'd been kidnapped. She should've left a note, not that she had been thinking clearly with the drugs Chris injected in her. Her mouth opened to say she was sorry. She wanted to apologize for worrying him, but she had to get away. Her hands were tied, bound by a man who'd not hesitate to kill again. She choked back a reply waiting for him to say something…anything.

"Why did you leave?"

A question he deserved an answer to. The next few minutes were going to be hell. How should she respond without endangering everyone dear to her? God damn Chris, if he was here and she had a gun, she'd shoot the bastard.

"Did you hear me or did you put me on ignore?" Tension had changed to annoyance.

Her mouth transformed into a dry cotton ball and all of the water in her body must have deadheaded to her eyes. The tears rolled down her cheeks like two faucets that had been turned on full blast.

A raspy, "Yes," escaped, not able to clarify it was the former rather than the latter and she chided herself. The last thing Kyle needed was an overwrought bawling woman. She ground her molars together, hoping for an emotional reprieve.

"Okay…I'd like you to come back under our protection, then I'll leave and you'll never have to see me again." His baritone words rattled her psyche.

"No…Oh God…Why?" Her world fell apart. The helpless feeling left her vulnerable, empty. Unable to change the past or correct the future, she staggered at how defenseless she'd become and would be for a long time. How many months would it take for all the stones to illuminate on Ten-Blue-Sun? What if it took several years, how would she be able to find the doll? Unless, she asked Kyle to give warrior woman back...or stuck around...Jesus, did she just consider using him?

"You're going to have to help me out here. I don't know what you want anymore."

Apparently his patience had thinned to the point his anger had increased exponentially, she shuddered. The heel of her hand swiped away the tears. She sniffled.

The only response she had and could honestly ask for, "Will you forgive me?"

Silence answered her question. She ended the call.

Another waitress sauntered over to fill her cup with fresh coffee. "Sometimes life is unfair and taking a stand all by your lonesome is hard and self-defeating. Many of us understand that you can get help in the most unlikely places. When you don't know what to do next, go and ask." Then she walked away.

Shelby added sugar and squinted at the black liquid swirling as she stirred. Did she look that bad for a stranger to give her advice? Unlikely places?

The original server brought her out of her reverie. "Anything else?"

"Who was the lady in the dark blue uniform and red hair? She refilled my—"

"Nobody by that description works here. We're only allowed to wear black pants and white shirts."

"I'm sure I must have been mistaken." She handed the ticket back with some money. "Keep the change." Shelby rose and left.

The messenger gave her instructions—to ask in the most unlikely places. At first she had considered the lady meant for her to question She-Who-Smiles. Most people had several spirit guides and she did too. Nevertheless of her own freewill, she'd opted out.

Crying wolf all the time wasn't smart because someday, she might need the cavalry.

As she walked back to her hotel, a truck skidded to a halt. Kyle jumped out and stood in front of her. The panic in his gaze changed to relief then simmered to fury.

Chapter Seventeen

Kyle held his temper and waited for Shelby to speak first. Her splotchy face and swollen eyes gave away she'd been weeping. He'd been pissed when she hung up on him, but more to the point, it scared the shit out of him. Sometimes he understood her perfectly and then there were other times, like right now, he didn't have a clue. This was one of those instances where he could kick himself in the ass for making a promise not to mind walk. It sure would come in handy, especially with Shelby.

"Where's your entourage?" Shelby's palm wiped her cheek.

"Didn't bring them." He glided his hand through his hair. "You never gave me a chance to answer your question."

He stalled until she connected her regard to his. "I forgive you, but you're not the only one who should be making amends."

She took a hesitant step toward him then stilled. "You're something else." She sniffed. "At times, I can't think straight. I'm sorry I caused you so many problems…If you never met me or I stayed away from you, then—"

"I would've lost too much."

He closed the distance between them and hugged Shelby. Her arms wrapped around his waist, and she softened against him. She was a damn strong woman to live in his life, to fit in his hellish existence and the crazy world of his ancestors.

"I want to take you...to stay with me."

Her fingertips dug into his back, her cheek rested on his chest, and she trembled. "I'm afraid, frightened for my family, for you and Jude." She gasped, her shoulders lurched, then her legs gave way.

He hung on to keep her from falling to the ground. As what-the-fuck moments went, this was one of them. "What's wrong?"

"Nothing." Her teeth ground together as if she was in pain.

"I'm taking you back and calling Chris again." He curled one arm underneath her knees while the other held her shoulders and lifted, carrying her to his pick-up.

She wiggled to free herself, screaming, "No, put me down."

It certainly was a study between balance and presence of mind to not hurt Shelby while he placed her in the vehicle and tried to calm her. He settled Shelby in the passenger seat. His foot rested on the floorboard while his hands shifted to gently hold her hips in place. "Stop fighting me and listen."

She quieted and fixed her gaze on his.

"Talk to me." When he had mentioned Chris' name, she freaked out, and he wanted answers, now.

Tears erupted and streaked down her cheek, then a stone-cold expression emerged. "All I'm going to say is...I don't want him near me...ever again."

If he did anything to her, he'd castrate the son-of-a-bitch's balls. "Did he hurt you?"

She shook her head. "Not like you're thinking...It's just I don't like him...Okay."

"All right." He caved at her request, but he'd find out what the problem was and correct it. "We should be heading back." He stepped away, straightened and panned looking for anyone or anything out of place. "We're like sitting ducks out here."

"My stuff is at the hotel."

"Not a problem." He closed the door and walked around to the driver's side. The hairs on his neck rose and his gut contracted violently. Instinct kicked his ass in gear, time to get the hell out of here.

****

"Damn, almost had her." He cursed Kyle Pressley's luck. Why the bastard didn't die rolling down that mountain, he'd never know.

He told his customers, he'd be able to handle the cowboy and his sweetheart, but they done circled their wagons.

"I'll git 'em, Dad, I'll git 'em. Kyle'll pay for what he done ta' ya'. I'll make sure of it." He missed his father and waited for the day he could have his revenge. He'd have to bide his time again, taking his cousin's advice, patience.

****

Kyle opened the penthouse door and followed Shelby upstairs to her room, then placed her backpack on the floor. He settled on the sofa and opened his arms wide inviting her to join him.

She sat beside him and he twisted, laying her back against his chest. Her rapid breaths spoke volumes. As much as he wanted to find out what happened, he'd wait until she calmed. Something had spooked the hell out of her and the source had to be Chris.

Chris was a lady's man, but he'd never seen or heard of him taking advantage of a woman. Women called him eye candy. With his wealth and single status, ladies vied for his attention. He'd pick one and let her dictate the game and how fast they played. In the end, he messed around, had a good time, enjoyed the liaison, and shied from a lasting affair or marriage.

Hell, he felt the same way about relationships since Christine. He inhaled the sweet aroma of Shelby's hair. The feminine fragrance reminded him that Shel had been able to turn the tide of his onerous conviction.

She shuddered again.

Kyle would sit tight a little longer. When he returned from the police station, the detectives had given their laptops to him. He'd talked to Jude first, swapping info. With nothing out of the ordinary, he'd checked on Shelby and she was asleep. He had stayed in her room until well after midnight then went to bed.

In the morning, he'd let her rest and given her some personal time. By noon, a sickening feeling rolled in his gut. He'd taken the steps two at a time and didn't knock, jerking the door open. The empty room confirmed his instinct. Havoc steamrolled through him until he inhaled several deep breaths to get a grip.

He'd made a number of calls to Shelby's cell leaving messages and to Alessa, who hadn't heard from her. Next came the hard part, biding his time. His mind played out graphic scenarios that got worse with each one.

When she answered her cell, he'd been surprised by the distance in her voice and words. After she hung up on his ass, he turned to Marcus tracing her call and asked for her position. The head of security gave him a several block area. He knew where to find her...Their restaurant.

Jude, Marcus, and Sam told him to wait for his security team. He'd told them to go fuck themselves. Later on, he would have to go downstairs and face their wrath, although he wouldn't apologize. He'd bet if any one of them had been in his boots, they would've done the same thing.

Finally, Shelby's head relaxed against his shoulder and she stretched her legs on the couch. Her tell signs signaled she was ready.

"Tell me what happened."

Shelby tensed. "I don't want to be drugged again."

"What?" This was the first he'd heard about any medication. Damn, that's why she'd slept so long and hard. He'd been worried because she hadn't moved. During the night, the shallow rise and fall of her chest concerned him enough to check on her several times. "Did he explain or give you a reason?"

She inhaled to answer, her shoulders bunched and she squeaked as if in pain. "I...I'm sure it was my fault."

That was the second time he'd seen her distressed reaction when talking about the bastard. If Chris was here, he'd deck him. "I can't believe your actions would dictate using a barbiturate, but you have my word, no more."

She settled against him.

"There's one more thing I need to discuss with you." Kyle waited for her answer.

She hesitated. "Yes?"

"I want you to promise me you'll never go

anywhere un-chaperoned, unless we talk and both agree beforehand that it's okay." When she didn't answer, he urged, "Baby?"

****

Shelby untangled from Kyle's embrace and stood. She met his gaze. "I have a few things to talk about too."

She crossed to the balcony doors. Her eyes strained but couldn't see anything but lingering shadows from the resort lights. "I'm confused...and worried about all that has happened."

And because of Chris, what would come to pass? She tried not to think about him and what he'd do to her family. The first time on the sidewalk in Jackson she'd come close to telling Kyle about the threats. When she had, the sudden pain of the talons clamping on her shoulders, the nails digging into her skin, the flesh burning, hurt like hell and scared the bejesus out of her.

The second time was a few moments ago on the sofa. She attempted to block the five-star general out of her mind hoping to inform and receive help from Kyle. But Chris won again. She didn't like the idea of hiding the truth from Kyle, but now with every fiber in her being, she'd guard him from harm. Even if it meant instant death, she'd protect the ones she loved.

"We promised to love one another, to spend more time together. This isn't exactly what I had in mind, but here we are. I can't believe I'm asking you this, but I need you to tell me what you want from me...Do you want a life-long commitment?" As Shelby whispered the words, moisture beaded on the glass pane, she swiped it away with one finger.

She spun to face him and held her palm up to stop

his answer. "Before you respond, I want to give you some of my thoughts."

In the back of her mind, she questioned her rationale. She wanted Kyle with all of her heart, but if their relationship lasted, they'd be put to Chris' test. One she wasn't sure who'd win the bloody battle.

For now, she'd go with her heart and not logic. Her reason screamed to run as fast and far as she could. Another thing she couldn't do was to promise Kyle she'd never disappear alone. Life wasn't like a parade route, planned and protected. When Chris set the time, she'd have to leave Kyle, taking Ten-Blue-Sun with her. She inhaled, took a leap of faith that her family would be safe and Kyle would forgive her in the end.

"I'm not someone who can voluntarily commit to a temporary situation. There are times I wished I were clairvoyant. If you only want me for a while then I suppose... friends are all we'll ever be."

Kyle crossed the room and halted in front of her. "You never answered my question, how am I to give you one without the other? I love and trust you. Because I've given you my heart and soul, I want to protect you. If something happened to you...I'd never forgive myself." His Adam's apple bobbed. "I'd be the one who'd have to tell your family you passed on to the First Realm. Christ, that'd kill me. I'd rather give my life for yours any day of the week before facing your grandchildren."

There was the confluence, a junction of wills. They'd both die for one another. An irrefutable fact. It wasn't if, but when the test came, one would overpower the other. Then all hell would break loose.

Or they would work together, become stronger,

better and forge on. She chose to believe in the positive.

"And mine for yours." She raised her arms, cupping her hands around the nape of his neck, drawing his lips to meet hers. The fusion of moist skin accelerated the hot jolts of desire to her belly then lowered. With a simple kiss, this man, her lover, turned her into mush.

His mouth nipped along her jaw to the sensitive flesh behind her ear. Goosebumps rose as his tongue streamed moisture along her flesh. He nibbled her collarbone then journeyed back to exchange breaths, him giving and taking while she accepted and bequeathed hers. A need to be loved and filled by him barreled through her body, her nerves strummed with sensual tension, waiting, anticipating.

His caresses changed from gently inviting to urgent, charged with pheromones, demanding possession and she accommodated.

He withdrew and released her. "Wait here, don't move."

Like she would or even could.

In three long strides, he had the door locked and pivoted. He flashed his luscious smile, his double dimples deepened. With each small step, he discarded a piece of clothing. His shirt fell to the floor first, revealing the broad expanse of sinew. The dusting of dark hair covering his chest trailed a path dipping below the waistband of his denims. Next his boots were discarded. He unfastened the singular button, unzipped his fly, and as his jeans slid over his muscular thighs he included his boxers and socks. Now before her, he resembled a god.

She'd definitely pay homage to this one,

impatience thrummed to every extremity. His body screamed with intense desire. Her gaze traveled to his darkened eyes full of passion. His pupils dilated as she stripped.

When he joined her, she matched his fervor. The fire in her loins burned for the ecstasy just out of her grasp. But there was more, fueled by the knowledge she'd have to leave him someday, her soul charged forward. With their combined energy, she navigated into their charted territories, the undefined boundaries she had yet to understand and a place that was exquisite.

He slowed the pace, whispered sweet words and cherished her with unhurried motions, yet each was expressed with acute potency. The power of his deliberate leisure carried her back from the edge. He granted her time to savor their joining and she did. Her inner muscles milked his shaft. His thumb found her swollen nub and his rhythm increased.

His hips pumped and with every thrust, he hit her sweet spot. Then he scooted his arms under her thighs, lifting to penetrate deeper while her folds opened. His advances struck her clit, and the immense pleasure contracted her core.

"I'm so close."

"Baby, right with you."

She catapulted and he plunged several more times then joined her in their world. A special place where their souls were free of the encumbrances of earth, in a location where erotic gratification passed beyond the physical realm, the bliss of fulfillment took her breath away.

Sated, under post-coital stupor, Kyle lay on top of

her, his weight a reassuring comfort no words could ever give.

After a few moments, Kyle rolled to his side and pulled her back against his chest. He stroked his hands over her arms. "I'm sorry those bastards bruised you. Does it hurt?"

"Hurt? No. More like sore. Nothing to worry about."

He laved every black, blue, and purple mark with his mouth, attended her palms and ended by sucking her fingertips. "Baby?"

"Mmm?"

"What am I going to do with you?"

She languished under his diligent attention. "Whatever you want."

He chuckled. "I'll take you up on that after we eat. Ready for a midnight snack?"

Not really sure if food was on the menu, either one would be fine with her. "Famished."

****

During the long shower, Kyle transported Shelby one more time. Her release always accompanied his favorite sounds, a mewling then a sigh. "You're beautiful...Your cheeks are flushed with afterglow."

Her rosy face changed to a flaming red.

He turned the water off. "Let's get dressed and head down stairs."

When Kyle followed Shelby into the kitchen, Jude sat at the bar tapping the keys of his computer.

His older brother peered over his reading glasses and his fingers stopped typing. "Mending and healing?"

"Shut up." Kyle grinned pleased when Jude nodded and smiled back.

231

"I'm going to call it a night." Jude closed his laptop and rose from the stool. "Shelby, I'm glad to see you're back safe. Contrary to my behavior and your thoughts, as long as Kyle's happy, so am I. I want you to feel comfortable and at home with us."

Shelby closed the distance between her and Jude. She stood on her tip toes, kissed his brother on the cheek and hugged him. "You don't know how much that means to me, thank you."

Jude cleared his throat. "Good night." And he left.

Shelby cocked her head to the side. "Mending and healing?"

He closed the refrigerator door, placed cold cuts, condiments and bread on the table then winked. "I believe we are."

She helped with the plates and silverware. "I guess we are… in more ways than one."

Their sandwiches made, they took two of the four stools at the bar.

Shelby glanced at him. "What were the messages in your house? What did they say?"

"I'm not going to repeat the words to a lady let alone my woman. No person in their right mind would ever write anything like that, they were reprehensible."

"Ah, that nasty." Her chin lifted an inch.

"Vile wouldn't come close."

"Your life is in danger because of Ten-Blue-Sun. But, we don't know who or why?" Shelby's finger tapped the bread crust.

"That's right."

"How many people knew you had the doll?"

"I can count on one hand who knew about Ten-Blue-Sun." He raised his glass to his mouth and drank.

"I'm a suspect for tampering with your truck, stealing property, issuing death threats, and attempted murder. Pressley, stop pussyfooting around and tell me what's going on."

He placed the tumbler on the table and pondered how much to tell her. If the detectives questioned her again and she was cognizant of more than they thought she should, he'd end up getting her into more trouble. "Part of the message asked for the doll, the other threatened both of our lives."

"Ours? You and me?" Her eyebrows rose.

"Yes."

"Anyone else?"

"Anyone trying to help us. Beyond Pressley International, that's another reason why Jude's here too."

Shelby chewed the bite she took, and what he had told her. She swallowed. "I've met four of your acquaintances. First, there was Mira Dent, but I can't imagine her having anything to do with this. Bobby Jo, David, and later Lisa. Do you really think they'd have done this to you, to us?"

"I've given those names to the detectives, as well as, some business colleagues."

"Have I met any people who work for you?"

"No." He shook his head once.

"How would your business colleagues know enough to write my name much less assign a death threat to it?"

"My answer is to wait on the detectives. Hopefully, they can figure out if the grievance is personal or a business vendetta. Of course, the life-bringer is still a problem."

"You have a state of the art security system. How did they get through all the safety mechanisms you have in place?"

"They knew enough to not set off some of the features. Others were activated, but they overcame them. I'm being vague until I know for sure the investigators have scratched you off their list as a person of interest. Only then, will I let you know the full extent of how they got around security."

"Fair enough. So, what do you want to do for the next couple of hours?"

"We could work out or—" Kyle winked. "Mend and heal."

Shelby smiled. "I should exercise, but I'd like the last better."

Chapter Eighteen

By the end of the week, Kyle received a phone call. Garrett had returned from a trip and offered his ranch to him and the crew. Kyle had jumped on the invitation. Even Jude was ready to blow the joint since the extra bodyguards never made it. Side by side with Marcus and his brother, he labored over the security details.

When Shelby entered the dining room, plans lay scattered on the table with the three of them huddled diligently working over the fine points. Kyle stood and the rest of the gentlemen chased his lead.

Hesitation eclipsed with Shelby because her mouth opened then closed. She cleared her throat. "I'm sorry to interrupt, but I'd like to speak to Kyle for a minute."

He grinned. "Excuse me…I have a beautiful lady who needs my attention." He strutted from the room feeling like the winning stud.

Following her into the living area, he leaned on one shoulder against the arched entry. "What's up?"

One-half of Shelby's curvaceous ass inched over the back of the sofa. "I've updated both of my sisters. When I told them about going to Garrett's ranch, Alessa wanted to come. She has some documents for me to sign, although, I think my little sister needs to reach out and touch me…kind of thing. Al wants to come as soon as it's okay. To be perfectly honest, immediately wouldn't be soon enough for her. Is this something

235

doable?"

"Sure it is. Pogonip used to be a dude ranch. Garrett has enough cabins for our security detail and his house is big enough for all of us. Until we know who we're dealing with, we'll have an army out there. The detectives believe their investigation is turning toward a positive direction. But I still want to discuss it with the crew in there." He tilted his head toward the dining area. "They may see a problem I don't. I'll let you know."

He strode to her, kissed her forehead and left. He fist pumped the air. "Yes." Meeting Shelby's family signaled a step in the right direction for their relationship and meant the world to him.

Earlier this week, he wouldn't have bet two cents in their involvement continuing, but mending and healing had done wonders. Another good thing about going to Garrett's ranch, he wanted to spend time outdoors with Shelby. He had a better perspective surrounded by nature, much better than the four walls that had a tendency to close in on him.

The last few days, he had his face glued to his laptop conducting his work via Pressley International's secure computer. Shelby worked on her book when she wasn't in contact with Alessa helping her little sister on various business problems. Even though she was in the same room, she never interrupted him. Shelby had given him the needed time to complete several projects so when she was with him, nothing was more important than each other.

The evenings were spent intimately and in the early morning hours, he'd convinced her to exercise with him. In so many ways, their bonds had grown, but in other aspects, they had a long way to go.

Shelby wasn't high maintenance and didn't demand his attention every waking moment like so many women he knew. He had a sneaking suspicion she still harbored secrets. Not criminal by nature or the psychologically demented kind, but the sort that kept her at a safe distance. If he had to describe her intentions, it was just in case she had to run, whether it was from Chris, the stifling rules his security team stipulated, and he hated to admit it, him.

She had appeared to have accepted all the precautionary measures to safeguard their lives. His primary concern, would she continue to carry out the protocols or would she suffocate under the constant pressures of his way of life?

Wait, he led an ordinary existence, didn't he? This just happened to be a worst case scenario. Other than needing a security team, or that his wealth kept him from doing mundane things he enjoyed, and there was his mom's kidnapping and murder...Well, he'd best stop there.

When he entered the living room, he found Shelby staring out the window. The thick Turkish rug gave a little under his feet as he crossed in between the two Italian leather sofas facing one another. He sidestepped the mahogany coffee table and grabbed a dark chocolate from the Waterford dish. Peeling the wrapper off, he popped the bite size treat in his mouth, where it instantly melted into nothing.

He circled his arms around her waist. "If we were alone, I would make love to you right here until you screamed my name begging me to stop."

She rested her hands on his forearms. "When I

scream your name, it's definitely not telling you to stop."

His long fingers dropped to her pelvic bone and angled his hips against her bottom. "Hmm, Shel, we fit perfectly. Baby, what you do to me." He chuckled releasing the pressure. "I'm not going to be able to walk out of here."

He kissed her right temple. "The crew felt it would be safe for Alessa to visit. Just let me know when she's supposed to arrive. It'll be great to meet your sister."

"Are you sure there's no problem?" She placed the back of her head against his chest.

"Alessa won't be an extra burden. If it were remotely unsafe, I'd never add your sister to the mix. You can call her when we get there. Plus, I'd like to know you'd have someone to keep you company if I have to take off."

As Shelby turned, he released her and she stood with her hands akimbo. "You'll be leaving?"

"There's always a possibility." He hugged her then eased back a few inches. "We'll be heading out this afternoon, are you packed?"

"Yes, I did that while I was talking to my sisters. Go figure, multi-tasking even when there isn't another item on the to-do list."

"I've got an idea to add to that list of yours."

"And that being?"

He cupped her breast and his cock strained against his zipper. "Guess?"

She slid her hand to his groin and massaged his hard-on. "Hmm, lets."

****

Shelby nestled beside Kyle. Her gaze panned

inside the armored stretch-suburban taking in the two men working on their laptops. The heat from Kyle's body added to the warmth from her computer fan. Like many moments in life to remember, this was one of them. She considered herself lucky to know both these guys. Her lover raised her temperature with a stroke of his finger and Jude was a gruff and commanding man, but once you got to past the tough exterior, he had a heart the size of Texas.

She looked forward to Garrett's ranch, a relaxed atmosphere of a home and the great outdoors, and she appreciated now what most people took for granted. She understood the freedom to come and go as you please without looking over your shoulder. The Pressley men couldn't afford to yield to any temptation, for if they did, the payment in full was injury and possibly death.

Garrett met the caravan of vans, trucks, cars, and what looked like a SWAT truck. He had aerial and topographical maps of his ranch for Marcus. The cabins, stables, barns, and outbuildings outlined the valley with the high mountains all around giving a serene, picturesque scene.

All the buildings were fashioned from hewn logs. The corrals and stables were the first structures specifically built for Garrett's clients, who boarded their horses in his first class accommodations.

Kyle and Jude shook Garrett's hand, then hugged him. Garrett's eyes twinkled when they connected with hers. The First Realm's kinship drizzled into her soul. Garrett prodded his brothers to take Shelby to the house. Kyle insisted on being her escort and would return to help oversee the security details, as well as the arrangements. Shelby smiled. It was the little things Kyle did that made her feel warm and fuzzy inside.

Everyone had agreed not to make a show of force, but rather to make it seem like they were here as guests. Garrett's clients could come and go working with their horses. They had several men who were knowledgeable and would work beside Uncle Grey. That was all she heard before Kyle closed the passenger door of Garrett's work truck.

Garrett's drive meandered up the mountain. They passed the cabins dotted along the stream and the house came into view a mile later. When Kyle pulled into the circle drive and stopped, Hilda scurried out the front door, sweeping down the steps in deference to her age followed by several other women.

Kyle chuckled. "I couldn't keep her away."

"She's a good person. I like her a lot."

Along with Kyle, she received Hilda's affectionate welcome. Hilda introduced the four other women, her nieces, Linda and Sophia along with Julia, Uncle Grey's wife, and Shay, their daughter.

Each of their auras had bright swirls of color radiating moral virtue, decency, and integrity. She was blessed to meet the women and honored they'd welcomed her with open arms.

They were all talking at once when Kyle grinned at Shelby then mouthed, "I'll be back."

She nodded to Kyle, then Hilda locked her elbow through Shelby's and guided her to Garrett's home.

The corner steps extended from the side to the front. High off the ground the porch wrapped around the entire length. The double doors led into a great room, which had high ceilings, log beams, and the tall windows from the floor to the wooden supports. The stacked stone fireplace and the hearth took up most of one wall. Shelby followed the women up the staircase. "How many bedrooms are there?"

Aunt Julia's soft voice spoke with a tender love. "Seven, all with their own baths and suites. Our cabin is right beyond the garage. Shay will be staying in our guest room with us. Linda and Sophia are staying with Hilda in the maid's quarters."

"This is beautiful," murmured Shelby.

"I'll give you a tour when you get settled. Come down when you're ready and I'll brew some coffee or tea and you can have a piece of cake." Kyle's aunt opened the bedroom door and the women crowded inside her suite.

Hilda fussed with the curtains. The nieces ran their hands over the handmade quilt covering the bed taking out non-existent wrinkles, shaking out pillows on the sofa and love seat, turning lights and lamps on. Finally Julia bid the women to leave. When the door closed, Shelby laughed out loud and hard. They were absolute dolls, had hearts of gold and took pride in their work, but most of all, it looked like they had fun together.

She unpacked the few clothes she had and freshened up for her next adventure, to find where the delicious aromas were coming from.

Situated in the back, Shelby found Julia preparing dinner. "I'm glad you decided to visit. We were worried."

"Where's everyone?"

"They left a couple of minutes ago. Shay, Hilda, and her two nieces are in charge of serving the three meals in the one of the outbuildings. It has a commercial kitchen for the cafeteria style dining. I wouldn't have finished all the work if it hadn't been for Hilda and her girls' help. All the necessary food and drinks were delivered and put away. They helped me clean and ready the cabins for the guests."

Julia whispered, "We were told to refer to them as guests."

Shelby giggled at her newfound friend sharing a secret. "Can I help you do anything?"

Julia reverted back to her normal voice. "No, help yourself to the fresh batch of coffee or tea, I made both and have some cake."

"Thanks, then I think I'll go outside for a bit."

"That's a good idea. The view is gorgeous. Go and make yourself at home. We'll be ready to eat shortly."

When Shelby opened the back door with her coffee in hand, the beautiful mountain range took her breath away. She bypassed the first level with the gourmet barbeque, bar, table, and chairs. Taking the couple of steps to the next area, lawn chairs and a fire pit created a comfy setting. The last half-level down, the pool and Jacuzzi invited and tantalized her for a future dip. Shelby opted for the second. Relaxed, she let her head rest on the back of the chair.

She jumped when her cell rang. Her fingertips grasped the phone from her back pocket. The ID read Al. "Hey, Sis."

"Are you there yet? What did they say? Can I come up? Is it safe? Hello, are you there?"

Shelby smiled. "Yes, to all."

"Yahoo, I can't wait to see you and meet Kyle. I'll start making arrangements for everything. What do I bring for clothes? Dress up or down? What's the mainstay there? Do I need to bring anything in particular for you? More clothes? Cat? Dog?"

Shelby laughed. "Alessa, this is a ranch, jeans will be the staple of your wardrobe. I'd be grateful if you could bring some stuff for me. I look forward to not washing every couple of days. I don't think the cat would be too thrilled traveling, but please bring Annie and you can drive my car up."

"Right, SUV, clothes, dog no cat, gotcha'. I'll see you in a few days and I'll call you when I get close for directions. Can't wait, luv ya', bye."

Shelby peered at her phone. Yep, end of call. "Love you too, you're a whirlwind."

"Who?" Kyle sat next to her.

"Alessa, she's a bundle of energy and can be exhausting if you're not used to her."

Kyle winked. "If she has that much stamina, we'll have her muck the stalls."

"I can help. Garrett was gracious enough for us to bombard him with all these people, it's the least I can do. I do know how to clean up after horses."

"I was kidding. Garrett has everything in hand, he's already high tailed it to furthest point of solitude. He prefers the company of horses to people."

"How's everything working out?"

"A three shift schedule has been instituted and everyone is settled. The command post is in the cafeteria. Hilda has taken over down there, making sure there is coffee and snacks to keep everyone happy and has started supper."

"She does like to take care of people."

"Want a tour of the house? Julia said she was going to give you one, but would be obliged if I did."

"Only if you want to, we have plenty of time. You don't have to right now."

"Come on, I'll show you around." Kyle slid her hand in his and led her inside.

****

Two days had passed and Shelby waited for Alessa's arrival on the porch swing. A dust cloud catapulted through the air and then was carried away by the northwest wind. In between the trees, she noticed her SUV speeding up the driveway. Shelby waved and bounced down the steps to meet her.

Alessa skidded to a stop. Gravel slung and crunched. Hopping out of the car with Annie on her heels, Al gave her a bear hug, while the happy canine sat patiently for her welcome.

She knelt, ruffled Annie's ears, consoling her whines. When Shelby stood, her sister encircled her again. "You scared me there for a little while. I'm glad to see you're all right."

"I'm fine. I'll show you what room you'll be staying in." Parental guidance tinged her words.

"You're forever taking care of everyone."

She zoomed to connect with Alessa's gaze. "I don't 'take care' of everyone. I think of you as my responsibility..." She paused and smiled to herself.

Al's face softened and whispered, "As a matter of fact you do, and I wouldn't have it any other way."

As Shelby helped with the suitcases, her mind cartwheeled. She'd accused Kyle of the exact same thing, berated him and then ignored her own actions. How did she miss the mark so badly?

With Alessa settled, she led her outside to the first level. She and Al occupied two of the eight chairs around the table, sipping warm mugs of hot cider when Garrett and Kyle joined them.

"Alessa, this is Kyle Pressley and Garrett Blackwell. Garrett and Kyle, Alessa Staley."

Kyle sat next to Shelby. "How was your trip?"

"Uneventful. My sincere thanks to you and Garrett for having me."

Garrett twisted the caps off two longnecks. The hiss of carbonation escaped and the aroma filled the air. "Everyone likes a smooth ride to their destination no matter the vehicle of transportation."

****

The next morning, Shelby followed Kyle into the stables. Her eyes adjusted and the intermingling scents of horses, leather, and hay tickled her nose. Last night, Alessa had promised to help Garrett. Which would be normally a good thing, but sometimes her little sister had a lot of energy roiling inside her and bubbled out. If Garrett wasn't used to Al's vigor and her zest for life, he'd be driven crazy.

Alessa leaned against one of the stalls while Garrett led a sorrel through the center aisle. He nodded at first to Kyle then Shelby.

"Good morning," Shelby greeted.

Al pushed off the wooden slatted frame with her foot. "This is a fantastic day, beautiful and so peaceful."

Garrett halted beside Kyle. Without a pretext of a whisper, Garrett rolled his eyes. "Peaceful? Not the word I'd choose to describe it."

Kyle rubbed the mare's ears. "What's the problem?"

Garrett zeroed a scathing gaze to Alessa. "Nothing, if you like to listen to a woman who has an insatiable appetite for chatting." Then Garrett ambled outside.

Alessa trailed behind the horse. "I'm just interested in what you're doing. Can I give you a hand?"

Kyle slipped his fingers through Shelby's. "I can't believe what I think I'm seeing…Come on, I don't want to miss a thing."

Inside the round pen, Garrett grunted, "Don't need your help." He put the sorrel through the paces.

Shelby propped her foot on the lowest bar of the piped fence in between Kyle, who had crossed his arms on the top rail and Alessa, who was perched on it.

Al continued with her queries and Garrett never replied. Not to be ignored, Alessa called his name.

Garrett's back straightened and he halted the workout. He clenched his fists, balled at each side then strode to Al. "What do you want?"

"You didn't hear me? Maybe we ought to make an appointment for you—with a doctor—for your hearing."

Garrett walked past her stopping in front of Kyle. "Shoot me now and put me out of my misery."

Shelby took the cue. "Al, let's go get some coffee."

"Sounds good to me." Alessa yelled to Garrett, "Can I bring you anything?"

"No, ma'am."

"Pastries?"

Garrett directed the horse into a trot. "No, ma'am."

"I'll be back to check on you."

"Don't bother, I'll be gone."

Alessa jumped and landed on both feet. "Did you get up on the wrong side of the bed this morning?"

Garrett didn't answer.

"I've never ran across someone who is

so…taciturn," Alessa acknowledged to Shelby. How does he do it, get through life without talking?"

Shelby declined to respond to Al. "Kyle, want to join us?"

"I'll be leaving for the Sheriff's office shortly."

She shoved her hands in her coat pockets. "What's going on?"

"They want to give me an update."

Shelby wasn't sure why he gave a cryptic answer, but she'd have to accept his explanation, for now.

After the caffeine boost, Shelby invited Alessa for a walk. The two guards accompanied them several paces behind.

Alessa whispered, "How can you stand it?"

"What?"

"Them…Being followed." Al tilted her head at the two men behind them.

Shelby shrugged. "The only break is when the bedroom door closes behind me or us."

"How is everything going in that department?"

Shelby grinned. "I don't kiss and tell, but Kyle's wonderful.

"And?"

"What?"

Al snorted.

"All right already. He makes sure I'm happy and satisfied. And we've seemed to come to an understanding about us."

Al's eyes twinkled. "That wasn't so difficult. You would've thought I was pulling your back teeth out." Her stride lessened, she squinted and her brows drew severe lines across her forehead.

Shelby met her steps. "What's wrong?"

"You know me, right? I mean, you raised Joni and I when our parents were too old to care or too stupid to take birth control measures."

Shelby sighed. "We've had this conversation before. Our parents—"

"That's not what I'm talking about. You didn't have a childhood. You made sure we had our homework done, clean clothes, and cooked our meals."

"Don't worry about it." Shelby flicked her wrist.

Alessa suddenly stopped as if to assure herself that her big sister would listen. "I've always felt guilty. You chose not to have any children with Tim…Was that choice a result from raising Joni and I?" Alessa's eyes shimmered with tears.

Chapter Nineteen

Shelby shuddered and remembered the morning she had dropped off Annie, she had given her little sister the big hug, but never had the chance to alleviate Al's guilt complex. Alessa had blamed herself all these years. Shelby gathered Al in an embrace and bear hugged her. "No honey. Every single decision I made with and without Tim came from my personal preference, me."

Shelby grasped Alessa's shoulders, opening the distance between them. "Look at me…"

When Al's gaze met hers, she wanted to quiet her fears and release her of any undue accountability she harbored. "I love you and that's why I took care of you and Joni. You remember Tim already had grown children and grandkids. We agreed to keep our family's size the same. Okay?" She released Alessa.

Her little sister nodded. "I need to talk to you about something else…I've been having a dream…the same one over and over again."

Shelby smirked. "Don't you think you're a little old for me to turn on the nightlight?"

"Stop. I'm serious." Alessa crossed her arms over her chest.

"I'm sorry. Tell me." Shelby's hand patted Al's elbow.

Al's gaze panned to the guards. She spun, putting

her back to them. "She's a Native American trying to tell me something, but she's communicating in another language or maybe telepathically to me. I've tried talking to her, but we're not connecting. She's frustrated that I'm not getting her message. Her look of dread is something I can't get over."

Goosebumps rose over Shelby's flesh. "Are your dreams the same every time or are they at different places with the identical...message?"

"Same everything...I don't know if this is important...I'm looking into the rising sun..."

Her description didn't sound like the First Realm. Shelby relaxed a little but remembered Ten-Blue-Sun's response to Alessa. The wooden doll's eyes glowed. "How do you know the sun's not setting?"

"This sounds sappy, but I understand her coming is a dawning...of...a new age or existence...like a new beginning is imminent or something is going to happen...hell, all I know is I'm facing east."

"Okay, you have a perception that she's warning you of some sort of future occurrence. Not only are you concerned for her, but she's distressed for you?"

"Yep, that pretty much sums it up." Alessa's unfolded her arms and her palms slapped each thigh.

"You don't feel threatened by her?"

"No, not even."

"Don't give up on her."

Al shrugged. "She's not giving me a choice. Her face is forever emblazoned in my memory. The woman is demanding my attention, recognizing we don't understand each other and at the same time, persuading me not to ignore her. I can't dismiss her...or her sadness...her tears...Am I losing my mind?"

"I've been meaning to share with you what's been happening."

When Al blew air out of her mouth, her bangs fluttered. "Why don't I have a good feeling about this?"

Shelby looped her arm through her sister's and continued walking. She held onto Al pondering all the implications. Why had the American Indian woman plagued Alessa's dreams and why couldn't she communicate to her?

At this point, Shelby assumed they were both chosen to fulfill quests although the reasons weren't altogether clear. The singular subject she refused to divulge was Chris. To not yield to the five-star general's threats would mean death to family members. She wouldn't put that kind of strain on her little sister and according to past experience, she couldn't anyway.

Whether she liked it or not, she had a responsibility eclipsing any she'd ever undertaken. It didn't take rocket science to figure out Chris would kill her in the end just like he had murdered Tim. For now, she'd share with Al, watch over her safety, while taking the time to listen and learn more from She-Who-Smiles.

Winding their way around the house and up the steps, Al seemed ready to conquer the world. Of course, she had a lot of questions. Both of them had concluded, the woman may be revealing the massacre during her lifetime and now, may possibly be Al's spirit guide. Al, being Al, likened the circumstances to an exciting adventure and looked forward to making a connection next time around.

Kyle met them at the front door. "We're having a meeting and I'd like both of you to join us."

He led them to the living room indicating to pick a

seat. Jude and Marcus stood with their arms crossed.

Kyle faced the group. "After meeting with the detectives today, they felt the problems are not directed toward Pressley International. The vendetta appears to be personal and only directed at me. I've volunteered for a sting tomorrow afternoon and hopefully the suspects will be captured. Most of the guards will be leaving except for a small contingent of off duty policemen and personal bodyguards. Any questions?" He stared straight at her.

She shook her head. Her belly roiled, scared for Kyle's life. What was he thinking?

"Good. Now if everyone will pardon me, I need to talk to Shelby privately." He extended his hand to help her stand.

Kyle led her to their room, closed the door behind him, and he strode across to the window.

She didn't like the idea of the sheriff putting him in danger. "Isn't there another way to handle this situation other than you being personally involved in this sting?"

"No. I'm the only one who can stop this. Then I have to deal with whoever found out about Ten-Blue-Sun." Kyle's words etched with exhaustion worried her.

"Do you know who these people are?"

His hand swiped through his hair. "Yes…and no I can't tell you."

"I see. After you catch the suspects, then what happens?"

"We can all go home."

Her breath hitched. "I understand."

When he didn't respond further, she murmured, "I'm going for a walk." Either he never heard or refused to acknowledge her comment, so she left.

Without a destination in mind, Shelby found the meandering creek beside the house. When the stream forked, she chose the left one. She focused on Kyle and how tired he seemed and expressed the need for everyone to be able to return home. He had a lot on his mind, the sting, along with the security details which included her and Alessa. But she couldn't shake the distance Kyle had placed between them.

When she came out of her reverie, she recognized her location. The big boulder bought back the memories of Kyle and Lisa. Was this divine intervention?

She couldn't shake off the lethargy. Climbing up, she adjusted her supine position, covered her eyes with her arm. With the babbling stream in the background, the warmth of the massive rock and a couple of hours of daylight left, she relaxed. Kyle's last response kept repeating like a skip on an old vinyl record. *We can all go back home.*

The commotion of men's voices and radios chirping stormed through her dreams, then the clop of hooves, the smell of horses and leather invaded her nostrils.

A man yelled, "We found her. Ms. Littleton, are you okay?"

His question penetrated her consciousness.

She lowered her arm, pins and needles throbbed from her shoulder to her fingertips, a groan escaped. When she sat up, a dull ache ran down her spine. A bright spotlight shined in her eyes. She squinted then shaded them with her hand and noticed the day had turned to night.

The same man demanded an answer. "Ms. Littleton?"

"Yes, of course, I'm okay. I just fell asleep. What's going on?"

He keyed the radio and replied, "Ms. Littleton has been found with no apparent injuries."

He released the button then spoke directly to her, "You were missing and several SAR parties were formed to find you."

"Oh no, I'm sorry." She climbed down from her perch.

Another gentleman from the search and rescue party led a horse to her. She stared at the mare and shook her head. "I can walk."

"Not at night, animals."

"All right." Shelby placed one foot in the stirrup and swung her other leg over and lagged behind the men. On several occasions, they stopped to let her catch up. Shelby wanted to shout she was a beginner and wasn't impeding them on purpose. This was when she wished she had Alessa's fortitude to say what was on her mind. Instead, she gulped and swallowed the words.

The searchers grumbled when they found out she went for a walk and fell asleep. Finally making it to the stables, she dismounted, and apologized to Marcus then thanked them all. Her face burned with the heat of embarrassment. She wanted to get back to the house and hide for the rest of her life.

Grey's understanding eyes locked onto hers, affirming the First Realm connection. "I'll take care of your horse."

"Thanks."

He slipped the reins from her hands. "Kyle's waiting for you."

She found Kyle right outside the door, he gunned

the ATV's engine and he didn't look happy.

"Get on." His words escaped between clenched teeth.

Shelby climbed on opting for his anger over the disapproving stares from the crew filing out of the stables.

Kyle braked and came to a complete stop in front of the house. She hiked her leg over the back and stood.

"Shelby, you promised me never to leave un-chaperoned." His gaze panned to the right then back to meet hers. "No, you didn't, did you."

No, she hadn't. "I told you I was going for a walk. I found the boulder where we had lunch and stopped to rest. I fell asleep. I apologized and thanked Marcus and the men in the search parties. After the security meeting, a bodyguard seemed ridiculous."

He grunted, and his wistful expression said it all. "I can't live like this. I'll be in later to talk." He revved the four-by-four, changed gears and took off.

Kyle was a force to be reckoned with. His love was as strong as the granite boulder she'd slept on earlier. Right now, she didn't have the strength to face his fury and disappointment. Odd, how life changed from one minute to the next. She inhaled a fortifying breath. She was a peacekeeper and refused to stick around for his wrath.

She pivoted and strode toward the house, opened the front door and bounded up the steps two at a time. Shelby found Alessa in her bedroom. "I'm leaving."

"What's up?"

"I'll be ready in fifteen." Shelby pushed off the threshold.

"Shelby, what happened?"

"Nothing."

Alessa sidled next to her sister. "Kyle was beside himself, I've never seen a man go crazy with worry before. I figured you'd be in each other's arms."

Shelby leaned her head and shoulder against the doorjamb. "No… just the opposite. Let me know when you're ready."

Alessa embraced her. "Okay."

Shelby marched to her room, packed her two bags and wrote Kyle a note.

Downstairs, Shelby told the two men assigned to her and Alessa they were leaving while giving them a signed release of liability. They didn't like it but in the end agreed to let them go.

Chapter Twenty

Kyle stalked through the front door. He waited at the team leader's desk as one of the guards recited all the updates and the other produced a ledger. He initialed the printout then patiently waited for them to complete their job. He already knew most of the long narrative. Tired and exhausted, he needed to find Shelby and talk to her.

"The last item I have—Shelby Littleton, Alessa Staley, and Annie, the dog, have departed and won't be returning."

Kyle grimaced. "Thanks."

Each step up the staircase sent a dark foreboding streaking down his spine and landed in his chest. Once in the bedroom they had shared, his heart pounded. The room contained nothing of her belongings. The breeze from an open window caught a piece of paper propped on the dresser and sent it fluttering to the floor. He crossed the space, picked it up and opened the halved sheet.

Tell everyone thank you. With your earlier assurance that it's safe, Alessa and I are going home. I've signed a release of liability for your records.

I'll let you know what decision I make about the doll and if the detectives have any more questions, they know where to find me.

I wish you well.
  Your friend,
  S

He grabbed his cell phone and tapped the speed dial. Voice mail. His jaws clenched as Shelby's articulate inflections offered instructions. He ended the call and jammed the mobile in his pocket and heaved a sigh.

His chest tightened…he blew it again. His temper and worry for her safety consumed their relationship. Why didn't she listen to him? He knew first-hand what families went through, the hell of losing a loved one by maniacs. Was Shelby unaware of the danger that surrounded his life or did she refused to accept it? Either way, didn't bode well.

He still remembered the rage at feeling powerless to help his mom. He was exhausted from trying to protect Shelby, the Pressley fortune and Ten-Blue-Sun from the crazy idiots of the world. With her in Texas, how the hell was he to guard her?

The sound of solitude ringing in his ears lent to despair and gut-wrenching honesty. How had his life fallen apart so quickly? His anger. It was time for him to be truthful. When he had asked Shelby to let him take care of her, she had changed the subject. He'd meant to redirect the conversation. Damn.

His displeasure dissipated into regret after rereading her letter. Maybe they should take a break, but he wanted more.

Almost as if she were there, nestled in his arms, he could feel her warm body cradled in his, fitting perfectly. The fruity scent of her hair curling to his nose while his lips sought the soft skin behind her ear, to taste the sweet nectar of her mound, creating a desire to take her, possess her, until he drove her past the edge, entering into another world they created together.

But he loved other things about her. Even though her fears of the First Realm loomed, leaving Ten-Blue-Sun with him meant she trusted him. Undoubtedly, she understood the enormity of the quest and opted for his help and support.

She had accepted the possible consequences of the interviews with the detectives. When she was mad, she'd plowed into him undaunted, giving her two cents worth and wouldn't allow him to coddle her.

He loved her resilience. She'd stood up to the bodyguards at the airport and Chris' medical practices. Not knowing if she would face his consternation, she'd told his ass to go pound sand when he overstepped her comfort level.

Tonight, he'd lost his temper, and she'd written a note thanking everyone, signed a release of liability, and chose to be friends with him. Now that was perseverance.

For now, he'd give her a break. He'd come up with a new game plan to include Shelby in his life. If she didn't want him, he'd walk away and never bother her again.

The next morning, the detectives called and the sting was postponed. The suspects were moving across the state and were being followed. A new strategy would unfold depending on where the perpetrators settled. For now, his life was on hold. Marcus and the crew evacuated Pogonip, and issued a thumbs-up for Garrett to fly him and Jude to New York for scheduled business meetings.

****

The meeting ended in the early evening and Garrett met Jude and him for dinner. Waiting for the maître d' to seat them, Lisa sauntered over.

"Mind if I join you guys?"

"Of course, wouldn't have it any other way." Kyle kissed one cheek, then the other. Garrett and Jude greeted her the same way.

Lisa reminisced about their childhood together, the parties her parents held. Hell, she even had Garrett laughing with nostalgia.

Kyle forked the last bite of grilled trout. "Do you remember at the clam bake when Lisa lost her bathing suit top in the ocean after she dove under a wave?" Then he popped the morsel in his mouth, grinning and waiting for everyone's reactions.

Garrett nodded. "I remember. She stayed in the water till, who was it finally got her a towel?"

Kyle grunted. "Not me, I wanted to see how long she could stay there. Revenge for when you stole my trunks when I went skinny dipping earlier that summer."

Jude's eyes widen. "I forgot about that. Sarah rescued her, when she realized why she had been in water for so long."

"Mom saved me. I was a wrinkled prune and cold...I nearly froze my...Not one of you lifted a finger to help me and I've never forgiven you guys for it either."

Jude wiped his mouth with the cloth napkin and placed it beside his empty plate. "We were young and foolish, will you forgive us?"

Lisa smiled. "I don't know. You three were not

very nice to me when I needed your help. But I could never stay mad for very long. Of course, I will."

Jude rose. "On that positive note, it's time for me to leave."

Garrett followed. "Same here."

"We could stay and have a few drinks at the bar and dance a little?" Lisa pleaded.

"Nope." Jude and Garrett responded at the same time.

Kyle hadn't had one-on-one time with Lisa in a while. The twenty-something brat had turned into a kinder woman. "Sure, sounds great."

Jude and Garrett kissed Lisa's cheek and said their goodbyes.

Kyle guided Lisa into the dimly lit room, the piano and violin playing soft jazz. He gently helped her petite body up on the stool. She placed her evening purse on the high table for two.

The cocktail waitress appeared. "Would you care for a drink?"

After giving their orders, Lisa asked, her sky-blue eyes hopeful. "Want to dance?"

He flashed back to the gangly girl of ten. Her jet-black hair plaited in a braid, dirt smudged along the smattering of freckles dotting her face asking to play with the guys. Back then, he'd always watched over her, protected her.

Of course, there was more history. Lisa and Christine had become lovers and chose another lifestyle, choices that would eventually be too much for Christine to live with. He'd finished his masters, withdrew from life into the bottle, until he had enough of alcohol-dazed memories. Then he had joined the

Navy, never looking back.

When he'd returned from his last mission, Lisa made a special point in contacting him. He'd helped her come to terms with what had happened. Life had a strange way of healing, at least for her. How could he refuse a simple dance with a long-time friend?

Although her feet gracefully caught her weight when she slid from the chair, he balanced her frame with his hands on her waist. He led her to the waxed floor, grasped her fingers and with his palm gently held the small of her back.

Moving to the music, he wished that Shelby was in his arms instead of Lisa. He missed Shelby. Her note designating him as a friend had sliced open new wounds he'd rather not analyze. He wanted her as a lover, a committed partner, a woman to share his days and nights, a wife.

A shudder traveled down his spine and landed low in his belly. His stomach tensed. What he truly wanted, she had denied him outright, walked away, and refused to answer his calls. Damn, he should be able to change her mind. There was only one way to alter her course to his benefit, mind walking, and admitting his desire to do so, ripped his soul apart.

No, he wouldn't use his ability. He'd given an oath, a vow. Besides that, he didn't want to alter Shelby's path. She had to freely give herself to him, relinquishing her body and spirit for a lifetime commitment. He wanted, no, *needed* the bond that would last not only here on earth, but in the next world, the First Realm.

Earlier, while waiting to be seated, he'd asked Garrett to head to Texas for a surprise visit. Of course,

Jude in his brief interrogation inquired exactly how he had planned to get back with Shelby. He didn't have a clue, but he'd think of something. With a brief, okay, it was damn well skimpy game plan, he relaxed.

Lisa laid her cheek against his chest. She stopped dancing, stood on her tiptoes and kissed the skin between the V of his shirt, making her way to his throat.

He released her and took one step back. "Don't. I'm in love with another woman."

Her chin lowered. "Are you speaking of Shelby?"

He shuffled marking more distance between them. "Yes."

"She's a lucky woman. Let's sit down for a while."

The last call issued, Kyle dropped from his stool and stumbled, but gained his feet again. The room spun. He grasped the table for support. "Whaa tha he-ell? Jus thwo dreenks...all naght."

Lisa steadied and lowered him to his seat. "I'll ask the maître d' for a cab."

****

Kyle blinked to relieve the blurry sheen covering his eyes. The sun's rays and heat penetrated through the windows. His head throbbed as he attempted to rise from the bed then fell to his back again. He studied his surroundings. Kyle panned the room with no recognition of where he was.

He lifted his back off the mattress. His abdomen muscles clenched holding a half sit-up. Kyle quickly placed his elbows to brace his upper body. Movement to his left drew his attention and the lacy cover drifted down revealing the small bump underneath the pink quilt.

"Lisa?" He licked his parched lips.

She stretched. "Good morning, how are you feeling?"

"What in the hell happened?"

"You don't recall?"

"Redundant question." He clenched his jaws together from the pounding headache.

"Oh my, you are grouchy this morning."

"Well?"

"You're breaking my heart. You wanted to get back together." Her seductive voice cooed. "You sure do know how to make a woman happy. You're an exquisite lover."

"What the hell are you talking about?"

"You asked me to call and break up with my fiancé, Bill, last night." Her lower lip pouted. "I'm truly hurt you don't remember."

He flung the covers off then slung his feet to the floor and sat. He swayed, waiting for his equilibrium to balance. Kyle peered at his body. He was buck naked. First thing in the morning, he normally had a boner, but his cock was flaccid. Strange he'd noticed that.

"My head is killing me." He rested his elbows on his knees, cradled his forehead in his palms. "This isn't good."

Lisa bounced out of bed. "Let me get you some aspirin and water."

The mattress coils rebounded, his belly churned, and he moaned. His pulse surged under an intense heart palpitation. He took a deep breath to level out the rapid beats. What Lisa told him didn't add up. His love for Shelby coursed through his veins into the very marrow of his bones. *What did I just do? What am I going to tell*

Shel and how am I to explain this to her?

Lisa returned without a fucking stitch of clothing on, he grimaced. She'd tried to hand him a glass and two pills, which he refused, then she bent down to kiss him.

Any other time when he accompanied women home and stayed the night, he would have initiated morning sex. His mind and his dick were in agreement, there was only one woman who rang his chimes. He turned away. "No. Don't. I don't know if you are telling me the truth, but I can assure you nothing will happen ever again. You should call your intended and try to make amends. I'm getting the hell out of here."

He stood. The room spun. This wasn't a hangover, it was something else.

"What are you saying? You said you loved me, not Shelby."

He fumbled into his pants, tucking his shirt tail inside his jeans. As he tugged, the metal zipper filled the silence because he declined to acknowledge such an inane comment.

"Please don't leave. I'll make some breakfast."

When he bent down to pull his boots on, his eyes watered. Thank God, they slipped on with relative ease. He found his cell and tapped Jude's speed number.

Without any modesty, she claimed a spot right in front of him. "Why are you being like this? Talk to me."

His brother's leave a message routine echoed in his ear. He gave Lisa his best go-to-hell look, which was pretty easy considering his state of mind and left.

Through the closed door, Lisa ranted. "You bastard, I loved you both with all my heart and soul.

We wanted you in our bed, not your stupid college friend, but you returned home early and destroyed my dreams. I would've done anything for you and for her. I wanted to be your sub." Then she cried out, "Christine, I miss you."

****

Kyle unlocked the door to his Manhattan penthouse apartment. The click of the deadbolt reverberated inside his head like a jack hammer breaking concrete. He wanted a shower and to lay his aching body down.

Jude lips curled into a smirk.

The ones he wanted to slap.

"Girl in every city?"

Yep, he would've liked to smack the shit-eating-grin off his face. "Something happened last night."

Jude gazed from his hand-combed hair to the eel boots that were now scuffed beyond repair. "Yeah, I would say so, thought you decided not to dip in that well again?"

"Kiss my—"

"Problem?"

He sighed. "I think Lisa gave me a mickey, a GHB, a fucking date drug. She told me we were together last night. I had two drinks all evening, and I don't have any recollection after the first thirty minutes at the bar."

Jude stoned his features. "You do understand the implications you are making?"

Kyle clenched his fists at his side. Sometimes Jude really pissed him off. "I'm fully aware."

"What are you going to do?"

"I can't prove a damn thing, so nothing, for right now. After we're done here, we're going to Texas."

Jude's brows drew together. "Are you sure that's

wise?"

Kyle shrugged. "Got to."

Garrett rose. "I'll get a flight plan scheduled and filed, when did you want to leave?"

"First thing tomorrow morning. We have a few more things to finish up here and I have a feeling I'll need tonight to get over this shit-ass headache."

Jude ran his hand through his military style haircut. "Think you can make it through the meetings this afternoon?"

"Yeah, but I'm going to lie down for a few hours." Out of the corner of his eye, Garrett had grasped the edge of the desk with both hands and sweat beaded his brow.

Kyle waited until Garrett relaxed. "A vision?"

"Yeah."

"Anything I need to know about?"

Garrett nodded. "I'm inclined to agree with you about Lisa. My images appeared like an old-time silent movie, you seem to be unaware of what's happening. At the bar, you are dancing and in the next sequences, your head is on Lisa's lap in a limo."

Garrett bit his lower lip then released it. "Your boots skidded across the concrete and marble tile. She had help getting you to her condo and your clothes off. They put you in a bed. A damn frilly one, I might add."

Garrett heaved. "I have to interpret the scenes, but I'm positive you were unconscious."

"I knew she played games, but not like this." Kyle shook his head once, then wished he hadn't.

Jude rose from the couch and growled. "You guys are full of shit."

Jude's eyes met Garrett's with condemnation.

"Visions."

Then his gaze panned to him with the same reproach. "Mind-walking." He whirled a one-eighty and strode to the door. "I'm fucking out of here. See you at four."

"Don't—" The door slammed shut. Kyle winced as the sound waves vibrated in his head, bouncing from one side to the other, then echoed in his ears. "—slam the door."

Garrett's eyebrow rose.

Kyle nodded. "One day he'll understand. Until that time comes, he's hell to live with."

That night, Kyle hung up with his conspirator in arms. Alessa had said Joni was in town, staying with Shelby and Joni would help. Together, they had come up with a plan, an impromptu barbeque dinner with friends. He'd rent a car and follow Alessa to Shelby's ranch.

The sisters reveled in their devious scheme. According to them, Shelby hadn't been the same since she returned from Wyoming. As much as he hated Shelby not doing well, he savored the idea that she'd had problems adjusting without him. It was like drinking an ice-cold beer on a hot, summer day, hydrating with liquid, but not quenching the thirst. The only way to relieve his dry mouth was to see Shelby, to ask for another chance, hold her again and never let go.

Chapter Twenty-One

Shelby placed the wine glasses on the counter and hoped she'd get through the evening.

Joni strode to the door. "Alessa and her friends just arrived. I'll help bring in the food."

Shelby inched her chin higher to acknowledge Joni.

"Why don't you open some Spanish red?"

"Got it." She trudged to the tiny wine room, more like a closet, but it was hers. The red digital temperature and humidity gauge read the space was perfect. She grabbed a bottle and plodded back to the kitchen.

Her sisters had been worried about her and she guessed this get together was for her benefit. She appreciated their concern, but wasn't in the mood for a supper gathering.

All she wanted to do tonight was to get a shower, read a book, preferably in her T-shirt and shorts. She sighed. Sprawled across her bed with pillows behind her back would be heaven, but that would have to come later.

They were driving her crazy. If her siblings didn't leave her alone soon, she'd take a week off and go be somewhere, anywhere.

She shook her head, yesterday was a prime example. They took her and her step grandchildren to see a comedy. Joni jabbed her elbow in her side to join in the laughter. She'd laughed and wanted to reciprocate the loving gesture except with a little more enthusiasm. Maybe then, she'd get a reprieve. Of course the children were oblivious, in their own cute worlds, enjoying the time with their aunts, but for her, the outing proved tiresome.

Her energy had hit the lowest level in years. She recognized the symptoms of emotional withdrawal; nonetheless, she didn't have the strength or fortitude to put the pieces of her heart together again. Maybe when she felt a little stronger, she'd forget the two men who had taken a piece of her soul. For right now, dark clouds with thunder and lightning stormed inside her mind and body. Unlike what glared at her through the window at this very second. The sun shone, the wispy clouds floated against the azure sky, she grasped the bottle tighter. She could get through this.

The commotion at the front door let her know Alessa's friends had arrived. She pasted a grin then her lips flattened in a straight line. Fake smiles wouldn't get her any brownie points and she wanted her sisters to stop hovering. She wiggled her cheeks, drew in a deep breath and tried again. Yep, this should work. Since she was a happy drinker, after a couple glasses of wine, the bogus act would come naturally.

Alessa yelled, "We have enough food to feed the cowboys on a month-long cattle drive."

Shelby shook her head and spun to help. "You always buy too much food. That's par for the—"

Jude held a sack in each arm. "We couldn't resist. Hope you don't mind?"

"Of course not, you're always welcome here."

Garrett peeked around Jude. "Me too?"

"You too."

She panned the room and zeroed in on Kyle. Awareness scuttled around her heart, she did an about face unwilling to define what was in his eyes. "I'll pour the wine, who would like some?"

Joni stepped up. "I'll do it. Alessa, would you start putting the food on the table?"

Jude and Garrett volunteered to help, removing the barbecue from the paper bags, leaving Shelby to weather the uneasy air floating in the room.

"I'll get some more wine." Shelby sidestepped Kyle.

Kyle's footsteps followed her. Her hand shook as she touched one bottle then the next, picking up a Tempranillo, she put it back. Or did she open a Rioja?

Kyle inched his way until he was beside her. He placed his palm over hers, settling the wine back on the rack. "You're trembling, baby, I'm—"

"Shh, Pressley."

Moisture welled. She blinked to keep the tears at bay. Unsuccessful, a stream ran down both cheeks, dropping on her blouse. Kyle gently grasped her shoulders and turned her to face him. He cradled his hands around her jawline and wiped the salty liquid with both thumbs.

She scrunched her eyelids shut. His touch radiated warmth, caring, and yes, she could feel his love. How was it possible? Her soul brightened with his light, the ugly storm was gone. With a simple brush of his fingers, a beacon of renewal shined. Her spirit wanted to hang on to his lifesaving gift. But she had to remember, this was the same man who could take her down to the pits of emotional hell. For survival, she had to be strong, without him. Did she have the strength?

He whispered, "I was an asshole, forgive—"

"Is that why you came?" She opened her eyes, squared her shoulders, taking one step away from him. "It doesn't matter. You're forgiven. Your work is done here so go back to the crew. I'll be there in a few minutes."

She needed more time than that to get it together, maybe a walk would help. To see him again, all the pain and sorrow roared back to life, rearing its hideous head, making fun of her failures. The lack of success surrounded her on a daily basis. Every day her inadequacies seared her skin and zapped her strength.

The knowledge of Chris paying a crony to kill Tim crushed her. Then the five-star general blackmailing her if she didn't follow through with his orders grated against everything she stood for.

She'd turned her back on the visions of the medicine man, walked away from the miscarriage of justice with Ten-Butterflies' baby and the infant to come. Shelby refused to believe she could handle the First Realm's quest and succumbed to the belief she could do nothing about the wretched curse of her Comanche grandfather.

The latter crawled all over her. Her spirit guide revealed she and her sisters were direct descendants of the nefarious man who used black magic against his own family. She didn't see any recourse but to accept what had been handed down by numerous generations.

Her hand traveled toward Kyle, and her palm rested over his heart. A significant milestone occurred, Shelby finally admitted she still loved Kyle even though he had hurt her and broke her heart. Of course, she would forgive him.

The problems they were encountering weren't his fault or hers. All of their strife had derived from a baneful man, her ancestor. They had wonderful times together enjoying passion and devotion, but their relationship had been doomed from the beginning.

"You are not to blame for any of this. At Garrett's, you were only trying to protect me. Although, I would've preferred a nicer response from you, but I understand you had more things on your mind than me." She nudged him marking additional distance.

"Don't push me away, not yet. Hear me out."

She stiffened then spun to face the wine rack, focusing on the myriad of colored wine tops.

His palms lightly touched her waist and she shoved them away. "No." To let Kyle pursue her would only lead to more heartache. The dictates of her forefather burned, grinding her soul to dust. She had to follow them to protect Kyle, to safeguard her love for him.

"Shel, I'm here to apologize. I'm used to people following my orders to the letter, without question and without me drawing a line for the boundaries. Yes, I had a lot on my mind, but that doesn't give me any excuses for how I acted. I blew it, but we deserve to be happy, together."

Shelby wheeled to face Kyle, raised her hand for him to cease. Anger coursed to every nerve ending, the hairs on the back of her neck rose. "Let me get this straight. You were angry because I didn't march to your tune? I'm not employed by Pressley International, nor am I a member of the Navy. You're a presumptuous man and you better get a grip on relationships."

"That's why I'm here. To tell you I made a

mistake."

Kyle knew he was wrong and was man enough to face her. He deserved to leave Texas with a clear conscience. She sighed. "We've all made mistakes, including me. I'm just as accountable for my actions."

Air hissed out of his lungs. "Thanks." Kyle pivoted, his boot heels striking the floor.

That's what she wanted...right? She lowered her chin, wrapped her arms around her waist and sniffed. No, that's not what she wanted.

"Will you forgive me?"

Kyle stopped. His footsteps were quiet as he closed the space between them.

His arms gently embraced her. A sob wrenched from her throat while his chest absorbed the horrible sound. He drew small comforting circles on the small of her back.

He murmured near her ear. "God, I've missed holding you."

She couldn't answer him except to nod. She missed his touch, his love and his sweet spirit. He was a take charge kind of guy and had to be to survive. Everyone had some control issues, including her. So they were going to tangle every once in a while. She was okay with that. Having come to that decision and along with his tender ministrations, her cries abated. She had buried her face under his jacket. His shirt was wet from her tears. She squeezed him. "I've never stopped loving you."

He eased backed with his palms planted on her hips. "Same here."

She met his gaze. Desire flamed in his eyes then something else, but it was gone before she could pinpoint the emotion. She swiped away the last remnants of moisture from her cheeks.

There it was again. "What are you thinking?"

He gathered her hands. "How is it that we can profess our love without any conditions and yet, we continue to hurt one another by our insecurities and our past history? What is the answer?"

She shrugged.

"Faith."

"What do you mean?" Her nerves were already wired, exponentially growing as he talked in riddles. His explanation would either kill her by breaking the pieces of her heart into tinier ones. If he did that, she would not survive. She wasn't the Brave-One. In fact, she was dying a small death with each second that ticked time from her life. Or would he give her a lifeline to hold onto? She hoped for a reprieve so she could live in peace. At least until the day when Dr. Chris Humphreys demanded she betray the First Realm, the spirit guides, and worst of all, Kyle.

"A belief if you will, a confidence that we can persevere through all of our problems together. A trust in that no matter what happens, we will stay and fight on the frontlines for each other. I'd call it an allegiance, a vow, and one hell-of-a promise. It'll be a bond that will be tested and stretched to our physical, emotional, and mental limits. However, the binding will never break because we'll be one, not only here on earth but in the First Realm. You have my assurance the trials will be considerable and tough to pull through. On the other hand, we'll have each other's back and the love in our hearts safely held in our souls. Do you believe we can do that for each other?"

His dark chocolate gaze searched, and at the same time, demanded an answer. His words made sense. They were beautiful, warming, and supportive. Her heavy heart responded becoming lighter. Her soul grasped for the beacon radiating from Kyle, the glimmer of hope she wanted desperately.

She blinked long. "Yes."

A flute played the notes she was familiar with. She-Who-Smiles centered inside her. "Brave-One, he speaks the truth."

"I know." Shelby grinned. Kyle had never lied to her and the special connection they shared was the real deal. The black hole within had been sucking her deeper into its depths, but Kyle had reversed the vacuum, releasing her bit by bit. She marveled at his ability to save her.

He dropped to one knee. "Will you do me the honor of marrying me? Will you be my wife, my woman, my soul mate for eternity?"

She stared in disbelief, stunned and speechless.

His brows shot several inches higher. "Do I need to repeat my question?"

"No," she whispered.

"Is that your–?" He jumped up, standing sure footed. "No, don't answer. You're hesitating, why?"

"What do you mean soul mate for eternity?"

His eyes panned the small room then the intense gaze met hers. "If Ten-Blue-Sun's stone illuminates when we marry, we'll be united forever. After our life on earth is complete, we'll be together in the First Realm, at our special place." He winked.

"Oh." She shook her head. "Wait. Let's talk about this life first. We have monumental disagreements.

What makes you think we can survive a marriage here on earth when we fight all the time?"

He hugged her and kissed her temple. His moist breath brushed across her ear. "We are driven by commitments. When we make a vow, we'll fight, but it'll be for one another. Remember what I said, we'll be tested beyond what any other normal couple could or would endure. The two things that will be in our favor are our spirit guides and us, you and me."

She blew out her breath. "I can't just walk away from my business."

Kyle eased back, his brown eyes connecting once again with hers, his hands settled on her shoulders. "That's it baby. Take one step at a time. I talked with Alessa, she seemed to think everything can be done by the net and telephone. After all, she's been running the corporation every time you were with me. You can come back here any time you want. I'll make sure of it. Is anything else worrying you?"

"Alessa? Who else do you have in your pocket? Never mind, I'll deal with her later. Come back here?"

"Well, I live in Wyoming."

Her voice quivered, "Oh God." *Nearer to Chris?* She didn't think that was a smart idea.

"Right, how about Texas in the winter and my home for the other three seasons?"

"I don't know." Heat scorched her shoulders reminding her to keep her mouth shut. The five-star general had long-ass talons.

"I have other houses in the States, Canada, and along each coastline, penthouses, several villas and flats abroad. You can choose any of them. Just as long as we're together, I don't care."

"You have that many and you prefer Wyoming?"

"Yes."

What if the wooden doll's crystal didn't light? She had to protect Kyle against Chris and save her family. Death was the likely outcome for her, but she wouldn't involve Kyle. She had to give him a reason to leave, to shield Kyle from the five-star general. "I feel like a fool. You deserve someone else, someone who understands your circles. I'm not cut from the same cloth. I've made terrible mistakes since I've met you. I thought I was a strong person, confident about who I am and what I wanted in life. But we have issues we'll never win, even together."

"Issues?"

"It doesn't matter."

"It does to me. I'll come back to that. I never told you how many places I own. Besides, I think you're a confident, smart, and a passionate woman. As for my family and business, that's who I am. If you accept me then you'll have to take that part too. I'm a low profile person and I don't run with the elite crowds having parties to be seen and heard. You'll do fine. Now, what else is on your mind?"

"Lisa, what is she to you?"

He hesitated. "She's a family friend, we grew up together and I don't want her. I love you. What else is bothering you?"

"What happened with the sting? Did you catch, whoever?"

"No, not yet. It's been postponed, but we'll be okay." He raised his eyebrows for the next hurdle.

"My grandchildren?"

"I'd like them to be a part of our lives. If they are

allowed to come during school breaks, we could show them a good time. Is there anything more?"

Her chin cranked up a notch. "Yes, everything imaginable is against us."

He squinted, drawing his brows together, furrowing lines crossed his forehead. "The issues…What are you talking about?"

Good, she had his full attention now. "When I was more of a positive person, She-Who-Smiles and Bear-Claws shared with me. Do you believe in reincarnation?"

He nodded whether he was agreeing or for her to continue she couldn't tell so she forged ahead. "We have been." Then she waited.

He schooled his facial features. "Go on."

"Remember when I told you about Many-Horses' second wife? She was a Comanche and her father, Tall-Man put a curse on her husband and his linage. Well, you're a Shoshone descendant of Many-Horses and I'm…" Tears welled and for the life of her, she couldn't maintain composure.

Her spirit guide always told the truth. It was hard to accept that she was a Comanche, a direct descendant of Tall-Man and the implications surrounding that revelation. Her sisters thought she had lost her will to live, but she'd still been trying to grasp that losing Kyle evolved directly from her ancestor. Choking down that bitter pill had left her empty. Slowly, she'd come to terms with who she was and why her relationship with Kyle should have ended a long time ago. Simply because…of who she was.

His hand lifted to touch her face and as though he thought better of it, he lowered his arm to his side.

"Comanche, yes I know. I'm well aware of my previous life and yours. That's what I was talking about a few moments ago. We won't be able to come back."

An uncontrolled gasp escaped. Screw coming back, she had to deal with now. "Then why did you ask me to marry you, knowing our lives are cursed and will be a living hell?"

Kyle extended his palm and caressed her cheek. "You're not worried about reincarnation? I thought you still wanted to…Never mind. We'll be blessed because of our true love and the possession of Ten-Blue-Sun. Have you accepted that the life bringer belongs to you, to us and our future, until the time comes when the doll will be forwarded?"

"Yes." And she did. Although Kyle made the situation seem black and white, she definitely had all the shades of gray blending into a dismal picture.

"We're an integral part of the spiritual battle that lies ahead, the steps are out of our hands. We can persevere, win this bloody war, and maybe find out who killed Tim, but the question remains, are you ready to stand with me, unified in spirit, as well as our bodies?"

He released her, gathered her hands and rested one knee on the floor. "Will you do me the honor of becoming my wife, Brave-One?" He winked. "I'll give a good bride price."

She whispered, "Mind-Walker, you know my name?"

"Yes, baby, I do and you know mine."

"What does yours mean?"

"Walking through minds is my gift from the Great Spirit. I don't use it anymore. Although, I did slip into yours one time. I was at one with your conscious and unconsciousness, your feelings, your very thoughts, I understood. I have the ability to change someone's actions by simply entering and giving them a nudge. Unlike others, when I was in your mental processes, you flow around, through and in me. To be honest, I miss being there with you."

Her spine straightened. "When did you do this?"

Kyle grasped her wrists and exhaled a long sigh. "The first time you visited my home. That's one of the reasons I shoved you away. I broke my oath."

"I wasn't aware, was I?"

He grinned. "No, but our spirits are connected because once, while you were in the throes of passion you called me Mind-Walker. You weren't cognizant that you said my name."

"I'm not aware of a lot of things when we make love. Do other people know you're inside their minds?"

"I choose whether they know or not."

She stilled as the memory of him taking his hand away paralyzed her, his haunted eyes, his words, telling her to leave. Now, she understood. "I made you break—"

"No." He stood. "You didn't make me do anything."

Kyle's eyes reaffirmed what he had said. They bored into her soul attesting to his declaration then gentled.

She lowered her chin. "As much as I love you, we shouldn't be together."

He cradled her jawline with his palm, lifting until she fixed on his gaze. "Maybe we are right for each other, destined to be together and to have our spirits

281

united to help in the upcoming battle. I can't ignore Ten-Blue-Sun's presence or that when we marry, our lineage will be joined again to protect a baby, Little-Dove-Feathers. In the end, it's your decision. But understand this—I want to give a life-long commitment to you, hope for our families, and to fill you with my love. Will you become one with me? And by all that I am, I hope it is forever."

Moved by his simple touch, his loving words and the connection, she smiled. The execrable emptiness inside was gone and Kyle's light filled the once barren recesses. She knew this was right. Shelby nodded and hugged him, capturing his warmth, his spirit and best of all, him.

He released her, plucking out a velvet box from his jacket pocket and opened it. Inside, a marquis-shaped yellow diamond with baguettes glistened on both sides of the single setting. "Alessa helped me on the ring size."

"It's beautiful."

"Are you ready to take off his wedding band?"

The memories of Tim rushed back. Her vision blurred as tears spilled into her eyes again. A hiccup followed and she bowed her head to her chest. "This is hard."

Kyle stilled. "I know. I'm not going to remove his ring. This is something you must do."

She inched her chin up until she gazed into the liquid depth of his brown eyes.

He closed the velvet top, tucking the case back into his pocket. His lips thinned. "I won't compete with him or his memories. You can't wear both and I can see you're not ready to give up his for mine."

Her voice quivered, tension raced to each individual cell. Even the roots of her hair tingled. "He was my other half. I never realized the strength he gave me and I didn't recognize…comprehend that until…When he passed, a part of me died with him. The days were long and the nights…an eternity, cold and dark. I've traveled a long road to fit into this world without him. He'll always be here." She rested the heel of her palm over her breast. "Safe in my heart and I'll never let him go. That's why I know you'll understand when I take his ring off, he'll still be a part of me."

"I don't want to take him away from you. I love all of you, not just bits and pieces. He had a part in making who you are today and that's the person I want."

She clasped the band and slid it off. Grasped between her finger and thumb, a symbol of a never ending circle for this life, she sighed. "I didn't think it would be this hard."

"You don't have—"

"No. Please." She slipped the ring into her jean pocket. "I've loved two men in my life. One has gone to another realm, I can no longer share. The other stands before me. You have my heart, my spirit, and you have filled me with a light that has saved my soul from eternal darkness. This you should know, there will come a time when you'll think I have betrayed you. I can only hope you will stand by me."

Kyle cloaked Shelby in an embrace. "I'll always be here for you."

He drew the comforting circles on her lower back. After a few silent moments, Kyle murmured in her ear, "Are you ready?"

She nodded.

He slipped the ring out of the box and slid the setting on her finger. "I'm glad you made the decision to be with me in this life and possibly for eternity."

"So am I."

Shelby threaded her fingers in his. "I love you."

"Me too, baby. From now on, you're mine. Damn, I'm a fuck—"

"Stop with the F bombs."

"I can do that." He laughed then cocked his head to the side. "Does this mean you'll tell me your birthday now?"

She shook her head. "Not yet."

His hands slid down her arms then meandered to her waist. "I stopped the private investigators from telling me your age. They thought I had lost my mind." He chuckled. "You're going to tell me someday, and I'm a patient man, Shelby Littleton." He nodded toward their families. "You ready to tell them."

"You'll have to...I don't know if I can, without bursting into tears again."

He released his hold, gently guided her by the small of her back to the dining table. Silence filled the room.

Kyle cleared his throat. "We would like to make an announcement." His luscious lip smile spread across his entire face setting off both dimples on each side. "We're tying the knot."

Cheers echoed along with the congratulatory hugs and cheek kisses of best wishes.

Alessa piped, "Took y'all long enough to figure out what everyone else already knew. You were made for one another. I have an idea. After you and Kyle eat, let's all go to Austin to celebrate."

Kyle pulled back a chair from the table for her. "Not a bad idea. Shel, do you feel like driving?"

"Sure."

Jude offered, "Joni and Alessa can hitch a ride with us in the rental and leave you two lovebirds alone."

Kyle grabbed a plate, forking the meat from the platter. "Deal."

After they ate, the guys helped stow the leftovers in the refrigerator. She and Kyle were the last ones out the door and met the crew waiting for them. On the driveway, Shelby questioned how well Garrett and Alessa would get along.

Garrett grasped Jude's elbow. "You're going to make me sit with her?"

Alessa stilled.

Jude glanced at his arm then to Garrett. "You're very astute this evening."

Alessa's eyes squinted. "Never mind, I'll take my own car." She wheeled, strode to her sports car, got in and sped away.

With Joni settled in the front seat, Jude closed the passenger door. "Way to go, Blackwell." He sauntered around the vehicle then slid behind the wheel.

Garrett shook his head and folded his very large frame in the back. He patted Joni on the shoulder saying something, maybe an apology she didn't know.

Chapter Twenty-Two

Kyle danced with the love of his life in his arms as the live band strummed a slow number. Across the way, Jude nestled Joni the same way while Garrett and Alessa sat at the table ignoring one another.

Even though the country-western bar was smoke-free, the smell of liquor mixed in with everyone's cologne and perfume filled the air. He lowered his head to Shelby's ear. Ahh, that's what he liked. Honey filtered to his nostrils. Inhaling her feminine, sweet spring scent, he edged her closer. She melted against him from her head to her thighs. He liked her hips snug to his groin, so did his cock. He'd have to think of something else before his boner would become public knowledge.

Earlier, when Shelby had asked him about Lisa, he wanted to discuss what had happened in New York, but hesitated. She'd set enough hurdles for him to jump over, for a whole damn track team. He would tell her at a later time. The years of Lisa's friendship had come to a screeching halt after what he figured she'd done, and to his way of thinking, Garrett's vision confirmed his suspicions. Lisa had crossed the line one too many times for him to turn the other cheek.

After he closed the door to her Manhattan apartment, Lisa sounded like a lunatic professing her love for him and Christine. Lisa had been the third with

Christine and his buddy. Although he accepted the people who made different lifestyle choices, that wasn't his. He'd tolerated Lisa throughout the years, understood she and Christine had a bond, but Lisa manipulated him. She lacked character, honor, and as far as he was concerned, all ties had been severed.

Shelby angled backward while her hands cradled the nape of his neck. "Are you okay?"

He cleared his throat. "Fine."

She tilted her head to the side and her palms cradled his jawline. "You're keeping something from me, Pressley. Your whole body tensed and you lost your erection."

Well at least he was successful at one thing. "Baby, losing my hard-on is probably a good thing right about now."

Shelby stopped in the middle of a step. Standing on her tiptoes, she inclined her lips to meet his.

He accommodated Shelby's wishes, lavishing his attention on her mouth. His tongue swept across her moist flesh, she opened and he tasted wine and welcomed her affection, her love. Damn, it didn't take long for him to respond to Shel.

Breaking contact, he whispered, "I'm so hard, wanting to be inside you, wanting your wet warmth surrounding me. Damn baby, I better sit down, and you need to lead the way."

"You got it cowboy."

Kyle held the chair for Shelby. Once she settled, he maneuvered his seat a little behind hers. He laid his arm over her shoulders and crossed his legs to hide the bulge straining against his zipper.

Garrett asked Alessa. "Would you like to dance?"

Al turned to face him. "I know you don't like me so leave it alone."

The hostility between them weighted the air until a gentleman sidled next to Alessa. "I'd like to dance with the gal unless she's with you."

Alessa stood. "I'd love to and he's not with me."

After several lively tunes, the cowboy guided Al back to their table and she introduced him as Travis. The young man sat beside Alessa.

Kyle balanced backwards in his chair until the two back legs carried his weight. He listened to the banter between the three sisters.

That's when Kyle noticed Garrett's stone face. His jaw clenched, and the pulse at his throat kicked into high gear. "Garrett?"

Garrett's gaze traveled to Travis, then met Kyle's again and shook his head. Garrett's alert eyes and an ancestral gift of keen awareness had noted something with Alessa's new friend.

Kyle nodded once to let him know he understood.

Another slow number thrummed, Travis led Alessa to the dance floor embracing her with too much familiarity in his opinion.

Garrett mumbled. "Not in this lifetime." He unfolded from his seat, strode to the couple and tapped Travis' shoulder.

Above the din of the music, Alessa answered, "No."

Travis puzzled by the situation relinquished Alessa to Garrett. Garrett clasped her arm and drew her flush with his body.

"Baby, did you just see that?"

Shelby smiled. "Yes. They're polar opposites, like

oil and water, but I think they look good together and would make pretty babies. Our niece or nephew would be beautiful with Garrett's black hair and Alessa's blue eyes or her blonde hair with his dark ones."

"Yeah, a little person, that'd be cool. Did you ever make up your mind about wanting children?"

Her eyebrows scooted higher. "Is this a decision that needs to be made right now?"

He chuckled. "No."

"Good. Now tell me what happened between you and Garrett that has to do with Travis."

Shelby honed in on everything. Maybe she could warn Alessa. "We want Al to stay away from the guy. Can you talk to her?"

"She's an adult and makes her own decisions, but I'll mention your concerns before we leave."

"Speaking of which, are you ready to go?"

"Yes, definitely. I have a wonderful cowboy, who I haven't seen in a really long time, and he and I have some major catching up to do."

His dick twitched. And he knew exactly how he wanted to make up for time lost, in several positions, all night long.

With his hand at Shelby's elbow, he helped her stand and bid everyone good evening. "Garrett, want us to drop you off at the hotel?"

Garrett stood. "I'd appreciate the ride."

Shelby grabbed her purse. "Alessa and I have to use the ladies' room and we'll meet you two at the front door."

Kyle whispered, "Good luck."

****

Kyle was in hog heaven. He had his brothers and

soon to be sisters sitting on Garrett's back patio, burgers on the grill, with drinks in hand.

Garrett raised his glass to toast. "To my favorite couple at Pogonip."

Annie groaned and rolled on her back, her feet raised in the air enjoying the peaceful evening.

Everyone laughed then cheered, "Here. Here."

Kyle squeezed Shelby's hand. She had blossomed the last several months. With the May wedding only three days away, she seemed relaxed. She and Joni had meticulously planned the details of the intimate ceremony to be held at an upscale restaurant. His requests and preferences had transformed Shelby into a tiger to insure he'd receive them. Conversely, whatever she wanted he commandeered anything and anyone to have her wishes met.

Joni had insisted on being their wedding coordinator because of her successful business on the west coast called Your Dreams Come True. The lady had connections. They'd agreed, with Joni's assurance, she wouldn't be taking time away from her clients and would conduct most of the details from her office in California.

Her clientele waited months to schedule around her openings. Joni demanded perfection from herself, as well as her vendors, insisting on impeccable service and products. The multi-million dollar weddings she planned required months of preparations and Joni had assured Shelby she could handle theirs with ease.

He understood why women liked a big blow-out celebration, but he'd been pleased when Shelby favored a more personal and family-oriented day. A piano maestro would play before they said their vows and during dinner. He'd hired a local country and western band for the evening dancing.

She'd tied up all the loose ends in Texas. Shelby had been completely flummoxed when she had to hire two people to replace Alessa's position. She promoted Al to president and had transferred the majority of the company stock to her.

Kyle winked at Shelby. "To my family."

"Salud." Everyone echoed.

Jude followed. "To Shelby, may you have the patience of Job. You're going to need it."

Alessa and Joni raised their goblets, but didn't speak while Garrett boldly proclaimed the cheer.

Alessa stood. "To my brothers." She pivoted toward Garrett, her eyes squinted and everyone stilled. "All of them."

Garrett's eyes changed from an intense black to a kinder onyx. He smiled and mouthed, "Thank you."

Kyle chuckled. He'd bet a considerable sum of money that if they ever got together, they'd fire up the heavens.

Shelby raised her glass of wine. "I love you all dearly and may you find happiness just as we have."

Tears welled in Joni's eyes and she held the stem, barely audible. "I love you all."

Another female voice rang over Shelby's sister. He recognized it and rose from the chair. Out of the corner of his eye, Jude did the same and grabbed his arm.

"Don't."

Lisa strode toward Garrett, gave him a hug and kissed each jaw. Jude was next then him. She stopped in front of Shelby. "I wanted to extend my congratulations and best wishes personally." She bent down and gave Shelby her right cheek. "You take care of him." And she gave her the other side. "You hear me?"

Shelby replied, "You can count on it."

Lisa straightened. "Kyle, I was hoping you'd allow me to give you and Shelby a party. Just a small get-together of family and friends, a way of saying I'm truly happy for you. Would you let me do that?"

Kyle stalled, what was she up to now? Was she trustworthy? Did he misjudge her in New York? Was he really a victim of foul play? Or did he say and do the things she enumerated on that God awful morning? He couldn't remember what happened. The aches and pains didn't subside until twenty-four hours later and he'd bet his last dollar, the hangover wasn't due to alcohol. He couldn't fault Lisa for his actions unless she was the one who slipped the mickey in his drink.

He'd not dwelled on what she'd said behind her closed door, all of it was history including her. Lisa needed to get on with her life. Only because there never seemed to be the right time or the correct opportunity, he still hadn't told Shel...yet. "It's up to Shelby."

Lisa tilted her head, batting her eye lashes. "Would you please let me do this as a way of making amends?"

Shelby shrugged. "Sure."

Kyle gleaned the admission of guilt and it ruffled his feathers. "Lisa...Never mind. Small, very small. Shelby and I don't want one of your blow-out parties."

Lisa smiled as if the cat ate the canary and strolled over to the grill. "Garrett, would you like to have it here? I noticed you still have some security."

"I'm not the one to ask. Fine with me, if it's all right with them."

Jude hiked up several inches of his jeans and sat. "Not my decision."

Kyle faced Shelby and she answered him with a nod. His stomach jerked.

Lisa beamed. "Great. How about Friday evening? Are you having a bachelor party or a wedding shower?"

Shelby responded. "No wedding shower and no presents."

Kyle slipped in his chair wanting to touch Shelby, needing the physical contact. He clasped his fingers over her thigh. "And no bachelor party, I prefer time with Shel and our family." Kyle had allowed Shelby to choose. Now, Lisa had one more chance to redeem herself. He had a feeling he'd regret this decision.

Garrett flipped the burgers. "I don't think they want that kind of get up. Leave the shindigs to your mom and dad."

"Well, a small get-together would be easier to handle and I'll be sure to mention no gifts."

With the spatula, Garrett chucked the last patty on a serving platter. His fingers tightened on the utensil, his knuckles turned white.

Lisa wrapped her hand over Garrett's. "Are you all right? Garrett? Are you having one of your visions?"

Garrett panted, sweat beaded on his upper lip and brow. "I'm fine. Yeah…It's… I'm going to go upstairs for a bit. Supper is ready. Everyone go ahead and eat. I'll be down later."

Kyle followed Garrett into the house. He wound his arm around Garrett's waist and helped him up the steps to his room and sat him on the bed. "What's going on?"

"I'm experiencing physical and mental exhaustion

after my visions. This one was a bitch, but fucking A, it's not good."

"Shit. What happened?"

"There was a dude with a gun, then he pointed and fired the weapon."

Chills slithered over his body. "Where was it? Who wielded the firearm and what the fuck did he shoot?"

"I can't replay the scenes like I use to. Going from my memory there's no distinguishable facial features and I can't tell the location. The only things I can recall are tree branches and a rental car."

"License? Make or Model?"

"No. Dammit. I'm losing control. You know I have the ability to manage my mental pictures, especially when I fly."

Garrett had the capability to stop the projections and summon them back at his discretion. The gift allowed him to hold and discern each snapshot. He dissected each scene, face and extrapolated where, who and most of the time could analyze motive. Kyle feared the battles of the First Realm had already begun.

Kyle heaved a sigh. "The cause?"

"The last two visions I've been powerless to stop. I'm unable to investigate each illustration."

"A common thread?"

"Each time, Lisa has been the topic of conversation or had been around. What would she have to do with this? She knows about my abilities."

"I'm not liking this one bit. Especially after what she did to me."

Garrett's hands clenched into fists and his angry gaze connected with his. "Three things don't bode well. Her dicking with you. We have a man who will shoot a pistol in our future and the possibility the connection is to Lisa, our supposed fucking friend."

Kyle shook his head. "Get some rest, and we'll try to figure out the mess later." He left Garrett and hoped like hell the vision was wrong.

Chapter Twenty-Three

The next morning Shelby shoveled Julia's southwestern scrambled eggs into her mouth. The spicy dish was delicious, and she'd asked for the recipe.

Dawn had not fully broken, and the crew had gathered in the kitchen watching the flat screen television. Casper's meteorologist promised a beautiful day ahead for the entire state.

Kyle had suggested a ride and Joni added a picnic to his idea. With everyone on board, Garrett texted Grey and his uncle replied, "c u @ daybreak."

By the time they arrived at the stables, Uncle Grey had the horses saddled and he promised if Lisa arrived he'd tell her where to meet them. To be honest, she could do without her presence, but she'd keep the peace.

Once mounted, Garrett led the group. Kyle kept to her side and she was glad he stayed near. More importantly, she appreciated his constant attention to details, both minor and the major ones. What would seem insignificant to some meant the world to her. The day before, he had massaged her temples when a stress headache had pounded her skull until she drifted off to sleep.

During her nap, the restaurant called with a problem. The chef had a death in the family and would be unable to prepare the menu for the wedding. Kyle had telephoned a friend and within the hour had another culinary artist on his way. Shelby could pull a lot of tricks out of the proverbial hat, but she wouldn't have been able to manage that one.

An eagle squawked circling high in the dawn sky, the silhouette contrasted against the bright sapphire blue streaked with pink. A few wispy clouds scattered here and there looked as though an artist had taken a palette knife and dabbed the oils on a canvas.

Annie, who had been diligently following the horses, woofed. A rabbit stood stock still in front of the caravan. The hare had to make a horrifying decision. Eagle or dog, either predator didn't bode well for the furry creature. The long, slender ears laid back, the bunny darted. Annie barked and gave chase. The white-cotton tail nosedived and Annie yelped her frustration. Shelby sighed. One life saved, but the hungry bird of prey had to continue to search for food.

Garrett made a few runs to check on water troughs. Each time, he easily caught up with the slow moving group. Finally arriving at the copse of trees outlining a beautiful stream, Kyle helped her dismount. He took care of the horses while everyone pitched in and unloaded the pack horses, except for Alessa.

This trip was the first time Al and Garrett had been together since the Austin fiasco. Her little sister had been trying to make amends and Shelby was proud of her. Sometimes pride was a hard pill to swallow, but Alessa had. Deep down Shelby had to admit, she wished for them to get together and make babies. Yeah, she was a sucker for romance. Shelby cast a sideways glance watching the couple without being too obvious.

Al held the reins of her horse, waiting for Garrett to

tether the mare. "It's beautiful here." When Garrett didn't respond, she put a hand on her hip. "Look, I'm trying to be civil at least until the wedding is over this Saturday, will you try also? Or should I just not talk to you at all?" Still no answer, Al stomped her foot. "Fine, I've put out the olive branch and you've rejected it."

She released the leather, leaving the horse to munch on the grass. Al spun and walked over to her. "He's so exasperating."

"Just give him his space and don't worry about it. As the host, he has a lot to do."

Alessa swiped her hat off her head and slapped her thigh with it. "I didn't realize talking interfered. You know, you're right, he's taking care of everyone...including me. I'll give him room. And then some."

Kyle reclined supine with his Stetson over his eyes while she lay prone basking in the sun. Everyone had eaten and rested on the pallets placed in a haphazard circle.

Kyle lifted his straw hat. "Let's take a walk along the creek."

Jude jumped to his feet and helped Joni to hers. "I'm going to show Joni the view of the valley from the mountain top.

Shelby hesitated and whispered to Kyle, "That leaves Alessa and Garrett alone. I don't want any trouble two days before our wedding."

Alessa rose. "I'm going for a walk too. See you all later."

Garrett grabbed her arm forcing her to sit again. "I accept your olive branch."

"Fine." She carried her gaze from his hand to his

eyes. "Let go, Blackwell."

"How do you know my last name?"

"We were introduced. You don't pay attention."

"When I want to. What else do you know about me?"

"You're a visionary and your Shoshone Mother named you Lone-Wolf. Your hobbies include your horses, running your ranch, and flying, the latter only because you choose to work, not because you have to. Oh, and I know you don't like me, but I'll survive."

He released Al and this time she sprung to her feet and marked distance between them. "Thanks for accepting my peace offering, but it doesn't give you the right to manhandle me." She briskly strode away.

Garrett rose. His strides were double in length and faster than Alessa's. He quickly caught up, grabbed her arm, and twirled her around, bringing her belly against his hips. He guided both of her legs to straddle his. Catching her bottom, he rubbed her womanly folds against his muscular thigh. He raised one hand to her back, gently pressing her breasts to his chest. Garrett lowered to kiss her, and she spun from him. His other hand caught her jaw, bringing her face to meet his.

Breathy, Al asked, "What in the hell are you doing?"

Garrett chuckled. "Isn't it obvious?"

Kyle grasped Shelby's elbow. "Come. They need to work this out and from the looks of it, privately."

Shelby nodded.

****

On the bank of Live Horse Creek, Shelby relaxed on a quilt beside Kyle. She inhaled, taking in the pleasant scents. The water flowed easily in the middle and burbled against the rocks along the edge while releasing fresh moisture to the air. The spring flowers perky and colorful blanketed the embankment. A cool breeze gently swayed the leaves on the nearby trees and the sunlight danced on the branches of the evergreens.

Shelby folded her arms around her tummy, snuggling against Kyle. "I love this time of year, but it's a little chilly in the shade."

Kyle encircled her. "I can keep you warm."

Her head tilted, looking into the mesmerizing depth of his eyes. "I'd like that."

He chuckled. "Come here." His lips brushed over hers. He lifted then slid her in his lap and enveloped her. "You are cold." Kyle opened his jacket, covering her as she cuddled against his chest. She curled her legs together while Kyle had crossed his making a warm cocoon of body heat.

Shelby rested her head in the crux of his shoulder. "You feel so good." She wiggled her bottom against his groin. "I'm glad we're going to stay at your house for our honeymoon."

Kyle whispered through her hair. "It's our house."

"No."

With his palm, he stroked up and down the length of her spine. "Yes, it is. I made some decisions in addition to the pre-nup you signed. I'm giving a gift to you. As soon as we are married, the house and the surrounding land become yours, but I am keeping the mineral rights."

She sucked a deep breath.

"Before you say anything to me, just listen. I want to do things for you and I will. You can be cognizant of it or I can hide what I do for you until you eventually find out. But I don't want to go behind your back. I want to be able to tell you everything without you berating me for my decisions. Mine, baby. And you're not going to change my mind."

"I don't want you to conceal anything from me." She struggled to sit upright and faced him. "It's not right for you to make arrangements without my input. Can we not do these things together?"

Kyle touched her forehead with his. "Why are you making a big deal out of this?"

"It's your house. You designed it. It's you. Everything about your home is you. I love your ranch and soon we will be sharing our lives there. I guess everything will slowly become a part of me only because it's a piece of you. Do you understand what I'm trying to tell you?"

He notched his chin in the air and lifted his gaze to hers. "You know I'm as stubborn as you are."

"You understand I'm not accepting this as the end. I can always gift it back to you." She curled her arms around his neck and hugged him. "I want to change the subject for a minute."

His chest rumbled with his muffled chuckle. "Shel, you've chosen well."

She released her hold. "Who are the suspects?"

He tapped his right-index finger against her temple. "You sure do switch gears on the fly."

"I want to know who might want to hurt you or worse, kill you."

"We still don't know for sure. It's all hypothetical and as a sting operation, it was to entice them into admitting their guilt."

"I understand. You're speaking of alleged

301

suspects."

Kyle exhaled fully. "I don't want to scare you, but you should know who my enemies are. The police think it is Bobby Jo and David."

"How do they know?"

"The detectives don't. The conjecture is based on several factors. I told the lead officer about them wanting money and then, they refused to a voluntary interview. That's when we planned the idea of a sting. Problem is they are constantly on the move and we're waiting for them to become complacent. At that point, we will institute an alternate strategy."

Shelby relaxed against him again. "I'm scared for you. I still don't like the idea of you participating in something where you could get hurt or killed."

"We've been over this. I want them off the streets. What if I'm not the only one they have done this to? What if the next couple has children and they escalate to violence? It's a small step to brute force and bloodshed. People do strange things whether they are in a bind for money, psychologically deranged, emotionally hurt, or whatever the case may be. It doesn't matter the reasoning behind Bobby Jo and David's actions, if I can stop them, I will. You're not going to change my mind and I'd rather you support me."

The only thing left to do was to give him her blessing. She cringed at the idea of him putting his life in danger. Even though she applauded Kyle for taking control and possibly saving other lives, she still feared for his wellbeing. She cupped his face with her hands. "I do support you. Just promise me one thing." His jaw clenched under her palms. "When this happens you have to tell me everything. The where, who, what and the why's of the whole situation and my last request, please come back to me safely."

"I'll do my best."

"That's all I can ask." Shelby lifted her mouth as he lowered to kiss her. Sweetly, his lips whispered over her face. He drew her closer to him and hugged her. Nudging the hair away from her ear, he nibbled on her ear lobe. His warm breath panned over her neck and sent tingles skittering over her flesh. With each touch, Kyle loved her, with each caress, he gave his heart and she'd give him back double.

He grazed across her throat with his tongue. "Your skin is smooth and you taste good." He lifted her hand to his mouth kissing her palm then traveled to her thumb. He opened his lips encasing her index finger then another. The warm suction of his cheeks accelerated the erotic sensations chasing up her arm, lowering to her clit. As he stroked and licked, his eyes darkened with desire and never left hers.

The motion increased her appetite to do the same for him, but not with his fingers. She wanted to taste his essence, to revel in her favorite flavor, his aroma. Her nipples hardened. Blood rushed to her already swollen clit. Every part of her body seemed connected to her fingertips. He sucked harder. She fell into his world, surrendering, knowing she would never get tired of being loved by him. A moan escaped. She was in heaven envisioning a future with a man who'd love her forever on this earth and maybe for eternity in the First Realm.

His tongue rolled over each tip. With each stroke, he delivered a wet and slick massage. Seductive waves pulsed through her from his ministrations and when he nipped her with his teeth, tremors erupted.

She trembled. "Kyle."

His pupils enlarged with passion. His mouth released her fingertips with a pop and greedily took her mouth, drinking as though parched, dueling not for control, but to quench his thirst.

Kyle mumbled. "Let me spread the blanket."

Once the quilt opened and fluttered to the ground, he held out his hand and smiled. She threaded her fingers through his and stepped onto the pallet. He sat and gently tugged, inviting her to join him.

She placed her feet beside each hip then lowered until her groin met his. A flood of lust zapped her clit. She slid her crotch up and down the erection bulging from his jeans. The rhythmic friction added to her already inundated senses, saturating every nerve ending, she was drowning in pleasure and didn't want to be saved.

Her wet panties lubricated her movements. She groaned at the same time Kyle had. Her hands cupped his nape while her mouth found and tasted man, pure unadulterated man. Heady from the powerful position she held, she took command, grabbing the blasted tiny piece of metal of his zipper. Why in God's name did they make them so small?

Kyle brushed her hand away. "Baby, if you touch me now, I'll come before the party gets started."

"It's way past midnight."

He chuckled, unbuttoning her jacket, lifting her layered shirts along with the lacy bra and her breasts fell into his waiting hands. Her hardened nipples tightened into turgid peaks. She arched and whimpered as his thumb and finger squeezed then flicked the buds.

Shelby drew up his T-shirt. He smelled like the fresh outdoors, leather, horses and best of all, completely masculine. Her core clenched as her hands caressed his chest and tweaked his nipples. A low rumble escaped from his chest. His mouth laved her breast, first one then the other. He knew where she was the most sensitive and explored new places. She liked the idea that her cowboy was a trailblazer, adventuring across her body, discovering new spots to turn her on, and new positions to stoke their passion.

He lightly bit her with his teeth. "Ahh, so good." Yep, he was one hell of a man and he was all hers. Her fingertips found the top button on his jeans. "Do not stop me."

His stomach muscles contracted. "It's got to be past one by now."

With a twist, the stud released. She continued her descent bringing his zipper down. Her fingers nudged inside to hold his velvet-hard shaft, and her thumb drew circles over the crown. Moisture beaded and while she spread his essence over the head, his hips bucked.

He grasped her palms and placed them on his chest. "Come here." Both of his hands clasped around her hips, scooting her forward. She rubbed her mound over his engorged shaft, stroking, taking and giving pleasure.

He released Shelby, his hungry eyes finding hers. "Damn woman, you have me so hard already. Can you stand up?"

She exhaled. "I'm not sure." And she really wasn't. So close to a climax, her tense muscles jerked when she tried to lift herself.

He helped her rise, removed her shoes, jeans and panties. Again she placed her feet to each side of his thighs, but he held her there.

"See if this helps." His hands rubbed her knees stroked up her legs holding her bottom firm. He brushed her clit with his mouth, using his tongue to separate her folds.

"Ohh."

A long-titillating lick from her opening to the enlarged bud stimulated another earthquake of ten on the Richter scale. Kyle suckled on the bundle of nerves, and swift pleasure overtook her. Shelby's knees wobbled, ready to fall over the edge. He stopped, taking her weight and gently lowered her. Her core widened to accept his beautiful erection. The bulbous head probed through the swollen walls, hitting her sweet spot.

He filled her completely. His hips rose lifting her until her breasts were level with his face and he eased one into his mouth. Ecstasy and pure pleasure trickled from her nipple to her clit. Another moan escaped her lips. She clamped her inner muscles around his shaft, milking his satin erection.

Kyle growled and the vibrations sizzled through her. She wanted fast and hard. Taking control, she pumped up and down before he joined the rhythm.

Two souls were now one. With each penetration, a euphoric spiritual connection consumed her. Her heart soared; this went beyond a physical union, and beyond their physical world. They were a part of a realm.

Her imminent release drew her back to the here and now. The aroma of their lovemaking intermingled with the spring flowers teased her nostrils. The slap of skin rallied her to the apex. She slipped her hand behind her and lowered, finding his tightened balls and gently squeezed.

Kyle's groans gave way to grunts, his release was near too.

He rubbed his thumb over her swollen clit, circling, adding the right amount of pressure then flicked. Her muscles tightened around him, he gave her another deep plunge and she tipped over the edge.

Kyle ground her swollen flesh, taking her higher. "Come with me, baby."

Now in another place, his fingers threaded hers. He led her into an open meadow, flowers and trees dotting the landscape. "Do you like it?"

"What? Where are we?"

"This is part your vision and mine of what we think our eternity would be like in the First Realm."

She shook her head. "I was in the throes of passion and an orgasm to die for and we end up here? Creepy, if you ask me."

Two seconds later, she was back, Kyle still suckling her breast and his finger and thumb twisted her clit. Tremors shook every muscle just before the erotic release blasted through her entire body. When she calmed, she opened her eyes. Her gaze met his.

He chuckled. "I like watching you come, but most of all, I love feeling you climax." He bucked again. "There's nothing finer."

"We'll talk about what happened, later." Shelby smiled. "Now for you." She used her inner muscles to clamp down, enveloping his shaft.

"Baby." Holding her, he leaned her back. He slid in, scraping her sweet-spot, her folds added friction. He advanced and held. Bringing her hips forward and back, her clit rubbed the dark hair surrounding his groin. When he released, so did she, never expecting a second so quickly. He shuddered and filled her with his seed. His glazed eyes connected with hers. After his last tremor, he hugged her.

His throaty whisper misted her ear with dampness. "Are you warm now?"

"What do you think?" Comfort, security, and best of all his love filled her through every channel of her being, here and obviously, beyond.

"I freaked out, earlier."

He kissed her jawline journeying to her chin then placed another on her forehead. "I know. I would never intentionally scare you. Throes of passion? An orgasm to die for? You sure know how to make a man feel like a god."

She groaned.

Kyle's hand stroked her spine then drew circles in the small of her back. "I could stay here forever, but we should be getting back."

"You're right."

Kyle stopped her from rising, still connected, his erection fading. "I want to remember this." His hips plunged one more time. "Me inside of you... and you glowing."

"I know it sounds corny but how could I not have an afterglow? I'm a glutton for...you."

He rose, then helped her stand.

"I'll be back."

Kyle yanked a handkerchief from his jacket pocket and walked to the stream. His tight ass and leg muscles rippled with each step. She gulped, wanting to curb the desire to stroke and taste his handsome flesh one more time. They needed to return before the men sent a search party. She grumbled, "Don't want to go there again."

He soaked the cloth and sauntered back with a shit eating grin. "You first, my lovely lady."

Chill bumps rose as he cleansed her. "That's fricking cold."

"Now for me. Jeez. I'd say fucking, but frickin' would keep me out of trouble."

He strolled back to rinse the western tie-dyed kerchief and spread it out on the ground to dry. Kneeling on the blanket, Kyle plucked her jeans from her grasp and held them for her to step into.

"I can do this myself. It's kind of you to help but…" She grabbed for the denims.

He whisked them behind his back and let go. Kyle whispered kisses up her sensitive thighs. His tongue glided over her skin, nipping her with his teeth then soothed the sweet pain with his tongue again.

His hands nudged her silk panties to the side and opened her folds. He laved over her clit then lowered, darting inside her.

He withdrew.

"Don't stop."

"You can't do *that* by yourself."

She collapsed and Kyle caught her. He settled onto his back and gingerly positioned her apex above his mouth.

Her pulse increased with each plunge of his fingers, his thumb stroking her clitoris. His pace changed as her fervor increased. Her clit enlarged, she spread her legs wider.

"Baby, come now." His warm breath and words

danced across her labia. She shattered with an explosive orgasm. This time, Kyle had not taken her to the other realm. He must have figured one freakish event today was all she could stand. To be truthful, maybe he was right.

Shelby scooted down lying on top of Kyle, while his hands wrapped around her shoulders.

He kissed the top of her head. "Every time you don't let me help you, won't let me share with you, I'll find something you can't do for yourself."

She giggled. "If it's anything like what you just did, I have a feeling, I'll say no forever."

"Now, will you let me help you put on your jeans?"

Her head still buried in the crook of his neck, she replied, "I want you, Pressley, and I don't want you helping me with my pants. I want you to make love to me because you are the only man I want and need, only you." Her hands traveled down and grasped the base of his shaft and stroked. His semi-erection lengthened, widened.

His hips bucked. "You're going to kill me woman."

He flipped her on her back, spread her legs with his knees and plunged, as far as she was concerned, home. The weight of his body on hers was a blanket of security. She wallowed in the knowledge that he'd always be there to protect her. He filled her core completely, taking away any emptiness, the joining tender and sweet. Soon, his thrusts ramped faster, deepened and the sound of their skin sang to her once again.

"Kyle, I'm so close."

With each advance, his balls slapped her ass. She

basked in the pure pleasure of him smacking her butt and his groin stroking her clit.

"Let's go. Kyle's head tilted back, his eyes closed. "Baby, you're mine."

As her climaxed erupted, she joined Kyle, not only in an orgasmic release but in their meadow. This time, she would pay attention instead of flipping out like she did before.

Kyle stood in front of her with his hand extended. He looked normal, she peered down, so did she. She intertwined her fingers with his and they walked to a nearby stream. They sat on the bank, discussing whether or not the Great Spirit would give them a bonding in eternity. She wasn't quite sure she understood it all. "Only the Father can bond us?"

Kyle nodded. "Instead of Cameahwait, I'd like to call this place, Sacred-Spring. What do you think?"

"Apropos."

"I love you, Shel."

He hadn't said the words, but she understood his thoughts. Could she do it, too? "If Ten-Blue-Sun's stone lights after we are married and we're set to be together, is this the place we'll stay? Is this how we'll communicate? Telepathically?"

"Fuc- damn well amazing, isn't it?" He smiled. "Caught myself just in time."

"You're doing pretty well with the F bombs. You know, you won't need to mind walk anymore."

"Except in our world."

"What?"

"Never mind. Ready to go back?"

Back on earth, they both shuddered as the last of their releases rippled throughout their bodies.

Shelby's gaze caught his. "By the way, Pressley, I love you too."

****

Shelby angled closer to Kyle's side, greeting the guests as they entered onto the veranda. Lisa's small get-together grew with every minute that passed. Thank heavens, Garrett had plenty of room.

She enjoyed the moderate temperature which made for a perfect Friday evening party. Jude and Joni situated themselves across from them to intercept the talkative ones who dallied too long in the line. While soft music filtered through the air, Julia served hors d'oeuvres and Grey tended the bar keeping the men who wore tailored suits and the women dressed in designer gowns occupied.

Shelby whispered to Kyle. "I feel out of place. Maybe I should go change."

"Don't worry about it. We agreed to be informal. If no one likes my blue jeans they can leave. By the way, you look scrumptious in yours." His hand curved over her bottom and squeezed.

She grasped Kyle's hand, threaded her fingers through his and drew them to her side. "How many people do you think she invited?"

"Don't know. But it looks like she took after her parents. Just enjoy the night." He wrapped an arm over her shoulders and gave a reassuring embrace. "Here comes some more. In a few minutes, we'll start mingling."

"I'm with you since I don't know a soul save the wedding party." She should've asked to oversee Lisa's guest list or given her a specific count. The rest of Shelby's family wouldn't arrive until tomorrow morning. Hopefully, the flight wouldn't be late or their bags lost. Then again, the limo could have a flat or get into an accident. *Jeez.* She exhaled and guessed she ought to chill instead of thinking about everything that could go wrong. Joni had told her not to fret. Her gaze connected with Joni's and Shelby rolled her eyes.

Joni winked and said something to Jude. Jude leaned toward her, his lips moved, but she couldn't hear the conversation. Hmm, maybe that was a good thing because Joni blushed as Jude slid his hand into hers and formed a line beside them. In between guests, Jude whispered to Kyle.

Kyle nodded and guided Shelby to the lower level. He held the chair for Shelby. "What would you like to drink?"

"A glass of Chardonnay would be nice."

"I'll be back as soon as I can get through Lisa's idea of an intimate party." Kyle smiled and kissed her cheek. "Keep my place for me."

Two seconds later, Alessa bounced into the seat next to her.

"Are you having fun, Al?"

"I really am. I'm meeting some interesting couples and then there are others who couldn't care less if they were here or on Mars.

"I'm glad you sat down for a while. If you didn't, you would have blisters on your feet, then where would you be for tomorrow."

"Jude and Joni saved us. I don't want to sound ungrateful, but after an hour and a half of standing, I needed to sit."

"Can I get you anything Sis? I see Kyle trying to make his way to you."

"No, I'm fine. Thanks."

Alessa shot from the chair and zigzagged toward the bar. She interrupted the gentleman who was speaking to Kyle. Kyle acknowledged Alessa and angled his way to Shelby.

Her sexy man handed the wine glass to her. "Alessa's good. She knew I didn't want to talk to him anymore about his high yield investment. There's always a few who want to talk business during a party. Those are the very same people I try to stay away from. I don't mind them giving me their business card and ask if they can call me. But damn, he felt it was his duty to warn me of my grand losses if I didn't jump on his band wagon. Anyway, enough of that, I'm glad she saved me." He grinned. His laugh lines lifted and his eyes twinkled.

"What are you thinking? You have the devil-may-care look." Shelby warmed at his spunky attitude.

"By this time tomorrow night, you'll be my wife. Right now, I'm the happiest man on earth."

She shivered from his gaze and wallowed in his sincerity. "And vice versa." How could she be so lucky? When her first husband died, she'd never considered falling in love again. She grasped Kyle's thigh and squeezed. Her eyes filled with tears. "I'm going to the restroom. I'll be right back."

"Shel, you okay?"

She smiled to reassure him. "I'm fine as long as you're beside me."

"I'll always be there for you. I need to start making the rounds and thank everyone for coming. Join me when you come back."

She nodded and headed around the crowd. Kyle's

family and friends had opened their hearts and homes to her. Life couldn't get much better than this. She sighed with contentment and proceeded around a table.

Garrett canted against the bar with his right cowboy boot hooked on the bottom rail of the stool beside him, talking with Grey. She wanted to tell him thank you and see how he was holding up with all the people surrounding him.

Lisa's arm wrapped around Garrett's abdomen, and laughed. She whirled to face him. "Do you like the party? I think I did a superb job considering I didn't have much time to put it together. Of course, I couldn't have done this without you." She placed her other hand on his chest and hugged him.

His eyebrows lifted several inches. "Sounds like you had one too many champagne cocktails."

"Not enough actually, I could use a few more. Grey would you be so kind and make me another?"

Grey eyed Garrett. Garrett nodded and shifted his weight to face Lisa, swiping her palms off of him. "Why don't we sit over here and talk a little bit? He'll bring your drink to you, won't you, Uncle Grey?"

Grey's shoulder rolled as Garrett shook his head once. Grey's chin lifted and acknowledged Garrett's request. No more alcohol for Lisa.

Lisa movements were graceful and fluid even when she appeared to be three sheets to the wind.

Shelby shifted closer.

Garrett held the chair for Lisa as she plopped down. He chuckled.

Shelby didn't have any problem hearing Lisa's question. "I noticed you increased your security."

"Yes."

"Still don't know who is thhhrenning them?" she slurred.

"Threatening…nope. Got any ideas?"

Lisa laughed. "How would I know? Not that I want them to marry anyways."

"Why?"

She shook her head. "I probably shouldn't have said that."

"Probably not. But you can talk to me."

Lisa lowered her chin, her lips pouted. "I just don't think she's good enough for him."

"We don't have a say in that do we?"

"No, I guess we don't. But I'd like to. What does he see in her?"

"We all see people differently. How do you see her?" Garrett squinted.

"As a—I need my drink." She hefted halfway out of her seat when Garrett gently tugged her arm and she fell into her chair.

"Hey, don't do that."

He chuckled. "Just sit here a bit and talk to me."

"Oh Garrett, what's wrong with me?"

"A loaded question, pun intended."

Lisa exhaled loudly and scrunched her face, missing the play on words. "Why doesn't Kyle like me?"

"You're asking the wrong man. Besides, aren't you engaged to a guy back east?"

"My fiancé is the perfect man according to my parents. His heritage is politically correct and just like our parents, he comes from old money. Old for us that is, I know we are still considered new money across the pond."

"Do you love him?"

Lisa's voice quivered. "Yes, I do...Kyle means everything to me...more than you know."

Garrett shifted toward Lisa and his eyes narrowed to slits. "I meant your fiancé. I'm not one to preach, but maybe it's time to take inventory of your own life and get yours straightened out first."

She bolted upright and hissed. "I have my life in order. You have no right—"

Garrett raised his palm. "You're right. I don't." He stood and waited for her drunken gaze to connect with his. "Don't do anything stupid, Lisa. I've known you too many years and seen you pull too many stunts. They ended badly...for everyone."

Lisa waved him off and teetered as she rose. "Don't worry about me. I can take care of myself."

"You usually do."

Shelby eased back into the crowd and shuddered. A bad feeling snaked to the pit of her tummy, coiling as if ready to strike.

The last of the guests had left. Kyle and Shelby slumped into a love seat.

Kyle shoved a hand through his hair. "I didn't think anyone would leave."

Shelby peered at her watch. "Two thirty in the morning, no wonder I'm so tired."

"I can remember someone saying to me the party was almost over at midnight. There was a time when two thirty meant the party was just getting started."

Heat surged to Shelby's cheeks remembering what she'd told Kyle at the stream while making love. "Yeah, maybe during our college days when we were know it all teenagers and a foolhardy twenty

317

something."

"Ah, I lasted longer than you."

"So what age were you when the night seemed to extend into infinity?"

"By nineteen, I had received my undergraduate degree, that sheepskin came easy to me."

"Are you serious?"

"Yeah, I challenged and passed most of my courses. But, it was when I was twenty, going to school for my masters, working full time, engaged, nights and days were just a blur to me. I grabbed forty winks here and there and kept on going. That's when I found Christine in my bed with...I slept for several days straight after that...not like Rip Van Winkle, but long enough to start a good beard." He scratched his jaw and chin.

"I can see you running like the proverbial energizer bunny, but I've never seen you sleep for that long. Just know if you ever do, I'll be there whenever you wake up."

His eyes shifted and glinted with humor. "Now that I'm older and wiser, want to head for the bedroom and sleep with this old man?"

Shelby grinned. "I'd love to."

****

The light from the morning sun brightened the room and the rays glimmered across their bed. Shelby stirred and spun toward Kyle. While he slept, the stress lines around his eyes were nonexistent and with the morning shadow of his beard, he appeared peaceful and masculine all rolled into one. She smiled at her soon-to-be husband. His right arm stretched above his head and the other still lay over her waist. She drank in his appearance and played with the wispy hair on his forearm.

This was the beginning of another chapter of her life. Excitement coursed through her and at the same time, butterflies tickled the inside of her tummy in anticipation of a new beginning with Kyle. He always seemed to know how to sooth her, love her and therein lay her contentment. She smiled again.

"Are you happy this morning?" Kyle murmured.

"Very."

"Today is the day. You'll become Shelby Pressley, my wife."

She burrowed under the covers. "Hmm."

"Come here." He gently drew her back to his chest and held her. "Let's go take a shower."

"I will in a minute."

He wrapped his muscular leg over her hip. "Don't overanalyze this day." He rocked her with his legs and arms. "Come on, time to wash the sleep from us."

"I wasn't analyzing today."

Kyle roared. His indignant laughter echoed in the room. "Oh, yes, you were. You were going over your mental to-do list and plotting out the next few hours. By the time we meandered into the shower, you would've completed your whole day. Am I right?"

She grinned and didn't say a word.

This time he shook her whole body bouncing both of them on the bed. "Am I right?"

She groaned.

"Ah-huh, I knew it." He tickled her.

She twisted in the sheets, spinning to the edge of the mattress.

"Oh no, you can't get away from me." With one

hand on her belly, he scooted her derriere against his groin. He embraced her from his chest to his feet. He whispered in her ear, "I want to hold you for the rest of my life...just like this, every morning that the Great Spirit gives us."

"Same here."

"You know it will be our last?"

"What are you talking about?"

"It'll be our last shower as Shelby Littleton and Kyle Pressley."

"You're getting sentimental."

"That I am, baby...that I am."

They retreated into the tiled bath, stroked, caressed, and loved each other not once, Kyle made sure she climaxed several times. They stood holding one another, letting all the nozzles spray over their bodies. With their desires slaked, their souls intertwined, they grew closer...deeper yet again.

Bam! Bam! Bam!

They both jumped and then laughed.

Kyle yelled, "Who's there? I'll go see who it is and what they want." He grabbed a towel and wrapped it around his waist.

Shelby ogled his fine frame. As he trotted off, the water drops ran down his broad back from his hair to his muscular thighs and calves. Yep, and his ass was still yummy. Shelby turned the nozzles, stepped out of the shower and donned her robe. Nearby, Kyle talked with someone and she smiled not because of what she could hear, but knowing he made her happy...very happy. She'd have this expression on her face all day long.

He sauntered into the bathroom. "It was Julia

bringing your breakfast tray. She said she'd be right back with another one. I think I surprised her."

"How sweet of her. Be sure and help her when she brings up the other."

"Nope. No, ma'am. It's your turn to get the evil eye from her. I felt like I was schoolboy caught with my pants down."

"Well, you were caught, with your pants off and I can vouch you're certainly not a young boy. Go ahead and get ready, I'll watch for her."

****

Kyle had leased the entire building of the five-star restaurant for the day and evening. Shelby panned the first level entrance. The open floor plan invited guests in to an old-fashioned bar that stretched the entire length of the wall. Tables and chairs surrounded the dais for live music. Normally, the musicians ranged from concert pianists to country and western bands.

The grand staircase to the second floor reminded her of old grandiose times. The interior decorator had an eye for exquisite detail. Wonderful smells met her at the top of the stairs, her stomach growled, but truthfully, she'd be surprised if she could eat. The restaurant buzzed with activity, everyone bustling to make their day perfect.

As she stepped onto the third level balcony, her heart warmed. In another hour, she'd be standing at the altar saying her vows to Kyle. The phalaenopsis orchids with live bamboo graced the entrances, each table, the support columns and wedding arch which matched her bouquet. The white canopies fluttered in the Wyoming zephyr. This was perfect. She'd favored the idea that less was more and Joni had pegged the concept beautifully.

The rooms off to the side were for meetings, gatherings, and each had dressing rooms. Joni had decorated both the men's and women's areas with white roses in honor of their parents.

Alessa, Joni, and Rain had helped Shelby dress. Shelby examined her image in the mirror. Her tea length, cream satin, A-line bridal gown gathered at the bodice adorned with seed pearls fit her frame to perfection. Although, the twenty-two dainty mother of pearl buttons fastened in the back were a beautiful addition, they were a pain in the butt. A gal from the local salon had her hair swept in an up-do with phalaenopsis orchids placed throughout. Kyle had requested those particular flowers. The beautician left a few tendrils of curled hair to feather around her face, giving her an ethereal air.

Joni gazed at Shelby's reflection. "You're absolutely beautiful and glowing."

Rain wore her ceremonial dress and her two sisters wore a dark purple, matching the orchid's splash of color. "Thank you and you look great too. The tea length is perfect."

Alessa held a serving tray with four glasses of champagne. "Here we go, Shelby...Rain...Joni...and me." Al set the silver server on the table. "I think we need a toast. I'll start. I've only seen you this happy one other time. I'm glad you've found someone to spend the rest of your life with."

Joni raised hers. "You've been blessed twice in this life. Not too many people get that chance."

Rain placed her drink on the tray. "I have something to show you." Paper wrestled inside a bag and she withdrew Ten-Blue-Sun. "Look at the top stone."

Shelby stiffened. "Oh my God, that's not the right color."

Rain placed the doll back in the sack. "Don't be swayed by what you see, fight for what you believe, who you love."

"It's blood red." Shelby shook her head once.

Rain patted her arm. "Several months ago in a restaurant, you trusted a total stranger. She told you to be strong, to seek answers in another place, to believe in those who love you. Above all, to be brave. I come to you again as your shaman and...your mom. Are willing to heed my advice?"

Shelby gasped. "That was you?"

"Are you going to fight for your man?"

Shelby took a deep breath. Dammit, everyone from the First Realm talked in riddles. A warning raged within her heart and threatened to overturn what should've been the happiest day of her life. She exhaled. Ten-Blue-Sun's prediction was ominous. Her sweaty palm clenched a fist in anger, the other around the long stem of her glass. She needed to see Kyle and get his reassurances. He was the strong one. His presence and words always calmed her.

A soft knock quieted the room. Kyle opened the door and gazed at her with those precious brown eyes she fell in love with. He wore a black suit tailored in Hong Kong. It hugged his wide chest, and the shirt matched Shelby's dress. The trousers formed to his muscular thighs and the black full-quill ostrich boots shined. His orchid boutonniere was an exact duplicate to the ones in her hair.

"You're beautiful." He strode to her and gave her a careful hug. "I have to talk to you."

She nodded. That's when she noticed Chris standing at the threshold scowling. Anger radiated from the five-star general's frame, a dark foreboding fell over her soul.

Joni's dress swished. "Alessa, Rain and I will check on…everything."

The soft click meant they were alone.

Chapter Twenty-Four

Anguish glittered from Kyle's eyes, covering every inch of her with rays of excruciating agony and sorrow.

He shifted, edging closer. "I love you…you know that…right?"

"What's wrong?"

"You never answered my question."

"Nor you mine."

"Do you want to sit down?"

"No." Her knees wobbled and her stomach pitched. "I don't know where to start."

Time stretched to infinity, there was no point dragging out the inevitable. "Usually the beginning helps, but you can skip to the end. I'm pretty sure that's where we…I come in."

"I meant to tell you a while ago."

She gathered her strength and waited.

"On one of my trips to New York…Lisa joined us for dinner. Jude and Garrett left, but we stayed to have a few drinks and listen to the live music." He cleared his throat. "I don't remember much about the night. In fact, after the first thirty minutes at the bar, my memory is blank. I believe I was drugged." He shook his head. "I woke up the next morning in Lisa's bed. She's here…said she's pregnant and I'm the father."

Shelby understood everything he had said, but she couldn't respond or move. It was as if time stood still and gravity cemented her in place. Rain's words crowded her mind. This situation didn't require her to be brave or to contest any actions. Kyle was needed elsewhere. An unborn babe depended on him, on his love and she would not be the one who took a father away. She had enough failures and guilt on her dinner plate to last a lifetime.

Her course had been set long ago when Tall-Man, her grandfather's grandfather, weaved his magic. Rain was right about one thing, she had to fight for—the baby—Kyle's baby. What if this child was the next shaman?

"Will you say something?"

After a long moment, she gathered the last vestiges of courage. "What a shame you don't remember creating your son or daughter. Lisa is a beautiful woman." Surely the strong-level voice wasn't hers. "She'll need not only your support, but you. I want to be alone, if you'll excuse me."

He grasped her shoulders, the warmth of his hands permeated through her gown. "If Lisa isn't lying and the child is mine, I'll take care of the little one. But I don't love Lisa, I love you. Why can't we be married and handle this together? Remember what we promised one another?"

"Don't you understand? We can never be together. The entities and curses are too powerful and we'll never be able to overcome them. The alpha man in you can't win this one. It's out of our hands."

He released her. She lifted the glass of champagne to her mouth, downing the contents. She stared at the fluted crystal watching the remaining alcohol glide down the sides. "Ten-Blue-Sun's stone wasn't the right color." She released the crystal letting it drop to the floor and met his gaze head on. "Go, you have other responsibilities now."

She twirled, giving her back to him. "Please leave." Kyle's footfalls whispered across the carpet. As he walked out of her life, she cringed at the bitter taste of life's cruelties. The second man she ever loved was gone, thanks to the vicious acts of her ancestor. She trembled at the hellish existence she'd have to endure until her grisly and untimely death.

A soft voice behind Shelby interrupted her morbid thoughts. "I'm sorry." Shelby turned to face the intruder. "Mrs. Dent?"

"Please, call me Mira."

The grandmother's eyes held sympathetic sorrow, but Shelby refused to acknowledge the pity.

"You know, Lisa and my granddaughter were very close. They were roommates in college and became lovers. When Christine committed suicide, Kyle sought his solace from the bottle then sobered and joined the Navy. Even though I don't believe it, Everett, my son, may have brought Christine's troubles, Lisa had plenty of her own input."

"I'm sorry—"

"My granddaughter wouldn't know a good thing if it slapped her on the face. But Lisa forgave her and blamed Kyle for years. I never gave a thought she'd be up to anything so deceitful."

"Mrs. Dent, forgive me. I'm not thinking clearly, could you help with your point and what this has to do with me?"

"Dear, I asked you to call me, Mira. Somehow, I think Christine's in the mix again compliments of

Lisa."

Shelby shook her head. "I—"

"Christine is my granddaughter."

Shelby's mouth rounded in an O.

"Just so you know, I think this is awful. Lisa's revenge tactics have gone too far. Christine's gone, Kyle doesn't want her and she needs to move on with her life."

"Mira…this has nothing to do with your granddaughter and everything to do with two consenting adults…and a relative, a man you don't even know. If I may be so bold as to ask for some time alone."

Mrs. Dent's hat bobbed. "You take care." Mira kissed each of her cheeks and left.

Her mind blanked. The pressure in her chest overpowered the ability to breathe. She struggled to inhale. Finally, she gasped a breath.

Shelby grabbed her suitcase, marched out the door into the world of loneliness Tall-Man special ordered for her.

The next cognizant thought she had was the darkness that surrounded her, both physically and mentally. Damn, how long had she been driving subconsciously. She had better find some place to stay for the night.

The flashing sign of a hotel caught her attention. When she walked into the lobby, the hotel clerk stared then recognition dawned and the lady smiled. "A room for two?"

"One." Her voice dropped to a whisper, silently pleading for no more questions. The woman frowned and seemed to understand, moving through the motions.

Shelby took the keycard, swiped her bag from the floor and through the fog and haze of her mind found her room. Cursing the twenty-two mother-of-pearl buttons, she slowly undressed. The orchid petals in her hair fell to the floor, discolored, dying a slow death.

Shouldn't she have some emotion inside her? Anger or hurt? There was nothing, not a single damn thing, just a void, like a zombie. She stepped into the shower and twisted the handle as far as it would go. The hot water beat on her tense muscles and ran over her back. Tears never came, odd that.

When Lisa acknowledged her with a nod as she left, something broke inside of her or had she mended? Or maybe she died and this was her hell? She grunted. Did it matter? Like viewing herself as an outsider, she could "see" herself. How strange. She likened this to a purgatory of sorts.

She donned a T-shirt as opposed to her silk honeymoon nightgown. One thing she had learned from Kyle, always have a change of clothes. She didn't turn on the TV or radio. When she laid her head down, staring at the ceiling, she realized she hadn't a clue what city or for that matter what state she was in, but like Scarlet O'Hara, she would think about it tomorrow. Her eyes closed, sleep, that's all she wanted, the dark abyss of another world.

Chapter Twenty-Five

Kyle had let Mira enter Shelby's dressing room. Rain and the wedding party marched toward him with concern etched on their faces while others marked their distance from him.

Jude scraped his hand through his new haircut. "Are you okay?"

Kyle choked. "Shelby canceled."

Garrett sidled beside him. "Kyle, I don't think you did anything in New York. I think Lisa is a manipulative and a conniving bit..." He cleared his throat. "Wench."

"Thanks, bro, but you're not the one I was going to marry today."

Jude straightened. "I'll get Lisa out of here. Garrett, take Mom with you and start moving people down to the restaurant, tell them to enjoy the rest of the day and evening on us. The limos can stay for the duration in case anyone needs a ride, security will help you. Joni and Alessa, get Kyle out of here and back to Pogonip. We'll meet you there."

Al whirled to face him. "Tell me what Garrett said is true, that you didn't sleep with Lisa."

He lowered his gaze to the floor, feeling like the lowest scum on earth. "I can't."

"I see."

He met Alessa's eyes. "No, you don't."

"I may not, but what I do know is your timing sucks. Exactly when were you going to tell my sister? After the vows of honor and truth? Or were you going to wait until Lisa came to your front door? Oh yeah, dear wife of mine, forgot to tell you, I knocked her up. Damn. You're not my favorite person right now. Let's go."

****

Kyle, settled in his truck, meandered through the maze of cars following Shelby's sisters out of the parking lot. Alessa and Joni turned right and he took a left weaving through the traffic. He didn't know where he wanted to go, but he sure in the hell didn't want to be around his family with their pitying looks and Shelby's sister's go-to-hell glances.

As though he was in another world, the miles and hours whisked by quickly and twenty-four plus hours later, he faced the salty breeze of the Pacific Ocean with Mt. Rainier behind him. The only plans he had made were to travel by ferry to Victoria, then head up to Alaska.

Before he left Seattle, he wanted to see his godson and daughter who were named after their grandpa and him. For right now, he succumbed to the hypnotic lap of the waves hitting the coastline.

****

The next day, the weather was perfect for the al fresco lunch he had planned with Aaron and Kat. Kyle handed Danielle Lee to her dad and Daniel Kyle to his mom. "I'm glad you all could join me."

Katherine settled Daniel into the baby carrier. "Where's Shelby? I thought she'd be with you."

Kyle cleared his throat. "Something came up and I

had to cancel the wedding."

Aaron, a spitting image of Dan, offered his condolences. "I'm sorry to hear that. Maybe when you reschedule, all of us and our better halves can be there."

Under the table, Kyle made a fist, his fingernails digging into his palm. "I'll let you know. How's Becca?" A dawn of understanding hit him like a freight train head-on. He was acutely aware of the hurt Dan had endured. Granted, his best friend had more years with his wife and children then he'd had with Shelby. But this was the first time he could honestly fathom the heart wrenching despair and torment Dan went through.

"She's remarried and living in New York." Aaron smiled. "She got hitched to fellow musician."

Kyle nodded. "I'm happy for her. Did you receive the information on Danielle's and Dan's accounts?"

Katherine inched her chair closer to him. "You didn't need to start a trust fund for them. Aaron and I still have the money you gave to us eleven years ago."

He rubbed his hand against his jeans relieving the indentations in his flesh. "I made a promise to your dad and I'm keeping it."

Kat shifted in her seat. "You gave us so much money our great grandchildren will be set for life. We're concerned about you...That you're driven by guilt."

The silence that followed held him like a vise. He planned to keep the two oaths he made that day. The twins would be set for life including the next several generations. And other than slipping into Shelby's mind for a split-second, the last time he walked was with Dan. "It's not out of remorse, it's because I want to do this for your families."

Danielle fussed and Aaron grasped the handle bouncing the stroller that he'd put her in. "Do you mind sharing with us, what happened in Columbia with Dad?"

Kyle tensed. They had every right to know what really happened, instead of the official watered-down version. He sighed and resigned to relive that day. "Our team had a mission a little north of the Ecuadorian border. We were to find one of the largest cocaine work-camps and follow a shipment to determine how they were getting the drugs into the U.S. The guerillas found us and opened fire. We were told later that our informant had been tortured and gave us up. Right after that, he was murdered."

He swallowed long and hard. "Dan, your dad, took a hit to his femoral artery." His breath hitched. "He loved you both. More than you…just imagine how you feel with your little ones." He cleared the lump in his throat. "The job had been successful in several areas. From what I hear, that particular work-camp no longer exists, plus they were able to figure out how the cartels were bringing the narcotics through our borders. The new equipment we tested has been refined for use by our soldiers today. Your father helped prepare a way for our guys to fight and live to see another day."

Katherine rose and bent over to hug his neck. "I miss him."

He scooted off the chair and stood, then embraced Kat. "So do I, princess."

Aaron surged out of his seat. "I for one, think you've left out an enormous chunk of information. I may have been fourteen, but I knew there were problems between Mom and Dad. When I asked her

333

about it, she always had the same reply, that it's ancient history and I should let it go."

Kat tensed in his arms and withdrew. "Don't, Aaron. What good can come of it?"

Aaron's chin notched several inches in the air and his gaze reflected a man who wanted no, *needed* answers. "I'm asking Kyle for the facts. You can go to the ladies' room if you don't want to hear the news of what our father was really like."

The comment crawled all over him. He intended to set the record straight. "I'm taking into consideration that you are my best friend's son and I'm the godfather of you and your daughter. But hear this, keep up that attitude and I'll stomp a mud hole in your chest and walk it dry. Stop puffing up like a bullfrog and sit."

Aaron perched on the edge of his seat while Katherine plopped in hers.

He slowly followed, which gave him time to come up with a reasonable response. "I won't speak for your dad."

Aaron grunted.

"You shouldn't blame a man who's not here to defend himself. What I do know is that your father loved each of you very much, including your mom. As adults, we don't always like the circumstances handed to us, but we can't change or manipulate them to suit our wishes. We can only accept." Fuck, maybe he should pay attention to his own words.

Kat sniffled. "You're right...Aaron and I have talked about Mom and Dad's situation for years and I'm ashamed of myself. As teenagers before he died, we'd listen to mom cry and babble about him not caring enough to take time for her and us." She peered over to her brother. "We were unfair to Dad. When he died, we unjustly accused him of not loving us and blamed him for anything that went wrong in our lives. Besides, I always felt Mom was the one who gave up on our family, not Dad."

Kyle shook his head. "To condemn Becca won't change a thing, will it?"

"No. But now as a wife in love with my husband, I can remember certain instances with Mom that don't ring true for me. I'm not placing fault at her feet; nevertheless, I am aware that she isn't an innocent bystander."

Aaron's arm stretched across the table and grasped Kat's hand. "You never told me that before…We'll talk later, okay? Even then, I can't promise I'll change my mind, but I'll listen and evaluate."

Kyle rested his palm on top of theirs and gently squeezed. "That's all I can ask." He let a long sigh escape. "I don't know about you all, but I'm famished. Is everyone ready to order? I bet Little Dan and Danielle could gum a big huge steak."

Dan's kids laughed and a new sense of peace seemed to filter down from the heavens. *You'd be damn proud of your children, Dan, damn proud.*

After several days, he was ready to head toward the forty-ninth state. Sam, his bodyguard, had been pissed for leaving without him. He told Sam to take some time off and be with his family. Family, that word had a new depth and a powerful meaning. He'd been able to visit with Aaron and Kat's spouses. They understood the bond between the twins and the unified spirits warmed his heart.

He had called the private detective agency and had

them follow Lisa. Once aware of Lisa's activities, conclusions could be drawn and he could come up with a plan of action. Had she seen a doctor to initiate prenatal care? Or was she still partying and calling his and Shelby's breakup a win?

He tapped the speed dial. "Hey, Jude, doing okay?"

"Fine. You?"

"Been better. I wanted to give you a heads-up, I've contacted the PI's—"

"I know. They've already talked to me for my take on the situation. I'm glad you're being proactive."

"I have a plan for my life and I'd like it to include Shelby. I want to give both of us some time, maybe even have proof from the detectives about Lisa then I'm heading to Texas. I'll keep you updated."

"And I'll call you if my group comes up with anything."

Kyle cleared his throat. "I didn't know you hired...Thanks, man. That means a lot."

"I'm still your big brother, and will always look after your six."

"Love ya', man." Kyle leaned back in his chair and smiled. Jude did believe him and was covering his ass.

****

Shelby awoke and showered. Dressed in her jeans and sweater, she ate breakfast and headed down Interstate Fifteen. She purchased a map in Idaho and outlined a trip through Utah and Arizona. After Flagstaff, she would head home on I-40. Her love of national parks and the outdoors were going to be the balm to sooth her soul and there were plenty on this route.

She had called her sisters so they wouldn't worry.

She thanked Alessa for taking Annie back home and Joni for all of the work she did. Joni had questioned Shelby's last request thinking she'd lost her marbles. Maybe she had, but she wanted to remember yesterday forever. Her savings account would have to be reconciled on a monthly basis. The lesson would arrive like clockwork, a constant reminder that she should have heeded the curse and that there are no second chances at love.

Both sisters had squawked at the idea she'd be inaccessible for the next couple of days, but they understood her need to be alone.

A week had gone by and she was doing better every day. She stopped at an overlook, sat on the hood of her car resting against the windshield. Her gaze panned the massive mountains of rock and the long valleys. An epiphany righted her senses. She now understood how insignificant her existence was compared to the overall juxtaposition of Mother Nature. She gasped as the moments of truth overwhelmed her to a point of reckoning.

The choices she had made were hers alone. She wasn't angry at Kyle or Lisa. If her life had brought them together, she accepted it. She wished it could have happened earlier, but in reality, she didn't have control over Lisa, Kyle, the fate of the First Realm or the curse.

Her cell phone jingled. A text message flashed on the screen from her late husband's daughter with a video attached. She tapped and viewed her six-year-old granddaughter sing and dance "We Are Family" by Sister Sledge. She smiled. Now, that's what her life was all about. She scrambled off her SUV. It was time to go home.

****

Shelby's day began as a typical Texas July morning. The sun blazed and the UV index climbed higher with each hour, Shelby tied the wide-brimmed hat under her chin and slipped into knee-high rubber boots to fix a water leak. She had turned the bivalve off earlier so the ground should be a little dryer for her next job. Grabbing a shovel, the bucket filled with all the transitions, plastic pipe, cleaner and glue from the tool shed, she marched to the horse's trough.

The mares were Tim's. He loved riding. Her fear kept her from sharing more time with him. She shuddered. Damn her trepidations.

Her cell rang. She placed the tools on the ground. Al's name splashed on the caller ID. "Hey. What's going on?"

"Wanna get together for a cup of coffee? Rev our engines."

"I can't. I have to fix a water pipe leak. But thanks for asking."

"Where?"

"The horse trough or thereabouts. Not sure exactly, but I'm about to find out."

"Ah. OK. Maybe another time. Do you need help?"

"No, I'm fine. I'll take a rain check on the caffeine train. Everything going well at the office?"

Chapter Twenty-Six

Kyle tensed and waited while patting Annie on her head. From the fresh scent emanating from Annie's coat, Aunt Alessa must have had her groomed today.

Alessa grinned. "Everything here is terrific. Talk to you soon." She lowered the phone to the cradle. She's at home. You'll find her near the stables or thereabouts repairing a water break."

Kyle smiled wide. "Thanks. I owe you one."

"Dude, you owe me for a couple…Kyle?"

He stilled.

"Make her happy."

He nodded. "That's my aim." Or he'd die trying. He spun and left.

****

Kyle found Shelby digging. With every shovel full of mud and water, she sank deeper into the mess. The horses ears perked then sniffed the air, their gazes landed on him. They were beautiful animals.

Shelby was covered in muck from her lovely head all the way down her delicious body. Her hat tied to the fence fluttered in the breeze. He shook his head. His love for her had grown more over the past two months. Together, he'd hoped they would wage the battles and the curse. He refused to surrender their relationship to an old man's bigotry or an asinine woman like Lisa.

"Did you find the break yet?"

Shelby jumped. "No." Her chin rose as she took a deep breath and gazed off into the horizon.

He chuckled. "Looks like you could use some help."

She jabbed the shovel back into the mire. "I can handle this."

He softened his voice. "Shel, it's not a sign of weakness to accept my assistance."

She twirled to face him. "What are you doing here?"

At least she didn't have any hate emanating from her eyes. Sadness, fear, joy—all of it swirled in the hazel depths. He placed his booted right foot on the bottom rail of the pipe fence. "I came to see you."

She glared at him. "You should be with Lisa and your unborn child."

"I chose to be with you."

"Pressley, I'm disappointed in you. Your baby needs you as well as your name."

"Shel, you have mud all over your face."

"People in your circles pay big money for facials. I'm sure Lisa's had a few." She held her palm up. "I was out of line." Her voice lowered. "And don't call me Shel."

Kyle laughed. "None of my friends get mud facials, let alone laced with horse manure."

Shelby exhaled. "I told you before I was country. Not my favorite job but I don't mind it. By the way, I appreciate you handling my boxes when I issued call tags for them."

His heart skipped a beat. "You already had your things sent back here?"

She drew her eyebrows together. "You didn't

know?"

"No. Hilda must have handled it. I haven't been home since..." He didn't want to say the words out loud.

"Where you've been is none of my concern. Next time you talk to her, thank her for me."

"I've been traveling the Pacific Northwest for a while. And for your information, if there is a baby and it's mine, I'll handle the responsibility. But I won't marry Lisa. The private investigator's report stated she hasn't been to a doctor or bought any prenatal vitamins. Her venue has been one party after another, no nesting or preparation of any sort for starting a family."

"I knew in my heart that you'd take care of your child. That was never the roadblock—I'm assuming you said your piece, Pressley. It's time for you to leave." Her eyes misted and she yanked the shovel out of the thick mud.

"I'm not going to desert you when you need my help." He climbed over the fence and hefted both legs to the side, clearing the top rail.

"Pressley, don't."

His boots landed and splattered the quagmire.

Ooze hit her T-shirt and she glowered. "What part of no don't you understand?"

"Maybe by the time we're finished with this project, you'll be calling me by my given name."

She shook her head. "Not a chance, Pressley. Before you get any more mud on you, I suggest you get in your truck and leave."

Kyle grabbed the shovel from her hand. "You don't have any rings on."

"I don't wear any jewelry while I'm doing ranch

work." She visibly stiffened. "Is that why you're here? To get your ring back?"

"Baby, it was merely an observation."

She put her hand up again to stop him and tugged the shovel out of his hands. "I'm not in possession of it. Talk to your lawyer, he should have it. I sent the blasted thing with a notarized packing slip. I'm sure I have the proof of delivery in my files. You see, I've already been accused of burglary and attempted murder. I don't want to travel that road again. If her eyes were knives, he would have been cut to shreds. "You need to leave, now."

"Lindbergh didn't tell me you sent it back. What he did mention was that you reimbursed all the money that I spent on our wedding. He double checked the bills. You paid them all."

"Penitence." She shoveled the sludge. "Penitence for being so stupid." Then she slung it and growled, "Now, get...out." She hefted another and snarled, "I said go." The third throw landed her butt in the muck. The shovel fell to the side and her hands grabbed more and threw it at him. She clutched again catapulting the mixture hitting him on the chest.

He stood unmoving waiting for her anger to subside. He deserved everything she was dishing out. Hurt. Rage. Disappointment. And horse shit. His heart broke to see what he had done to the love of his life.

She finally resigned. "Please, go."

He picked up the shovel and didn't respond. She wasn't giving him an inch. He had a long way to go with her. Nor he guessed did he deserve any latitude, but he would find the right way to reach out to her. Maybe he would take a bit longer than necessary to find the leak.

She worked right beside him, not talking but handing the necessary items to finish the job. His hands held the pipe while she swabbed the cleaner. He wanted to kiss her. Her lips beckoned him to taste her sweet mouth.

"Pressley, what do you need?"

He cleared his throat. "The glue and transition."

He mopped the adhesive over the plastic, slid the conversion in place and applied the few seconds of pressure. "Okay. In a couple of hours, we'll turn the water back on to make sure we have a good seal. Let's go clean up."

Kyle waited for Shelby to finish rinsing off the caked mud with the garden hose. He offered to help, but she had refused. She held the spray nozzle toward him and he stepped into the water allowing her to assist. He continued to watch her clean his boots and jeans. Her ministrations were damn near given with care.

"I'm glad I was able to help. I didn't think we'd ever find it."

Her gaze met his. There was affection in them. "Thank you." Then her stomach rumbled. "I'm famished. What about you?"

"I could go for something."

She shut off the spigot. "I suppose you have a change of clothes?"

"Always."

"Go get them. You can shower in the guest bathroom. After we get cleaned up, I'll fix a sandwich for us."

Shelby trotted off not waiting for him. He smiled at her sexy ass swaying with each step. She had invited him into her house. A good feeling skittered into his soul and he wanted to roar and beat on his chest. Maybe, there was a chance, howbeit a long shot, but it looked like he had some odds in his favor.

After his shower, he stepped into the dining room. Her eyes traveled from his wet hair to his bare feet, lingering at his midsection. His cock twitched.

She sat at the table and lowered her gaze to her plate. "Smoked turkey sandwich with chips and iced tea." She pointed to his place setting opposite of hers.

"Looks great. Thanks." At least she invited him to share her table. She could've shoved the food in his hands and told him to leave. Things were definitely looking up.

"You said you took in the Pacific Northwest. Where did you go?"

He took a long drought of his tea then set his glass down. "Seattle, Victoria, then on to Alaska."

"Flew with Garrett?"

"Drove to Seattle. Chartered a plane to catch some of Alaska's port cities."

"I bet your trip was beautiful."

"Very."

He consumed another lengthy drink. "What about you? What have you been doing?"

She lifted her finger to ask for a moment and swallowed hard.

He nodded.

"Nothing." Shelby slid her plate to the side.

About to pop the last bite in his month, he held onto the remnants. "Will you forgive me?"

Her gaze glared. "That's why you're here?"

He didn't want to break the contact. "Some of it."

She fiddled with the edge of the tablecloth. "We've been here before. You shouldn't have driven all this way to ask me. I'm not angry with you."

"Are you saying you do then?"

"If that's what you need to get back to your life and raise your child, yes."

"Yes, what? I want to hear you say it out loud."

"Pressley, I forgive you." She grabbed her plate and rose. "There you've got it. It's time for you to leave."

As she walked passed him, he touched her arm. She stopped.

"Thank you, Shel."

Her eyes misted, sadness had crept into them. She dropped her gaze to focus on her feet. "Not a problem. I'm glad I could give it to you."

He stood, closing the distance between them and placed both hands on each shoulder. "That's just a start of why I'm here."

Backing out of his light grasp, those hazel orbs shuttered. She turned and headed toward the kitchen.

He followed then angled his hip against the counter to watch and wait for her decision to either throw him out or talk. Of course, he needed more than forgiveness and dialogue to address their problems. He had to convince Shelby their relationship was worth the effort to work through the doubts, difficulties and overcome their major obstacles. He wanted her, here and in Sacred-Spring. Damn, he craved her touch and her love.

She'd had taken his plate from him then shoved the remaining items in the dishwasher. "Would you like to go outside? I have a picnic table and benches under the tree. It's nice this time of day."

"Sure."

Beneath the towering red oak, he gambled again. "What did you do afterwards?"

"Afterwards? Ah, my thoughts weren't there. I came home."

His stomach bounced. Home—damn, he wanted her to think of his house as her home. Every muscle tensed, he had to know more. "I heard Alessa left Garrett's place soon after and she was back before you were, so where did you go?"

"Idaho, Utah, and Arizona."

"Did you stop and see anything?"

"Several national parks."

"Which ones?"

"Why do you want to know? I may not be angry with you, but I'm still hurt. It didn't take rocket science to figure out that you had just been with Lisa in New York when you came here. Asking me to marry—you had the gall to—Damn you." Shelby sighed. "I'm sorry—"

"Don't be. It's not your fault. I take full responsibility."

She shook her head as though she didn't agree with him. The lines on her face relaxed. "Well, I don't remember all the places I stopped. I guess I shifted into a self-defense mode. Maybe I self-induced a hypnotic trance to get through the emotional upheaval. I don't know."

"What do you remember?"

Her gaze met his. He recognized the minute Shelby's resolve bounced back.

"I spent a lot of time by myself, Pressley."

He traveled down a precarious road, but the more

she talked about what had happened, the possibility existed, he could rebuild their relationship. "What made you decide to come back hom—here?"

Shelby smiled. From her back pocket of her blue jeans, she retrieved her smart phone. "I saved it." Tapping her way to the library of videos, she handed the cell to him. "This was the message that led me back."

He grinned as he viewed the little girl sing "We Are Family" by Sister Sledge. "She's cute as a button." He handed the mobile back to Shelby.

She nodded. "Yes, she is." Shelby's back straightened, the grip she still had on the device whitened her knuckles. "You'll be making your own memories shortly."

"I don't think she's pregnant."

"Pressley, why would she lie?"

"That's a question I can't answer. But—"

She raised her hand. "I don't want to hear it."

He stopped his line of reasoning and proceeded on another. "Will you give us another chance?"

Her lips thinned to a fine line. "Pressley, there will never be an *us*."

Gravel sprayed Shelby's back. A car skidded to a stop beside the table. Four doors swung open.

Kyle squinted from a white arc of light. A gun. He rose and grabbed Shelby, placing her behind him.

The man's graveled voice disclosed a command. "Don't move."

Kyle recognized the timbre. Swordfish. "We're not. What do you want?"

"Dead. Peckerhead."

Kyle addressed the asshole holding the Glock.

"Who are you?"

Bobby Jo stepped forward. "I...we didn't want this. They're making us."

Swordfish screeched, "Shut up, bitch."

Bobby Jo cried. "I don't want any part of this. It's gone too far."

David's head bobbed. "I agree."

"I'm going to ask one more time. What do you want? Where have I met you before?"

"My dad. He gave ya' his blood, sweat, and all them years of service and ya' upped and fired him. When ya' gave him the boot, he couldn't handle it and now he's in a loony bin. So I'm figurin' a life for a life. Yer suppos' to die in that truck accident. But I'm countin' on ya' ain't got no more lives in ya'. Yer worse than a cat."

Recognition dawned; memories flooded his mind and Kyle's muscles tensed. "I had to call security to remove you from the Christmas Ball. You were drunk, a violent one."

"Good ol' Pressley International givin' to charity and can't take care of yer own."

"Your father knew he was wrong. That's why he resigned on his own."

"Bullshit. That ain't what he tol' me. Yer still gonna' die anyhow."

David stepped forward. "He's serious. I didn't want it to go this far. I just did your house. I don't want anything to do with this." He nodded toward Haines.

Kyle growled disgusted. "It's a little late for regrets."

Haines eyed Kyle then swung his pistol toward David. "Ya' ain't gonna' have no more regrets when I get through wit' ya'."

"All right, Haines. That's enough. I'm paying you to do as I say."

Kyle shook his head. "What are you paying him for, Mira?"

Mira hissed, "That's not important."

Haines yelled, "I want him dead and she has ta' go too."

Mira's voice lowered. "Then kill her, dear."

David grabbed Swordfish's arm. "That's it. You guys are certifiable crazy. This ain't what I bargained for. I may spend time in the pen, but Texas is a capital punishment state. I don't want to lose my life over this shit."

Haines pointed the gun on David and squeezed the trigger. "Ya' just did."

Bobby Jo screamed. "We did everything you asked. Why? Why? We broke into Kyle's house like you said to do. All we needed was money. We didn't want to kill them."

Mira grabbed Haines' arm. "I can't believe you did that, but you saved me some money. Kill him! He's the one who should die for his transgressions against my granddaughter. Poor Shelby, I'm sorry, you see, he'll have to dispatch you too. For some reason, I became very fond of you, dear. Later, when I knew Lisa lied about her pregnancy—Just like I thought—You see she confided and told me she wasn't with Kyle in New York. Lisa will be dealt with also."

Speak of the devil, Lisa approached. She sidled beside him and at the same time, Shelby stepped away giving them wide berth.

Lisa angled her way in front of Kyle. "Mira. Stop.

This isn't going to bring back Christine."

"Get away, child, you disgust me. When you became Christine's lover you only lowered her self-esteem…How she loved you, I'll never know.

"Mira, Christine had far worse problems. Her father, your son molested her."

"You're lying."

Lisa advanced toward Mira. "I've made a mess of things, but I intend on correcting them."

Lisa pivoted to Shelby. "I'm sorry I should've known when I first saw Kyle with you at Pogonip. He loves you and I never had a chance."

Lisa's gaze met his. "I'm sorry. I've been out of line for most of my life. Christine had major issues that she never shared with you. Dear God, I begged her to tell you, but she always thought you'd view her as damaged or dirty.

He swiped a hand through his hair. "I didn't know…I'm not a monster, I would've understood."

Lisa lightly touched his forearm. "I told her…But—"

Lisa swiveled to Mira. "You turned a blind eye and refused to stop the perversions by your own husband to your son. Christine's mom did the exact same thing. Christine didn't understand love or what constituted a stable relationship. You, Mira, could have saved your son and your granddaughter, but you never did."

Mira's eyes shifted from anger to sadness. "Lisa, maybe we can discuss this later." By the time he'd finished the sentence, Mira's gaze hardened to a glaze that possessed nothing.

Shit, he recognized Mira's reaction. With one hand he grabbed Lisa's shirt to pull her behind him while his other extended to Shelby.

Mira pulled a thirty-eight out of her purse, pointed, and squeezed the trigger.

The momentum of the bullet catapulted Lisa's body into his. He steadied his foothold and held onto her.

Mira swung her arm and tapped again.

Shelby collapsed. The sickening thud of lead ripping apart her skin and tissue kicked his SEAL instincts in gear. He lowered Lisa, laying her on the ground.

Kyle lunged for Mira. She shot Swordfish then placed the tip of the gun to her chest and tugged.

Kyle landed on his feet and wheeled to help Shelby. Out of the corner of his eye, Garrett, Jude and Alessa appeared.

Garrett kicked the pistol from Haines and tied his hands with a rope. Garrett growled, "Shut up before I give you something to cry about."

Kyle gathered the handguns. "I don't know where you guys came from, but I'm glad to see you."

His older brother took the weapons and nestled them in his waistband. "The authorities and ambulances are on their way."

Kyle crossed the five feet to Shelby and carefully lifted her in his arms. "Shel?" She wasn't responding. He flashbacked to Dan and his gut twisted into a triple knot. He stood with Shelby cradled against his body. "We don't have time to wait for the medics."

Alessa unhooked the D-ring holding his truck keys from his belt loop. "I'll drive."

Chapter Twenty-Seven

Forty-eight hours later in the ICU waiting room, Kyle bided his time waiting for his ten-minute turn. Numb from Shelby's prognosis and lack of sleep, he prayed for divine intervention.

Alessa plopped in the seat next to him and put her arm through his. "She's still not breathing on her own and the doctors want a decision...I'm not going to make it...I can't."

His stomach curled into tighter knots. "And Joni?"

"She's more of a basket case than I am."

"How about we give everyone more time?"

Alessa released him, her tears running freely down her cheeks. "Go...see her."

Garrett followed him into Shelby's room and stood off to the side. Kyle held her fingers in his hand because the intravenous lines snaked from the top of hers. "Shel, fight for me, fight to live and die another day."

The heart monitor thrummed a steady beat. The breathing machine's screen scrolled the amount of oxygen it was giving to her, one hundred percent. Even his voice had no effect.

Garrett inclined against the wall. "You could mind walk and maybe help her."

He sighed. "Or not. It didn't make a difference with Dan."

"So you're not going to do *your* thing? That's not the man I know."

Kyle released Shelby and strode to the door. He grabbed the handle. "Fuck off."

Garrett's eyebrows rose in unison.

He left Garrett in the wake of his anger and trekked down the hall. Garrett understood the frustrations of his gift, and had the ability to persevere his storms. Garrett would have his back just like he'd always have Garrett's six.

He had to escape from a situation he had no control over. Alessa and Joni allowed him to see her stating to the staff that he was Shelby's fiancé. The decision to remove her ventilator wasn't his either. On the path of Shelby's life, he was a bump in the road, a distraction and a bad one at that.

Outside, he meandered along a trail to a garden. No one was around. He parked his ass on the bench and closed his eyes. The shade was a welcome reprieve from the scorching sun. The breeze gave little relief, but it was better than nothing. He stretched his legs and peered at his boots that had dried conforming once again to his feet.

Two days ago, Lisa had saved his life by giving her own. In his mind, she had righted all her wrongs. He'd been surprised by Lisa's revelation about Christine's past. Mira hadn't helped her only son from her husband's sexual abuse. Then once again, she turned away from her granddaughter. He shook his head. Not only did he forgive Lisa, but also Christine and accepted the fact he couldn't save everyone.

The detectives had come by for statements. They'd found out Swordfish was hired by Mira and someone else, but he'd lawyered up before the investigators received any more information. Somehow David and Haines had survived, recovering in this very hospital, handcuffed to the bed with an armed guard outside their rooms.

Kyle was grateful for his family's help. Lisa had been the one to ask for their assistance. When she told Mira that she had lied, Christine's grandmother had hinted at her next move. Lisa had inquired with a buddy of hers and found Mira had hired a private contractor to fly her and several associates to Killeen.

Annie yelped. Her front paws hit his chest. He ruffled her ears. Rain stepped over his legs then folded her tiny frame sitting beside him. He scooted his rear back, straightened his spine, and pushed Annie's feet to the ground.

"Hey, Mom. When did you get in?"

"This morning. Garrett thought everyone could use an extra hand and called Holt to fly me down. We left Missoula pretty early because there was a storm system heading our way."

He wrapped his arm around her shoulder and squeezed. "Thanks."

"Son?"

From her tone, he could tell he was about to be put in his place. Where, he wasn't sure. By the end of her lecture and soft words, he would. He lifted his chin for her to continue.

"Garrett said you refused to mind walk with Shelby. Is there a reason you'd like to share with me?"

He released his embrace. "There are several topics in my life that are not up for discussion. That's one of them."

"I see."

He jumped off the bench, shoved his hands in his pockets, clutching his personal medicine bag, Bear-Claws had instructed him to make long ago. "No, you don't."

"What makes you think I wasn't there when you locked away your gift?"

The dog whined and Annie nudged her nose at his thigh. He unclenched the leather pouch and swiped his palm along the tuft of hair on top of her head. "You shouldn't have been there."

"I was called upon to go by my spirit guide."

He lowered and rested his weight on his heels, continuing to stroke the red coat, gleaming even in the shade. "Then you know I failed. Not only there, but damn well through my entire life. Christine assumed I couldn't handle her history. Mind walking wasn't enough to save Dan. My SEAL training didn't kick in fast enough which gave Mira the wherewithal to kill Lisa. And Shelby is hanging on by a thread."

His gaze connected with Rain's. "Damn...Mom, I'm not looking for your pity."

She snorted. "I'm not giving you any."

"Always direct and to the point."

"Not yet."

He stood. "I gave my word."

"In remorse. Not a wise choice."

"Nevertheless."

"You're one stubborn man."

He shrugged.

"Okay that's it. The gloves come off." She rose to her feet, her finger poked his chest and her fingernail jabbed his skin. "You listen here, buster. I would remove any obstacle within my means to help my sons and daughters or any other family member for that matter. I'd tear apart any barrier, any impediment that would hamper my assistance. Why? Because love is unconditional. You've put a price tag on Shelby's life. Your word of honor is your own self-centered encumbrance and I'm disappointed in you. Furthermore, how dare you take away the key to save her."

He grabbed her hand and held her palm over his heart. "Mom, what kind of man gives a promise than breaks it to suit his wishes?"

Rain's voice softened. "When he saves a soul? A damn fine one."

He embraced and held her.

A moment passed and Rain stepped back. "One other thing you may want to consider…if you don't do anything, you'll always wonder…" Then she left, taking Annie with her.

He slid onto the bench and stared at a hummingbird as it fed. Even birds and creatures in this world needed help and he'd never denied sustenance or shelter for any animal.

"Is this seat taken?"

Kyle scooted to the left. "Nope." He glimpsed at the gentleman then did a double take. "Dan?"

As a solid full-bodied apparition, Dan settled beside him. "Kinda' crazy, huh?"

"Not in my world."

"I can't stay long."

Moisture gathered in the back of Kyle's eyes. "I've missed you, man."

"The First Realm is a cool place…You know why

I'm here."

Kyle chuckled. "Who called in the mission?"

Dan laughed. "There's a whole team of us covering you and it's a full-time fucking job."

"You need something to keep your wimpy ass busy."

"Do I have to show you again what a wimpy ass can do?"

Kyle raised both hands. "I surrender."

Dan's laughter subsided and his lips turned into a straight line. "I want to thank you for taking care of Aaron and Kat."

Kyle swallowed the hard lump in his throat. "I told you I would."

"What do you think of my two grandchildren?"

"Cute and awesome all wrapped in pink and blue blankets. You can be a proud grandfather."

Dan grinned. "I am." Then he scowled. "You're the one with the problem."

"What?"

"Your gift is mind walking, not healing."

"I failed you and your children."

"Still playing God?"

Kyle cut his eyes to Dan. "Prick."

"Dick."

Dan broke the long silence. "Talk to me."

"There's nothing that needs to be said, but I'm sure you're going to give me your two cents worth, everybody else has."

"I would've died anyway. You read the autopsy report, yet you still blame yourself."

Kyle shrugged his right shoulder. He had heard the same song and dance before.

"When I was shot, the pain of the wound was a welcome relief from the ache I had inside from losing Becca, and I gave up. After your lecture about my kids graduating and having grandchildren, I wanted to fight and live. By then, I had lost too much blood, wasn't going to survive. If you'd be honest with yourself, you knew too. As a soldier, you wouldn't admit to defeat and you willed your strength to me…Any other time, I would've made it. You realize you have another ability that can save lives?"

Kyle refused to answer his question and grimaced.

Dan crossed his arms over his chest. "That's what I thought. You stubborn bastard."

"Someone else called me that, but she was nicer. Are you finished?"

"Not by a longshot. You're not going to use me—"

Kyle leapt from the bench. "I'm not—"

Dan followed and grasped his arm. "Yes, you are. Visit your woman and see if you can help her, but I'll be damned if you're going to use me as an excuse. Believe me, I'll haunt your ass until you take your last breath."

"An oath is something that I can't bend just because I want to."

"This isn't about you. It's about Shelby. If you don't do anything, you're going to lose her. By the way, that's inside information. What you do with it is on you…I have to go."

Kyle hugged Dan. "I love ya', man."

Dan returned his embrace. "I love you. I'm proud to call you my brother. Remember, never retreat, always pursue."

As his spirit evaporated, Kyle's hands held nothing

but air. Damn, it was good seeing him again. He eyed the bench and sat.

"You have another gift and the ability to give your woman another chance at life."

Kyle glanced at Garrett standing by the edge of the garden. "So I hear."

"If she was mine, I'd fight for her." Then he strode off.

Kyle sighed. Every time he got close to a lady, she died. He didn't want to accept a life without Shelby. Life. A simple four-letter word that had more impact than the others he had in his vocabulary.

What if he wasn't successful and she died. Failing Shelby again scared the shit out of him. His stomach double knotted. He'd tackled missions with far less odds and won. According to Dan's intel, he could help Shelby and if he didn't, she'd die.

His next step was a no-brainer. If she survived and thought less of him because he had broken his vow, that meant she had lived to see another day, to be surrounded by her family, and have loving memories of hugging her grandchildren and celebrating their birthdays.

He hoped like hell...He closed his eyes and slipped in.

Chapter Twenty-Eight

Kyle growled. *"Tim? What are you doing here?"*

"What took you so damn long? She's been trying to cross over and I won't allow her."

"Detained."

Now one with Shelby, Kyle burrowed into her memory. He smiled at her happiness with her grandchildren, her writing, then grimaced at her hurt when Tim died.

Kyle glanced at Tim. *"She still loves you."*

Tim crossed his arms. *"Shelby is a strong lady. It will take one hell of a man to hold onto her steadfast commitment."*

"Stop talking about me like I'm not here."

Kyle's breath hitched. The love she had for him showered over his soul like a blanket of pure bliss. *"Baby, you still love me."*

She nodded. *"Always will."*

Kyle turned to Tim, waiting for him to throw the first punch.

Tim offered, *"You are the one she has chosen."*

Shelby's gaze met Tim's. *"I never deserved your love."* She looked at Kyle. *"Or yours. I've made a mess of things."* A tear rolled down Shelby's cheek and Tim wiped it away.

Tim's hand caressed Shelby's jawline. *"I'll always have your heart here."* His palm rested over his chest.

"Don't let our memories hinder our growth. How about we let them be a part of who we are. We were chosen to help in the upcoming battle."

Shelby hugged Tim until he released her hold. *"Kyle is a dedicated man, resilient in every sense of the word. He'll keep his pledges. You both have my blessing."*

Kyle delved deeper into Shelby's mind. Anger and rage swelled inside him. *"I know why you didn't tell me about Chris. I'll kill the sonofabitch."*

Tim drew his attention. *"His time will come, but not by your hands."*

"And meanwhile, he'll continue to harm her? Not on my watch."

Bear-Claws joined them, bringing Chris' spirit guide, Spotted-Owl. *"Listen to Tim."*

Kyle gritted his teeth. *"How can Spotted-Owl help? You can only direct, not lead."*

Spotted-Owl vouched. *"We are allowing Chris to be used as a puppet. He doesn't see a way out of his predicament. He thinks he doesn't have a choice, but I'm counting on him to see there is an answer."*

Kyle scowled. *"All right, but if no one takes him down, understand this…I will slip into his mind and kill the bastard."*

Bear-Claws shook his head. *"I'm glad you decided to start using your ability again."*

"Just to take care of Dr. Chris Humphreys."

Bear-Claws harrumphed. *"Leave it alone."*

Kyle scowled again. *"Don't you guys have something better to do? It's a bit crowded in here."*

Tim laughed while Bear-Claws grunted and both disappeared with Spotted Owl.

"Shel, do you really want to cross over?"

"Now that you know about Chris and my obligations to hand over Ten-Blue-Sun, no. But we still have the curse to deal with...I'm frightened. I'm not brave at all."

Kyle gathered her hands in his. *"On the contrary, you are very brave...As for your grandfather's curse, if we marry and the first stone lights; we will have stronger powers than his black magic can dish out."*

"Maybe...Did Lisa make it?"

"No."

"I'm sorry. I'm sorry about a lot of things...I believed Lisa's lies and didn't fight for the one person who I held dear to my heart...you. Rain told me, but I ignored her wisdom and fell for what I had seen. Ten-Blue-Sun's stone changed to an awful shade of red which I now know stood for the bloodshed. Will you forgive me?"

"Baby, a very wise woman reminded me that my love for you is unconditional."

"Oh Kyle, do you think we'll make it?"

"Fight, baby. Fight for your family, for me and yourself. Then I have plans. You have another love I forgot about, writing. When you're healthy, we'll travel and I want you to write." He winked. *"Of course, I'll be demanding some of your time."*

Shelby laughed. *"Sounds wonderful."* Then she sobered. *"If I don't make it, promise me to use your gift to help other people."*

He choked. *"You'll be fine."*

"You have a wonderful ability and a big heart. I'm counting on you to follow Bear-Claws and get the bad guys."

Kyle smiled at Shelby's innocence. *"I'll try my best to use my gift for the benefit of mankind and the First Realm on one condition."*

"Which is?"

"You have to come back to me."

"You got it."

"Then you have my word."

"I hope to see you...physically, in our world. I love you."

He embraced her. *"Shel, I love you too, baby."*

He harvested all the positive energy within him and called upon the universe. Answering his plea, the potent power of his spirit guides and angels flowed, filling him with the needed force. With all of his might, he launched the life giving essence into Shelby, willing her to fight and survive. God he hoped Dan was telling the truth. His soul was wrapped inside this one woman.

Epilogue

Kyle's Veranda—Jackson, WY
Three Months Later

"I, Kyle Lee Pressley, take you, Shelby Jayne Littleton to be my wife, my partner in life, and my one true love. I will cherish our union and love you more each day than I did the day before. I will trust you and respect you, laugh and cry with you, loving you faithfully through good times and bad, regardless of the obstacles we may face together. I give you my hand, my heart, and my love, from this day forward for as long as we both shall live because I love you and can't live without you."

"I, Shelby Jayne Littleton, take you, Kyle Lee Pressley to be my husband, my partner in life, and my one true love. I will cherish our union and love you more each day than I did the day before."

She stopped.

His heart skipped a beat.

"Pressley, I trust you and respect you, will always like I do now, laugh and cry with you, faithfully loving you through good times and bad especially in this world and the next regardless of the battles we will face. From this day forward, I give to you my soul, for within me everything else follows for as long as we both shall live."

"Nice. Very nice."

He slid the band on her finger. "This ring is a symbol of my commitment to you, giving my heart, my love, and my life to you as long as I live."

Shelby's hands shook.

Kyle helped her with his ring then her gaze met his. "What you just said."

Laughter filled the veranda as Rain quieted the crowd. "I have something to show all of you."

In her left hand, she held Ten-Blue-Sun then extended her arm above her head. The first midnight-blue stone illuminated to an azure luminescence.

Shelby had told him about her experience with One-Who-Soars-With-Eagles making the Kachina doll in the cave. The medicine man had lifted the doll in the air, sang, and cried at the same time. The many meanings of the warrior woman would make a strong man shake in his boots. One thing was certain; his woman would be with him throughout eternity and he was damn glad he walked not only in her mind but into her heart.

Annie barked beside him and nosed his hand. Kyle stroked the top of her head. He gazed at the happy canine with a smile. Annie's brown eyes sparkled then changed to amber while pinpoints of white light danced about.

Kyle nodded. He understood and ruffled her ears. Annie was of the First Realm.

Rain lowered the doll. "You may kiss your eternal bride."

And he did. Her luscious mouth tasted sweet. He nibbled his way across her jawline to the swirl of her ear. "Now will you tell me when your birthday is?"

She angled and nipped his earlobe with her teeth, then whispered, "It's…"

Kyle eased back. "Well, I'll be damned. A winter solstice baby."

A word about the author...

Susan JP Owens lives on a ranch in Texas with her wonderful husband. After work and leaving the dangerous & sizzlin' hot world of her stories, Susan enjoys skydiving, the great outdoors and a fine glass of wine from time to time.

She enjoys hearing from her readers. You can contact her by email at:

Susan@SusanJPOwens.com

or learn more on her website

www.SusanJPOwens.com.